PIECES
and
MEMORIES
of a
LIFE

USA TODAY & WALL STREET JOURNAL BESTELLING AUTHOR

JEWEL E. ANN

PIECES AND MEMORIES OF A LIFE

COLTEN & JOSIE

JEWEL E. ANN

Copyright © 2022 by Jewel E. Ann

ISBN 978-1-955520-23-2

Print Edition

Cover Designer: Murphy Rae

Formatting: Jenn Beach

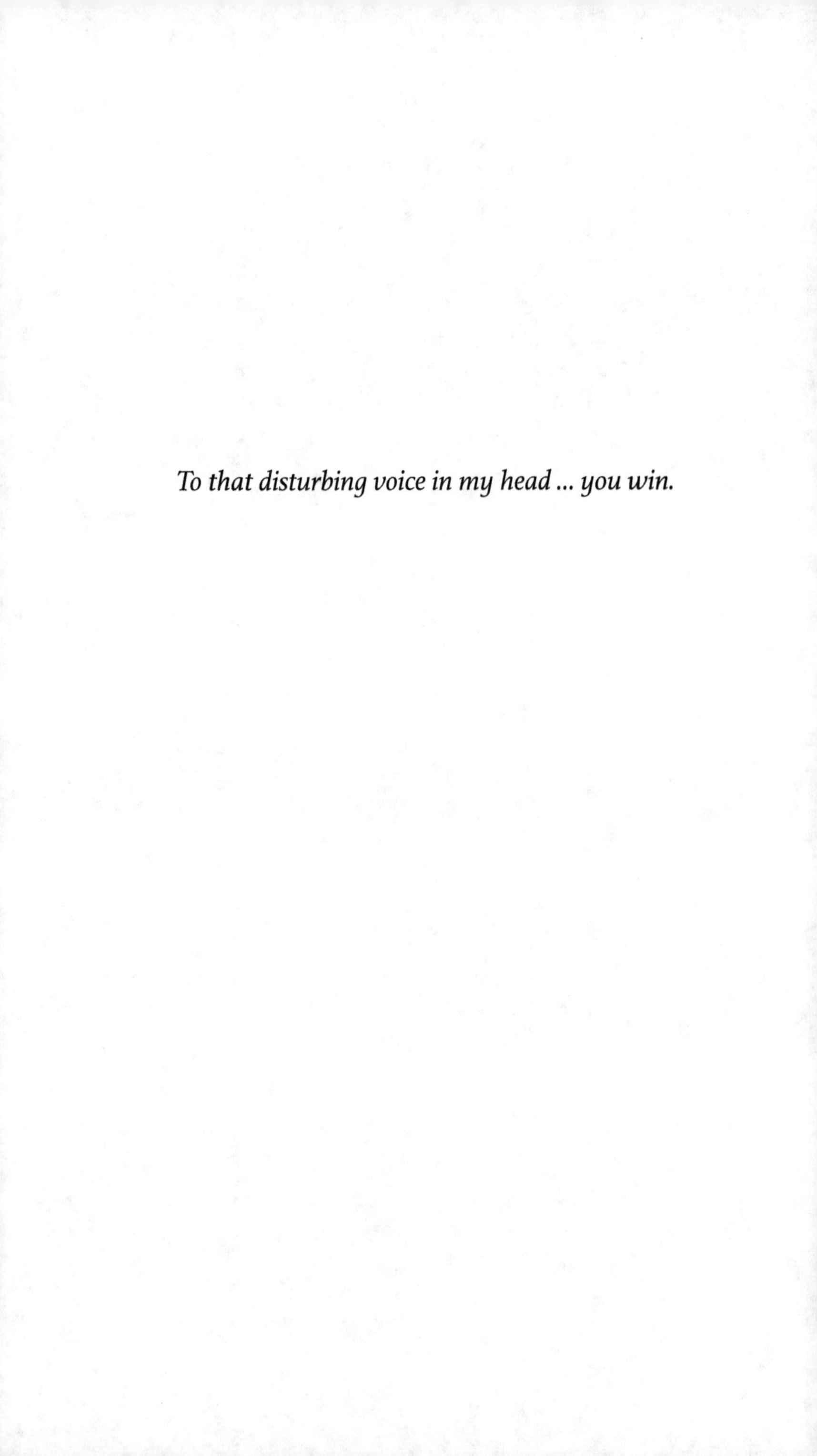

To that disturbing voice in my head ... you win.

PIECES OF A LIFE

COLTEN & JOSIE: PART ONE

Prologue

"My dad said I need to stay close to you until my mom comes back. He's afraid a bad person will hurt me."

While my mom zips the back of my white gown, I stare at the little girl before me.

So innocent.

So loved.

So beautiful.

Her dad is right. There are bad people who do bad things to children.

However, we are at a private venue surrounded by family and close friends. Whether it's right or not, this is the perfect example of allowing kids to roam freely until corralled at the last possible minute—there's an assumption that *someone* is watching them.

Her dad is feeling extra protective today because Winston Jeffries preyed on little girls running around at family events, like weddings, between 1892 and 1901. Nearly a decade of kidnapping. Nearly a decade of long hair hanging from trees in churchyards. Just the hair.

The bodies were never found.

Jeffries was convicted of thirty-seven counts of first-degree murder and hanged in Owensboro, Kentucky, on February 10, 1902 without a single body discovered.

He took the location of the bodies to his grave.

"A bad person, huh?"

The young girl nods, her long, dark curls and pink ribbons bouncing with each tip of her chin.

Her father's not worried about a mysterious "bad person." He's worried his bride might flee at the last second.

This girl has been sent here to keep an eye on me.

But why scare her? Why not just tell her I need help getting dressed? Why send her to deliver the one message that would make me want to kick off my heels, toss aside my veil, and run until my heart gives out?

"Mom, will you give us a minute?" I ask.

She straightens the skirt of my gown. "Sure. I need to check on your dad anyway."

When it's just the young girl and me, I bend down so we're at eye level. "Do you trust me?"

She nods slowly, eyes wide.

"I think your dad is scared. Will you help him not to be so scared?"

Another slow nod.

"It means you have to be brave too. You have to do something really brave and trust me that it's for the best. Can you do that?"

"I think so," she whispers.

I riffle through my mom's bag. She packed everything we could possibly need for any hiccup. My fingers curl around the orange-handled scissors, and I turn back to the girl. "Are you sure you're brave?"

She stares at the scissors and nods.

"And you trust me?"

"Y-yes ..."

"Come here."

She shuffles her pink shoes toward me.

"Turn around."

She turns around.

I remove the ribbon from the partial ponytail on the crown of her head. Then I tie it low, right above the nape of her neck.

She jumps when I cut her hair just above the tied ribbon, and the rest of her hair falls into a short bob around her chin when she turns toward me.

I smile, ignoring her parted lips and bugged-out eyes. "Take this to your dad and tell him you are safe. Then tell him I am just a star. If he takes a step back, he'll see the whole galaxy."

She hesitantly wraps her hand around the tail of hair.

"One more favor?" I turn and squat in front of her. "Unzip my dress."

CHAPTER
One

Seven months earlier ...

I COULD USE a naked body with a pulse. This thought summarizes my love life as I approach Paul Turner, my first swipe right in over a month.

Full head of blond hair neatly parted to the side.

Clean shaven.

Jeans, white button-down, and a navy blazer.

He'll work. My standards are at an all-time low.

Paul sips his water and surveys the restaurant, blue-eyed gaze snagging on me as I weave my way through the chattering crowd, clinking dinnerware, and the tantalizing aroma of garlic. When he smiles, the tension vanishes, leaving nothing but relief. He not only looks like his profile picture; he looks better than his profile picture. This never happens.

"Josephine?" He stands.

"Paul?" I smile as he nods. "You can call me Josie."

Paul gives me a hug instead of a handshake. We've been chatting online for weeks. I don't get a lot of hugs, which makes it easy to sink into his warm body.

A warm body ... I could use one of those too.

Warm.

Naked.

With a pulse.

"It's nice to finally meet in person," I say, taking a seat across from him.

"You look better than your profile picture." Appreciation seeps through his words.

My grin doubles. "Funny. I was thinking the same thing about you as I approached the table." In less than thirty seconds, I have a good feeling about Paul Turner. He doesn't appear nervous or awkward. Confident, but not overly so.

"Can I get you something to drink?" he asks.

"Water is fine. Thank you."

"Are you sure? They have an amazing house wine here."

"I'm sure. Please, however, order yourself a glass of wine. I'm going to jump straight into an appetizer because I skipped lunch today."

He laughs. "Sounds good."

We order drinks and appetizers while I contemplate my main course. He smiles a lot. I smile a lot. All the good vibes buzz around us.

"Did your niece have a nice birthday party?" I ask, lifting my gaze from the menu.

He narrows his eyes for a second. "Oh, that's right. I forgot I told you about that. Yes. It was extravagant. I fear when she turns five, anything short of a trip to Paris will be an epic disappointment."

"Is she an only child?"

Paul gives me a few more details about his family, and his love for them bleeds through each word. He's originally from Vermont, and he's lived here in Chicago for five years as a cosmetic chemist. Paul swiped right because we both have degrees in the sciences.

"So how do you like Chicago? It has to be quite the change of pace from Des Moines."

My head bobs several times as my stomach growls waiting for the appetizers. "It is, but I feel at home with my job."

"And you like your job?"

I sip my water before nodding. "I do."

"That's good." Paul sets his menu aside and unwraps his silverware, depositing the cloth napkin on his lap. "It takes the right kind of personality to work in a lab. My friends think I have a cool job. I mean ... I formulate cosmetics, but when they find out I'm tucked away in a lab all day, it loses its luster. I bet you get the same thing."

"Yeah, it's not as uh..." I clear my throat "...glamorous as other jobs."

"I can imagine people perk up when they hear you're a doctor. You think doctor and immediately you think *saving lives*. But I suppose working in pathology you're catching things like early stages of cancer, and in some ways, you're saving lives as much if not more than other doctors. Right?"

Saving lives? Not exactly.

I find a subtle smile to accompany my slight nod. "I worked in surgery for just under a year. So I'd never take anything away from other doctors. I solve mysteries."

"What's the hardest part?" Paul asks, and I wish we could steer the conversation in a different direction. Talking about jobs this much on a first date is as disappointing as talking about the weather until the main meal arrives.

"The hardest part is dealing with the death of young children."

"Yeah, I can see that."

"So, Paul, do you travel much?" I make the conversation go in a more acceptable direction. Paul bites, gobbling up my questions like Pac-Man. There are no awkward moments of silence. We cruise through dinner and dessert with each topic of conversation smoothly shifting to a new topic. This is how a date is supposed to go, and I'm hopeful that it won't end when we leave the restaurant.

"I'm going to use the men's room quickly." Paul

stands after paying the check, even though I argue that the first date should be separate checks.

Feeling good about the start to my weekend, I watch his smooth gait drift toward the back of the restaurant.

"Josie Watts?"

No.

No. No. No.

That familiar voice at my back—familiar like a paper cut eliciting a grimace and a silent expletive— brings every hair on my neck to attention, ready for battle.

Turning, my lips find a neutral position short of an actual smile. That dark hair is as unkempt as it was the last time I saw it, nearly seventeen years ago. Same irritating smirk. Same glimmer of antagonism in his monster-like brown and gold eyes. He's a dimple shy of being that guy every girl swoons over in high school then despises the rest of her life. "Colten." His name still leaves a sour taste in my mouth.

"Wow! How long has it been?" he asks.

Not long enough is my answer, but I don't offer it to him.

"I heard you went to medical school."

"Did you?" I press my lips together for a beat. "I heard that too."

He laughs, angling his body a little more.

"Eating alone?" I eye his table set for one.

"I am. I'm comfortable in my own skin. Besides, I like listening to the interesting conversations around me. A pathologist. That's impressive, Josie. Well done. I can see you hunched over a microscope."

"Good to know you *heard* I went to medical school, and you can *see* me hunched over a microscope. Are your other senses working well too?"

Colten laughs again.

I've always been his favorite source of amusement. It started in fourth grade. The seventeen-year break from his torment has been nice.

"Still quick-witted. I'd forgotten how much I loved your feistiness."

"Ready?" Paul saves the day with his return.

"Absolutely." I stand, tossing my napkin on the table.

"Aren't you going to introduce me to your friend?" Colten has the nerve to ask me.

"No," I say, hooking my handbag onto my shoulder while glaring at him. More than a decade and a half should be long enough to bury all hatchets, yet I feel eighteen again and equally as livid. No scientist has been able to prove the existence of time, so in some ways, I am and always will be eighteen and despise Colten Mosley.

He knows what he did. And he knows where he can go for it.

As soon as I escape Colten and step out into the early June sunset, Paul invites me to his place. It's a no-brainer. I'm thirty-five. What I do with my body is no longer a measure of my virtue. However, when Paul makes me breakfast Saturday morning, it's a positive measure of his virtue. After a long kiss at his door, we make plans for dinner midweek. This might be something.

***

MONDAY MORNING, I sweat at Pilates, grab a breakfast sandwich and coffee, meet in the conference room with twelve other pathologists, and then gown up in the county medical examiner's locker room in time to meet my two bodies for the day.

A possible overdose and a suspected homicide.

I start with the suspected homicide because there's something about the missing legs that calls to me. An hour later, I nearly bobble the liver right onto the floor when I hear an unwelcome voice behind me.

"Never saw this coming. Dr. Josephine Watts, M.D. Assistant Medical Examiner? No fucking way." Colten Mosley chuckles.

I recover the liver before it slips past my clawing fingers and secure it at the end of the table where the decedent's legs should be. Then I glance over my shoulder while a masked Colten makes his way into my view—suit, tie, and that messy excuse for a hairstyle. "What are you doing here?"

"Detective Mosley..." he flashes his badge "...homicide. I started last week after working in Indianapolis for five years. I wanted to move closer to home. The real question is what are *you* doing?"

"What does it look like I'm doing?"

"I'd say you're up to your elbows in vital organs, but you told your Friday night fling that you work in a lab. A nerd hunched over a microscope. This is … not the same thing, Josie."

"I'm a pathologist. And I do have a lab with a microscope. What's your point?" I glance up and reach for my scalpel.

"*This* is not what your date pictured. I can guarantee that. Not gonna lie … this isn't what I pictured either when my mom told me you got into medical school."

"I don't care what you pic—"

"I pictured…" he cuts me off, sliding his hands into his pockets "…a dress hugging your curves, stopping right above the knees, high heels, sexy lab coat, hair down, maybe nerdy glasses sitting low on your nose. Not this astronaut getup with a black apron, goggles, and a face shield. And I guarantee Mr. Friday Night didn't picture you in this. Unless … did you tell him the rest? Did you tell him you're not *just* a pathologist, but a forensic pathologist who plays around in the cavities of dead bodies like a toddler in a sandbox?"

"What do you want, Mosley? I'm too busy with my real job to play cops and robbers with you today. So if that badge is real, then you'd better have a good reason for interrupting me." I glance around the autopsy suite for Alicia or one of the other assistants, someone to force *Detective Mosley* to get to his point and leave me alone.

"We canvassed the entire area, and we can't find a

weapon. I thought you might tell me what we're looking for."

"An eighteen-volt circular saw with a seven-and-a-quarter inch blade. Six-foot cord. Zero to fifty-one degree bevel angle range. Adjustable cutting depth. Red handle."

"How do you know the handle's red?" Colten asks.

I grin behind my mask and shield. I've waited for what seems like forever to be the one on top. "Because you don't saw off two legs without a little blood splatter. But really, your question should be how I know the cord is six feet long."

"How do you know that?"

Glancing up again, I wait for him to realize I just ate his lunch.

"Jesus … you don't know shit about the weapon, do you?" he asks.

"Weapon or tool? If the cause of death didn't involve a weapon, then you're merely looking for the tool that was used to remove the legs. Now … get out of here. When I know something that you need to know, I'll let you know. Breathing down my neck won't expedite anything."

"Oh, Watts, I'm not breathing down your neck." He heads toward the exit. "If I were, you'd feel weak in the knees."

"Or … I'd vomit." My comeback bounces off the door that shuts before my words stumble out of my mouth.

I hate him. He's always one step ahead of me.

CHAPTER
Two

I MET Josephine Watts the summer before fourth grade. While I wasn't thrilled about moving to Des Moines, my dad landed the head boys' basketball coaching job at the high school, and the cost of living allowed us to have a bigger house—aka my own bedroom.

"Better stay out of trouble," Dad said, squeezing my shoulder as my older brother and I helped Mom unpack the dishes. "Our new neighbor is the Chief of Police. Just met him while he and his son were getting ready to go fishing. They hunt too."

"Great. Neighbors who are gun obsessed," Mom murmured.

"Not everyone hunts with a gun, Becca." Dad slapped her butt like he did to his players. Then, he winked at me like I needed to take notes so I could slap my wife's butt someday too.

"How old is their son? Do they have other kids?" Mom quizzed Dad. He opened the fridge as if some food fairy filled it before our arrival. No such luck.

"I don't know if they have other kids. I didn't ask. His son, Joe, is Colten's age."

"Really? My age?" I perked up. Hunting and fishing weren't my favorite pastimes; in fact, I knew nothing about either one. However, the idea of making a friend before school started easing my anxiety a bit.

As soon as Mom dismissed me from helping her in the kitchen, I ran up to my room. Mine. It was all mine. No more bunkbeds. No more of Chad's dirty underwear being tossed on my pillow, streak side down. No more "accidentally" breaking my Lego creations or wiping boogers on my baseball glove.

It took me the better part of the afternoon to get my room organized. Mom was a stickler on cleanliness, except with Chad. Apparently, his ADHD diagnosis gave him an exemption from hanging up his shirts and dumping his dirty underwear in the hamper.

I tacked up my final poster to the wall, Hank Aaron, while the neighbors pulled into their driveway. The police chief climbed out of the black pickup truck as his son jumped down from the other side. A fishing hat with dangling lures covered his head.

Tan, scrawny legs, baggy shorts, and a green tee— nothing like his intimidating father with shoulders twice as broad as my dad's and calves the size of tree trunks. The kid had to be the runt of the litter. My enthusiasm lost momentum. My *one* friend for the first day of school wasn't going to be the most popular kid, that was for sure.

With no lack of confidence, I headed downstairs and straight to the door. "Mom, I'm going to meet the boy next door." Figured I might as well befriend him early. Without at least one friend, it was going to be a long summer. And I sure as heck wasn't going to rely on Chad to entertain me. All he did was play stupid video games. I wasn't sure his skin ever saw the sun.

"Don't play with any weapons," Mom replied.

I rolled my eyes. "Okay."

Their garage door was open, and my steps faltered for a second when two freaky eyes peered at me. It was a deer head mounted to the garage wall. Before I could make it to the front door, it opened.

"Hi. Are you the new kid?" A girl in jean shorts and a pink tee grinned at me. Her teeth looked extra white behind her deep red lips and tan skin. Hair as black as my brother's fingernail (the one Mom said might fall off) caught in the breeze and blew into her face as she peeled it away.

"Yeah. I wanted to meet your brother. I guess we're going to be in the same grade."

"I don't have a brother."

I stepped onto the stoop and shoved my hands into the pockets of my shorts. "Haha. My dad already talked to your dad, so I know you have a brother. And I watched him get out of the truck a few minutes ago..." I turned to point at my window facing the street "...from my bedroom window."

"That was me."

"Why are you being weird?" I tilted my head to the side. "I know what I saw. And my dad's not a liar. And I know your brother's name is Joe."

"You saw *me*. And my name is Josephine. My friends call me Josie. And my dad calls me Jo because I was supposed to be a boy."

I shake my head. "The kid who got out of the truck was wearing shorts and a green shirt."

"Yeah. And it smelled like fish, so I changed my clothes. Do you want to come inside?"

"Not if you don't have a brother."

"That's ..." She twisted her lips together as her fists perched onto her hips. "Rude."

"I'm not being rude."

"You don't want to be my friend because I'm a girl. That's rude."

"I don't play with dolls and dress up stuffed animals."

"Do you eat cookies and drink chocolate milk?"

After thinking about it for a few seconds, I nodded.

"Good. So do I. Come on." She turned and left the door open, disappearing to the right.

I glanced back at the street, giving a quick look right then left before taking slow steps into the house. More animal heads mounted to the wall peered at me along with a big fish and some kind of bird on a shelf that looked quite real.

"Where are your parents?" I asked, peeking around the corner into the kitchen as she poured two glasses of chocolate milk.

"My dad's rubbing my mom's feet in the bedroom. They're huge! She's pregnant, and I guess being pregnant makes your feet and ankles get really big, and that makes them hurt."

I nodded slowly while she climbed onto the kitchen stool and opened a Tupperware container of chocolate chip cookies.

"So what's your name?" Josie asked, setting a cookie on a napkin for me right next to hers.

"Colten."

"Where did you come from?"

"Across the street."

"Duh. Where did you live before you moved into the house across the street?"

I stammered a second. She had me flustered because she was a girl, a pretty girl, with as much if not more confidence than I had. "Houston, Texas."

"Are you a cowboy?"

"No. Why?"

She lifted a shoulder and dropped it just as quickly while dipping part of her cookie into her chocolate milk. "I thought there were a lot of cowboys in Texas ... which is weird because we have a lot of cows here in Iowa, but I don't see that many cowboys."

I couldn't start my first day of school with only one friend—a girl. But school wasn't starting for two months, so I didn't see anything wrong with being

Josie's "neighborhood friend" just until I found boys my age. After all, the cookies were the best thing I'd ever tasted, and I liked watching Josie.

Her smile.

The way she flipped her hair over her shoulder.

Even the way she whisper-counted to ten every time she dipped her cookie in milk.

"Have you ever seen the exoskeleton of a cockroach under a magnifying glass?" she asked before starting her silent count again with her next bite of cookie dipped into the milk.

"I don't know if I've ever seen a live cockroach."

"Oh, it's not alive, silly. It's dead. I have a lot of dead stuff in my room. Want to see?"

And just like that ... the hair-tossing and whisper-counting became the least fascinating thing about Josephine Watts.

CHAPTER
Three

"You're breaking my heart, Dr. Watts."

On the verge of grabbing my bag and heading home for the day, I glance up from my desk. The irony …

I'm breaking his heart? I'm pretty sure he obliterated mine on more than one occasion, which proves one thing: he has no heart.

"Who keeps the citizens of Chicago safe while you're stalking me, Detective Mosley?"

"I bet it felt nice to put on makeup and wear a bra for your date the other night?"

I'm wearing a bra. *Asshole.*

Glancing down at my chest, I curl my shoulders inward when I notice my nipples. I'm wearing a *thin* bra.

But still … he's an asshole.

"You were supposed to call me with the results of the autopsy."

"I talked to Detective Rains. Cardiac arrest due to major blood loss. The decedent was alive when his legs were amputated."

"Why?" Uninvited, Colten takes a seat in the chair across from me.

"It's extremely hard to profile a ghost. When you catch your killer, plenty of qualified people will dissect his life and motives."

"No." Colten shakes his head. "Why did you talk to Detective Rains instead of me?"

"Because I like him better than I like you."

"Oh ..." He nods and smirks. "So you do, in fact, like me?"

"I like your parents ..." My scowl softens as I keep my gaze on my computer screen. "I liked your parents. I haven't talked to your mom in years, but I was brokenhearted when I heard about your dad. I'm sorry, Colten."

"Good old dad hung himself." He blows out a long breath, staring at my framed certificates on the wall. "I didn't even come home for the funeral. Fuck it. If I mattered to him, he wouldn't have killed himself."

I deal with a lot of grief in my job. I talk to families daily, explaining *what* and sometimes *why* something happened to their loved ones. But suicide doesn't usually come with a clear "why" answer. "I know you weren't there."

Colten returns his attention to me. "My mom told

me you were at the funeral."

With a slow nod, I shut off my computer. "I wasn't there for you."

He grunts. "Of course you weren't. Nobody gave a shit about me, especially my dad."

"How rich of you to play that part."

"What part?" Those monster-like eyes narrow at me.

"You're fine with people being shit on as long as it's not you."

Colten's dark brows lift a fraction. "Oh, this is about that? You think I shit on you."

I *know* he shit ... shat ... crapped all over me.

"I'm referring to your mom and brother. When you don't show up to be with them—the living—that's pretty shitty. Even for you."

"I visited them the following week. I helped go through his stuff."

I open my mouth to say more, exchange another barb, but I close it just as quickly. "Detective Rains has everything you need to know. And for the record, I was right about the weapon. And if you find it, and it has a red handle and a six-foot cord, I expect something like a fruit and chocolate bouquet with a note that says I'm the goddamn queen of forensic pathology." Standing, I sling my bag over my shoulder, give him a tight-lipped grin, and fish my keys out of the side pocket.

"I knew you were smart to a fault, Watts. But this..." Colten stands and takes several steps toward the door before glancing over his shoulder "...is a godlike arrogance I never saw coming from you. I imagine you're a pain in the ass to work with. We should grab dinner sometime."

"Can't. I'm busy." I usher him out the door so I can close and lock it.

"I didn't say when."

"I know." I pass him on my way to the stairs. "I meant I'm busy *never* having dinner with you. Not having dinner or any interaction with you outside of work is officially my new pastime."

"Jesus, Watts. You're still boring as fuck if avoiding me is your pastime. But I'm flattered that you're spending so much time thinking about me. Feels like old times."

I race down the stairs. "I'm not thinking about you. I'm actively *not* thinking about YOUUUUUU!" My foot catches and I fall down the final four steps.

My head. Oh, my aching head. My fingers reach for the laceration at my temple.

"Josie, just ... don't move. You could have broken something." Colten flies down the stairs after me.

I broke something alright. My pride, her sister Dignity, and Dignity's cousin Self-Esteem. It's taken Colten less than a week to reduce me to the young, shattered-ego girl I was the day I left for college. He's a perpetual thorn in my side. He's necrotizing fasciitis— a flesh eating infection that can't be contained.

"I'm fine." I search for my feet to get them under me so I can make another mad dash.

"You really need to hold still and let me call for

help."

"When you…" standing, I grimace "…finish medical school, I'll let you give me advice on my health. In the meantime, just stay away. You're nothing but bad luck."

"Are you blaming your clumsiness on me?" Colten's jaw unhinges like I offended his fragile, Good Samaritan soul.

I blame everything bad in my life on Colten Mosley. Always have. Why stop now?

As I dig into my bag for a tissue, Colten grabs my arm and pulls me toward the restroom. The men's room.

"Let go of me. I don't appreciate being manhandled."

"Really?" He opens the door and forces me inside without checking for occupants. Luckily there are none. "Huh. You used to love my hands on you. Handling you."

Asshole.

"I have an open wound, and you think the best idea is to get me closer to urinals?"

He grabs a wad of paper towels and runs them under the water. "I'm pretty sure I can assess your wound and decide if you need stitches without an actual medical degree. Basic first aid training, Watts. Or did you become a forensic pathologist because you couldn't save lives? Did you get demoted to the morgue? Can't kill anyone if everyone's already dead."

"Asshole." I could only keep it in my head for so

long. He's the *worst!* And when I'm in his presence, I'm the worst version of myself too.

"You remember what I used to do when you called me that?" He presses the wet towels to my injured head.

He used to kiss me. I'd get mad. Call him an asshole. And he'd kiss me until I lost all my fight. He called me a stubborn overthinker. As if one can really think too much.

"You manhandled me. And I hated it." I frown, averting my gaze to the side.

"You loved it."

"That's what your inflated ego said to ease your conscience of the burden of truth."

"And what was the truth?"

I force myself to look at him. "You were a control freak. And clearly you never grew out of it."

He flinches.

Colten's mom called his dad a control freak. I know Colten doesn't want anyone comparing him to his dad, but it's the truth. It doesn't mean Colten will hang himself while his wife and oldest son pick up Friday night pizza. It's just an unavoidable mix of genetics and years of learned behavior.

"You'll need a couple stitches. Or glue. They glue shit now, right?"

I grab his wrist as he blots my temple. "Give this to me." Facing the mirror, I frown. "This is why you don't chase people downstairs."

"You're not seriously blaming this on me?" He lifts

his right eyebrow.

"I was trying to get away from you." I press the wet towels to my temple and open the door with my other hand.

"Why are you always trying to run away from me?"

I turn back toward him with such speed that he nearly bumps into me. "You're too old to be asking why the grass is green and the sky is blue."

Rubbing his stupid lips together, he hides his grin. They're stupid lips because I always stare at them. They were my first kiss. I still feel robbed.

"Look at you. You're a goddamn medical doctor, Josie. That's a shit-ton of school. So much hard work and determination. However, here you are ... assistant chief medical examiner in the third largest city in the US. Even if your job is creepy as fuck, it's a huge feat. Not very many people can do what you do. But a lot of people can get a bachelor's degree to be an accountant or some certificate to sell real estate. A lot of women get pregnant and forego their professional aspirations to stay home and a raise a family." He shakes his head slowly, face a little more somber. "You weren't that girl."

I never said I wanted to be that person. I hated him then and a part of me still hates him now for assuming he knows everything about me. Colten meant something to me, but he wasn't a drug that took away my ability to make sensible decisions. He's still so fucking full of himself.

"Oh my god." My head rears back. "Please tell me

you're not trying to take credit for who I am and what I've become."

"Well ..." he says slowly.

"You..." I jab my finger into his chest "...are still an asshole. I became a doctor, and you stayed an asshole."

He inhales my words like they give him some sort of high. It doesn't matter if it's a compliment or not. The bastard gets off on pushing my buttons. "I'll drive you to urgent care."

"You won't." I pivot and stomp my feet toward the parking lot.

"You're going to hold that to your head *and* drive?"

"Yes. And I might even chew a piece of gum at the same time."

He chuckles. "I wouldn't expect anything less, Watts."

Even when I'm showing strength and independence, he has a way of making it seem like I'm stubborn, which feels like a weakness. I can't explain it. And nobody else has ever noticed it. Everyone thinks Colten Mosley is a classic nice guy which means my reaction to his constant goading seems extreme.

I'm the bitch.

I'm overreacting.

I don't know how to take a joke.

Not true.

Not true.

Definitely not true.

I get along well with others.

I've always excelled at group activities.

And most people find my sense of humor endearing. I can laugh at myself.

Except ... when Colten pokes and prods at me. He toys with me like I'm a cat batting my paw at a dangling ball of yarn that only he and I can see.

"Colten's going to miss you, Josie. He's making a sacrifice so you can pursue your dreams and he can find his way. It's noble. Friends do that for each other. You'll be better ... stronger for it someday."

My mom had *all* the great mom lines and philosophies.

Boys are mean to you when they like you.

Girls are catty because they are jealous of you.

You'll look back and be so grateful that you didn't try to fit in with the cliques.

You're smarter than them, and that's intimidating.

You might be the only girl in your class who hunts, but that just means you'd be the only one to survive if you're ever stranded on a desert island.

That one was always my favorite.

How many people actually get stranded on desert islands? I grew up in the Midwest. Was that really a danger?

I drive to urgent care, grab groceries after that, and get in a workout just to prove that I'm not anyone's damsel in distress.

Then I pull out my photo albums because I can't believe Colten Mosley actually got better looking with age.

I really, really hate him.

CHAPTER
Four

Josie wasn't the worst friend ever—for a girl.

"You sure do like balls," she said as we rode our bikes to the batting cages.

I laughed. "That sounds bad."

"Why?"

I made a quick glance behind me as her dark hair blew in the wind. "Because it sounds like you're talking about parts of a body."

"You mean testicles? If I meant testicles, I would have said it. I know all the parts of the human body."

"Yeah." I faced forward again to hide my grin. "I know you do."

Josie didn't look like a nerd, but she acted like one. It's not that I didn't like to read, but that's *all* she did. Well, that and fish with her dad. I probably had no room to talk; I spent a lot of hours practicing piano.

Mom was determined to have one of her boys play the piano. Chad wouldn't even consider it.

"Am I your only friend?"

"No," she scoffed.

"Because I haven't seen you play with anyone else since I moved in next door to you."

"Do you stare out your window and watch me all the time?"

"No." Yes. Watching her house was my favorite pastime. Her dad seemed to like me. He ruffled my hair a lot the same way my dad ruffled my hair. Chief Watts looked intimidating in his uniform. He always appeared ready to crush something or someone. They had a two-stall garage attached to the house and another two-stall detached garage where he kept all kinds of free weights, a bench press, and a pull-up bar. Sometimes Josie would go ask him for permission to play with me while he was lifting barbells that I swore weighed more than Josie and I combined. Angry veins riddled his skin like the Hulk. And a really big one bulged along his forehead while his face turned as red as the cherry tomatoes Josie's mom grew in five-gallon buckets on their porch.

"Jenn and Adrianna, my two best friends, are gone for the summer to Jenn's grandparents' house. They have a cabin on a lake in Wisconsin."

"And they didn't invite you?" I made another quick glance back at her, not at all hiding my grin. I liked picking on Josie. Whenever my mom heard me doing it, she rolled her eyes and assured Josie I was just pretending that I didn't have a crush on her. Of course, I adamantly disagreed, but not because my mom was wrong.

She was right. However, I would rather have died than admitted it.

"They invited me. I just couldn't go."

"Why not?"

"Because Jenn's dad got arrested for drinking and driving, and now my stupid dad won't let me ride in the car with them, even though Jenn's mom was going to do the driving."

Why did it disappoint me that Josie had two best friends? Why did I secretly hope I was her only friend?

Oh, right ... I had a huge crush on her.

We locked up our bikes and headed toward the cages.

"My dad said to always be careful if you're here close to dark because a few years ago a boy our age was kidnapped. They never found him."

"Then how do they know he was kidnapped?" I asked.

"Because he's gone, stupid."

"Maybe he didn't like his family, and he ran away."

"He was nine. Where does a nine-year-old go?" She pulled my bat out of my backpack and turned quickly before I could grab it back from her.

"If I ran away, I'd hide in the woods during the night and get free samples at the grocery store during the day. Sometimes, the gas station will give you free pizza and donuts if it's the end of the day, and you pretend you forgot your wallet at home. They just throw them out anyway." I shrugged.

"He's dead. Someone took him and cut up his body. He's in the woods, buried in pieces."

I tried to hide my shock. Josie looked so innocent, but the things that came out of her mouth were not things most kids our age said. Her dad must have discussed his job around her. Of course, that didn't explain why she had a collection of dead insects in her room or why she liked to hang out around the funeral home in hopes of seeing Roland Tompkins, the undertaker, to ask him a slew of questions.

"Anyone die today?"

"Have you ever put two people in one casket?"

"Are you going to be cremated or buried when you die?"

"Can you put ashes in a casket if you want to be cremated but still want to be buried too?"

Roland tolerated her because she was the police chief's daughter. After the third or fourth question, he nodded toward our bikes and asked us if we had somewhere we needed to be. I would say "yes" at the same time Josie would say "no."

"Thanks, Josie. Now, every time I come here, I'll think about someone kidnaping me, cutting up my body, and burying me in the woods." I managed to snatch the bat away from her.

"Well, that's what I always think about when I'm here with you," she said matter-of-factly.

"You think about *me* being kidnapped or you?"

She didn't answer me, not until I was in the batting

cage hitting my third ball. Her fingers curled around the chain links as she leaned against the cage to watch me. "Both. I think we'll be kidnapped and killed together. Or ... what if our kidnapper makes us choose? What if only one of us can live? Would you choose me or yourself?"

"I don't know." I swung and missed. "Who would you choose?"

"I asked you first."

"I'm not answering unless you answer first," I said.

"Then let's answer at the same time. I'll count to three. Who would you save? One. Two. Three."

We both said "me" at the same time. Then we shared an offended look at the same time.

"You'd let me die?" Josie's jaw dropped.

I laughed and hit the next ball. "You'd let *me* die."

"Yeah, but ..." She had nothing.

"I don't think the kidnapper would let us choose. He'd make us run, and the fastest one would get away."

"Well ..." She took several steps back from the cage. "That means you would die."

"Uh ..." I missed the next ball because I was looking at her overly confident grin. "No. That means you would die. I can run faster than you."

"Why? Because you're a boy?"

"Yes."

"Let's race."

I shook my head.

"Scared you're gonna lose?"

"No. I just don't want you crying when I beat you."

"I won't cry."

"Fine." I dropped my bat and sighed as I exited the cage.

We found a strip of grass to the north of the fields and made a starting line with a few sticks pushed end to end. Then we did the same for the finish line.

"It's like capture the flag." Josie set a bigger stick right behind the finish line. "First to get the stick wins."

"Promise you won't cry?" I said as she hunched into a ready position at the starting line.

"Shut up, stupid. Mark. Set. Go!" Josie took off like a shot. Arms pumping furiously.

I can't lie. She nearly beat me. *Nearly.*

And maybe she would have had she not tripped three feet before the finish line and scraped her hands and knees along the ground until they were grass-stained and a little bloodied.

"Are you okay?" I tossed the winning stick aside and knelt beside her as she pulled her knees to her chest and inspected her hands. I couldn't see her face because her hair hung like a dark, silky veil around it.

"I'm fine," she said just above a whisper in a shaky voice.

"Are you crying?"

"No." She sniffled.

"If you are, it's okay. You're bleeding."

"I'm not crying!" Her head whipped up straight. She wasn't crying, but she had tears in her eyes, and she clenched her jaw so hard it made her whole upper body shake.

I didn't know what to say, so I grabbed the prize stick and handed it to her. "Here. If you wouldn't have tripped, you would have won."

She stared at the stick for a few seconds and sniffled again before taking it from me. "I'll be your girlfriend."

"What?"

She shrugged one shoulder. "I said I'll be your girlfriend. Your mom said you have a crush on me. And my dad said I should never like a boy who isn't nice to me. You did the right thing. I won, and you gave me the stick. So I'll be your girlfriend for the rest of the summer."

My young brain didn't know how to respond. She packed so much into her little speech. She wasn't faster than me. She simply got a head start because she said "mark, set, go" so quickly. And I never said I wanted her to be my girlfriend. Then there was the summer part. She'd be my girlfriend for the rest of the summer? Why? Why did I need a girlfriend for the rest of the summer?

"But you should get a skateboard. Jenn had a boyfriend last summer, and they rode to the skate park all the time. Sometimes they kissed. We're not kissing because you lick your lips a lot, and I'm not kissing your lips after you've licked them."

"No thank you." I stood and headed back to the batting cage to get my bat and bag.

"What do you mean *no thank you*?"

"If we're not going to kiss, then I don't need you to

be my girlfriend. And I already have a skateboard, but one of its wheels got busted off when my dad accidentally ran over it with his car. And you're not faster than me. And I shouldn't have given you the stick because now you're acting weird. Well ... weirder than you already are."

"Colten Mosley. What's that supposed to mean? You think I'm weird?" She chased after me.

"Yes. You collect dead stuff, and you talk a lot about death. That's weird."

"Maybe it's unique. My mom says I'm unique."

I shoved my bat into my bag and headed toward our bikes. "She says you're unique because your skin is not the same color as hers or your dads." I turned just before reaching our bikes. "My parents told me not to say anything to you in case you didn't know, but if it were me ... I'd want to know."

"Know what?" She crossed her arms over her chest and flipped out her hip.

"You're adopted. That's why your skin and hair are darker than theirs."

"I'm not adopted, stupid."

"Um ..." My nose wrinkled. "Yes. You are. My mom said it looks as though you have a little Native American in your bloodline. And don't tell anyone I told you. I don't want to get into trouble."

"My mom had sex with someone else. That's why my skin is darker."

"What do you know about sex?" I asked. I knew only

what my brother had told me. A man pushes his penis between a woman's legs and pumps his hips. I asked why. He said because it feels good like when I touch myself. But ... I hadn't touched myself in a feel-good way. Not yet. That came (pun intended) the following summer when Josie let me see her tits for three seconds in exchange for half of my Twix bar. I later learned it was frowned upon to trade things for glances at titties. They really needed a handbook for stuff like that. I couldn't keep track of all the unspoken rules.

"Sex is how two people make a baby, stupid. Why don't you know that?"

"I do know that." I ignored her "stupid" label. My mom, the relationship expert, said Josie calling me stupid was actually an endearing term—just a little immature and unrefined. Mom said "silly" might be a better word, but she assured me Josie didn't really think I was stupid.

"Then why did you ask me?"

I turned away from her and unlocked my bike. "Because my bro—" No. I stopped myself. I wasn't giving my brother credit for my knowledge of sex. If my mom was wrong and Josie did think I was stupid, I didn't want to give her anymore ammunition to tease me. "Because I'm pretty sure people have sex for other reasons too."

"Other reasons?" Josie eyed me as she unlocked her bike.

I didn't make direct eye contact because my cheeks

were catching fire from talking about something that felt taboo. "Yeah. Sex feels good."

"What do you mean?"

By that point, I couldn't remember how we got on the conversation of sex, but I would have given my right arm to talk about anything else. "You'll find out someday."

"Tell me."

"No."

We hopped onto our bikes.

"Tell me, Colten."

"Nope."

"If you don't tell me, I'm telling my dad you pushed me down."

I slammed on my brakes, skidding to a stop. My gaze flitted from her scraped knees to her grass-stained hands. Before I could say anything, I think she read my reaction and withdrew her threat. That was the first of what would be many withdrawn threats.

"Fine." She sighed. "I won't tell my dad that. Just … tell me. If you don't tell me, I'm not going to be your friend."

Again, I gave her a look.

Again, she huffed a breath and withdrew her threat.

"We'll be friends, but I'm never coming back here with you. And that's no lie. So if someone tries to kidnap you, tough luck, Mr. Duck."

After a few more blinks, I laughed. "Tough luck, Mr. Duck?"

She hated it when I laughed at her, but I couldn't help it. Who said, "tough luck, Mr. Duck?"

Josie. That was who.

I was too young to recognize it, but I started falling in love with Josephine Watts before I had any idea what that really meant. By the time my adult self figured it out, she was gone, and it was my fault.

She frowned at me, a rain cloud ruining her baseball game, and wrinkled her nose while bolting ahead of me, down the street. I easily caught up to her.

"I'm kidding. Are you mad?"

"I'm kidding. Are you mad?" she parroted in a mocking voice.

"You're mad."

The second we turned onto our street, Josie kicked it into overdrive, dropped her bike in the front lawn, and ran inside her house.

"Did you and Josie have fun at the batting cages?" my mom asked as I kicked off my high-tops at the front door.

"I don't know."

She glanced up from the sofa, folding laundry and sorting it into piles around her. "Did something happen?"

I pulled off my baseball cap and hooked it on the banister before plodding my way to the faded leather recliner next to her.

"Don't sit on my folded bath towels."

"I won't," I said, managing to wedge myself into a small open gap next to them. "Josie's mad."

"Why?"

I shrugged. "She's a girl. Girls get mad about stupid stuff."

"Like?"

"Like I was joking about something she said, and that made her mad. And she said she'd be my girlfriend for the rest of the summer, and I said no. Maybe she's mad about that. I don't know."

Mom chuckled. "She offered to be your girlfriend for the rest of the summer?"

"Yes. Because I let her win a race."

"You're a little too young to have a girlfriend. And I really like Josie, so I think it's best that you stay friends."

I didn't mention that I would have said yes to her being my girlfriend had she not made the no kissing stipulation.

That night, my eyes were glued to the window, hoping to catch a glimpse of Josie. Just when I was about to give up and close my blinds, she ran out the front door and grabbed her bike. As she walked it toward the garage, she glanced back at my window. I jumped to the side so she wouldn't see me. My heart pounded, and I wasn't sure why.

What was the point of hoping to see her if I didn't want her to see me too?

Over the next nine years, I spent a lot of time at that window hoping to catch a glimpse of Josie Watts. Hiding from her. Hiding my feelings for her.

CHAPTER
Five

"Dr. Watts, do you believe in God?" Dr. Cornwell, the Chief Medical Examiner, asks me as he documents tattoos from the decedent on his table at the opposite end of the autopsy suite. A flock of interns surround his table, church mice with perked ears and curious eyes while four other forensic pathologists dissect their first cases of the day.

I focus on my table holding a male teenager who took a round of ammunition in his chest last night. "I like the idea of God."

"So that's a no?" Cornwell asks.

I glance up, eyeing him through my goggles and face shield—what tiny sliver I can see of him through the congested parameter of interns. "Depends. Do you define the word 'believe' as something you hold as a truth or opinion?"

"Does it matter?"

"Yes. I can be more liberal—in a nonpolitical sense —with my beliefs if others willingly interpret them as my opinions. But if they are interpreted as what I believe to be truths or facts, then I find it best to limit my beliefs to things that have little disputable evidence. So saying I like the idea of God is my way of saying I acknowledge that I can't prove God's existence, but I wish I could because it's comforting to think there's something greater than us ... than this life."

"Now, I know why you're still single," Dr. Cornwell says, eliciting some chuckles from the peanut gallery. "You don't always have to be right, Watts. Well, I need you to always be right here, when it counts. But outside of work, it wouldn't kill you to indulge a little."

I bite my tongue. I think he just implied I'm a prude or someone quite boring, not so adventurous. "I indulge."

"Now I'm curious. Tell me you follow your horoscope or get your palm read. Do you avoid black cats and walking under ladders? Have you ever had bad luck after breaking a mirror? Do you believe in ghosts?"

"Vampires and werewolves. Not ghosts. Come on, Dr. Cornwell. Ghosts ... what are you? Eighty?"

He turns seventy next month, and he's really sensitive about his age, not as sensitive as he is about losing his hair, but still ... I think he'll always be young at heart.

"Have you ever autopsied a vampire, Dr. Watts?"

"No. That would be nearly impossible," I say.

"Because they don't exist?"

"No. Because they don't really die. I don't think they can be killed either. They have to be destroyed which means there would not be anything left to autopsy." It's my turn to elicit laughter from the peanut gallery.

God, I wish I could see Dr. Cornwell's face behind his mask. Is he smirking? He rarely smiles, so a smirk would feel like a total win for me today.

"Dr. Watts graduated top of her class. She thought she wanted to stare at diseased tissue all day through a microscope and diagnose diseases. Then she tried her hand at general surgery. Then ... she met me. I've trained a lot of young doctors in my life, but none have shown as much natural talent for ... dare I say, disassembling and reassembling the human body quite like Dr. Watts."

A few of the interns navigate from his table to mine. I'm now the interesting one in the room, and they're curious. What do I have that they might see in themselves?

"Spooky," I say.

One of the other pathologists uses a bone saw for a bit before the room returns to its normal white noise from the ventilation system.

"What's that, Watts?"

"Spooky. The first time you watched me perform my first solo autopsy, you said it was almost spooky."

He grunts. "It was. I think I also asked you if you'd lived on a farm and slaughtered animals. Nothing about the process seemed to phase you one bit. I'm not sure I've met anyone in this profession who hasn't taken a moment's pause when working with a dead body for the first time to let subtle realities sink in such as how cold the bodies are. You know it in your head, but it doesn't register until you actually feel it. Not with you. I didn't see you take a millisecond pause or so much as exhibit the tiniest of flinches. In fact, you whistled the whole time. You still do."

"Only when I'm alone." I follow the next bullet track.

"Not true. You were doing it just before I asked you if you believed in God."

"No. I wasn't."

"Can I get a witness testimony?" Dr. Cornwell asks the interns.

A few brave souls nod their heads and mumble, "You were."

"'Pumped Up Kicks,'" one of the interns adds. "Yesterday," he continues, "you were whistling 'If I Die Young' during your first autopsy of a young woman who died of a suspected drug overdose, and you whistled 'Pumped up Kicks' during your second autopsy—a gunshot victim as well. I assume you have certain songs for different causes of death."

I do?

How have I not realized this?

"Funny." I retrieve the bullet. "I never realized I did that."

"A song for different causes of death," Dr. Cornwell

says. "I like that. What do you whistle for heart attacks?"

I chuckle. "I don't know."

"Duh." The same observant intern pipes up again. "Demi Lovato's 'Heart Attack.'"

His fellow interns laugh, and I smile behind my mask. It's interesting how much we learn about ourselves from the observations of people around us. This shouldn't surprise me. I often learn more about the deceased from talking with their family than I do from performing an autopsy. There's so much in life that's not black and white—so many things that require explanation before one can make accurate inferences. What if we learned to reserve judgment until we knew the whole story? I think I'd like that world.

TWO HOURS LATER, I take my lunch outside, in need of some fresh air.

"Watts," Detective Mosley says my name and grins as I strut past him in the lobby. "Just the person I'm looking for."

"I'm on a lunch break."

He pivots and follows me outside. "Does your profession get a lunch break? I know mine does not. Is it hard to eat after seeing the things you see daily? I bet you're a vegetarian."

"I bet I'm not." I cross the gated entrance to find a spot on the grass behind the building's sign.

"Do you still hunt?"

"No." I take a seat and dig my sandwich out of my thermal lunch bag.

Colten slips his hands into the pockets of his suit. I never imagined him in a job that required a suit. I can see him in a uniform, but not an actual suit. It's weird. I don't let on that I'm the least bit interested in what he's wearing or anything else about him.

"Did you put 'field dressing a deer' on your resumé?"

"Did you put asshole on yours?"

"Ouch. That's harsh. You're not still holding a grudge, are you?"

Leave it to him to make my feelings seem ridiculous.

"What do you want, Detective Mosley?"

"What were your findings with Jacob Marsh?"

"Who's Jacob Marsh?" I know who he's referencing, but I'm not his personal medical examiner. Jacob Marsh was brought in this morning. I haven't autopsied him yet. And I wouldn't be surprised if Dr. Cornwell jumped in and stole him from me.

"Missing legs. Most likely a chainsaw. Seeing any connection? That's two in the past month."

"Good to know. I'll have to get back to you after I conduct the autopsy."

"Why didn't you do it this morning?"

I chew the bite of my sandwich and stare up at him,

squinting against the sun. "Because I was busy," I mumble with my mouth full.

"Don't you prioritize?"

"That's what your boss said when he wanted the results of this morning's gunshot victim. Now, he has to sit on his thumbs and wait for ballistics. I suggest you go see if your thumbs will fit up your ass too because I'll get to it when I get to it."

"Did you speak to my boss like you're speaking to me?"

Just his presence has stolen my appetite. I shove the other half of my sandwich in my bag. He's relentless. Always has been. I know he won't stop nipping at my ankles anytime soon.

"You can finish your lunch first. I'm not a monster."

"You are." I march back to the building.

He grabs my arm like he did before I fell down the stairs.

I yank it out of his grip as I turn back toward him.

"I'm sorry, Josie."

I don't want to be the person who holds a grudge. Not because he deserves my forgiveness, because I deserve to live without this awful feeling weighing on my conscience. Anger is an unrelenting weight on one's soul. It's suffocating. And it's been too long. I need to let this go.

"It's no big deal." It is. Or at least it was a huge fucking deal. He ended us—a near decade of friendship—and it crushed me. I told no one. I suffered in silence.

"Well ..." He shrugs with an innocent and somber expression I haven't seen since our recent reunion. It's a glimpse of the Colten I once knew. And maybe that Colten is still inside of him, the way that young Josie girl still resides in my heart. "It was a big deal to me then. And you knowing that I'm truly sorry for how it ended ... even if it was for the best..." his eyebrows pull together as he bites the inside of his cheek for a few seconds "...that means something to me now."

I don't walk away. It feels physically impossible. All these emotions that have been locked away for so long are on the verge of coming out. Things I should have said seventeen years ago. "Did you get married?"

His head eases side to side slowly.

Maybe that should make me feel better, but it doesn't. I hope he didn't get married because he *is* the asshole I thought he was, and no woman in her right mind would marry him. The thought of him searching for me in someone else, the way I've spent the last seventeen years looking for him in every failed relationship, makes me feel a little less broken.

"I have a daughter," he says.

Never mind. I'm shattered. Again.

"No wife. But you have a daughter. I hope you're just rejecting marriage and not a deadbeat dad who didn't stick around and do the right thing."

Colten winces.

I don't. Not externally.

If I nailed the truth on the head, that's his problem.

Not mine, although I find it disheartening to think that he fathered a child and abandoned her and her mom.

"It's complicated," Colten says.

"Yes. Children complicate things." I force myself to turn again and head back into the building. It's his life. *We* ended a long time ago. What he's chosen to do with his life is none of my business.

"Call me about Jacob Marsh. There's a killer on the loose."

"There's always a killer on the loose," I say as the door closes behind me.

CHAPTER
Six

I AGREED to let Josie be my girlfriend. Then she broke up with me right before school started. Two weeks later, Annie Nelson asked me to be her boyfriend. Being one of the new kids at school made me an enigma of sorts. All the girls wanted to be my girlfriend.

"You can't be Annie's boyfriend." Josie ran to catch up to me after the school bus dropped us off at the end of the street.

"Why not?" I didn't bother turning to look at her. The sting of her breaking up with me made it difficult to make eye contact with her. Unfortunately, our parents had become friends, and we lived across the street from each other, so totally avoiding her wasn't an option.

"Because she's so annoying."

"Maybe I think you're annoying."

"That's not very nice."

"But it's nice of you to call Annie annoying?"

Josie's shoes slapped against the sidewalk as I picked up my pace forcing her to jog behind me. "Because she *is* annoying. All she ever talks about is her stupid brother who plays football in college. *Ethan goes to school for free because he's so good at football. Ethan's going to be in the NFL and make millions of dollars. Ethan ... Ethan ... Ethan.* It's SO annoying!"

"What I do is none of your business, Josie."

"We're friends. So it's kind of my business."

"We *were* friends."

"Colten, we still are."

"You broke up with me."

"Yes. But I said we should just be friends."

I darted across the street to my driveway, hiking my backpack farther up my back. "I think we should just be neighbors."

"Colten ..."

"Josie ..." I mimicked her with the same tone she always used to mimic me.

"Derek asked me to be his girlfriend. I think I'm going to say yes," she goaded me. God ... she always goaded me.

I didn't give a shit about "Derek, brace-faced, thick glasses Hoffman." But his family was rich, and that made him one of the cool kids. It was too early to determine my status at school, but Annie was more popular than Josie, probably *because* her brother was a big deal, and that meant I'd be popular too if she was my girlfriend.

So I became Annie's boyfriend, and Josie became Derek's girlfriend. We didn't talk for the month she spent holding hands with Derek from the school to the bus stop, nor did we talk for the two weeks after they broke up while I was still Annie's boyfriend.

All that changed the Saturday Annie rode her bike to my house. My parents were gone, and Chad was supposed to be keeping an eye on me, but that was always a joke. I sneaked outside to meet Annie behind our garage.

"Hi." I grinned.

She looked pretty in her pink hoodie and jeans with flowers on the legs. She had straight blond hair and high bangs. The opposite of Josie's dark, unruly hair that always had waves in it and long bangs that she sometimes clipped to one side with a barrette.

"Hi." Annie smiled and wet her lips several times because the whole purpose of her riding her bike to my house the morning my parents were gone was to kiss me. And unlike Josie, I didn't mind kissing someone who licked their lips.

"Ready?" I asked because ten-year-olds asked to kiss each other. They excessively wet their lips. And they hid behind garages to do it.

"Are *you* ready?"

I nodded. I was ready. It had nothing to do with Annie and everything to do with kissing a girl before Josie kissed a boy. I wasn't one hundred percent sure she hadn't kissed Derek, but I felt pretty sure she hadn't kissed a kid with braces after her unwillingness to kiss me for licking my lips.

I leaned in a few inches. Annie leaned in a few inches. We stayed there, separated by another three inches for what felt like forever. Finally, I went the rest of the way and pressed my lips to hers. We both kept our eyes open, and that was really weird. She blinked, and I pulled away. There was no sound. No suction. I'm not sure it counted as a kiss, but she smiled like it did, so who was I to argue? I wasn't exactly an expert on kissing at that point.

"Oh my gosh!"

Annie glanced over my shoulder. Then, I turned around to Josie and her gaping mouth catching flies while her eyes swelled to big brown saucers.

"Did you really kiss her?" Josie tripped over her words.

"Get out of here," I said.

"I'm telling your parents." Josie pivoted and stomped toward the front door.

"I'd better go. I hope you don't get into trouble." Annie's face wrinkled.

Yes, we were hiding behind the garage to kiss, but not because I was worried about getting in trouble. It's not like my parents specifically ever told me I couldn't kiss a girl. I just didn't want my stupid brother to see us. Or Josie.

"I'll call you tonight," I said while chasing after tattletale Josie. She wasn't at my front door. She was, instead, running into the wooded area behind her house that backed up to a dirt trail where people walked their dogs or sometimes road dirt bikes.

"Josie ... stop!" I jogged after her.

She jumped up and grabbed the lowest branch of her favorite tree. Then she climbed up three more branches to her favorite perch where she often spied on people along the trail. It was also where she escaped to when her parents would fight. Josie climbed trees, fished, hunted, and rode a skateboard. She was the definition of a tomboy. She also wore girly clothes and painted her fingernails and toenails. She was a mix of ... perfection.

I never told her that.

"That's gross, Colten. Just stay away from me."

"Kissing a girl is gross?"

"Kissing Annie is gross. Why did you do that?"

I laughed as I climbed the tree and sat next to her, our legs dangling in sync. "Because she's my girlfriend. Why did you hold Derek's hand every day after school while walking to the bus?"

She kept her expression neutral and her tongue mute as she stared ahead at the empty dirt trail.

"Are you going to tell my parents?" I didn't care. Well, I kind of cared, but I didn't understand why she'd tell them. Did her parents know about the hand-holding?

"Why?" she whispered.

"Because if you're just going to tell on me, I'm going to tell them first."

"No." She shook her head. "Why did you kiss her?"

"I told you. She's my girlfriend."

"Ugh!" Josie maneuvered past me, nearly knocking me out of the tree to get to the trunk and shimmy down it. "I *hate* that she's your stupid girlfriend." She marched back toward her house while I hopped out of the tree.

"Why?" I ran behind her.

"Because."

"Because why?"

"Because now you can't be my boyfriend."

"You broke up with me."

"Ugh ... you're so stupid. Boys are so stupid." She ran up the deck stairs.

I was really confused. And I had no idea that moment was a tiny glimpse into a lifetime of not understanding women. I thought it was just Josie being Josie. Wrong. It was Josie being a female.

As usual, I needed my mom to interpret things for me. She spoke female.

"She likes you. That's why she's upset that you have another girlfriend," Mom explained as if it should have been crystal clear to me.

"But she broke up with me."

"Yes. But that doesn't mean she's ready to see you with another girlfriend."

"But she had a boyfriend for a month."

"Doesn't matter."

That made no sense to me. It *did* matter.

"You never said what made her mad to begin with.

Why did she run off to her tree? Did you say something? Did someone at school say something?"

I hadn't told my mom about the kiss behind the garage. Even if I didn't think she'd be mad, I also didn't think she'd exactly be happy either.

"I don't know," I mumbled as I escaped to my room before she asked anymore questions.

Taking my usual spot on my beanbag chair by the window, I pretended to read the book we were supposed to be reading for English while keeping surveillance of the Watts's house in hopes of catching a glimpse of the *stupid* girl I had a chronic crush on.

The next day, I broke up with Annie.

Josie still ignored me on the bus ride home, even though I sat right next to her. When the bus dropped us off at our stop, I waited for Josie to get her bag, and we exited the bus together. Instead of walking toward home, she just stood there, watching the bus close its door and pull away from the curb as the rest of the kids scattered in different directions toward their respective houses.

When it was just the two of us, I broke the silence. "Aren't you coming?"

Josie turned ninety degrees from the curb toward me. After a few slow blinks, she clenched the straps of her backpack, lifted onto her toes, and leaned forward, our lips pressing together. But this wasn't like the Annie kiss. This was different. It was a real kiss.

My lips moved, latching onto her top lip for a few seconds, and then her lips moved and did the same thing to my bottom lip. There was suction and movement.

It was definitely a real kiss.

When she dropped flat onto her feet again, she smiled. "Let's go home."

That wasn't the day she became my girlfriend, again. Not in any official capacity. That was just the day I started kissing Josie Watts.

We kissed a lot.

We held hands.

We hung out at the batting cages, in the woods behind her house, and in her dad's garage where he exercised or worked on his old Chevelle. That was the year I learned to change a tire and change the oil in a car. My dad thought I was a bit young when I told him, but I think he was just jealous that Josie's dad taught me instead of him.

Josie and I were friends, but of a different kind. At school, I had my friends, and she had her friends. I played sports and the piano. Josie stayed after school to help the librarian put the returned books back on the shelves. And sometimes, she lay in her front yard under the maple tree and read. Josie read so many books.

Then there was *our* time. It felt like everything else was just an obstacle to navigate to make it to our time. That place where our hands searched for each other. That place where she'd nudge my arm with hers, and I'd bend down to give her a quick kiss. We'd smile and I knew she thought the same thing I did: we weren't each other's world—the world was simply ours when it was just the two of us.

Josie Watts was unlike any other human I had ever met. She'd call me stupid one minute and bring me cookies she made with her mom the next minute with a handwritten apology.

Passionate.

I'd say she was passionate, even if at the time I didn't know what the word really meant. There were a lot of words that fit Josie that didn't come to mind until after I'd already lost her.

Inquisitive.

Generous.

Authentic.

"I heard something," Josie said one night as we were stargazing from her mom's hammock on their deck. Her parents were inside, tending to her baby brother.

"I didn't hear anything."

"No." She gently rolled toward me as I did the same, so we didn't fall out of the hammock. With her face a few inches from mine, her lips pulled into a sad smile. "I heard my dad telling my mom something about your dad."

I narrowed my eyes. "What?"

"I'm not sure I should tell you."

"You have to tell me. We tell each other everything."

"Yeah." Her gaze shifted to my chin. "But this is something that's sad."

"What? Just tell me."

She forced her eyes, the color of night, to look into mine again. "My dad said he saw your dad kissing a woman that wasn't your mom."

"That's a lie." I sat up, and Josie had to quickly put her feet on the ground, so she didn't fall off the other side.

"I'm just telling you what my dad said."

"Well ... he's lying," I murmured with my back to her, and my heart pounding against my ribs the way it did when I thought I was in trouble or when I jumped off the high diving board at the pool. It made it hard to breathe, and it felt painful and a little scary.

I was too young to understand, or maybe I didn't want to think about what that meant. "I have to go home."

"Don't tell your dad I told you. I don't want him to be mad at my dad or at me."

My unpredictable relationship with Josie should have prepared me for that moment—the one where things that seemed upright were actually upside down. Where the sky was green and the grass was blue. It was like Josie breaking up with me then kissing me. Maybe I wasn't supposed to understand everything; I just needed to nod and accept it. Whatever *it* was.

CHAPTER
Seven

"Wʜᴀᴛ's up with you and the detective?" Alicia, one of the morgue techs, asks me as we change into our PPE in the locker room.

"I don't know. What do you mean?"

She smirks. "I heard he calls and always wants to talk to you, not Dr. Cornwell. And I saw the two of you having lunch outside the other day."

"We weren't having lunch outside. *I* was trying to eat my lunch outside, and he insisted on ruining it by asking me questions about an autopsy I haven't performed."

"You sound angry." She laughs. "I take it you don't care for him?"

"Astute observation. We went to school together." I tie my black apron.

"I see. Childhood archenemies?"

"Not exactly. The enemy part came after we graduated and went our separate ways. For the most part, we were … friends growing up." Who am I kidding? We were more than friends. I would have been fine saying goodbye to my *friend* Colten Mosley after we graduated, but we were a lot more than friends. Or maybe that was a miscalculation on my part.

"What happened?" Alicia pulls her booties on over her tennis shoes and all the way up her legs, close to her knees.

"It's a long story." I lie. It's a rather short story. With the grace of a dirty bomb, he obliterated my heart and wished me good luck at college. There were a few pathetic moments that I blamed his dad. Had his dad been a better role model, maybe Colten would have known how to treat someone you supposedly love.

Maybe his dad didn't really love his mom, just like Colten didn't really love me.

"We should get a drink sometime, and you can tell me all about your long story."

"I don't drink alcohol." I shut my locker door.

"Why? You've seen too many ugly livers?"

I laugh. "Ironically, no. That's not it. I've just never had any desire to drink alcohol."

"Ever?"

I shake my head.

"Were either one of your parents an alcoholic?"

"Nope."

"You didn't drink in college? At all?"

"Nope. Cough syrup and kombucha is the extent of my alcohol consumption."

"That's ... crazy." Alicia follows me to the autopsy suite.

"I know. But it's true."

"Well, I've seen you eat, so we'll talk about your juicy past over greasy onion rings and two virgin margaritas."

"Deal."

I half expect to see Detective Mosley waiting for me in the autopsy suite because my first case today is another body missing its legs from what investigators believe was likely a saw. That makes three. By the end of the morning, we might officially have a serial killer on our hands.

Before I take lunch, I make a courtesy call to Detective Mosley.

"Circular saw. Red handle. Six-foot cord. Am I right, Dr. Watts?"

"Something like that." I roll my eyes and plop down into my desk chair, shaking my mouse to wake up my computer screen.

"Do I get brownie points for waiting for your call instead of visiting you?"

"I don't know, Detective. Are you a Girl Scout?"

"Just a do-gooder. Run-of-the-mill nice guy who happens to catch killers and put them in prison to keep citizens like yourself safe."

I should have left on my PPE; the shit's getting deep.

"You might catch the killer with the help of me and my team, but you don't put anyone in prison. I'm pretty sure that's the DA's job."

"I don't remember your ego being so sensitive, Watts."

"I don't remember your arrogance hogging all the credit, Mosley."

He chuckles. "Okay. I'd love to spend the day flirting with you like this, but I have a job to do. Give me the rundown."

I open my mouth to protest his ridiculous accusation that I'm flirting with him, but I, too, have things to do, so I get back to business and confirm everything he already suspects.

"Why cut off the legs if you're not planning on burying it or transporting it?" he asks.

"Well, I'm a forensic pathologist not a forensic psychologist, but it's possible that he or she had something happen to them in their past. If my husband beat me, *kicked* me repeatedly, and I decided to kill him, I might remove his legs."

After a few seconds, Colten hums. "Mmm ... maybe. So you think the victims abused their killer at some point?"

"No." I chuckle. "It's unlikely the victims did anything to the killer. They just might have resembled someone who did do something to the killer."

"I've thought about that, but there's nothing that stands out other than all three victims are men. One black, two white. Ages twenty-three, twenty-nine, and forty-seven. One was married with kids. One was in grad school. And one just married his business partner in a civil service."

"Keep looking. There's something. There's always a *something*. But ... I have other mysteries to solve, so you're on your own now."

"Did you talk to the families?"

"I haven't talked to Matthew Roslow's family yet. Why?"

"Just wondering."

I frown. I don't have to see Colten to know from the sound of his voice that he's formulating a theory he's not ready to share yet. When we were younger, he used to torture me with his half-thoughts. He'd ask me something that seemed random and out of the blue, only to answer my "why" with "just wondering."

The bait's similar, but I'm no longer biting. Colten Mosley is no longer my keeper of secrets, my favorite confidant. And if my heart knows what's good for it, it will keep my relationship with him professional.

"I don't know if the family will give me anything they haven't already shared with the police, but I'll let you know. Otherwise, good luck." I cringe as I say those two words.

"Good luck, Josie. You're going to be a huge success." The past echoes in my mind.

"Thanks."

"Bye—"

"Josie?"

I bite my lips together and close my eyes. "Yeah?"

"How would you feel about getting dinner with me sometime? We could catch up."

Catching up with my past is a terrible idea. I'm still running from it. "Thanks, but I'm good. I feel all caught up."

"You still with that same guy I met at the restaurant?"

"You didn't meet him. I never introduced you to him. And yes, I still see him."

"And he knows your real job?"

"Bye, Detective." I end the call and give my phone the middle finger. Colten thinks he knows me. He thinks he knows my date whom he's never met. How is this possible? We've spent more time apart than we ever did together. Nine years together. Seventeen years apart.

Seventeen adult years.

Seventeen years of dating other people—having sex with other people.

And ... having a baby with someone else. I still can't believe he has a daughter.

"Wow! I didn't expect to hear from you again. I thought you were ghosting me." Paul's spot-on analysis of my behavior makes me cringe.

"Work has been crazy. That's all."

"Long days looking through a microscope?" he asks with a hint of sarcasm.

"I'm free tonight if you want to have dinner or just hang out."

Have sex. If he wants to have sex.

For some disturbing reason, the more interaction I have with Detective Mosley, the more I feel the need to have sex with ... anyone. Well, not anyone. I'm not that desperate, *yet*. Someone. I want to have sex with someone.

Angry sex.

Revenge sex.

Screw-you-Colten-Mosley sex.

And I really want to have sex with someone and *not* think of Colten, but at this point, it's unlikely. That sucks too.

Still ... *still* ... after all these years, he has this invisible hold on me. I'm too educated, too mature, too confident to be this pathetic. It's because I don't like unsolved mysteries. I hate when I can't determine the cause or manner of death. I hate marking that stupid box. It makes me feel like a failure. And I hate that Colten broke my heart, and I don't know why. I *need* to know why, but I can't ask him. There's no way I'm giving him that level of satisfaction.

"We can order in pizza. Your place?" Paul invites himself to my place.

I think of a million excuses, then I think of Colten. "I'll order the pizza now. Can you be here in an hour?"

"I can. Should I ..."

"Should you what?" I ask while picking up some dirty dishes around my kitchen.

"Should I pack an overnight bag?"

Why did he ask me? It knocked his confidence level down a good ten notches. *Don't ask if you're staying. Assume you're staying. Make me want you to stay—beg you to stay.*

"I don't know. Should you?" I try to flip it, acting flirty, giving him the opportunity to play along.

"That's why I asked you. It's your place. I don't want to assume I'm staying."

Sometimes ... just sometimes ... chivalry kills the moment.

"Actually, I have to meet someone early tomorrow morning."

"No overnight bag. Got it." Paul tries to sound cool. He's not. I'm not that cool either, so I don't judge him too harshly. We're both science geeks. "See you within the hour. Text me your address."

"I will. Bye."

Paul arrives in less than twenty minutes. I'm flattered that he's so excited to see me. Devoting more than a decade to achieve your professional goals leaves little time to cultivate meaningful relationships. I've started to feel broken in that area of my life. Can I find a man who finds my love for my job an attractive quality?

We'll see.

"The pizza is on its way. And I don't have a drop of alcohol to offer you. So make yourself at home on the sofa while I get you a bottle of water." I bite my lips together to hide my ridiculously embarrassing smile.

"You can choose sparkling or still." Not only have I neglected my love life for the past decade, but I've also failed to stock my apartment with anything that might make me look like a good hostess.

"I feel like living on the edge tonight, so I'll take sparkling. Thank you." Paul slips his shoes off just inside my door and saunters to the sofa.

His ass looks good in jeans. It looks good without any too.

"You okay?"

I glance up as he turns toward me just before taking a seat on my sofa. *Busted!* Yes, I was looking at his ass, and he knows it.

"I'm good." I tame my grin, but I'm sure he sees the truth in my flushed cheeks.

"Do you have some lime to go with the sparkling water?"

I open my fridge as if I'm checking, but I know the answer already. "Shoot. I think I used my last lime yesterday. I have a tangelo. Would you like a slice of that instead?"

He laughs. "No. I'm good."

I hand him the sparkling water and sit at the opposite end of the sofa as if I'm shy—as if we haven't had sex. My mistake. I should have kept things going, but I'm terrible at keeping shit alive. That's why I don't have house plants. It's also why I work with dead people.

"I've missed seeing you. I'm so glad you called."

I shake my head. "I'm terrible at dating. I'm

surprised you even took my call. I get so distracted with work. Really, I'm sorry. I should have made a better effort because I did enjoy..." I smirk and laugh a little "...hanging out with you."

Sex.

I enjoyed the sex. I enjoyed the company of a *warm,* naked body.

"Well..." he scoots a little closer to me, angling his body a few degrees to face me "...I enjoyed hanging with you too." Paul makes me feel good. Normal. Relaxed.

The pizza arrives, and we eat nearly the whole thing while sharing funny stories from our childhood. We were both a little "different." I've been searching for someone who is not like me—probably not a great strategy—so it's not surprising that I'm still single. Paul gets me. Or so I think ... until I slip up and overshare.

"Oh ... this feels good." I toss the crust of my pizza onto my plate and set it on the coffee table. "It was a long day. I needed this. I don't think I'll ever get used to having a child on my table." The second I say it, my sluggish mind catches up. Paul doesn't know. I can't keep it from him forever, but I'd planned on sharing the truth with a little more tact and a lot more explanation.

"Child? On your table? Do you still work directly with patients? I assumed you just worked in the lab."

My lips curl together, face wrinkled with a hint of a cringe. "I do work in a lab sometimes. I ... God, please don't take this the wrong way like I intentionally lied to you. I just feel like sharing the truth too soon ends things before they really begin."

"You're not a doctor."

I shake my head. "No. I'm a doctor. And I'm a pathologist."

"So ..." Paul raises a single eyebrow.

"I'm a forensic pathologist."

He blinks several times before nodding slowly. "That's ... you ..."

"I'm an assistant medical examiner."

Paul continues to inspect me between his slow blinks. He leans forward, setting his nearly empty bottle of sparkling water next to his plate on the coffee table. "You perform autopsies?"

"Correct." I smile softly.

"So the child on your table was ..."

"Deceased." I nod several times.

"That's ..." Paul clears his throat.

"Sad," I say. "But if you're referring to my job, it's necessary. There's actually a shortage of forensic pathologists in the United States." I shrug. "Somebody has to do it. It's not glamorous, but it's necessary."

"Of course. I just didn't see that coming. I had a vision of you in a lab."

"Well, sometimes I'm in the lab."

He scratches the back of his head. "How did you uh ... decide to become a medical examiner? Surely you didn't dream of it as a young child."

I really like Paul. And I think he likes me. This doesn't have to be a dealbreaker. And he deserves my honesty, but I think he needs it in small doses. I don't tell him that I'm incredibly good at my job. A natural at something so very unnatural. I have a gift for separating the body and soul. I don't see a person. I see a body that housed a soul. Even when I see a child on my table, it's only a little harder because I know there is a family (usually) who feels like the order of death didn't go as intended. Children shouldn't die before their parents. But sometimes they do. And that's life.

It's my job to determine the why and the how. And while it won't bring them back, sometimes it gives the family a sense of closure.

"The Chief ME, Dr. Cornwell, recruited me. He made me feel special and needed. He knew I could do what a lot of other doctors can't do. So no, I didn't dream of becoming a medical examiner. I don't think most people end up taking the path they dreamed of as a child. Did you?"

"Yes." Paul gives me a serious face for a few seconds before grinning. "It's true. I'm a purebred nerd. I've dreamed of being a chemist since I got my first chemistry set for Christmas when I was eight. But ..." He nods. "You're right. It's probably the exception not the norm that someone actually becomes what they dream about as a child. That probably makes me boring and tragically predictable."

It really does. I bite my bottom lip, and he leans into me, stopping just before our mouths meet. I grin, so elated that he knows the truth and it's no big deal. I'm so glad I called Paul. I should have done it sooner.

We kiss, letting the need build. He slides his hand from my leg to my waist, from my waist to my breast. I hum into the kiss. My hands reach for the button to his jeans, and I push him back onto the sofa, straddling his waist.

My shirt comes off. His shirt follows.

My hands work the zipper to his jeans. He grips my hips.

I smile. He ... cringes. Winces. Something *not* sexy.

His gaze goes right to my hands. "Is it weird for you..." he grabs my wrists to stop my hands from doing anything else "...to separate what you do at work from your personal life?"

My gaze narrows. "Uh ..." I shake my head. "What do you mean?"

"I mean ... you use these hands to cut open dead bodies. But now you're using them to touch me. I bet you've done things to a man's..." he nods toward his erection "...*part* that's not exactly sexy. Is it weird for you? Do you think about it when you're not at work?"

My hands, the same ones I use in my job, rub my face as I chuckle because it's better than what I really want to do—cry. "No. I don't think about work when I'm with you like this—the way male OBGYNs don't think about their patients' vaginas while making love to their wives." I drop my hands from my face and rest them on my legs to keep from touching him since it seems to make him uneasy. "At least, most male OBGYNs probably don't think about work when they're having sex."

"But you've seen a lot of naked men."

Oh my god. This isn't happening. "It's an occupational hazard. It's not a perk. And can I just say that a lot of doctors who work on living people see them naked. Surgeons cut into people. They hold their organs in their hands. They put them together and sew them back up. But for whatever reason, it's much easier for surgeons to get laid than forensic pathologists." As my words escalate in volume, I climb off his lap and pull on my shirt.

"I'm sorry." He sits up. "I know how ridiculous it is. And you're a great person ..."

Here we go. I refrain from rolling my eyes, but it's not easy.

"But I can't shut off my brain now. All I can think about is you opening dead bodies like it's no big deal."

"It is a big deal, Paul. It's someone's son or daughter. Someone's friend. Someone's significant other. Someone's parent. I don't ever take that for granted. And while I'm not saving their life, I'm finding answers to questions that might help give the family closure or comfort if they know their loved one didn't suffer. And you know ... sometimes I do save lives. Sometimes I discover a hereditary condition that the family can use as knowledge for early prevention. I help the police solve murder mysteries, and I help put dangerous people in prison. There's nothing about my job that I don't take seriously. There's never a day that I don't feel like I'm making a difference in someone's life. I never make a cut and think it's *no big deal.*"

He tucks in his shirt as he stands, head bowed. "I'm so sorry. I'm a bastard. And this is one hundred percent me, not—"

"Me, not you. Yeah. Yeah. I've heard it a million times. Get the fuck out."

Paul's head snaps up, lips set into an O of shock. "Josie—"

"It's Dr. Watts to you. Get out. And pray you never show up on my table, or you will be the exception to my high level of professionalism as I gut you like a fish."

Paul keeps a sharp eye on me as he scurries to the door and shoves his feet into his shoes. "You're a crazy bitch."

Pressing my lips together, I nod a half dozen times while he flies out of my house. This is a first. I've never reacted like this before now. I've been rejected a lot, but never have I lost it. My usual MO is a few shy nods and a "thanks anyway" like someone's refusing to buy something I'm trying to sell.

If I'm honest, it's Colten Mosley's fault. He's had me on edge since the moment he said my name at the restaurant with Paul. I'm not mad at Paul. I'm mad at Colten.

And I'm sexually frustrated at the moment.

And I'm ... I don't know. Something. I'm definitely something at the moment.

CHAPTER
Eight

A WEEK after losing my shit with Paul, I have to testify in a murder trial. I *get* to testify. Dr. Cornwell hates this part of the job, but I don't mind it. I don't get nervous on the stand, and I find the whole legal process fascinating. If I didn't have to get back to work all the time, I'd enjoy watching murder trials all day.

"You're good."

I turn as the hair along my neck stands erect from the irritating sound of his deep voice. "Detective." I pull my shoulders back and challenge all my senses to act unaffected by Colten in his sharp navy suit and crisp white dress shirt. Perfectly knotted tie.

"On the stand, you're very put-together and confident."

I nod. "Of course. Why wouldn't I be? I'm an expert witness." My days of trying to impress Colten Mosley should be long over, yet they're not. I'm still singing my own praises with him. Only with him.

One side of his mouth lifts into a half smile that some women probably find sexy. I imagine.

Not me. Nope.

"I was actually a little nervous." He shrugs, looking innocent when I know he's far from it. "Rafferty can be a real dick on his cross examinations, regardless of your level of expertise. But you held your own."

"Thanks. I don't mind testifying, unlike Dr. Cornwell. I swear he's been passing any case on to me that he thinks might lead to giving testimony."

"I don't blame him. I hate being questioned."

"You hate someone questioning your authority, not necessarily questioning you," I say.

"Who does like having their authority questioned?" The elevator doors open, and we step into it.

"Me. I like when some hotshot attorney questions my authority and level of expertise. Because regardless of how much research they did in advance to sound intelligent while asking the right questions, they have a law degree and I have a medical degree with hundreds of autopsies under my belt. I like scrutinizing everything they say, looking for little discrepancies—an opportunity to show their lack of knowledge and therefore their vulnerability."

The doors open to the main floor. "You're sadistic."

"I'm not." I laugh.

"Which is weird..." Colten ignores my reply "...

because you were much nicer to people when we were younger."

There is a lot to unpack here. "You did not just say that to *me*."

"It's true. You were honest but considerate of people's feelings."

I exit the courthouse and cringe when a blast of humidity fills my lungs and fucks up my hair. "Yes, *I* was considerate of other people's feelings."

"That's a jab at me. I get it. That's fair. I was an asshole sometimes." Colten follows me. "You should let me buy you lunch to make up for the past."

There's not much that leaves me speechless anymore. I've heard and seen just about everything, but Colten is certifiably insane if he thinks lunch makes up for what he did to me. Maybe ... just maybe something like his testicle catching a bullet or early onset male pattern baldness with a scalp covered in scaly eczema would make up for the past. I'm going to think on this one.

"Wow, that's kind of like a murderer buying the victim's family a puppy and calling it good."

"Now you're comparing me to a murderer?" His eyebrows shoot up his forehead.

"No. Murderers eventually put their victims out of their misery. I have to get back to work." I pivot, taking quick strides to my car.

"My mom's coming for a visit this weekend. She'd love to see you."

I slow my pace, closing my eyes for a brief moment.

He's not playing fairly. "Tell her to call me, and I'll meet *her* for lunch."

"That's just rude, Josie."

Glancing back at him, my lips pull into a tight smile. "Rude?" I nod slowly as if I'm giving his word choice some careful thought. I'm not. I'm giving myself a few breaths to remain calm because I could kill him about now. "Tell *her* to call me."

FRIDAY, I swipe right on the hottest guy I can find. I need to clear my mind after a week of sorting through the cluttered memories of Colten. Tonight, I'm a doctor, an ER doctor who's going to get some mindless, meaningless, sex.

Jared supposedly manages hedge funds. I'm not sure I buy it based on our brief conversation over dinner, but he's not lying about his obsession with working out.

A full head of hair, nice abs, and my favorite flavor of breath mints goes a long way when I'm feeling ... easy. Jared checks off all three of those boxes. The next morning, he passes up the coffee I offer him and opts to head straight to the gym.

"It was nice meeting you," he says on the way to my front door as I slide on my robe and practically crawl to the coffee maker.

Nice meeting me? We had sex. Granted, I'm not wanting anything beyond last night, but throw me a bone. Lie to me and say you'll call me, or message me, or something. Cordial is not the best morning attitude.

I much prefer the awkwardness of fake intentions. A simple "see ya around" is something I can work with even if I know he won't see me around.

"Yeah." That's my reply. I could have said "you too" and matched his level of enthusiasm, but with a caffeine deficiency in my blood, I just don't have the energy to go the extra mile and give him more than one syllable.

"Oh, excuse me," Jared mumbles and the expected *click* of my door shutting never happens.

I don't make it three steps before I hear the *click*. By the fourth step, I see an intruder in my entry ... and his mom.

"Becca ..." I say her name slowly.

"Josie!" She hugs me, and I hold out my mug of coffee so I don't spill it on her.

"What a surprise." I give her a tight grin and wide eyes.

"So good to see you, dear. I hate to ask, but do you mind if I use your bathroom? We had breakfast, and I should have used the ladies' room after my second cup of tea."

I nod. "Down the hall on the left."

As soon as the bathroom door shuts, I shoot Colten a scowl. "You'd better have a warrant, Detective. You're in my house uninvited. And what the hell? You brought your mom without a freakin' heads-up?"

"Watts..." his head gestures to my door, ignoring my rant "...that's not the dude from the restaurant."

"Brilliant observation. Chicago is so lucky to have you as one if its best and brightest on the force. Why are you here?"

"What does he know about you?"

"He knows I'm not married, and I supply the condoms. What more does he need to know?" I sip my steaming coffee when it's obvious that he's not going to answer my questions.

Colten's thick eyebrows inch up his tan forehead. "Giving it away, huh?"

I shrug a shoulder and pad my way back to the kitchen. "I can't sell it in Illinois. You should know that, Detective."

"I like when you call me detective."

"I like when you call before coming to my house *with your mom*. What part about 'have her call me' was most confusing?"

The bathroom door opens, forcing me to find a welcoming smile again.

"You have a lovely place, Josie."

"Thanks, Becca." I set my mug of coffee onto the island and readjust my robe's sash.

"Not a single hunting trophy." Colten shakes his head slowly. "Not even a bearskin rug."

I'm ready to mount his head on my wall and skin *him* for a rug. Instead, I ignore him. "Had I known you were coming, I would have made a point to be showered and dressed."

"Was that your boyfriend leaving? I haven't seen or talked to your mom in years to find out what you've been up to. Well, I saw your parents at..." Becca pauses for a second like she needs a big breath to continue "... the funeral. But I don't remember much from that day."

Colten's gaze affixes to the window with a hardened expression. I don't think he likes to think or talk about his father's funeral or anything about his father for that matter.

I contemplate reminding her that I was at the funeral as well, but I can read the room. It's not a subject that deserves anymore time. "Jared. That's the guy you saw leaving my apartment. And our relationship is fairly new, so I don't know if he's my boyfriend yet."

I will never see him again. When the most prominent photo of a guy on a dating app is of him with a towel hanging so low on his waist that half of his closely trimmed pubic hair is visible, it's a given that he's only looking for a quick hookup. He was a good way to get Colten out of my head for a night. I thought I'd enjoy a full cup of coffee while thinking of Jared's warm body and strong pulse.

No such luck.

Colten nods to the sofa for Becca to take a seat like it's his place. Then he collapses onto the cushion at the opposite end. Okay ... I guess they're staying for a bit. I need a shower to wash Jared from my body. Brush my teeth. Put on actual clothes.

Deciding to save those as an excuse to get them to leave after a bit, I sit in the armchair adjacent to the sofa, tucking my feet beneath me and holding my coffee mug with both hands while Colten eyes me like I'm his next case to solve.

"Has Colten told you about Reagan?"

Biting my lips together, my head inches side to side. Colten adjusts in his seat as Becca gazes at him for a few seconds with a soft smile on her face.

"Reagan is five. And she's the most beautiful little girl I have ever seen. I didn't think either one of my boys would make me a grandma. They've been too preoccupied with pursuing careers. So imagine my surprise when I found out I was going to be a grandma."

I study Colten's expression. The constant bobbing of his throat. His unfocused gaze flitting all around the room. His hands slowly rubbing his denim clad thighs.

"I'd love to meet her." The words fly off my tongue before I give them much thought.

Colten eyes me, his fidgety hands stilling for a few beats.

"Does she live around here?"

He says nothing. Not a single word. It's been seventeen years, but I can still read him. He's in pain. I'm not sure I'm ready to muster sympathy for him since I'm still dealing with my own pain that's been renewed with his reappearance in my life.

"Against my better judgment, he gave up custody.

But he sees her every month or so. Katy's very generous."

Colten clears his throat, but he only responds to Becca with a few tiny nods.

Her smile swells and excitement shines in her eyes, but I'm not sure why since he looks so miserable. "And she's coming tomorrow," his mom squeaks.

I can't contain my own smile. After seeing the lifeless expression on Becca's face at her husband's funeral, this is a nice contrast. Well-deserved happiness.

Colten forces a grin, giving her a quick glance.

"I'm staying for two weeks to watch her while Katy and her new husband honeymoon in Europe."

"That's awesome," I say, earning me a slight scowl from Colten. It only makes my enthusiasm grow. If he thinks he gets to show up at my house uninvited on a Saturday morning with his mother and earn an ounce of sympathy from me for his life's decisions ... he is delusional.

"The four of us should go to the zoo." Becca's palpable enthusiasm is hard to ignore.

Still, I need to ignore it. I'm happy for her. She's earned this joy a million times over. Colten? I'm not sure what he deserves. Clearly, he doesn't deserve his daughter if he gave up custody.

Colten's expression softens as he makes eye contact with me. "We should."

We? No. I'm not part of any "we."

"I'm busy, but I'm sure you'll have a great time." My

fake smile stretches my lips, exposing the teeth I need to brush.

"You and your blanket statements about being busy." Colten has the nerve to challenge me in front of Becca.

"Well, Detective, as someone who harasses me on a daily basis, rushing me to give you information, you should know I'm very busy. Then there's Jared and that budding relationship. I'm a woman in demand."

"Oh! Colten said you're a medical examiner. Years ago, your mom said you were going to medical school, but I never knew you were interested in working with dead bodies. That has to take a very special mindset."

"Josie's always had a special mindset. An affinity for dead things." Colten smirks.

Apparently, he's all smiles as long as we're not talking about his role as a father, or lack thereof.

"It's a very in-demand profession. It takes someone with a high level of intelligence, laser focus, and well-honed communication skills to do what I do. Often, studying death unravels many mysteries of the living. Colten's had the pleasure and good fortune to work with me and learn from my expertise."

Right there.

That look on his face is the most satisfying reward I've received in a very long time, and that's saying a lot because I do, in fact, find my job incredibly rewarding. I can't quite decipher his expression, but it's either a classic case of "cat got your tongue" or good old fashion defeat. Either way, it's beautiful.

"Josie ... I'm so proud of you. I bet your parents are too. You work with law enforcement. That has to make your father happy. And I'm sure Colten is smitten to reconnect with you after all these years and get to witness firsthand all of your accomplishments." Becca gives her son an expectant look.

Colten eyes her briefly before clearing his throat. It's reminiscent of the times she thought he hadn't been nice to me and made him apologize or say something kind.

Also like old times, I don't say a word. I wait patiently whether I deserve it or not. Only this time, we won't run out of the house to the back woods, climb the tree, and fight over who was really right or wrong.

One of us won't hold up a big sheet of paper to our bedroom window at bedtime with the words *I'M SORRY* scribbled in all caps. One of us won't offer a giant-sized Snickers bar as a truce.

"Smitten isn't the right word, Mom." Colten's gaze flits to mine, sliding down my face and over my entire body as he maintains a contemplative expression. There's a newness interwoven with the old familiar parts of Colten Mosley, a tiny glimpse of those missing seventeen years when he transformed from a boy to a man.

A lanky teen to a filled-out man with a thick scruff along his jaw and face.

A dreamer without purpose to a professional with stature.

A heartbreaker to … what sometimes feels like a glimpse of the brokenhearted.

Did his daughter's mom break his heart?

"Happy," Colten says, returning his gaze to mine, the hint of a sincere smile touching his lips. "I'm happy that Josie has found her calling in life. It would have been a shame for her to settle for anything less than her dreams."

Fuck you, Mosley.

My dreams? Is he serious?

"How are your parents, Josie? I feel so out of touch since Trenton died. Is your dad still Chief of Police? Are they still in Des Moines? Does your mom still teach sign language at the community college?"

"My dad took early retirement two years ago, and my mom retired six months later. Dad sold the fifth wheel even though he still hunts, and they bought an RV. They still have their house in Des Moines, but they're on the road more than they're home."

Becca tries to smile, but it's a failed attempt. I always wondered why she stayed with Trenton after he cheated on her. More than once, I overheard my parents talking about it. I never caught the "why" part, but I remember my mom always saying Becca was a better woman than most. Years later, it occurred to me that my mom was giving my father a subtle warning that she would not be tolerant or forgiving if he was ever unfaithful.

"I always thought Trenton and I would move to Florida when he retired, maybe Sanibel Island."

The muscles in Colten's jaw work overtime at the mention of his father's name. This visit has reached its limit.

I stand. "I hate to be such a terrible hostess. Had I known you were coming, I would have planned accordingly, but I need a shower. My day is filled with plans."

"We really must have dinner when Reagan gets here," Becca says, taking Colten's proffered hand to help her up from the sofa. It's a kind gesture. He's always been a mama's boy.

I choose a smile as my response. It's friendly and noncommittal. There's no way I'm going down the Mosley rabbit hole again, but I'm not a complete asshole who says it to Becca's face.

"Do you remember when I used to make chicken enchiladas? Those were your favorite."

Tightening my smile, I nod once. My mom made the best baked goods, but Becca's meals were better. I basically invited myself to dinner on chicken enchilada night.

"I hope you enjoy your time with your granddaughter."

"Oh, I can't wait." Becca beams like a bright star.

I remind myself that it's been seventeen years. Colten's level of discomfort with this conversation is not my concern. Whatever he did to fuck up his personal life is none of my business. But there's no denying that his daughter brings much-needed joy to Becca's life.

When we reach my front door, Becca pulls me in for another hug, leaving Colten in my line of sight over her shoulder. With his hands in the front pockets of his jeans, his gaze flits around the space, anywhere but meeting mine. Becca always loved me. By our senior year, I felt certain she thought I'd be her daughter-in-law.

And if I'm being honest and peeling back the scar tissue covering seventeen-year-old wounds, I'll admit I thought the same thing.

As Becca heads toward the street, Colten hangs back a minute, preventing me from closing my door. "Thanks. She really wanted to see you."

I nod.

"I'm glad you're well, Josie. Really." He lifts his hand and traces the healing cut on my forehead. A breath later, he drops his hand.

I manage one last nod. I much prefer dealing with Detective Mosley on my turf at work where I feel a good ten steps ahead of him unless he's chasing me down a flight of stairs. Bringing his mom to my house, uninvited, on a Saturday morning is out of bounds.

Just as I think he's going to say something else, his phone chimes, and he answers it. "Mosley." He winks at me and struts toward the street.

Closing the door, I march toward the bathroom to shower, feeling a mix of anger and that familiar attraction. That wink. That stupid wink. It's just like the first time he winked at me when we were younger.

CHAPTER
Nine

Colten Mosley, starting as pitcher for the varsity baseball team as a freshman, was a sight to behold. He exuded so much confidence, and nobody loved that confidence more than Heather Peterson, his girlfriend who was a year older than us.

I hated her. That was a given.

My relationship with Colten flickered on and off more than the dying florescent light in the laundry room. It was easy to blame Colten. He was guilty of so many things.

Too cute.

Too nice.

A stellar athlete.

Coach Mosley's son.

And he played the piano like Hélène Grimaud.

Of course, nobody our age knew who Hélène

Grimaud was, except Colten. Our neighbor said he played with a similar "expressive freedom." Whatever that meant.

After the team's first win of the season with their freshman pitcher, Heather Peterson squealed while throwing herself into Colten's arms the second he emerged from the dugout with his lucky glove and shit-eating grin.

"Baby!" She just had to call him baby.

I rolled my eyes, taking slow steps descending the top of the bleachers with a cherry Tootsie Pop in my mouth, squinting at *him* as he stared at me over Heather's shoulder.

That was the first time he winked at me.

That asshole had the nerve to wink at me while hugging *her* to his sweaty body. I knew they'd already kissed. Heather had told Ronnie as much, and telling Ronnie was the equivalent of announcing something over the PA system.

The only thing I hated as much as Heather Peterson was that wink. The first of many. And he always did it over the shoulder of some girl hugged to him like a bear in a tree.

After games.

The homecoming dance.

In the school parking lot.

Just outside of the locker room.

The problem with Colten Mosley's stupid wink was I never saw him do it to anyone but me. Not once.

"Thanks for coming to my game," Colten yelled as I

scuffed my sneakers along the dirt toward the parking lot.

Halting, I turned slowly, bringing my sucker out of my mouth with a *POP!*

"Baby, I'm going to talk to Jenna and Ronnie. Meet you at my car." Heather blew him a kiss before blowing me off without so much as a smile or a "hi."

Colten stopped his dusty cleats mere inches from my sneakers as he eyed me with a smug satisfaction. He had an older girlfriend who called him "baby," and she had her driver's license. So what?

"Watts."

"Mosley."

"Need a ride home?" he asked.

"My mom's picking me up."

"Heather and I could give you a ride."

I scoffed. "I'd walk home before I'd get in the car with that psycho."

"Psycho?"

"She backed into the dumpster behind the school last month. Ronnie told everyone she barely passed Driver's Ed. And she rear-ended Mr. Leach at the four-way stop after last Tuesday's softball game."

"You think you're going to be a better driver?" Colten stole my Tootsie Pop and sucked it into his mouth—the same mouth he used to kiss Heather Peterson.

"I start Driver's Ed next week. But I already am a better driver. My parents let me drive everywhere. My dad lets me drive his truck. I've backed his fishing boat onto the trailer in and out of the loading ramp a million times. It's a stupid question and you know it."

Colten rolled my Tootsie Pop in his mouth while canting his head to the side. "Are you wearing lip gloss?" he mumbled over the sucker.

I rubbed my lips together. "No. It's from the red sucker, stupid."

"Looks like lip gloss."

So what if I was wearing lip gloss? Heather wore a whole paint palette on her face.

"Never seen you wear makeup before."

It irked me that he had to point out all the ways I was different than the other girls ... the girls who hugged and kissed him. The girls who cheered from the fence by the dugout and squealed while throwing themselves into his arms. The girls who called him "baby" and dissed me because I was younger.

"We're the same age in case you've forgotten. If you can play varsity baseball and suck face with the worst driver in the whole school, then I can wear lip gloss or an entire mask of makeup for that matter, without you making such a big deal of it."

Colten pulled the Tootsie Pop from his mouth. "I know." He shrugged a shoulder before bringing the sucker to my lips, a mischievous glint in his eyes daring me to put it back into my mouth.

"Colten!" Heather called.

My lips parted, accepting the sucker. His grin spread wider than I'd ever seen it.

Two seconds after brushing past me, he turned.

"My mom's making chicken enchiladas tonight. She felt bad for missing my game, so she promised to make my favorite dinner to make up for it. You should come."

"Three's a crowd, Colten. I don't think Heather wants to have dinner with me."

"Who said I was inviting Heather?" His tongue slid out to wet his lips before he rubbed them together as if he needed to hide his grin.

As Heather the angry badger charged in our direction, doing a terrible job of hiding her distaste for me, I smirked around the sucker and mumbled, "See you at dinner."

"Josie, come in, hon." Becca opened the door, a yellow kitchen towel draped over her shoulder as she smiled before heading back to the kitchen. "You don't have to knock. You know that."

"Smells amazing." I ignored her comment. Colten had a girlfriend who was not me. I no longer felt like I should enter their house unannounced.

"Colten's upstairs. Dinner will be another twenty minutes or so."

"Okay. Thanks." I crept up the stairs as I had done many times before.

"Mosley," I leaned against the doorframe of his bedroom as he scribbled on a page of music at his keyboard.

Becca bought him a keyboard after his dad took a sledgehammer to the piano when Colten called him a "fucking bastard" for cheating on his mom. Trenton Mosley wasn't a patient man by nature. After spending years trying to destroy his marriage, his career, and all credibility with his two sons, the last thing he expected was his youngest son having a moment of brutal honesty after reconciling with Becca.

"Watts." He glanced over his shoulder, flashing me a big grin.

"Where's your dad and brother?"

That beautiful grin? It fell right off his face, a big chunk of an iceberg breaking off and falling into frigid waters. "Don't know. Don't care." Returning his attention to his sheet music, he continued to scribble notes.

Padding my way to him, I glanced around his room, looking for signs of Heather. A photo. A gift she might have given him. A friendship bracelet since she wore approximately a dozen on each wrist. "Play me something," I said, sitting next to him in the opposite direction on the edge of the narrow bench.

"What do you want me to play?"

I shrugged. "Anything."

His long fingers rested on the keys, caressing them lightly before pressing a single key. Then he started to play the very familiar beginning to "Fallin" by Alicia Keys.

How ironic.

Did I keep falling in and out of love with Colten Mosley? It was too early to say. Still, I'd known him for what felt like forever. Living across the street for five years, same school, sharing a seat on the bus, spending every free moment with him ... it made it hard to remember what my life was like before he and his family moved to Des Moines from Houston, Texas.

"Do you play that for Heather?"

He stopped playing as if my words made him forget the notes. Glancing over at me, he narrowed his eyes a fraction. "Heather hasn't been in my bedroom."

"Well, she's been to your house."

"Are you spying on me, Watts?" One corner of his mouth turned up into a slight grin.

I rolled my eyes. "You wish. I'm not spying on you. I'm simply not blind. I've seen her car in your driveway. That's all."

He maintained his smirk of skepticism. Did I once (maybe twice) use binoculars to spy on him to see if he did, in fact, take Heather to his room? Maybe. If I had, I never would have admitted it to anyone.

"You did good today. Freshman starting varsity. Can you believe it? You know you'll get lots of offers to play in college. Right?" Once again, I managed to say something that dissolved all joy from his handsome face.

"Yeah, I mean ... it's possible. My dad sure thinks so."

"I'd imagine he's pretty proud of you."

Colten grunted, flipping off the power switch to his keyboard. "His pride is the least motivating thing in my life. In fact, when I think about something making him happy or proud, all I want to do is the exact opposite."

"Sounds like a great plan for completely blowing your future."

He sighed, scooting off the bench before moseying to the window, stuffing his hands into the pockets of his sweatpants. "Baseball isn't everything. There are a lot of happy and successful people who didn't choose to play baseball in college."

"True ..." I stood and followed him, stopping a foot or two from his backside. "But a very small percentage of the population has your talent at playing baseball."

He turned, eyeing me for a few seconds. "You've said I'm good at playing the piano."

I nodded several times.

Colten's head slanted to the side. "You said I'm good at climbing trees and skateboarding—almost as good as you."

It became increasingly difficult to not offer a submissive smile as he listed off his talents.

"Maybe I'm one of those people who will be good at whatever I set out to do."

Lifting a shoulder like I didn't want to give him a total pass on ignoring the obvious fact that he would be pursued hard by colleges wanting to recruit him, I offered a murmured, "Maybe."

"Not everyone's future is mapped out from birth like yours."

"What are you talking about?" I took a step backward to give us some space. It was hard to be in his *space* and not feel transparent with my feelings.

The jealousy.

The envy.

The true feelings hidden beneath mounds of stubborn pride.

The fear of telling him the truth only to be rejected.

"A hunter. A goddess like Artemis."

I scoffed at Colten's comparison. "Are you seriously still reading Greek mythology? I can recommend much better books."

"Ancient literature, thank you very much. And yes, I'm still reading it. So don't roll your googly eyes at me. I'm complimenting you. I realize there's a little controversy when it comes to Artemis, but true scholars believe she was fiercely protective of those who were considered weak. Reclusive but passionately defensive. A champion of purity ... the virgin kind." He smirked. "However, she was quite temperamental and rather unsympathetic to men. Sound familiar?"

"No. Not really. I'm very sympathetic to men. I mean ... we're still friends, right? Something tells me Heather wouldn't be near as tolerant of your nerdy side. She's a fan of your jock side. You know, the side you actively try to repress and secretly despise just to spite your father?"

"Look at you effortlessly proving my point, Watts. Again, just like Artemis, you possess a lack of mercy and an overabundance of pride. Sadly, those were her greatest weaknesses, and I think they're yours as well."

"I don't possess a lack of mercy." I scoffed.

"You kill Bambi." Colten's nose wrinkled.

"Bambi's dad, dumbass. Nobody kills Bambi, not even my dad. Hunters have compassion, Mr. High and Mighty, who gives not a single thought to the true brutality your double cheeseburger lunch suffered to make it into your fast-food sack next to a pile of cold fries and ten billion packets of ketchup."

"Dinner, kiddos!" Becca called upstairs.

We stared at each other through a series of silent blinks. It wasn't the first time the dinner bell interrupted our meaningless conversation. Neither Colten nor I ever participated in debate club, but we both would have excelled. We spent hours, sometimes days, debating the most ridiculous topics.

"Do store-bought chickens suffer more than hunted chickens? I think the enchiladas are made with store-bought chickens. I've never seen my mom snap a chicken's neck, so I assume it died by some other means. Lethal injection? Personally, I think I'd prefer the injection to someone snapping my neck."

My head eased side to side. "You don't see the neck snap coming. No fear. Just ... *snap*. Done. Dead. No suffering. But you know something bad is about to happen when you're restrained, and a needle's shoved into your vein. Ticktock ... the end is slowly approaching, and you can't stop it. The fear is terrifying and crippling. And no ... chickens don't die from lethal injection."

Colten had a way of looking at me for several silent seconds after I'd speak. And just as his face threatened to morph into amusement, he rubbed the pads of his fingers over his lips to erase all signs of a grin because he knew I'd lose my shit if I thought he was making fun of me.

"Do you think you'll ever let me give you a compliment without it turning into the most ridiculous argument?"

"We're not arguing," I ... *argued*. "Do you think you'll ever give me a compliment without presenting it in the form of a saga?"

"You're a skilled huntress." He gave me a sharp nod, a nonverbal period to his simple compliment.

It was my turn to hide my amusement. Huntress. Everything about that word implied something mythical in my head. "Thank you." I almost choked on those two words. I wanted to tell him the word huntress was a little extreme for me. I occasionally went hunting or fishing with my dad. I'd never been hunting on my own for anything besides insects, okay ... I might have happened upon some roadkill here and there.

"You're welcome. Let's eat."

As he reached the door, I spewed the words I told myself I wouldn't say. "Why did you wink at me? After the game, Heather hugged you, and you winked at me. If you were my boyfriend, and you hugged me while winking at another girl, you'd be my *ex*-boyfriend."

Colten turned a few degrees, his head twisted but not fully looking at me. "I've been your boyfriend ... a lot. And I've been your ex-boyfriend ... a lot. And when

I was your boyfriend, I never winked at another girl." He shrugged a shoulder.

I bit my tongue because I didn't have the courage to tell him that I never felt like the girl he deserved. He could spin things all day long, trying to explain away my personality and passions under the guise of mythical goddess likenesses. Guys like Colten Mosley were genetically bred to be with Annies and Heathers, even cheer squad captains like Kaitlyn.

The Josephine Wattses of the world (of which I knew there were very few) didn't fit in with anyone.

CHAPTER
Ten

"Just a preliminary guess, but I don't think this is a homicide case, Detective Mosley," I say without glancing up from the body on my table, ignoring the few students crowded around me.

"The victim's mom swears on her life that it wasn't suicide," he says.

"Bereaved mothers don't want to believe their children are capable of suicide, of hanging themselves. It takes premeditation. Preparation. Even a little practice to get the right type of knot, secure the ... extension cord in this case ... to something that won't break or collapse under their weight, and execute it without fail. But ... his face was paler than his torso which means the blood supply was cut off to his head, and therefore it's likely that within seconds he lost consciousness which means he didn't suffer that long. It doesn't always go that way."

When Colten doesn't respond with a single word, I meet his fixed gaze.

Shit.

His dad hanged himself.

"I'll talk to the family," I say.

Still, he doesn't move.

"Detective Mosley?"

Nothing.

"Colten?"

His head jerks, eyes on me.

"I'll talk to the family. Is that all you needed?"

In another delayed response, he nods slowly.

When we finish up with the sixteen-year-old boy who made an impulsive, irrevocable decision to take his life, I strip out of my PPE, complete some paperwork, and take my lunch break outside in my usual spot. Two bites into my sandwich, I slip in my earbuds and call Colten.

"Detective Mosley," he answers in a clipped tone. Either he didn't look at his screen closely or I'm not saved under his contacts.

"It's Josie. I uh ... just wanted to make sure you're okay. Earlier, I said more than needed to be said because I was in work mode, talking through things aloud for the students, and I completely spaced on your dad. I'm sorry."

"Don't worry about it."

I shouldn't worry about it because it was an honest

mistake, and I don't owe Colten special treatment seventeen years after he made me feel anything but special. We've exchanged so many barbs over the years, they should no longer break the skin. We should be calloused to them. But I didn't mean to cut him, not with the tragedy of his father's suicide. Even I know there are lines that shouldn't be crossed. Sometimes I just ... don't see them.

"Is Reagan with your mom?"

"Yeah."

"That's good. I'll ... let you go. Just wanted to make sure—"

"I'm fine, Josie. He was a fucking selfish asshole for as long as I can remember. I shouldn't have expected his death to be any different than his life. Did you talk to the family?"

I pick at the crust to my sandwich. "I will this afternoon."

"You should come to dinner tonight. I'm picking up pizza on the way home. Then we're watching a princess movie."

"I'm not a big princess movie person."

"But you love pizza."

"I used to love pizza."

He chuckles and I let the sound of it *not* irritate me this time because I need to know I didn't unearth too many memories of his dad's suicide. "Josie, there are a few things in life that you love forever no matter what. Pizza is one of them."

And the boy next door ...

"Popcorn too. I'll even see if I can scrounge some deer jerky to go with it."

"Shut up." I chuckle.

"She's perfect, Josie." His voice softens. The chattering in the background disappears. He's moved away from the people around him. "I look at her and I can't believe she's part of me. She's just too perfect."

Leaning my head back and closing my eyes against the sun, I try to imagine what a little female version of Colten would look like ... or act like. "No onions."

He laughs. "Cheese. She's five. It's just cheese. I'll text you my address. Six work?"

I nod to myself and smile. "Yeah."

Colten's unfairly using his daughter and his mom to get me to spend time with him outside of work. And for whatever reason, I'm letting him. It's nothing more than curiosity. His having a daughter who lives primarily with her mom has my curiosity piqued.

"Josie! Come in, honey. Colten isn't home yet, but he's on his way."

"Daddy!" A little girl comes barreling down the stairs, long, flowing dark hair pulled partially away from her face and secured with a red bow.

"No, sweetie. It's not your daddy."

Reagan hugs Becca's legs and peeks up at me with rich brownish-gold eyes and long lashes. Those are

Colten's eyes and his full lips that seem to smile a little crooked on one side.

"Reagan, this is your daddy's friend, Josie. She met your daddy when they were just a few years older than you."

"Hi, Reagan." This is awkward. I'm a little intimidated by a five-year-old because I work with adults and dead people, and I have no children of my own. I used to be better with kids when I had to babysit my little brother. That was a long time ago.

"Are you going to marry my daddy?"

My eyes bug out. Every word I was going to say dies on the end of my tongue and evaporates into thin air through my parted lips.

"Mommy married Sean. She said Daddy didn't want to marry her."

Well shit. This girl's a little too smart for her own good.

Becca doesn't seem to offer words either. Her cheeks flush as she clears her throat. "Oh, sweetie, it's not that your daddy didn't want to marry your mommy. They just had different plans for the future. And sometimes grown-ups have to raise their kids apart while they follow their dreams and work hard to buy little girls cute stuffed animals and big swing sets for the backyard."

That's a terrible explanation, but I applaud Becca for thinking on her toes and finding literally anything to say. I still have nothing.

"Um ..." I fumble my words. "Reagan, I'm your

dad's friend. He might get married someday like your mom got married, but he won't marry me. We're just friends."

Friends is a stretch at this point, but she doesn't need to know the finer details of how her daddy broke my heart. She'll probably have her own version of a Colten Mosley to teach her those hard lessons in life. For now, she can leave her daddy on a pedestal. I'm not a dream crusher.

Becca gives me a sad smile. I think she always imagined me with her son—forever. I imagined it too.

"Hello. Hello ..." Colten's voice carries from another door.

Reagan sprints toward him. "Daddy!"

Becca gestures for me to follow her.

For someone who doesn't have custody of his daughter, he sure has her love. We turn the corner into the kitchen where Colten has Reagan hugged to him with one hand and a pizza box in his other hand.

Becca takes the pizza box from him, and he winks at me.

"I just want you to know that no matter what girl lays claim to me, I'm still yours, Josie."

I can't help it, not that I want to. A big smile spreads across my face. Reagan is his girl. *The* girl. I'm not sure why he's winking at me.

Relinquishing a grin, I give him a slight headshake and eye roll.

"Daddy, your friend is here, but she's not going to marry you."

Jesus, little girl ... you're killing me.

He sets her on her feet, eyeing me the whole time. "Is that so?"

I laugh it off and file it under "kids say the darnedest things" as I nod. "She's correct."

Colten loosens his tie, eyeing me head to toe. "A shame," he mumbles.

I clear my throat, turning my attention to Becca as she tries to slow down Reagan's grabby hands reaching for the pizza box. "What can I do?"

"Plates are in the cabinet to the right of the oven," she says.

"Got it." I head to the cabinet.

"I'm going to run upstairs and change my clothes. Save me some pizza," Colten murmurs as he saunters toward the stairs looking unfairly handsome in his suit. I have a flashback of seeing him in a suit for the first time at a piano recital. He hated it, but Becca insisted he wear it.

By the time Becca and I get the plates, pizza, and drinks set on the dining room table, Colten emerges in a pair of jeans and a white tee.

"Sit by me, Daddy."

"Of course, Button." He bops her nose, and she scrunches it.

I sit across from him, next to Becca, as he gets Reagan a slice of pizza on her plate and starts to cut it into pieces with a fork.

"No, Daddy. Don't cut it."

His eyebrows lift a fraction. "Sorry. I didn't realize you were such a big girl now."

Reagan's little lips pucker to blow on the pizza before taking a tiny nibble. Colten drapes a paper napkin onto his leg while eyeing me and wearing a cocky grin.

I avert my gaze to the pizza on my plate.

"How's your boyfriend?" Becca asks.

I press my napkin to my mouth to keep from spitting it out at her unexpected question. Boyfriend ... she means hookup, only she doesn't know that's what she means.

Colten smirks, and I give him a quick narrowing of my eyes—one or two daggers shot at him.

"Uh ... that didn't work out. Most all dating these days is online dating, and to be honest, it's pretty brutal out there. Sometimes, I'm just looking for a night out with good conversation."

"Well..." Becca lowers her voice, talking like a ventriloquist as if Reagan won't pick up on anything if she talks that way "...he was at your place the next day. I assumed that meant it was serious."

Colten coughs, fisting a hand at his mouth.

"Yeah, well, I might have read that wrong." I shrug. "So what did you and Reagan do all day while Colten was at work?"

"We had tea and cake!" Reagan spits a little pizza out of her mouth with her excitement.

Becca and Colten chuckle.

"Colten made us reservations at a tearoom. So we

got dressed up and had three o'clock tea. Scones. Little sandwiches. And cakes. It was really ..." She eyes Colten and I swear I see tears in her eyes. "It was a wonderful gift. I raised such a thoughtful young man."

We're just going to agree to disagree on that one for a while, even if I find it really sweet that he did that for his mom and daughter.

"What about you, Josie? Did you have a good day?" Colten asks as if he didn't see me this morning and talk to me on the phone at lunch.

I nod several times, eyeing him suspiciously. "You?" I feel compelled to ask in return.

He takes a bite of pizza and chews it while nodding. "It was okay. Better now that I have my three favorite girls all at the dinner table with me."

No. Nope. Uh-uh. He's not allowed to say that. Seventeen years. Seventy years. Five hundred lifetimes. It doesn't matter. He crushed me, and I'll *always* feel it.

Becca gives her son the expected adoring gaze. Reagan's too busy eating her pizza in micro bites to pay any attention to his comment. I ... well, I ignore him, gulping down my water like I haven't drank a drop all day.

After dinner, Becca takes Reagan upstairs for her bath while I help Colten clean up the small mess from dinner.

"I talked to the family this afternoon." I hand him the last plate to load into the dishwasher. "It was incredibly hard, but I think reassuring them he probably didn't suffer was a little comforting. I don't know how long it will take for them to really process that it happened in the first place."

"Never," Colten mutters, closing the dishwasher. "You never fully process it."

I wipe my hands on a towel before setting it aside and sliding my fingers into the pockets of my gray linen capris. "I wanted to call you. After it happened, and you weren't at the funeral, I wanted to call you. But ..." I press my lips together, not really sure how far I can or should go with this. Where will it end?

"But you hated me."

Staring at my feet, I inch my head side to side. "I didn't have your number."

"And you hated me. You did. You *do*. I won't make you say it. And I take full responsibility. I can't change it. And I haven't decided if I would change it if I had the chance."

The only thing worse than feeling rejected is hearing his confession that it wasn't an accident. It was intentional. No remorse.

He hurt me, and he feels no remorse.

"Tell your mom and Reagan goodbye for me. I'm going to head home."

"Josie ..."

I make my way to the front door without actually running, but I want to. Boy, do I ever want to run away from Colten Mosley and never see him again. With him, I'm not a doctor. I'm not a well-respected medical examiner. I'm barely a woman. With Colten Mosley, I will always be the girl in love with the boy. The girl who he thought was a boy. The default friend.

"No. Just … no." I bolt out the front door, slinging my purse over my shoulder.

"Josephine Watts, *look* at yourself." He takes long strides, following me to my car. "You are more … so much more than I imagined. Without me, you became everything you never were *with* me."

I stop at the driver's door, keeping my back to him, taking one deep breath after another.

He's right, but not in the way he thinks. I will *never* tell him that.

"If we choose to live with regret, then I have to regret Reagan. I have to regret my job. I have to regret too many things that are good in my life *because* my life went in directions no one could have ever imagined. And I'm tired of regret. It's the heaviest anchor, the most unbearable feeling of drowning … of suffocating. My dad tied a rope around his neck because of regret. If I regret, then I'm chasing a ghost. If I regret, it might be *my* neck inside that noose."

Pressing my fingers to the corners of my eyes, I wipe away every outwardly physical sign of pain. My other hand grips the door handle. "If I can't look back, you are nothing more than a detective like Detective Rains. I don't eat dinner with him. I don't visit his mom and meet his children. So…" I open the door "…good night, Detective Mosley."

CHAPTER
Eleven

WHEN JOSIE SAID my dad had kissed another woman, I was mortified.

Angry.

Embarrassed.

But mostly ... confused.

I ran home without another word to her and tore through the house looking for my parents.

"Where's Mom and Dad?" I quizzed Chad.

He was too deep in his video game to acknowledge me.

"Where's Mom and Dad?" I plucked the controller from his hands.

"Hey! I don't know." He lunged for me.

I tossed the controller onto the floor, and Chad dove for it like a lifeline. Feeling frantic and confused, I checked the basement, the backyard, and finally the garage. Upon hearing raised voices, I cracked open the side access door less than an inch.

"I'm sorry, Becca ..." I barely recognized my dad's voice, the desperation and the way each word sounded like a stutter because he was crying. It was the first time I witnessed my father crying.

Mom stood in front of him with a blank expression, gaze fixed on his chest like it was too unbearable to look up at him.

"Honey ..." He grabbed her shoulders, and she jerked away from him, stumbling back a few steps until the Volkswagen door stopped her from going any farther. "It just happened. It wasn't planned."

"Did you fuck her?"

Mom didn't swear ... ever. And even if my young mind could have imagined a cuss word falling from her lips, it never would have been the F-word. The king of all swear words. I felt pretty sure I was not only forbidden to say it, but forbidden to even think it.

What confused me the most was what she meant when she said it. I had heard the word a few times. I knew it was bad and forbidden. But I'd never asked anyone for a definition. The few times I had heard someone use it was "fuck you." And not in a nice way. It was an angry "fuck you." So if my mom was asking my dad if he fucked "her," the woman I assumed he kissed, then he must not have liked said woman that much. So why did he kiss her?

I had so much to learn, and hindsight ended up being one very haunting bitch.

"Becca ..." my dad said, just above a whisper. I didn't recognize him. The strict father. The militant coach. The man of the house.

"How c-could y-you?" She sobbed.

Things were bad. How bad? I didn't know until I started to close the door and the hinges squeaked, drawing their attention to me.

"Jesus Christ ..." Dad mumbled, wiping his face while turning his back to me. "Go to your room!"

"Colten ..." Mom chased me as I did what my father told me to do.

In the house.

Up the stairs.

Door slammed shut.

Face planted into my pillow.

And then ... I cried.

"WAIT UP!" Josie called as I marched toward the bus stop the next morning.

Mom tried to console me for nearly an hour the night before, but I didn't want to talk, so I pretended to fall asleep.

The next morning, there was no sign of Dad. Mom's eyes were swollen, but she put on a fake smile and tried to serve Chad and me French toast like everything was okay. I wasn't hungry. And it wasn't okay.

I envied Chad's ability to tune out the world so easily, or so I thought. Come to find out, Chad absorbed everything; he just processed it differently. Not better, but differently.

"Colten?" Josie's shoes slapped the sidewalk, and she ran to catch up to me. "Hey, why are you ignoring me?"

"I'm not ignoring you. I'm getting on the school bus."

"You're ignoring me. Is this about last night?"

"Just ... shut up, Josie. I don't want to talk about it." As soon as the school bus pulled up to the curb, I raced onto it, taking the first available seat.

Two seconds later, Josie plopped down next to me, hugging her pink, black, and green camo bag to her chest. Slumped next to the window, I closed my eyes, hoping she would not say another word.

A few blocks later, she slid her hand under my bag and grabbed my hand, giving it a squeeze while keeping her eyes trained to the front of the bus and her mouth shut.

I lost track of how many times Josie squeezed my hand over the next few years after my dad moved out.

After my mom had a breakdown.

After my brother tried to set a stranger's house on fire.

Every little silent squeeze seemed to say *I've got you. You're not alone. This will pass.*

The news. Yes, I watch the local news. Most of the time. This morning, I spent too much time convincing my get-Colten-out-of-my-head hookup from last night that he needed to leave my apartment. No time for the news.

"Our serial killer strikes again."

I perk up before a single sip of coffee.

He smirks. "She's all yours."

"She?" I narrow my eyes while taking a drink of coffee.

"She. You need to find something, Josie. I'm sure you'll have several detectives breathing down your neck before you even get on your PPE."

Colten.

He means Detective Mosley will be breathing down my neck.

It's been five days since I walked out of his house, fumbling with my emotions and tripping over the parts of my ego that are still a little jagged.

Thirty minutes later, I'm in the autopsy suite with a nice gathering of students.

"Dr. Watts is the best I've seen," Dr. Cornwell announces as he passes my table on his way to an eight-year-old girl found dead in her room just after dinner last night. "Want to know why?" he asks the peanut gallery.

Cronk mumbles something just before speaking into the microphone hanging above the table to dictate. I know it was a jab at me.

"Because she thinks like a detective," the young

male student just to my right says, his eyes alight with confidence.

Cornwell and I have played this game. He's prouder of the "correct" answer than I am.

"Partial credit, Hoffler. All forensic pathologists have to think like detectives. It's the part that should come naturally in this field. Dr. Watts thinks like a killer—*that's* what makes her so special."

"My parents prefer 'hunter,' but thanks, Dr. Cornwell. I'm honored you think so highly of me."

The students laugh.

Alicia winks at me when I glance up from my camera lens. I roll my eyes, swapping her the camera for my sketch pad and blue pen.

Over the next hour, we lose three of the students. Newcomers. There's something about a mutilated body mixed with the stench of feces and stomach acid that gives even the most devoted students a moment's pause. Or ... a few moments to vomit or come to after passing out.

I finish my two assigned autopsies, shower in the locker room, and eat my lunch in my office while typing up case notes.

"Bet you expected to see me sooner." Detective Mosley pokes his head into my office before taking a seat opposite me.

I lean to the side, eyeing him behind my computer monitor. "Or not at all." I frown before returning my attention to my screen. "Did Detective Rains break up with me?"

"He has one of those..." Colten snaps his fingers several times "...camera up the ass appointments."

"Colonoscopy. Good for him. Early detection is good."

"You couldn't pay me to do that shit."

Again, I lean to the side, peaking a single eyebrow.

He shrugs, drumming his fingers on his legs clad in black pants. "Listen, about the other night ..."

I clear my throat and take a bite of my sandwich, finding refuge behind the monitor again while mumbling, "You mean ... about this morning. Did I find anything? Yes. I found a fetus. Fifteen weeks."

"Jesus ..."

Chewing another bite of my sandwich, I nod a few times. "They're alive. All of the victims have been alive when their legs have been amputated. You have an angry killer on your hands."

"Angry? Are you implying some killers are not angry?"

I shrug. "You know the answer to that. Kevin Gleason. Necrophile. Lust killer."

Twisting his lips, he nods slowly.

"Sorry," I say. "I haven't found anything to connect the victims. I'm afraid this will be on you. Friends. Family. Co-workers. What do you know about them? Did the victims belong to the same gym? Shop at the same grocery store? See the same massage therapist?"

"You're assuming we're dealing with an organized killer? Seems pretty random at the moment. Wrong place. Wrong time. Voices in their head."

"You have no DNA that does not belong to the victim or the victim's family. Four bodies. Always in a dumpster. No camera footage. Nothing. I think you have a highly intelligent person who is methodical, cautious, and patient."

"What are you doing tonight?"

My nose wrinkles. "What?"

"I'm taking Reagan to the park for a little T-ball practice."

"Okay. Have fun." I wad up my sandwich wrapper and shove it into the sack.

"I thought you could come with us. Unless ... you're hooking up with someone tonight."

"Detective Mosley, I'm pretty sure my personal life is none of your business."

"Listen, I couldn't care less if you go with us or not. It was Reagan's idea."

"Bullshit." I flip up the straw to my water bottle and take several long swigs while eyeing him.

"Ask her yourself."

"Sorry, I don't have her phone number."

"Call her dad around six, and he'll let you speak to her. Say 'Hi, Reagan. It's me, Josie. Do you want me to play T-ball at the park with you and your dad?' And I promise you she'll say yes."

"Why did Katy marry Sean instead of you?"

The gleam in Colten's eyes dies along with his smile. "Wow." He stands, buttoning his suit jacket. "You really know how to ruin a good day, don't you?"

"I'm the person who tells families how their loved

ones died. Ruining people's days is kinda my thing. And I don't really care why you didn't marry Reagan's mom. I'm just reminding you that we are not friends, so your incessant attempts will always be met with my incessant need for answers."

He shakes his head while finding the door to my office, stopping at the threshold with his back to me. "She asked me if I loved her."

I glance up at the door.

"I hesitated," he says. "Two seconds ... maybe three. Then I started to answer, but it was too late. She said she would never marry a man who hesitated ... but more than that ... she wouldn't marry me *because* she had to ask."

Leaning back in my chair, I hug my arms to my chest. "Text me the park and the time."

I HIDE behind a tree like a creeper watching Colten and Reagan play T-ball. This was a bad idea. Everything that involves being with Colten Mosley outside of work is a bad idea.

Some things never change. I spent most of my childhood entertaining bad ideas when it came to Colten.

On a deep breath, I step into view and smile at Reagan as she runs the bases of the small field.

"You came." Colten's smile gobbles up his whole face.

I shrug. "It's a nice night. Not as humid. And I could use a little fresh air."

"Daddy, it's her." Reagan runs right into Colten's leg, hugging it while pointing at me.

"Yes, it's Josie."

"Hi, Josie!" She gives me a quick wave before grabbing the bat.

"Hi, Reagan."

Colten sets the ball back on the tee. Reagan smacks it and starts running the bases again, stopping at third base to chase a butterfly.

"No attention span." Colten shakes his head.

I chuckle.

He slides his hands in his pockets and watches her. "Do you remember when we said we'd never have kids?"

Yes. I remember. Colten said he'd never bring children into the world because he was afraid he'd inherited the loser dad gene. I just ... never wanted to be a mom even though I've had a great family. I wanted a career.

And Colten ... I wanted Colten Mosley. Had he wanted to marry me and have ten kids, I would have said yes.

"Well ..." I clear my throat. "I didn't have kids. She's all yours."

His head inches side to side several times before looking at me. "What about now? Are you dating a new guy every night because you're looking for love? A husband? A family?"

Rubbing my lips together, I shake my head and watch Reagan and the butterfly. "Just sex, Mosley. I don't want or need a husband. And we know I'm not exactly maternal, so I'll leave the childrearing up to women who are more nurturing."

"Occupational hazard?"

I smirk. "Something like that."

"Well..." he blows out a long breath "...I hope the sex is good."

I snort. "Yeah. I'm sure you do."

Reagan runs toward us, and Colten hunches down, letting her tackle him. "Oof!" He falls backward, and she straddles his chest, pressing her hands to his cheeks.

"Love you, Daddy."

"Oh, Button." He jackknives to sitting and grabs her tiny head, giving her a loud smooch on her forehead. "I love you too."

"I'm hungry."

"Okay. Let's hit a few more balls then we'll grab dinner."

Reagan softens all his rough edges. I need those rough edges to remind me to keep a safe distance from him. The dad version of Colten Mosley is too much.

We find some great Tex-Mex a few blocks from the park. My treat. Then he fastens Reagan into his Tahoe and starts the engine before stepping outside with me again, back resting against the closed door. "Thank you for meeting us tonight."

I cross my arms over my chest and nod several

times. "It was fun. Reagan is great. I'm amazed at how close you two are given the fact that you don't have shared custody."

"We FaceTime almost every day." His brows knit together as he stares at his feet for a second. "I gave Katy full custody because it was better for Reagan. No need to shuffle a baby back and forth between two homes. And I trusted that she'd do the right thing when Reagan got older."

"The right thing?"

He glances up at me. "Katy is a better person than I am. Even if I couldn't love her like..." his gaze averts to the side "...like she deserved to be loved; it wasn't a reflection of her. I trusted her to either let me into Reagan's life if it was best for our daughter or to raise her with someone else. She chose me." He shrugs a shoulder.

"You're not your father. That's why she trusted you. That's why she chose you."

When his gaze meets mine again, he smirks. "You giving me a compliment?"

"I'm ..." I hold up my hands and take a step backward. "I'm ... leaving. That's what I'm doing."

"Got a date tonight?"

I shake my head. "Why? Are you jealous?"

Colten scratches his jaw. "Watts ... I'm not sure there will come a day that the idea of you with some other guy doesn't make me a little jealous. It's in my DNA."

I study him, looking for an ounce of sincerity. Then

I turn and make my way to the driver's side of my car. "You hesitate." I glance up at him as I open my door.

His eyes narrow.

"You're a single dad because you hesitate. You pause. You always leave the door cracked open. Certainty is sexy. Nobody wants to be anyone's second thought."

Me. I was his second thought.

CHAPTER
thirteen

I TURNED thirteen two weeks before the start of eighth grade. My dad was out of town for a camp. Mom was recovering from an appendectomy. And Chad managed to pull his head out of his ass long enough to help Mom while Mrs. Watts (Savannah) made me a birthday dinner and cake.

"How's your mom?" Chief Isaac Watts asked as I strode up their driveway. He was working on his 1970 Chevelle SS 454. Blue. White striped hood. His true baby.

"She's okay. Chad's with her."

"Your dad still gone?"

I nodded.

Chief Watts frowned for a second before ducking back under the hood. He didn't approve of my dad's extramarital affair or the way he failed to teach me and

Chad basic skills like changing a tire, fishing, or how to use a gun.

"Sports aren't going to help you in the real world," Chief Watts would casually say when our families got together to grill or play yard darts.

My dad always had the same comeback. *"Colten's going to go pro someday. He'll pay someone to fix his car. Hire a bodyguard. And eat at fancy restaurants where someone else caught the fish."*

Go pro? In what? I wasn't sure. Literally any sport. All coaches had big dreams of their kids achieving what they never could. I had no interest in letting my dad live vicariously through me or making him happy at all for that matter.

"Need some help?" I asked Chief Watts.

He glanced back at me and grinned. "Dinner won't be ready for a bit. Might as well get your hands dirty first."

I didn't care to fish or hunt. But I liked his Chevelle and how willing and patient he was to show me everything about it.

Only minutes later, Josie opened the back door. "Oh ... you are here." I bumped my head on the hood because her voice startled me. It did things to me every time I heard it.

"Yeah, I'm helping your dad."

"You could help too, Jo," Chief Watts said.

She sighed, taking a seat on the garage step. "I could, but that's why you have Colten until Benji gets older. Oh ... and happy birthday."

Savannah offering to make me birthday dinner didn't come at the best time. Josie hadn't talked to me in three weeks. I called her bluff on an ultimatum. She wanted me to lie to her parents if they asked about her whereabouts the night she said she was supposed to be with a friend but was actually with Roland Tompkins at the funeral home. Of course, she told Roland her parents said she could help him prepare things for a visitation that night.

They did not.

So ... when I said I wouldn't lie for her, she broke up with me. It was something like breakup number ten billion and one. Our relationship changed like a blinking red light.

On.

Off.

On.

Off.

I don't remember falling in love with Josephine Watts. I just remember the day we met and the day I let her go for good. For me, she wasn't really my girlfriend. She was my everything. Every other girlfriend was just a game to get her back. Every fight was a prelude to treehouse kisses, "I'M SORRY" signs in the window, and shared cookies and milk.

I lived with my family, but I lived *for* Josephine Watts.

"Thanks, Josie." I played it cool like my birthday wasn't a big deal. Like her mom making me dinner or her dad letting me work with him wasn't a big deal.

Like *she* wasn't a big deal. Who was I kidding? If my birthday was the excuse she needed to break her silence, then that was the only birthday present I needed.

"Isaac? I need you to start the grill," Savannah said before shutting the door.

As he passed Josie perched on the stair, he gave her ponytail a little tug. "Be good."

With a dramatic eye roll, she mumbled, "Duh."

I grabbed a rag and wiped my hands while Josie rested her elbows on her knees and her face in her hands.

"My mom said your dad is gone for your birthday. That's pretty lame."

I shrugged. "I don't care."

"What did you get for your birthday? A new bat? New glove?"

"Nothing. I'm not sure my dad even remembers that it's my birthday, and since my mom was in the hospital, she hasn't had time to get me anything."

Josie's nose wrinkled. "That sucks. What do you want for your birthday?"

"Nothing."

"Liar."

"I'm not lying."

"Can you believe you could be driving by this time next year? My dad said I can drive his car when I turn fourteen. Jealous?"

Jealous? Yes. I was always jealous of Josie and her family.

"No."

"I'll go to the batting cages with you after dinner."

Again, I shrugged. It didn't come naturally to me, but I sure as hell tried to act unaffected by her.

"Jo, go inside and help watch your brother while your mom tends to the burgers on the grill. I need to finish up so I can take Colten for a ride after dinner." Chief Watts ruffled my hair before taking the rag from me.

"Really?" I couldn't help my excitement.

"We're going to the batting cages. Right, Colten?" Josie said, cocking her head to the side. A test. The head-cock was always a test.

My gaze flitted between Josie and her dad. "Uh … we can go to the batting cages anytime. But your dad's not working tonight, so …"

"So what?" Josie played hardball.

"We might find an empty parking lot where you can get in a little driving practice," Chief Watts said, showing me exactly where Josie got her persistence and competitive nature.

What was she going to do? We were already broken up.

"Batting cages tomorrow," I said.

Chief Watts gave me a wink.

Josie stormed into the house.

"Give her time. She's spicy just like her mom. But she'll come around. She always does. Right?"

I nodded slowly.

Josie didn't even look at me during dinner. She

didn't sing "Happy Birthday" when I blew out the candles on the cake. And she took her cake and ice cream to her bedroom, ignoring her dad's offer to go for a ride with us.

As promised, Chief Watts let me drive his car in the empty parking lot of the community college. There was something really cool about the chief of police breaking the law with me.

"I took leftover cake to your mom and brother," Savannah said to me when we entered the house.

"Thanks. Um ... where's Josie?"

"Out back."

"I'm going to go check on her. Thanks for a great birthday dinner."

Savannah picked up Benjamin and kissed his head. "Anytime, Colten. Happy birthday."

"And thank you, Chief Watts. It was awesome."

"You can call me Isaac."

I shook my head, eyes wide.

He chuckled. "Whatever. Go tell Josie she needs to come in by nine."

"Okay." I shot out the door, but Josie wasn't in the backyard. She was past the trail in her tree.

"Go away. You chose my dad over me."

I jumped up to grab the branch and pull myself up into the tree with her. "I chose driving over the batting cages."

"Same thing." She pouted.

"It's not. Besides, what are you going to do? Break up with me?" I laughed.

She did not laugh.

"I break up with you, so you don't break up with me first."

"That makes no sense."

"It does. Amy said Josh said you feel sorry for me, and you're afraid of my dad. That's why you let me be your girlfriend. I don't want you feeling sorry for me."

"I never said that. Josh is an idiot."

"Well, you must have said something like that. I'm sure he didn't make up a lie for no reason. Just be honest ... do you think I'm weird? Do you think it's weird that I hunt with my dad? Do you think it's weird that I hang out at the funeral home? Do you think I'm ugly because I don't wear makeup like the other girls?"

"No."

"Then why do you want me to be your girlfriend?"

Thirteen wasn't the best age for me. The whole girls-mature-faster-than-boys was never more magnified than in that moment. I had no clue. Well, I had a little clue, but it was nonsensical. So I blurted out the first thing that popped into my head, which wasn't a lie, but it wasn't totally true either. "Because you keep telling me I'm your boyfriend. And I like you, so I say 'okay.' Then you get mad at me and tell me we're breaking up. So I say 'okay' because I just don't like it when you're mad at me. And I don't like it when you let other guys hold your hand and kiss you."

Josie took a moment to stare at her dangling black Nikes, and I waited for her to tell me what to do. Life was easier when Josie was happy, and when she told me how to make her happy instead of making me guess what I did to upset her.

"Why don't you like it when other guys kiss me and hold my hand?" she mumbled, keeping her chin tucked.

"Because it's what I like to do."

Ever so slowly, she glanced over at me and grinned. "Do you want to kiss me now?"

Wetting my lips, I nodded.

"Okay," she whispered.

Leaning to the side, my lips brushed hers. I closed my eyes. And ...

"Collltennn!"

Thunk!

Josie fell out of the tree.

"Oh, fuck!"

It took me a few seconds to move my body and climb out of the tree. I wasn't expecting her to fall. And I definitely wasn't expecting her to say the F-word.

"My arm ..." She cradled her left arm to her chest and cried.

"Josie! Oh my god. Are you okay?"

"M-my a-arm ..." She cried more.

"Is it broken?"

"I don't k-know."

"Can you stand? Do you want me to get your parents?"

She sobbed and nodded. I assumed it was a yes to getting her parents, so I ran to the house.

"Josie fell out of the tree and hurt her arm," I

blurted the second I charged into the house, but nobody was in the room. Panicked, I ran up the stairs. Her brother was already asleep in his room with the door cracked, and his white noise machine playing.

I didn't think. I really *really* should have thought before opening her parents' bedroom door without so much as a knock.

Up until Josie asked me if I wanted to kiss her, the highlight of my thirteenth birthday was Chief Watts letting me drive his car. Then Josie said those words, and I forgot about the Chevelle.

Until she fell ...

That was the new unforgettable memory from my thirteenth birthday.

Until ...

I barged into Josie's parents' bedroom and witnessed Chief Watts standing in front of the television with the remote in one hand and Savannah's ponytail in his other hand. Her on her knees. His penis in her mouth.

The infamous blow job.

I had only heard about it from friends. Never experienced it. Never witnessed it.

"Colten!" Chief Watts boomed.

"Oh my god!" Savannah scurried to her feet and ran into the bathroom.

Me? Oh, I couldn't tear my eyes from the chief's larger-than-life penis. He reeled that long thing back into his pants with the swiftness of a fire engine after the last ember was extinguished.

He was angry.

Josie was sobbing in the woods.

Yet, all I could think was will mine be that big?

God, I hoped so.

Benji cried. For some reason that was what brought me back to reality, that and Chief Watts's big hands on my shoulders guiding me out of his bedroom.

"What the hell are you doing, Colten?" There was a tightness in his voice that I hadn't heard before. A constraint.

"Oh ..."

Savannah, with her flushed face breezed past us to Benji's room. "Shh ... it's okay, baby."

"I ..." My gaze gathered enough courage to look Chief Watts in the eyes. My new idol. "Josie fell out of the tree. I think she broke her arm."

He winced. "Shit ..." he murmured, brushing past me to the stairs.

"Josie?" Savannah called behind us as I followed Chief Watts to the woods.

With the strength, only a large-penised man would have, he carried Josie straight to his truck.

"Josie ..." Savannah held a grumpy Benji while kissing Josie's head before Chief Watts put her in the back seat.

"We'll get an X-ray, and I'll call you," Chief Watts said to Savannah. "Get in, Colten."

He wanted me to go. Why? I wasn't sure, but I had a sneaking suspicion it had something to do with the infamous blow job.

I sat next to Josie, and she leaned her head on me as she occasionally sniffled and whimpered. My hand slid to hers and squeezed it.

"So what exactly happened?" Chief Watts asked as we headed toward the emergency room.

When Josie remained quiet, I cleared my throat. "Well ... we were in the tree, and she fell out."

"Why did she fall out?" He eyed me in his rearview mirror.

"Because I said he could kiss me for his birthday," Josie murmured.

I felt less intimidated watching Chief Watts shove all three feet of his penis back into his pants than I did as he scowled at me in the mirror. I'd kissed her so many times before that day; it wasn't a big deal. She showed me her tits. That was kind of a big deal, but not anything Chief Watts needed to know.

Why did Josie rat me out? Was it payback for me not lying to her parents about the funeral home?

"B-but ... I didn't. We uh ... we didn't ... Sir."

Chief.

Master.

King.

Please don't put me in jail!

He grumbled something indecipherable.

While the nurse took Josie for an X-ray, Chief Watts pulled me aside in the waiting room. "Listen, Colten ..."

I had run a lot of bases, sprinted many fifty-yard dashes, but never had my heart pounded so quickly and violently in my chest as it did beneath the formidable man towering over me.

"I don't know if your parents have had 'the talk' with you, but ..."

I nodded then shook my head. "No. I mean ... yeah, I know about *that*. I should have knocked, and ..."

"You saw something you weren't supposed to see."

"I-I'm ... sorry." I closed my eyes and shook my head.

"Hey, look at me."

Again, I dragged my gaze to his. "I need you to make me a promise."

I nodded at least a half dozen times. Anything. I would do anything if it didn't involve going to jail.

"You forget about what you saw."

More nodding.

"And you never kiss my daughter again."

I kept nodding. His words barely registered.

"So we're clear? We're good?"

A hundred more nods. "Y-yeah ..."

He rested his hand on my shoulder and squeezed it. "I'm going to talk to your dad. I think it's about time you learn how to use a rifle."

Forget about the large penis.

Never kiss Josie again.

Use a rifle.

Got it.

CHAPTER
Fourteen

"I've never felt normal. But what is normal? How does one end up in this profession?" I ask.

Alicia sips her drink while I stir my lemonade with my straw. I've needed this girls' night out, especially since I don't have a lot of girlfriends. Never have.

"I have a seven-year-old son who tells his friends I sew up dead people." She rolls her eyes.

I laugh.

Alicia shrugs. "Someone has to do it, right? It's not for everyone, that's for sure. I wasn't exactly a 'normal' child either. I didn't hunt with my dad like you did, but I was never grossed out by things. Not gory movies. Not grotesque odors. Nothing."

"Did you have a fascination with death?"

She shakes her head. "No. Did you?"

I think about it, eyes narrowed at my drink.

"Kind of. Yeah. I hung around the funeral home. I asked my dad a slew of questions every time I overheard him talking about a death. I wanted to know all the details. When I'd ride my bike near ponds or creeks, I'd scour the area for dead bodies."

Alicia snorts. "You grew up in Iowa, right?"

"Yes. I didn't say I found any dead bodies, but ..."

"A girl can dream, right?"

My eyes widen as she returns a wry grin and shrugs. "If you know, you know."

On a chuckle, I nod. "I brought home a dead badger from the woods behind our house when I was seven. My mom was beside herself. Later, I overheard them talking about the incident, saying it was something one might expect from a dog, not a young girl."

Alicia gives me a wide-eyed, unblinking stare. "A badger?"

I nod and shrug a shoulder. "I wanted to see if I could find its heart."

"Why? Had you watched something on television that made you curious? Did one of your parents have a zoology book lying around the house?"

"No. One night, our neighbor's Bichon got attacked by something. They had to put it down. My dad suspected it was a badger. He said badgers can be 'heartless bastards.' Well, I didn't believe any animal could live without a heart, so I wanted to see for myself."

Choking on her drink, Alicia coughs and pats her

chest as laughter assaults her ability to speak or breathe. "You're ... k-kidding."

"No. That was when I learned everything about rabies and all other diseases carried by animals. My dad told me I could no longer bring home anything that wasn't a bird, snake, or fish since they can't carry or transmit rabies."

"Oh my gosh ... your dad is too much. I can't imagine what it must have been like to grow up as the police chief's daughter. Were you allowed to date before you went to college?"

On a slight chuckle, I shake my head. "It wasn't easy. The only boy he cared for was the neighbor boy, but he didn't want me with him. He simply wanted a son my age. My dad adored him. Took him under his wing. They worked on my dad's Chevelle together. When we were in high school, my dad worked out with him. Morning runs. Weight lifting. They became quite competitive. Never got him to hunt, but he taught him how to shoot a gun."

"You must have been envious of the neighbor boy."

"Mmm ... I had strong feelings for him, but I'm not sure envy is the right word."

"You liked him?"

I nod. "Too much." Do I tell her it was Detective Mosley?

"But your dad wouldn't let you date him?"

"No. Well, I don't know the answer to that. We had a unique relationship where his loyalties were split between my dad and me since my dad made him promise to never kiss me again after an incident. So whenever our relationship breached the more-than-friends zone, we had to keep it from my dad. And I'm not going to lie ... I was all over the place. Protecting my heart wasn't easy. I kept him at arm's length, which kept me miserable for years."

Alicia frowns. "What happened when you graduated? Were you friends or more than friends?"

"We were ..." I stare at the bar over her shoulder, wondering if abstaining from alcohol all these years was a good idea with Colten Mosley living rent free in my brain. "We were over. He ended us. Blew up my heart. Ran over it with his car. Poured gasoline onto it. Then flicked a lit match at the wreckage."

Nose wrinkled, Alicia mouths the word "ouch."

"Yeah."

"Have you seen him since then? High school reunions? Facebook friends?"

Really, I should tell Alicia it's Colten, but I don't want her to think I'm still pining for him ... because I'm not.

"Yes, we've run into each other."

"Was it awkward? Is he married with a family? Really successful? A total loser?"

I chuckle while the waiter brings us our food. "A mix of all of the above."

After the waiter leaves, Alicia pops a cherry tomato into her mouth. "You're so successful and brilliant at your job; I'm sure he's envious of you. I'm sure he regrets everything he did."

"Sadly ... no." I dig into my meal.

After dinner, I offer to give Alicia a ride, so she doesn't have to take the train.

"It's out of your way."

"Nonsense." I reach into my purse as we round the corner of the building to the parking lot.

Alicia makes a weird noise behind me, and I turn.

Her eyes bulge from her head as a man in a hoodie holds his hand over her mouth and a knife to her throat.

"Wallets," he says. "Nice and slow, sweetheart. Or your friend won't see the sunrise."

Alicia drops her purse on the ground.

He kicks it a few feet to the right and nods to me to toss mine there as well.

With my hand still in my purse, fingers wrapped around my key fob, I shift my hand to my gun and quickly toss the purse. His gaze follows my purse instead of focusing on my hand ... on the gun.

The bullet hits his knee the second he releases Alicia to grab our purses.

"AHH!" Alicia screams when he releases her.

He grunts and falls to the ground like a wounded animal. "You shot me, you fucking bitch!"

Keeping the gun aimed at him, I sidestep and retrieve our purses.

"Oh my god!" Alicia shakes, hands cupping her neck where the knife had been.

With my free hand, I call 9-1-1.

An hour later, we're at the police station, giving our

statements. Alicia's husband picks her up, and I stay a little longer since it was my gun. To make my night better, my old neighbor shows up.

"Watts ... did you shoot a man tonight?"

Resisting an eye roll, I angle in my chair to see Detective Mosley at the door to the office, looking smug as usual.

"She's all yours." The officer questioning me grins at Colten.

I stand and exit the office, brushing past Colten. "I'm not his," I murmur.

"How's Alicia?" He tails me.

"Shook," I say, reaching the elevator.

"How are you?"

I shrug as the doors open. "Fine. Why?"

He follows me as I step into the elevator. "Because you shot a man tonight. Doesn't that give you a moment's pause?"

"I didn't kill him."

Colten lifts a single brow. "No ... but still. You discharged your weapon. I didn't know you carried."

"Sorry. Had I mentioned that earlier in our reunion, would you have given me more space?"

Colten stands next to me, giving me very little space while staring at the doors. "He's going to be fine. The guy you shot. If you were concerned."

"Pfft ... of course he's going to be fine. I didn't shoot to kill."

"Have you shot anyone before?"

The elevator doors open, and I make a mad dash for the exit. "Not to my knowledge."

He chuckles. "That's not exactly reassuring."

When I get to my car, I turn because I sense him less than two steps behind me. Colten engulfs nearly all the space between us. It's hard to breathe in his close proximity—another thing that hasn't changed in seventeen years.

His smile fades a fraction. "You were brave. And a little stupid. You didn't know he was alone. There could have been someone else. They could have had a gun. If he wanted your wallets, you should have given him your wallets and not risked things escalating."

"Thanks, Dad." I turn to open my car door.

"Josie ..." He rests his hand on my hip.

I freeze. The perpetrator didn't frighten me, but Colten Mosley's touch scares me to death.

"Are you okay?"

"He didn't touch me. I'm fine."

"Your voice is shaking. That doesn't tell me you're fine."

I clear my throat and force confidence into my voice. "How exactly did you find out? I don't think homicide is called for an attempted robbery and a shot fired that doesn't result in ... homicide." Turning to force his hand away from my hip, I hug my handbag to my chest. A shield from him.

"When the assistant ME shoots a man in the leg, news travels fast."

"Gossip."

"Official Chicago PD notifications," he says, but his words are nothing more than mumbled syllables with no meaning behind them because he's too busy staring at my mouth, and that's mind-numbingly distracting.

"I'm gonna kiss you, Josie."

"Don't tell me. Just do it."

"I'm not going to kiss you." He grins.

I scoff. "Why would I think that?"

"Because you drag your teeth along your lower lip when you think I'm going to kiss you ... when you want me to kiss you."

"Seventeen years ..." I turn and open my door, forcing him to take a step backward. "It's been seventeen years. You know nothing about me. A lot has changed." I slide into the driver's seat.

Colten wedges himself between me and the door, resting his forearms on my car. "Sure ... you've turned into a successful doctor. Maybe you've even mastered dating apps and finding random guys to hook up with, but that look..." he bites his lower lip, dragging his teeth along it to mimic me "...time will never change that look."

"People often see what they want to see, not what's really there." I start my car.

"Take the day off tomorrow. You need to process what happened tonight."

I laugh. "If you shot someone in the knee, would you take a day off to process it?"

"That's different."

"I'll be at work tomorrow. If you need to take the

day off, then do it. You're clearly more bothered by the incident than I am."

"I bet Alicia takes the day off," he says.

I glance up at him. "She had a knife at her throat. I did not."

"Had it been you with a knife at your throat, would you take the day off?"

"Bad people don't scare me." I reach for the door handle.

"Well they should."

"Well they don't."

"That's fucked-up, Josie."

"It's just me. See ... you don't remember me as well as you think you do."

Colten steps back and lets me shut the door. I make the mistake of giving him one last glance. Of course, he knows me. And I know him. That's what makes this seventeen-year reunion a recipe for disaster.

When I get home, I jump on my stationary bike for forty-five minutes before showering. As the hot water washes over me, I attempt to make a mental and emotional assessment of myself.

The conclusion? I feel fine.

Maybe I'll have nightmares about the situation, but I doubt it.

CHAPTER Fifteen

CHIEF WATTS ASKED me to take his daughter to the homecoming dance. Neither Josie nor I were dating anyone else. It was our sophomore year, and, honestly, I was fine not going to the dance. However, at the last minute, Ryan Wilkenson asked Josie to the dance.

A senior.

Josie said yes.

Chief Watts said, "Over my dead body."

I agreed with her dad, but I didn't tell her that. Ryan was a player in every sense. Not that I wasn't a player in my own right, but I wasn't in the business of collecting V-cards like Ryan.

"Dad! I hate this. You don't trust me. He's two years older, not ten. We're just friends."

I helped my mom bag yard waste while listening to Josie and her dad in their garage.

"Colten?" Josie yelled my name.

Shit.

"Tell my dad that Ryan Wilkenson and I are just friends."

Since Josie broke her arm, I refused to be her official boyfriend. Yeah, I made a promise to her dad, and I valued my life, so I kept it as best as I could. She still unofficially decided when we were together and when we were not.

Did she kiss me just to torture me? Absolutely.

Did I want her to kiss me? Did I love the torture? Absolutely.

Did I date other girls just to piss her off? You betcha.

As a result, she used me to manipulate her dad. Fair? Probably.

"They're just friends," I mumbled.

"He can't hear you!" She was ... fiery. "Come here, please."

Mom smirked at me.

Drawing in a long breath, I blew it out while crossing the street.

Josie sat perched on the step to the back door, her usual spot, while Chief Watts finished wiping down his Chevelle with a rag.

"Tell him," she repeated.

I rolled my eyes. "They're just friends."

"Don't care," Chief Watts said in a tone that sounded as uninterested as my own. "My little girl isn't going out with a senior."

"I'm not your little girl."

"Then whose are you?" He shot her a stern look over his shoulder.

Josie grumbled.

"You take her to the dance, Colten," Chief Watts said. "Problem solved."

"I ..." I shook my head while Josie's smile took over her face. "I'm not going to the dance."

"Yeah, Dad ... he's not going," Josie said behind her dad's back while running her teeth along her lower lip, that thing she did when she wanted me to kiss her.

"Either Colten takes you, or you're not going."

"I already bought a dress." She made an amusing attempt at batting her eyelashes at me.

I shook my head. "I'd have to see if one of my parents could drive us."

"I'll drive you in the Chevelle." He turned around and winked. "Your very own police escort."

Josie immediately played the disgruntled daughter. "Fine. Guess I'll have to tell Ryan that my dad doesn't trust him." She stormed into the house, slamming the door behind her.

An act ... it was all an act.

"Thanks, son." Chief Watts rested his hand on my shoulder and squeezed it. I wasn't his son, but most days I wished he were my dad. Except then Josie would have been my sister, and all of our kissing would have been really inappropriate.

TWO WEEKS LATER, Chief Watts drove us to dinner. He and Savannah sat two tables away. It sucked not having our driver's licenses yet.

An hour and a half later, he dropped us off at the dance. We had until midnight. We spent most of the time chatting with friends and fast dancing. When the DJ played a slow song, Darren Hayes's "Insatiable," I asked Josie to dance.

She smelled like cool mint gum and a really strong perfume. Josie wore a white strapless dress; and her hair was straighter than usual and silky. Her eyes had a bronze shadow and her lashes were heavy with mascara.

"After this song, let's leave," she said while draping her arms over my shoulders as I kept my hands a safe distance above her butt.

"Your dad's not picking us up until midnight. It's only ten."

"When my dad picks us up, he'll take us home. You'll go to your house, and I'll go to mine. How are you supposed to kiss me goodnight?"

"It's not going to take me two hours to kiss you goodnight."

She smirked. The pink lip gloss she wore earlier that night had worn off. "Then you're not doing it right, Mosley." That was the sexiest thing Josie had ever said to me.

I grinned. "I think our ride is here now."

Josie's grin matched mine. I took her hand and led her to the exit.

"It's cold, Josie. Where are we going?" I slipped off my jacket and draped it over her shoulders.

"You don't trust me. That sucks for you." She pulled me toward the football field and under the bleachers where there was a folded blanket hidden at one end.

"Did you leave this after the game last night?"

She nodded, handing me the blanket. I shook it out and wrapped it around my back before taking a seat against one of the rails. Josie hiked up her dress and straddled my lap. I hugged her with the blanket, wrapping us in a cocoon.

"I'm gonna kiss you, Josie."

She grinned, leaning in and rubbing her cold nose against mine. "Don't tell me. Just do it."

That was an awkward time in our lives. We were either fighting, pretending to ignore each other, or making out like our existence revolved around each other's tongue probing the other one's mouth.

The problem?

Josie gave me a perpetual hard-on. The way she hummed when we kissed.

Her fingers in my hair.

Her warm crotch and thin panties just on the other side of said hard-on and strained fly.

We didn't move against each other at that point, but surely, she felt the difference between first sitting on me, and thirty seconds later when her tongue slid against mine and every ounce of blood in my body shot straight to my dick.

I only knew of a handful of boys in my class who had already lost their virginity. All of them to girls a year or two older. I wasn't going to have sex with Josie, probably ever, if Chief Watts got his way. Had he known where we were that night and what we were doing, I would have been a lifeless body in the cemetery just down the street from our houses.

As if she could read my mind, Josie pulled away a fraction, breathless, eyes wide, lips slightly parted. "I want you to be my first," she whispered.

I shook my head half a dozen times.

Josie grinned. "Not now. Just ... when it happens, I want you to be my first, and I want to be your first."

"Your dad will kill me."

On a laugh, she threw her head back, fingers laced behind my neck. "Duh, Colten. We're not going to tell him when it happens."

Never. *If* it happened, we would never tell him.

But fuck ... did I trust her not to let it slip? After all, everything changed when she felt the need to tell him she fell out of the tree because I leaned over to kiss her.

"What if I'm dating someone else when that time comes? Or what if you have a boyfriend?" I asked.

She shrugged a shoulder. "Doesn't matter. We agree to be each other's firsts, and that's that."

"So ..." I narrowed my eyes. "If I have a girlfriend and she wants to have sex with me, I have to find you and have sex with you first?"

Josie gave me a firm nod. "Yes."

It was my turn to bark a laugh. "And if you have a

boyfriend, you think he's going to be okay with you telling him you have to have sex with me before you can have it with him?"

"I'll just say tough luck, Mr. Duck."

I tried to conceal my amusement. She hadn't said that in years. "You can't say that to him."

"Why?" She slanted her head to the side.

"Because you say that to me."

She nipped at my lower lip and whispered, "You don't own me."

I rested my hands on her ass. "Not all of you." My lips found her neck, and I kissed my way to her bare shoulder. "Just the best of you."

CHAPTER
Sixteen

"You good?" Dr. Cornwell asks when he saunters into the conference room.

"Of course. Not Alicia, though."

"One shot, right to his knee. You never cease to amaze me, Watts." Dr. Cornwell slides on his reading glasses and taps his tablet as the others file into the room.

"I've been called to testify. It's kind of last minute. I'll be back after lunch. If you're not done—"

"Go." He shoos me with one hand while keeping his focus on his tablet.

I grab my handbag and a case file from the table for court. "Is it weird that shooting a man in the knee didn't faze me?"

Several of my asshole colleagues mumble a "yes."

"Weird?" Cornwell eyes me over the top of his reading glasses sitting low on his prominent nose.

"Should I feel remorse? Fear of retaliation? Shock that I did it so easily? Something? I mean ... I don't really feel anything about it. I didn't panic. I just did it like someone does something on autopilot or instinct. Gave my account to the police. Drove home. Cycled. Showered. And slept like a corpse."

After a few silent seconds, he removes his glasses. "Frankly, I don't know. I've never shot anyone. I don't own a gun. I've removed too many bullets to feel like I'd ever want to put one into another human being. But consider all the people who think we are emotionless because of the job we do. Nothing could be further from the truth. We are methodical and controlled with our emotions. I'm sure that carries over to other parts of your life. My wife says I ground her because she's a ball of unchecked emotions, and I'm silently contemplative to the point she often feels the need to see if I still have a pulse."

I chuckle. "I don't feel so bad now." I head toward the door.

"Because I'm your idol?"

"Sure, sure, sure ..."

<hr>

AFTER A MORNING OF TESTIMONY, I grab lunch at a food truck and head toward my car. I half expect Detective Mosley to call me, but he doesn't.

Not today.

Not the following day.

Or the following day.

I'm good. Or so I tell myself. How does his new existence in my life transport me back to the young girl spying out my window, waiting for Colten to come home from baseball practice?

On my way home (*so* far out of my way), I drive by his house, slowing down to see if I see anyone through the front window. When I don't, I continue to the end of the street.

My phone rings. I hit the handsfree button on my steering wheel when I see it's Detective Moseley. Does he have a sixth sense that I'm spying on him?

"Hello?"

"You're a little out of your neighborhood, Watts. What's up?"

I cringe, glancing in my rearview mirror just as he pulls into his driveway. "Uh ... I know your mom is leaving soon, so I was going to say goodbye, but it didn't look like anyone was home, so ..."

"I'm home."

On a nervous laugh, I nod to myself. "Yeah. I see that."

"Reagan and my mom go home tomorrow. You should come for dinner."

"It's your last night together. I'm not intruding on that."

"The way I intruded on dinner at your house

nearly every night for months after my parents separated?"

"That was different. My mom invited you."

"True. Hold on a sec ..." I hear a few indistinguishable sounds then the click of a door shutting. "Hey, Mom ... can Josie come to dinner?"

Oh my god ...

I'm embarrassed, and I'm not even in the house. He's acting like a child inviting a friend to dinner.

"She said yes. Come over. After the old and the young go to bed, you can hang out in the garage with me."

I turn the corner to circle around the block. "I'll come to dinner, but then I have to go home."

"Curfew?" he asks.

I grin. "Something like that."

When I pull into the driveway, he's standing on his porch, tie loose, jacket open, and his hands planted in his front pockets.

He's ... a sight.

"I'm intruding," I say for a lack of other words as I approach him.

"My mom would be disappointed if she didn't get to say goodbye. It's like you knew."

I offer a genuine smile as he opens the door.

"You have the best smile, Watts. You really should show it off more often."

I slip off my shoes. "I smile a lot ... in the right company."

"I used to be the right company." He slides off his suit jacket and heads toward the stairs.

"You used to be a lot of things," I say, feeling a million more emotions than I did the night I shot a man in the leg because my friend had a knife held to her throat.

Colten pauses, but he doesn't look back at me. "Have I mentioned how proud I am of your accomplishments?"

It rubs me wrong ... in the worst way. He keeps parroting that sentiment. "Have I mentioned that you had nothing to do with my accomplishments?" I head toward the kitchen and the sound of a five-year-old giggling.

"Josie!" Becca smiles, setting a steaming casserole dish onto the stove. "I'm so glad you could join us." She takes off her oven mitts.

"I feel like I'm intruding, but I wanted to get a chance to say goodbye before you left. Hey, Reagan. I heard you're going home with your mom tomorrow."

She glances up from her coloring book and nods. "Uh-huh."

"Well, it's been fun getting to know you. I hope we get to see each other again."

"Uh-huh."

"Reagan, go see if your dad wants a salad with his dinner," Becca says.

"I'm coloring."

Becca shakes her head. "You're killing my knees with these stairs."

"I'll go." I wink at Becca.

"Thanks, dear."

When I reach the top of the stairs, I glance in each bedroom. The primary bedroom is the last on the right. And the second I realize that, I'm staring at a half-dressed man. Jeans on but unbuttoned with the zipper down. A gray tee with his arms through it but not pulled over his head yet.

Damn ...

Everything about Colten Mosley is all grown up. I much prefer a living, breathing, *perfect* human specimen.

After my gaze goes right to his unbuttoned jeans, it slides up a few inches to the long scar on his abdomen.

"Watts?"

My gaze snaps up to his, and I swallow before clearing my throat. "Do you want a salad? Your uh ... mom wants to know."

"A salad sounds good." He threads the shirt over his head and pulls it down his torso before buttoning his jeans. He wasn't this muscular the last time I saw so much of his body. I've seen a lot of bodies, so it's strange that I'm visually enamored with his, but ... I am.

Since my brain has decided to completely go off the rails, I go ahead and take a quick scan of his bedroom.

King bed.

Striped bedding.

Tall dresser.

Nothing special.

No photos on the wall, just a coat of gray paint.

How many women has he had in his bed? More than the number of men who have been in mine? Am I really thinking it's a competition?

"I'll tell her I want a salad if you need a few more minutes to check out my bedroom."

"No." I refocus on him and shake my head. "I'm going. Take your time."

"Did I ever tell you what I saw the day you fell out of the tree and broke your arm?"

I turn back toward him. He rubs his fingers over his lips like he's trying to hide his grin.

"What you saw?"

He nods, taking a seat on the end of his bed. "I ran into the house, but nobody was downstairs. So I ran upstairs. Benji was in his bed, and I was panicked over you, so I opened the door to your parents' bedroom. I didn't knock because it was an emergency, and really ... what would they be doing anyway?"

My nose wrinkles. I'm afraid of where this is going.

On a nervous laugh, he runs a hand through his dark hair. "I witnessed your mom giving your dad head."

Blink.

Blink.

Blink.

I didn't hear him correctly. I was crying in the woods with a broken arm, and my mom was giving my dad a quick blow job before my curfew ended? I have seen and smelled the most grotesque and vile things, but this image that's now in my head is far worse.

"It was kinda crazy," Colten continues.

I don't know if I want him to continue. I think I want him to stop. Better yet, I would have preferred he never *ever* tell me this. He hates me. This proves it.

"You were injured, waiting for help, and I was supposed to be the one getting help, but then I walked in on them, and your mom ran into their bathroom, while I just ... stared at your dad's cock. I had never seen one so damn big."

A little bile works its way up my throat as I shake my head repeatedly, silently pleading for him to stop. My dad peed a lot on our hunting and fishing trips, but his back was always to me. I never saw his penis, until now.

Now, I'm imagining the largest penises I have ever seen and mentally placing them onto my dad like part of a Mr. Potato Head. I'm ruined. Scarred for life.

Colten Fucking Mosley.

"At the hospital, while you were getting an X-ray, he made me promise to never mention what I witnessed. And that's when I had to promise to never kiss you again, and he suggested I learn to shoot a rifle. As of this very moment, the rifle promise is the only one I kept."

In med school, I had to help separate two people who were stuck together. His penis piercing got caught on her tongue piercing, and very sensitive skin was ripping apart. That image is more pleasant than the one Colten just planted in my brain.

"I need to tell your mom that you want a salad, and you need to never speak to me again." My head continues its back-and-forth swivel. "Like ... ever. Got it?"

Colten takes several steps toward me, fingers tucked into his front pockets. "Did you ever think of me? In the past seventeen years, have you thought about me much?" He glances at the floor for a second before returning his gaze to mine. It's the innocent, boyish thing he used to do. He's no longer a boy nor is he innocent.

I purse my lips for a moment.

"I did," he says before I find my answer. "I thought about you so many times. I wondered how you were doing. I hoped you were okay."

"Okay?" I ask, grunting a tiny laugh. "Did you think I wouldn't be okay without you? Did you honestly think you were my everything? If that's what you thought, then it only makes the way you treated me that much crueler. Doesn't it?"

Pursing his lips to the side, he takes a quick glance over my shoulder and nods slowly before meeting my gaze again. "I knew you'd be fine without me. I never doubted that. I knew that no man, including me, would be the be-all and end-all of your life and success. That didn't make me think about you any less. Other things can happen in life that might make one *not okay*. A car accident. Someone pulling a knife on you. Cancer ... so many things. When we graduated, my mom said if I was going to let you go, I had to *really* let you go. She didn't tell me much about your life, and I knew she kept in touch with your parents for a long time."

He shrugs. "I assumed she'd let me know if you died, but beyond that ... I had only my thoughts, my curiosity, and my hopes that you were, in fact, okay. I'm not sure I've gone a full day without thinking of you."

Why is he telling me this?

"I'm going to tell your mom you're having salad." I turn and head toward the stairs.

"Josie?"

I ignore him. For someone who can't look back with any sort of regret, he sure does have a lot of things to say about the past.

"He wants salad," I announce just as Becca sets the casserole on the table along with a serving spoon.

"That took a while." She eyes me with a knowing look on her face. I'm not sure what she thinks she knows, but probably as much as I do.

"He's chatty."

She chuckles. "He has his best friend back in his life. The last time I saw him, he wasn't this happy."

I transfer the plates from the counter to the table. "Miss Reagan is here. Happiness personified."

"I know his Reagan high. This is different." Becca transfers salad from a bag into bowls. "You owe him nothing. I love my son, but I've always thought of you like a daughter. So as someone who shares a motherly love for you, believe me when I say you owe him nothing. Unless ..."

I set the last plate in its spot and glance up at Becca while Reagan shoves her crayons back into the box. "Unless what?"

She shakes a bottle of ranch dressing. "Unless you feel good about him being back in your life too."

"I'm here for you, Becca. I don't have dinner with him alone. He's in my life as someone in my work world. That's it."

"Daddy play piano!" Reagan runs to Colten as soon as he comes down the stairs.

"After dinner." He picks her up and tosses her over his shoulder, and she giggles. When he sets her down at the table, he nuzzles his face into her neck and kisses her over and over.

Reagan squeals and giggles more.

Becca leans in and whispers, "I don't think that's how one looks at someone in their work world," while brushing past me to the table with three salad bowls in her hands.

I quickly glance away when she looks over her shoulder and gives me another knowing look. It's as familiar as the looks Colten gives me. Becca used to settle fights between us and gave me a look when I said I hated Colten. The look that said she knew I was crazy about him, and that's why I let him under my skin so often.

"Coming to Texas for Labor Day?" Becca asks Colten as we take our seats for dinner.

"Can't. Working."

"Halloween?" She follows up with him.

"Working."

"Thanksgiving?" She frowns.

He lifts a shoulder while dishing up casserole for Reagan. "I can put in for time off for Thanksgiving or Christmas, but not both."

"Well, choose whichever one you can bring Reagan with you."

"That might be neither." He eyes his mom.

She gives him a slow nod and sad smile. He has no official custody of her. Whatever time he gets with his daughter is granted by her mom.

I can't purge this one little thought from my head. It's on a continuous loop.

Colten Mosley is a dad.

CHAPTER
Seventeen

"Want to go for a drive?" Colten asks as he makes his way down the stairs after reading Reagan a bedtime story.

"I should go. When your mom comes back downstairs, I'm going to tell her goodbye and head home."

"She decided to take a shower because I told her we were going for a drive, and you'd say goodbye when we got back."

I frown. "Pretty presumptuous of you."

"Hopeful." He grins.

"Colten ..."

"Quick drive. We'll be back in twenty minutes. It will take my mom that long to shower and get ready for bed."

This is a terrible idea, but I find myself nodding.

With that winning smile that I've never been able to resist, he nods toward the door, opening it for me.

"This way." He heads toward the garage while I head toward his car.

"I'm not riding on the back of your bicycle, Mosley."

Colten chuckles. "You used to be more fun, Watts." He digs his keys out of his pocket and opens the side access door.

As I step behind him, he flips on the light, causing my next step to falter. There's a sunken floor and a car lift with a Corvette suspended in the air.

"Doesn't look drivable."

"Not yet." He eyes me over his shoulder and smirks.

I follow him around the car, stopping in my tracks for a second time when I see a blue Chevelle. Not *a* blue Chevelle, my dad's blue Chevelle. I don't know this for certain, but my gut tells me it's the same car, or maybe it's the beaming expression on Colten's face that leaks the truth.

"You bought my dad's car? When? Why? How did I not know this?"

"He sold it to me when I went into the police academy after serving in the Marines."

"You kept in touch with my dad after you enlisted?"

"Sure."

Sure ... he says it like it's no big deal.

"Do you remember when your dad took us to homecoming our sophomore year in this car?"

I nod several times, ambling around the car, giving it a slow inspection.

"Remember when we left early?"

My gaze finds his over the top of the car. Colten grins. I do all I can to keep my face neutral.

"Under the bleachers?" He continues to ask questions that don't need to be asked.

That's it. No more eye contact for him. There's nothing wrong with my memory, and he knows it.

"I'm trying hard to figure out," he continues, "how we spent nine years together and seventeen apart, but I feel like my whole life has been defined more by those nine years than the following seventeen." He shakes his head, running his hands through his hair. "You taught me so many things about life ... about love. And I didn't fully see those revelations until you were gone."

"Well..." I release a nervous laugh "...no regrets. Right? Your words. I don't recall saying those exact ones, so I didn't have *that* big of an impact on your life." I make my way around the car in the direction that will keep me the farthest from him. There's no way I'm getting in that car with him. "I bet your mom is out of the shower. And it's late ..."

"And I could have taken a job anywhere, so could have you. Still here we are in the same city, working in professions that overlap on a regular basis. Really, Josie, what are the odds of that?" He catches up to me just as I reach the door.

His fingers slide around my wrist.

And just like that ... I'm eighteen.

I can't breathe.

The deafening thud of my heart makes it hard to focus on anything but how his touch didn't age one bit. I've not acquired an ounce of immunity to it.

"Seventeen years, Josie ..." he whispers. "You can't stay mad at me for *seventeen years*."

Wrong.

My grudge is the eternal kind.

On my headstone, they'll write:

Josephine Watts

Mother of zero.

Loved by a few.

Friend to several.

Good with dead bodies.

Emotionally humiliated by Colten Mosley.

"You don't know anything about me," I say.

"I know the best parts of you."

God ... why does his warm touch feel so good? Oh, that's right ... dead bodies for a living.

I'm not going to forgive him. I'm sure as hell not going to forget what he did to me. But I might let his touch linger a few more seconds.

Colten tugs my arm a little until I face him. He takes a tiny step closer leaving no more steps to take. His hand slides up my bare arm, and I feel my resolve slipping. I don't like that feeling.

I need the anger.

The resentment.

The grudge.

Without it, I am too vulnerable.

"You killed the best part of me," I whisper.

His other hand cups my cheek. "I set it free."

My head eases side to side. "I hate you."

"If only it were that easy." He tips my head up and ducks his, pausing a breath from my lips.

Certain feelings, deep emotions—the haunting kind—can't be outrun. Colten has been the unshakable shadow of my existence since the day I met him.

"If only …" I echo him.

We kiss.

And it's … purgatory. It's poison. So why has my soul never felt more at home? *What is wrong with me?*

He's only feeding the hate and the resentment, even while my hands thread through his hair.

While I lean into his body.

While I let him back me into a slat wall of coats, coveralls, and hats.

"Josephine Watts," he mumbles, kissing down my neck, his hands palming my ass. "Jo … se … phine … Watts …"

I don't care how much agony his words hold; the grudge is eternal.

Hate sex was invented for this exact situation. Yes, my mind skips ahead a few steps to sex. It's not that I've been waiting seventeen years to have sex with Colten Mosley. Well, that's eighty percent true.

Kicking my heart to the curb to wait for me at a safe distance from Colten, I reach for his belt, giving it a hard tug to unbuckle it. He lifts his head from the crook of my neck.

He's going to stop me. That's his MO. I can see it in his eyes.

I blow out a long breath, unable to hide my frustration. "Some things never change," I murmur attempting to escape the confines of his much larger body pinning me to the wall.

His head cocks to the side as he smirks. "You don't know anything about me." He tosses my words right back at me while his gaze slides down my face to my chest. In the next breath, his fingers flick the button of my shorts, and he eases down the zipper.

Curling my fingers around the hem of his shirt, I work it up his torso. He grabs it with one hand and shrugs it off, letting it fall to the floor beside us while smashing his mouth to mine again.

Yeah ... I definitely waited seventeen years to have sex with Colten Mosley.

My hands return to his pants, unbuttoning them and giving the waist a slight nudge, sending them a few inches over his ass to his thick thighs.

His tongue makes a slow stroke against mine while his right hand sneaks inside my panties, palming my ass again.

Gone are the days of the cautious teenager, scared to death of my father. Where was this Colten when I needed him?

This changes nothing. This doesn't erase the jilted lover I've been for seventeen years. Still, it makes me deliriously happy to get the one thing he never gave me before we ended.

He spins me around, pressing my chest to a thick winter jacket. Hunching behind me, his fingers curl into my shorts and panties, slowly sliding them down my legs; his lips press to the curve of my ass while he hums.

"You are fucking perfection," he murmurs.

He's ...

So intoxicating.

So sexy.

So everything.

My eyes close, teeth digging into my bottom lip when I draw in a sharp breath and arch my back. He nudges my legs apart until my shorts and panties stop them, and he grips my ass with his hands, his lips skipping over my flesh, teasing me.

"Colten?" Becca says, opening the garage door two feet to our left.

History has a way of repeating itself. It's not a cliche. It's true.

Colten abandons me.

Abandons. Me!

He yanks up his jeans in less than a second and snags his shirt from the floor.

"What is it, Mom?" he asks her from beneath his shirt as he tugs it over his head.

My hands dive for my shorts and panties and wiggle them over my hips with my back to Becca. I cannot turn around.

Ever.

A few seconds of silence blankets the room. Why is

it silent? Are they talking in sign language? Is it a stare-off? Are they waiting for me to swallow the last drop of my pride and turn to face them?

"I'm going to bed. I wanted to say goodbye to Josie. Do you two need a few more minutes?"

Pinching the bridge of my nose, my face wrinkles into a grimace. A few more minutes? Is she serious?

"Maybe another ten?"

I whip around when Colten makes his stupid request. The floor becomes the most fascinating part of the garage. Giving it all my attention, I shuffle my feet to Becca and glance up only when I have her in a hug. "I should get going. It was great seeing you. Have a safe trip home."

That's it.

I release her and escape out the garage in one quick move.

CHAPTER
Eighteen

Mom and I spend a good minute or two staring at each other. I'm fairly certain thirty-five-year-old men can't be grounded, but she might prove that theory wrong.

I hear Josie's car door shut and her car pull out of the driveway. Mom tilts her head a fraction like she's listening to the same thing.

"Thought you two were going for a drive."

I return an easy nod. "That was the plan."

"And ... what happened? Your pants fell down on the way to the car? And ... you were helping Josie pull up her pants because you're a gentleman like that?"

Clicking my tongue twice, I wink at her. "Exactly."

She frowns. My humor's not everyone's taste.

Crossing her arms over her chest, she flicks out her hip. "Do you know what it means to court a woman? Because I feel like I failed you as a mother. You've never had any control around Josie. And I have a granddaughter (whom I love beyond words) because you think sex is the equivalent of holding hands. It's not."

"It was Josie's idea."

"Colten Wilson Mosley, you are a grown man. Stop blaming Josie for everything like you're still a child."

I've taken a life. Twice. Once as a Marine and once on the police force. I know martial arts. I have elite combat skills. I track down killers, risking my life to keep the public safe. How am I having this conversation with my mother?

I rub my mouth to keep her from seeing my grin.

"You have to grow up and take responsibility for your actions. You are a father now. And Josie deserves a man who's got it all together."

"I take offense to that. I have it together. I have a job. I pay my child support on time every month. I take my own bags to the grocery store. And I always have a condom in my pocket. Katy wasn't a one-night stand. We were dating."

Mom's expression wrinkles into a map of confusion. "So you were dating Katy, but you didn't love each other enough to get married for Reagan's sake?"

"I asked her to marry me."

Her jaw unhinges.

I nod several times before blowing a quick breath out my nose. "She didn't sense my love for her was what she deserved, and she was right."

"Why didn't you ever tell me that?"

I shrug. "Katy and I felt a little irresponsible, and we felt like it wasn't anyone's business. She knew her parents would try to talk her into marrying me, and I ... well, I wasn't sure what you would say."

Pursing her lips, she offers a slow nod. "Compare Katy to Josie."

My head inches side to side. Then I lace my fingers behind my head and gaze at the ceiling. "Apples and oranges. Really, I can't compare them. Katy is the mother of my daughter. Josie's the ..."

"The what?"

"I don't know," I whisper. "I never saw this coming. Her path and mine running side-by-side again. And when I see her ..." I return my attention to my mom. The gravity of my feelings seems to wipe the amusement from my face. "When I see her, I feel like our story is still untold. Seventeen years feel like seventeen seconds."

I can't remember the last time my mom looked at me with anything but concern on her face. She's always been worried that I'd be my dad. I'm not him.

"Go to bed, Colten."

Again ... I'm thirty-five, but I nod and shut off the garage lights behind us.

CHAPTER
Nineteen

THREE DEAD TEENAGERS waiting in the morgue.

Not my idea of a perfect Monday morning.

"Everybody gets a gun. You get a gun. She gets a gun. Every human gets a gun."

If I didn't already know where Dr. Cornwell stood on gun rights, I do now.

Alicia eyes me as she assists him. It's the you-saved-my-life-with-your-gun look. I don't think I saved her life. I think I saved us from being robbed, but I know from her incessant thank-you's that she feels like I saved her.

"If drugs were decriminalized, we wouldn't have to do this so much," I respond while removing drugs in the tied fingers of latex gloves.

"Guns *and* drugs, Watts? How did I not know about your dark side?" Dr. Cornwell laughs.

I smirk behind my mask. "We all have a dark side. I carry a gun. You hide a large bag of beef jerky in your desk next to a bag of peanut M&Ms. I'm likely to take someone else's life. You're likely to take your own."

I love Cornwell's chuckle. It's genuine, like a father finding his daughter's antics amusing. "Touché."

When my exhausting morning bleeds into the afternoon, all the way until two o'clock, I retire to my office for lunch and reporting.

"Oh god ..." I murmur to myself when I spy Detective Mosley waiting outside my office. Head bowed to his phone. One leg crossed over the other.

When he glances up, I bite my lips together, lifting my eyebrows in a silent question: *What are you doing here?*

"Hi." He grins. "I was about ready to give up on you."

"Three teenagers riddled with bullets were waiting for us this morning. I've been busy." I unlock my door and squeeze past him. "Last I heard, you worked homicide. Shouldn't you be busy too?"

"That's why I was about to give up on you. You've been ignoring my phone calls and texts. Don't you think we're too old for that?"

"Just the opposite, Detective." I take a seat at my desk and fish my lunch out of my bag. "I had more time on my hands when we were younger. Now, I'm busy. I'll give you five minutes. What do you need?"

"Have dinner with me tonight."

"Terrible idea."

"I could shut your door, and we could finish what we started in my garage."

Opening the lid to my nori rolls, I shake my head without giving him the tiniest of glances. "I've blocked that near mistake out of my head. Are we done here? Three dead teenagers ... do you have a suspect in custody yet?"

"We don't. State took over, anyway. I feel like the mistake we made was not accepting the extra time alone my mom offered us."

I chew my bite of food and blot my mouth with my folded paper towel. "I had a temporary lapse in judgment. I let my feelings for your mom and your adorable daughter blur my true feelings for you."

"True feelings?" One side of his mouth curls into a smile.

"I hate you. But your mom and Reagan humanize you."

"Ouch." Colten grips his shirt, pulling the invisible knife from his chest. "Hate is a strong word. Just say you have strong feelings for me after all these years and let me interpret those strong feelings on my own." He stands, moving in the wrong direction around my desk to me. When he leans his backside on the edge and crosses his arms over his chest, I scoot a bit to my left.

"We're here for a reason. You're back in my life for a reason," he says.

My attention remains affixed to the computer screen with the occasional glance at my nori roll. "I'm in Chicago. We're in the same city. I fear you're reading into that."

"If my mom would have had better timing, we would have—"

"Thank god for your mom. She had perfect timing." I frown, picking a carrot sticking out of my nori roll. "Well, perfect timing would have been five minutes earlier before we ..."

"Kissed? Lost our clothes?"

I grunt, shaking my head. "Lost our minds."

"What are you afraid of, Josie? Are you afraid if we go too far, you won't be able to hate me?"

"No. I can go as far as I want *and* hate you. I'm good at multitasking."

"Great." He knocks on the top of my desk twice. "My place at eight. I won't even buy you dinner first since there's no point."

My head whips in his direction as he saunters to the door. "You can't tell me what to do."

He glances over his shoulder. "I can. It's my turn."

"Your turn?"

"After you broke your arm, you said I could be the bossy one in approximately twenty years. It's been twenty-one years since you promised me control. It's past due. Eight o'clock. If you're late, I'm going to handcuff you to the bed."

My lips part, fresh out of words, and he exits my office with a frightening level of confidence.

AFTER WORK, I do what any good self-preserving woman would do—I line up a last-minute date for the night. Garrett is a nice guy. We've chatted off and on for months. It's time I do the irresponsible thing and invite him to my place after dinner.

He says something funny as I unlock the front door and toe off my shoes.

"The fuck ..." Garrett stiffens, glancing over my shoulder when I turn on the light.

My hand dives into my purse, fingers curling around my gun as I whip around.

Shoulder casually propped up against the wall, arms crossed over his T-shirt-clad chest, Colten returns a frigid look to Garrett before glancing at his watch. "It's nine o'clock."

Tipping my chin up and easing my grip on my gun, I narrow my eyes at him. "Go home."

"So you can fuck this dude?"

"Yes."

"Um ... I thought you were single," Garrett says. "And you have a gun?"

"I am. And I do."

"Then who's this guy?"

"Nobody," I murmur.

My response draws a tiny grin from Colten. "Do you have a gun on you?" He eyes Garrett.

"N-no ..."

"Well, I do and so does Josie. So I'm thinking you should go home, have some warm milk, jerk off to your favorite porn site, and forget about her."

Garrett takes a step back, closer to the door. Without looking behind me, I grab his shirt and make a tight fist. "Stay, Garrett. Detective Mosley is out of his jurisdiction and out of his mind."

"*Garrett* ..." Colten clicks his tongue a few times. "You are a placeholder. A stand-in. A knockoff of the real thing. Go before you embarrass yourself anymore."

Garrett breaks free from my grip. "I'm out of here. I'm not down with this stupid shit."

When Garrett's no longer at my back, and I can't seem to find a word to say, Colten shifts his attention from Garrett's vacant spot to my unblinking eyes. He shrugs. "You were right. We can't end."

CHAPTER
Twenty

BY THE END of our junior year, Tessa was the flavor of the month—Josie's label, not mine.

A senior, Tessa Hart declared her intention to give me her virginity after just three weeks of dating.

"I'm going to college in the fall. I don't want to be a virgin. And I don't want a boyfriend. You still have a year left. And you're experienced, so what do you say?" Tessa pinned me to the side of the concession stand with her big boobs after my first baseball game of the season. Her fake fingernails teased my groin area, and she frowned when she realized my cock was safely tucked into my jock strap and covered with a cup.

Just the thought of her trying to touch me there had my dick at attention. As for her assumption that I was experienced … I didn't know where she heard that.

And what was I supposed to say? That I needed to go have sex with Josie first?

Did I mention Josie had a boyfriend?

"Say yes, Colten," she whispered, lifting onto her toes and licking my lower lip until I took the bait and kissed her.

"Get a room," Tami said as she and a group of girls turned the corner of the concession stand, sports drinks and candy in their hands.

Bringing up the end of the cluster of giggles? Josephine Watts. But she wasn't giggling. Or smiling. The look on her face could only be described as murder.

"Maybe we will get a room. My bedroom. Maybe this weekend when my parents are at the lake," Tessa said, looking at me, but the volume of her voice was unmistakably announcing her intentions to the rest of the world—or at least to the group of girls.

My relationship with Josie was complicated ... flat-out fucked-up by that point. I felt loyal to baseball. My mom and her desire for me to get a musical scholarship. Chief Watts and keeping my balance on the tall pedestal where he put me. And ... there was Josie.

The reason my unconventional relationship with Josie seemed to work was because there was nothing conventional about Josephine Watts.

One minute I thought she understood my need to keep my promise to her dad (or at least the illusion of it), and the next minute I feared that she would take my life long before her dad ever got the chance to do it.

To say I had a love-hate-fear relationship with the Watts family might have been a gigantic understatement.

Tessa kissed me, closing her eyes.

I kept mine open, watching Josie toss her drink and bag of licorice into the trash before sprinting toward the parking lot.

"I gotta go," I said, turning my head to break Tessa's suction on my mouth before grabbing my duffle bag and running after Josie.

"Colten!"

Ignoring Tessa, I sped up. "Josie!" I smacked the side of her red Honda Civic as she sped out of the parking lot. "Fuck ..." I mumbled, dropping my bag to the ground in the cloud of dust she kicked up speeding past me.

By the time I made it home, Josie was in her house, and Chief Watts was home, sorting through his tackle boxes in the garage. As soon as I grabbed my bag from the back seat of my blue, rusty Chevy Silverado, he called my name.

Every time he called me into his garage, which was quite often, I dragged my feet, wondering if that was the moment he was going to break the news to me that Josie told him everything about us.

Break the news to me that he no longer thought of me as his son, and I would have to make amends with my own dad.

Break the news to me that I would soon die because I knew what Josie's nipples looked like.

There would be no lenience for staying out of her pants. I would die. And Roland Tompkins would cremate me and keep Chief Watts's secret because Roland had three daughters and would kill anyone who violated his daughters.

For the record, I didn't violate Josie.

"Congrats on your win," Chief Watts said.

I breathed a sigh of relief, knowing I'd live another day. "Thanks."

"Josie ran into the house mad as hell. Savannah is gone for the evening with Benji. Would you mind talking to her? She won't talk to me."

Jabbing my thumb over my shoulder, I fumbled my words. "Uh ... I ... it's ... my mom's waiting on me. Dinner. And homework."

"Five minutes, son. Just find out what happened so I know if I need to deal with someone or if it's just stupid friend stuff."

Deal with someone ...

Calling me "son" only tightened his grip on me, on my loyalty to him.

"Five minutes. But if she's really upset, she might not talk to me either." My shoulders curled inward while making my way to the door.

"I appreciate you trying."

"Mmm-hmm ..."

As soon as I shut the door behind me, I froze. Josie stood in the kitchen, a glass of milk in one hand, a cookie in her other hand, and that same evil glare boring a hole into my head.

I opened my mouth to speak, but before I could get a word out, her head shook several times in a sharp motion while making her way to me. "I hope Tessa has herpes or crabs or something that kills you. Then I'm going to dissect you and bury you in the woods next to my favorite tree so I can spit on you every day for the rest of my life." She tossed her whole glass of milk in my face.

And I stood there and said nothing while she took a slow bite of her cookie, giving me a blank expression for a few seconds before pivoting and heading upstairs.

"She's not in the mood to talk to anyone," I said to Chief Watts, not skipping a beat as I trod my way past him.

"Colten, what's all over you?"

"Milk." *And rage.* I kept walking.

"She threw her milk on you?"

"Mmm-hmm."

I managed to sneak past my mom without her focusing on my milk face.

"Sorry I missed your game, sweetie. How'd you do?" she called from the laundry room next to the kitchen.

My feet stomped their way upstairs. "Fine."

"Hungry?"

"I don't know."

It was a stupid question but so was my answer. I was always hungry. There was only one force stronger than my hunger— Josephine Watts's wrath.

The second I emerged from the bathroom, freshly

showered, Mom shouted upstairs. "Colten? Tessa called and Josie's here."

That sentence rubbed along my nerves to the point of making me shudder. Tessa and Josie in the same sentence just didn't belong. Oil and water. Heaven and Hell.

"Go on up, Josie. Tell him I put a frozen pizza in the oven for him, and it will take about ten minutes," Mom said as I stood at the top of the stairs contemplating going down them or climbing out my window, risking my fate from a second story jump and hoping I could wobble my way as far from home as possible.

Instead, I crossed the hall into my bedroom and took a seat at my keyboard, playing Beethoven's *Moonlight Sonata*.

Josie stood silent in my doorway.

Then she sat on my bed.

Finally, she made her way to the piano bench beside me, sitting in the opposite direction as usual.

I didn't skip a beat. Not a single note.

"My dad said I had to come apologize to you for the milk incident."

I ignored her, my fingers caressing the keys as my body swayed ever so slightly like the easy bob of my head.

"But I'm not going to apologize, and we both know why."

Did I though? I wasn't so sure.

After I played a few more measures, she sighed.

"I'm not ready to have sex, so you can't have sex with Tessa. Sorry."

For the first time since she came into my bedroom, I lost track of my location in the song, and my fingers stopped, idly hovering over the keys for a few breaths until they dropped to my thighs.

"Tessa's here!" Mom called, an official declaration of God's contempt for me.

"Oh ..." Tessa's voice chimed at my back. "What are you doing here?" she asked Josie in a catty tone.

"Whatever I want."

I grimaced at Josie's response even if it made me want to puff out my chest in pride that she stood up for herself with another girl from school, an older classman at that.

"What's that supposed to mean?" Tessa moved in on us.

I glanced over my shoulder and started to speak, but Josie cut me off.

"You are a placeholder. A stand-in. A knockoff of the real thing. Go before you embarrass yourself anymore," Josie said while standing, hands planted on her hips, chin up.

Tessa's jaw unhinged as she looked to me for confirmation that Josie was my official spokesperson. "Colten, are you and *her* a thing?"

We were *something*.

"Can I call you later, Tessa?"

"No," Tessa *and* Josie replied in unison.

Gritting her teeth, Tessa pointed a stiff finger at

Josie. "I am not a placeholder. A knockoff. I am the real thing. So why don't you go home and find a better way to stuff your little training bra so it doesn't make your chest look so lumpy. Then go ask your boyfriend to take a little pity on you and tell you about the birds and the bees. Colten, tell her to go home and leave us alone."

Focusing on my fingers, I continued my sonata. "Tessa, go home."

She gasped. I wasn't sure what Josie did, but if she had a reaction, it was silent.

"We. Are. Over!" Tessa stomped down the hallway and right down the stairs. A few seconds later, the front door slammed shut.

I moved to the middle of the song, leaning into the increasing tempo of the homophonic texture. Josie leaned her head on my shoulder.

"Are you the real thing? Does every other girl hold your place?" I asked her.

She drew in a slow breath and released it even slower. I couldn't see her eyes, but I imagined them drifting shut. "I hope so."

With that reply, I leaned my head on hers and finished the song. After the final note, her hand slid to my lap, taking my hand and guiding it to her stomach.

Beneath her shirt.

To her chest.

Into the cup of her bra.

Another girl was giving me an erection that day, only it wasn't just any girl. Josephine Watts was *the* girl.

My hand remained idle for several breaths, her chest pulsing in and out ... faster, deeper. When the pad of my thumb brushed her nipple, she released an audible breath.

"Close your bedroom door," she whispered.

She didn't have to ask me twice. I slid off the bench and closed the door. When I turned back toward her, she was sliding down her shorts *and* her panties, leaving her shirt on as she sat on the piano bench again. Her hands rested on her bare legs, her gaze struggling to meet mine as she chewed her lower lip.

"Have you had oral sex?" she asked, forcing her gaze to meet mine while her voice wobbled with uncertainty.

I shook my head slowly, unsure where I needed to keep my gaze. It wanted to track south.

"Do you want to?" I had never heard Josie sound so afraid, so nervous.

I nodded since my voice seemed to be on vacation. If this was her idea of an apology for the milk incident, I welcomed our next fight. My heart thrashed around in my chest so violently I thought it might explode while I took a few steps toward her.

"Here?" I whispered. The bed seemed like a more logical option, but for whatever reason, she sat back down on my piano bench after exposing herself.

Josie returned several tiny nods, lips pressed together while she took a hard swallow. I lowered to my knees in front of her. Her eyes flared, unblinking.

Leaning forward, my hands rested on the bench beside her.

We kissed.

Josie was familiar, but not "the same." Nothing about her got old. In fact, she grounded me. Even on the days she left me dizzy with her rules and sudden mood changes, I was unequivocally the best version of myself.

Our kiss was slow. So was her hand guiding mine between her legs, inching it along her inner thigh.

Up ... up ... up ...

With every micro-movement, whooshes of air pushed out of her nose. I wasn't as well versed in oral sex as some of my friends, so I had a little apprehension, hence the long kiss. When the tip of my finger reached the apex of her slightly spread legs, she gripped my hand, a vise stopping me from going any farther.

Our kiss broke, and we breathed into each other's mouths. Had she let go of my hand, she would have felt it shaking as much as her legs. If she wasn't sure about me touching her with my fingers, how was she going to let me put my mouth in that very spot?

I nearly came in my pants just thinking about it.

"Maybe I should do it to you first," she whispered over my lips.

"That's ... um ... f-fine. If you ... uh ... want to." How did I think I was going to have sex with Tessa (who thought I was experienced) when I could barely express a coherent thought with Josie? I couldn't imagine Josie giving me a blow job, if I were being honest. I never asked Chief Watts what Savannah usually did with his load. Did it go into her mouth? Was swallowing involved? My friend, Bart, deposited his jizz onto his girlfriend's chest. But Josie had her shirt on. Was I supposed to ask her to take it off? It couldn't go onto her shirt. Savannah would see it in the laundry. I had a hand towel tucked under my mattress, but if I grabbed it, Josie would've seen how well-used that hand towel was, and I wasn't ready to be *that* honest with her.

"Or I could just touch you with my fingers," I whispered back to her. We seemed to be stuck mere millimeters apart, my hand still *so* close to the goal line. I considered saying, "I could finger you," but I wasn't sure that was an expression girls liked to hear. It was commonly referenced in the boys' locker room, but so were a lot of other crude comments.

"Can you make me come?"

I gulped and thought about that for a second. My instinct was to say yes. Sex was one of the most basic acts of humanity; I couldn't imagine making a girl orgasm required any sort of special sorcery. Then I considered how many times I fell off my bike before learning to ride without training wheels. Biking seemed pretty basic too.

"I guess there's only one way to find out." I faked sixty percent of my confidence and managed a smile that matched at least forty percent of that confidence.

That made Josie relinquish a tiny grin and loosen

her grip on my hand just enough to enter uncharted territory.

By a fucking millimeter at the very most.

Because ...

My mom decided to come into my room. Nope. I did not lock the door. I never locked my door because it was an unspoken rule to knock. I wasn't five anymore. It was a given that behind a closed door someone could be half naked. If the bathroom door was closed, we knocked. We never just opened the door.

Etiquette.

Rules.

Protocol.

Come on!

"Oh!" Mom gasped.

Really, everything happened at once.

The gasp.

Josie closing her legs so damn tight, I could barely withdraw my hand from between them. Then she lurched forward, grabbing her shorts and panties while I stood with my back to my mom so I could adjust my dying erection.

My dad used to say my mom spewed the most nonsensical things at the worst moments. I wasn't sure what he meant until that moment.

"Condom. Do you have ... do you want me to get a condom? No! I mean ... this is wrong. Colten, this is wrong!"

When I turned around, her hands were covering

her face.

"Mom! Get out." I grabbed her shoulders, turned her around, and guided her out of my room.

"Dinner's ready," she squeaked.

I closed the door behind me and leaned against it. My head eased back while I closed my eyes to Josie zipping her shorts with frantic hands.

"Your mom has impeccable timing."

When I opened my eyes, Josie rolled her lips inward into a closed-mouth grin.

"Are you going to be in trouble? Do you think she's going to tell my parents? Should I tell them first before she gets a chance to tell them?"

"No!" I shook my head a dozen times. "Do not tell them anything. I'll talk to my mom. She won't say anything. Just promise me you won't tell them."

"Colten touched me between my legs. I was half naked on his piano bench, and we decided to do the finger thing instead of having oral sex. What's that, Dad? Oh ... you're getting your gun. What are you going to do with your gun?"

"Colten, I want to tell them before she does. I can make them understand."

"She's not going to tell them. And what's to understand? How are you going to sugarcoat what just happened?"

Josie shrugged a shoulder. "I'll tell them we were heavy petting. That's what their generation called it. And no one can get pregnant from heavy petting, so it's not the worst sin in the world."

Seriously?

I'd felt my life slipping through my hands years earlier when Josie ratted me out for kissing her when she fell out of the tree. Heavy petting? Every cell in my body physically ached and shook with fear at the thought of what Chief Watts would do to me for that.

"Josephine Watts ..." I took two big strides forward and cupped her face, tipping her head back so she had no choice but to give me her full attention. "Do. Not. Tell. Them. We will be over. We won't even be friends. We'll be nothing. Less than nothing. Is that what you want?"

She blinked several times before easing her head side to side the tiny fraction my hands allowed.

"Go home. I'll talk to my mom. And we won't ever discuss it again."

"K," she whispered.

I released her and blew out a big sigh of relief.

"Colten?" She stopped at my door.

"Yeah?" I looked up at her as I followed her lead.

"We can't end."

I didn't know what that really meant for sure, but I nodded anyway.

"I never felt normal and accepted until I met you. So ... we can't end."

CHAPTER
Twenty-One

"You ended us. We are over," I reply to Colten's regurgitation of the words I fed him so many years ago. "There is no *we*. There is you, and there is me. Even if you've managed to run off my date tonight, it doesn't change anything."

He studies me in silence for several seconds. "Do you remember Tessa? The day she came to my house, and you were there?"

I remember everything. Every word. Every breath. Even the tiny spaces between breaths. He doesn't need to know that, so I give him nothing but several bored blinks and a straight face.

Easing his head side to side, he grins. "I was fucking drowning. Trying to figure out who I was, where my life was meant to go, why my dad was such an asshole, and how to be what my mom needed me to be. Then there was you, Josephine Watts. When I was with you, nothing else mattered. Until Reagan came into my life, I couldn't imagine ever meeting someone who made me feel so ..." His face contorts into a slightly painful expression while he averts his gaze to the floor for a second. "I ... I can't even find the right word. It's not 'important' or 'purposeful.' It's like I just knew I was meant to be your friend, the way I just knew when I held Reagan that I was meant to be her father. Not that you needed me or that she needed me. Just that I knew I was part of something ..."

His gaze meets mine, and I hate him for not being awful. I'll forever hate him for so many reasons. "Something life-changing," he whispers. "And I felt so damn lucky. Always have. Always will."

Colten has never played by the rules, not that I ever have either, but I have a healthy respect for them. I'm more judicious when it comes to breaking them. He dives in before checking to see if the pool is two feet or ten feet deep.

"You ran away. *That* was life changing. Being with me?" I shake my head. "That was nothing special to you."

"Yes—"

"No!" I cut him off. "You took a nine-year friendship ..." I steady my words, needing them to be as clear as they've been in my head for so many years. "It was more than friendship. You ended it with ten fucking words. And then you went to the one place you knew I wouldn't follow you. And you never made an effort to speak to me again." As my words rip from my chest, they lose all confidence. Seventeen years has done very little to mend the broken pieces of my heart.

"I don't watch baseball. I don't own a bike. I can't stand listening to the piano, let alone Beethoven. I haven't had milk and chocolate chip cookies in seventeen years. You took everything that was wonderful in my life and made it ugly and painful."

He winces. "I'm so sorry."

"Nope. You don't get to be sorry. Not now. Sorry expired approximately a year after you left. I thought … surely you'd get homesick for me. You'd realize your fake altruism was nothing but fear. You'd be back. You'd call. Write. Something …" I shake my head slowly. "Undergrad. Med school. Residency. Your dad dying. Your mom moving. Your brother stuck in treatment. Earthquakes. Hurricanes. Fires. Terrorist attacks. Mass shootings. The world going to shit. Nothing triggered your need for me. So now that we've stumbled into each other, you think the universe is telling you that I'm in your life again and ready to spread my legs for you?"

The smile has vanished from his face.

"Colten, you are a drug. I won't deny that. I've seen the catastrophic side of addiction too many times. I'm no longer your addict. You knew I was destined for greatness, right? Your words? Well, here I am. Being great all by myself. I didn't …" The lump in my throat swells, exposing my weakness. Him. "I didn't need you …" I blink back my tears. "I just really wanted you."

I have *never* felt this vulnerable.

The pain in my chest breaking free with those five words that have been looping in my head for years.

"I'm going to fix this." With two steps, he gazes down at me.

My eyes focus on his chest for a few seconds before risking a glance up at his sad face. "Some things can't be fixed. That's my area of expertise. I study all the things that went wrong. I answer questions. I solve mysteries. I might even give a little peace of mind and closure, but none of it fixes anything. We died."

"What if we didn't?" Colten whispers, eyeing my lips, the ones I won't give him again. "Or what if death isn't the end?"

"What's after death?"

He studies me for a few breaths before slowly shrugging one shoulder. "A second chance. A fresh start where the past doesn't matter because ... time stole the anger, the resentment, the grief, the heartache."

Rubbing my lips together, I return a single nod. "We'll talk in another life, but eternal is eternal, and my feelings toward you are eternal." I sidestep him and toss my purse onto the floor along with my shoes.

Colten opens the door. "So you'll love me forever."

"I'll hate you forever."

"Not without loving me more. We were young. Young people are malleable, impressionable. What happens to us when we're young leaves a bigger mark than anything that happens to us as adults. Those nine years were an infinity to the following seventeen years." The door clicks shut behind him.

After running my fingers through my hair …

After wincing at my heart constricting in my chest …

After grumbling like I did as a child …

I turn and run after him, but I don't get a step farther than opening the door. He's less than a foot from me, smirking like he knew I'd cave. I'm not caving. I just need to ask him—

He grabs my face and kisses me like he did in his garage only harder, obliterating my thoughts. My conscience feels the sting of submission while my body refuses to listen to reason. It wants Colten Mosley naked. Right. Now.

We back into the house, his hands keeping a death grip on my face as mine grab his shirt and wad it into my fists.

His shirt … off.

My shirt … off.

I'm not thirty-five. I'm not a doctor. Or a well-respected professional.

I'm a teenager driven out of control by hormones and all the impulsive emotions that go with them.

Our legs tangle, and his hand shoots out to grip the wall, holding me to him with his other hand while keeping us from falling to the floor.

Doesn't matter. We hit the wall and melt to the floor anyway.

Colten hovers over me, hitting the pause button for

a few labored breaths. He's not a homicide detective. He's not the young man who left me. He's not a father. He's ... the teenaged boy who I chased, pushed away, hated, loved.

Dipping his head, he kisses my neck while cupping my breast over my bra. My hips lift off the floor as if my body's entire purpose in life has been to feel Colten Mosley between my legs.

While his lips brush the swell of my breast, he releases a soft chuckle.

"Shut up, Mosley," I murmur as heat fills my cheeks. I'm a lot of things, but immune to his physical touch is not one of them. "Just shut ..." I lose my words and my breath when he yanks my bra cup to the side, and his hot mouth devours my flesh.

My other breast.

My abdomen.

He unbuttons my pants and removes them along with my panties.

If his mom magically appears, I might take her life.

His right hand slides up my stomach, squeezing my breast again while his left hand grips my leg, guiding it to the side while his mouth plants between my legs.

"Dear godddd ..." I arch my back, and he pinches my nipple.

Lick. Suck.

One finger. Two fingers.

I'm dizzy. So ... damn ... dizzy.

Colten's not the hesitant sixteen-year-old who played Beethoven like a boss only to nervously inch his fingers up my inner thighs as I sat on his piano bench with shaky legs and racing breaths.

I close my eyes, and I swear I can still hear *Moonlight Sonata*.

I gasp ... then I moan, lips parted, hips rocking into his touch. One hand grabs his hair while my other hand covers his hand on my breast, squeezing it.

He pinches my nipple until my body jerks from the pain.

A good pain.

That pain crashes into an explosion of pleasure when his tongue and his fingers move faster, harder ... and just ... so ... perfectly ...

"Col-Colten ... Colten ..." I chant with the arrival of my orgasm.

He slows his tongue while lifting his hips and working the button and zipper to his jeans.

I chided him for hesitating with Katy when she asked him if he loved her. I said women like confident men.

With all the confidence in this world, and maybe a few other worlds too, Colten fits between my legs. Kisses me with breathtaking vigor. And drives his cock into me with a hard thrust.

"Fuckkk ..." I cry.

He groans into my mouth, but he doesn't slow down. Not one. Single. Bit.

Has he thought about this for seventeen years like I've thought about it? Has my name and image popped into his mind with every other woman he's been with? Did he think of me the night he conceived his daughter? And if so, how would I feel about that?

I'm going to have bruises on my back consistent with fucking on a hardwood floor. If I die in the next twenty-four hours, that's not what the medical examiner will write in his notes, but that's what he'll think.

"Jesus ... Josie ..." He breathes in my ear before biting my earlobe. "This can't end ... I want to fuck you all night ..." His teeth dig into my shoulder next.

He angles his hips lower ... even lower until his pelvis strokes my clit with each thrust.

My fingertips curl into his back, my teeth into his shoulder ...

Seventeen years of fantasizing about this moment that I thought would never happen.

Again, I orgasm a few seconds before a moan escapes him. He pumps into me harder than any man has done before him. Then he stills. A mass of rigid muscles and bones going limp over my body. The world's heaviest weighted blanket.

"Josephine," he whispers against my ear. It's a sigh. Or maybe something more reverent, more desperate.

Whatever the meaning, it gives me goose bumps.

It fills my eyes with tears.

There's no way I'm crying after sex.

Still, this doesn't feel real.

I'd sit up. Grab my clothes. And run to my bathroom to shore up the wall around my heart. But Colten's large frame has my body pinned to the floor.

With his chest pressed to mine, I feel his heart beating, compromising the strength of mine.

"I need you to go," I whisper past the lump in my throat. I suppose it's bad form to ask a guy to leave after sex while he's physically still inside you. It's all about survival, and sometimes survival mode isn't flattering.

"I'm not a guy you picked up off the internet. Sorry." He deposits soft kisses along my neck to my jaw … to my mouth. Then he relinquishes a grin. "I broke into your house. So just plan on being held hostage the rest of the night. Then I'll leave in the morning. After coffee."

"It's just sex."

Again, he chuckles. "Yeah, yeah … it's *just* sex. The way it was always *just* a kiss. *Just* my hand up your shirt. *Just* your fingertips slipping into the back pocket of my jeans. You've failed miserably at minimizing everything about us when it suited you." He lifts his head and rolls us so he's on his back.

I sit up, straddling him while I tuck my breasts back into my bra. "Just is *just* a word, no matter how I've ever used it." I stand, snagging my clothes from the ground, and make my way to the bathroom. "You minimized us to nothing when you left." I shut the door behind me.

After a good fifteen minutes, I open the door, ready to kick him out of my house. He's not here. "Colten?"

Nothing. Peeking out the front window, I don't see his vehicle. After a deep sigh, I head to bed. That's that. I had sex with Colten Mosley. Now I know.

I can check that box off some ridiculous list in the back of my head before I crawl into bed, curling into a ball, wrapping my arms around my midsection. With my eyes closed, I imagine my arms are his arms. I imagine what it would feel like to only feel the good things.

His touch.

The warmth of his smile.

The caress of his words at my ear.

He made me hate him. It's a poison that won't leave my body.

CHAPTER
Twenty-Two

"Plans for the weekend?" Alicia asks Friday afternoon.

It's been four days since Colten left my house without a goodbye. His usual MO. Detective Rains visited yesterday, but Colten hasn't so much as sent a text to me.

"I'm driving to Des Moines early in the morning. My parents' neighbor died. She was like another grandma to me. She moved in right after my brother was born, and she was his babysitter for years. Vera made the best blackberry jam from her blackberry bushes."

"Sorry to hear about her death."

I shrug, stuffing my PPE in the trash. "Colon cancer. She was seventy-two."

"Well, have a safe trip."

I smile. "Thanks. See you Monday."

I ARRIVE in Des Moines a little before eleven Saturday morning. The funeral's at three, and I need a shower after leaving so early this morning.

"Hey, hon." Mom pulls me in for a hug after I set my overnight bag by the stairs. "How was the drive?"

"Fine."

She releases me. "Benji called this morning. His flight was canceled, so he won't make it."

I frown. "That's too bad. I was looking forward to seeing him."

"Well, now Colten can sleep in his room instead of on the sofa sleeper."

"What?" I nearly choke on my words.

Mom heads into the kitchen. "He should be here soon. I'm surprised you two didn't ride together. I can't believe you didn't tell me you two reconnected after he moved to Chicago. I had to hear it from Becca. She called me after visiting with you there. Gosh, I hadn't talked to her in ... well, too long. She sounded good."

I watch her cut potatoes for the grill. "He ... he's a homicide detective, so our paths occasionally cross. He said his mom was in town, so we had dinner one night. I'm not sure that's reconnecting. And uh ... why is he staying here?"

"He's coming for Vera's funeral, of course."

I shake my head slowly and mumble, "Wow. He

couldn't make it to his own father's funeral, but he'll come home for a neighbor's funeral."

"What's that, Josie?"

"Nothing. What I meant was, why is he staying *here?*"

"It's just for one night. Your dad and I thought it would be silly for him to get a hotel room. He's always felt like a son to us anyway." She glances up from the cutting board, stilling her hands. "Is everything good between you two now?" Her brow furrows. "I know that's probably a silly question. What's it been? Seventeen? Eighteen years? I hope you've both had a chance to laugh it off and move on."

"Laugh what off?"

"The whole fiasco of him choosing to enlist when you were heading off to college. You never said anything, but I knew you were upset that your friend was leaving to enlist. But look how everything turned out for the best?"

Friend?

"You know, there are a lot of affordable hotels around here. Benji's bed is a twin bed. Colten would probably be more comfortable in a hotel. I bet he only accepted your offer because he was afraid of hurting your feelings."

Before she can respond to my brilliant suggestion, there's three knocks at the door, and it creaks open behind me.

"There's my boy." Mom wipes her hands and takes quick steps past me to the front door.

"Hey, Savannah."

I roll my eyes at all of it.

My boy? Pfft ...

Slowly turning, I plaster on a fake smile as he releases my mom and grins at me.

"Hey, Josie. I got to thinking about it, and it's crazy that we didn't just ride together."

"Mmm ... well, I had no idea you were coming to Vera's funeral."

"It was a last-minute decision."

"As are most deaths."

Colten's smile swells a little more, but I'm not giving him the satisfaction of admitting that I'm in a snarky mood.

"Take your bags upstairs, you two, then let's get lunch ready." Mom heads back to the kitchen.

I grab my bag and head upstairs without giving Colten another glance.

"How's your back?" Colten asks from my bedroom doorway before I even get my bag deposited onto the bed.

"It's fine." I turn, crossing my arms over my chest.

Bruised. Heavily bruised.

"Have you already bitched to your mom about the unfairness of me coming to Vera's funeral but not my father's funeral?" he asks, moseying into my room, right to the window that faces his old house and his old bedroom window.

"No."

"Liar." He glances over his shoulder at me.

I avert my gaze to my feet. "It *is* rather insensitive."

He returns his attention to the window. "Yeah, well, so is fucking around on his family."

"Funerals are not for the dead; they're for the living."

"I know."

"Yet you didn't care enough about your mom and brother to show up."

"I grieved him before he ever died, and nobody planned a fancy gathering to offer their condolences to me. My mom and Chad made excuses. Excuses are lies. They lied. When I made the decision to not come to his funeral, I didn't lie. I was honest."

I scoff but don't follow it up with anything.

Colten turns, eyeing me with suspicion before simply eyeing me everywhere. All men have a signature expression that says they've seen you naked. It's sly and cocky. "I left because you asked me to leave. In case you were wondering."

"I wasn't," I say.

"Liar."

"Stop calling me a liar."

"Or what?" His wandering gaze snaps to my face. "Are you going to tell on me?"

I sit on the edge of the bed. "I'd like it if you could behave this weekend. My parents don't need to know that I ... slipped."

"Slipped?" He coughs a laugh. "Are you calling what happened at your house a slip? Like you're a sex addict and you slipped? Or like you physically slipped and landed on my dick?"

He's not going to bait me. Nope. I keep a neutral expression. Rewarding him with any sort of response will only feed his obnoxiously huge ego.

Our silent standoff leads him to me. Not what I want. He squats, lowering to his knees then sitting back on his heels in front of me, hands resting on his thighs. "I'm sorry, Josie. Even if I can't bring myself to regret the path my life has taken, I can promise you that I've lived with the pain of knowing that I hurt you."

I shake my head and start to stand, but he lifts onto his knees and grabs my wrists, guiding me to sit back down on the bed.

"There has to be a way to make things right."

"There's not."

"There must be a way to make things a little less wrong. On the floor in your entry, things felt a little less wrong." He tries to hide his grin, but a half one pulls at his lips.

This grudge is heavy. It's exhausting. It's sticky. I can't shake it. I don't want it, but I can't get past it. An uncrossable sea. I've never been able to let things go. Maybe this grudge-holding curse is in my DNA.

"Best sex of my life," he says.

"I don't doubt that, but it doesn't change anything."

There it is, that showstopping grin. "It's amazing you're still single, Josie. With your winning personality and humble spirit, it's really just ... baffling."

"I need to help my mom with lunch. I'm sure my dad is in the garage. He'll want to see you first since he likes you better than me."

"Because he sold me his car?"

"Because you have a penis."

"Josie, I don't think your dad has any use for my penis. I mean ... I owe him a debt of gratitude for not cutting it off when we were teenagers, but I don't think he thinks about my penis. But I hope you do. God ..." He bites his lip and closes his eyes while easing his head side to side. "I really hope you think about it. I hope you miss it because it sure does miss you." When he opens his eyes, he frowns. "And can we call it something less clinical than penis?"

"It's a penis."

"It's your best friend."

"This conversation is over." I shove his shoulders, and this time he lets me go.

"To Vera." My dad raises his beer bottle while we eat lunch on the three-season porch.

"To Vera," Mom, Colten, and I echo.

"Still not drinking, huh?" Dad eyes my water glass while he and Colten enjoy their beer and my mom sips a glass of wine.

"Still not drinking." I set my water glass on the table.

"Never? You've never taken a drink, Jo?" Dad continues to probe.

I don't know why he thinks I would lie about it. "No, Dad."

"Why do you think you've had such an aversion to alcohol?"

"I'm not sure it's an aversion. I simply have no desire to have it. Never have. I don't know why, but it's not exactly a bad habit to avoid."

"Are you dating, hon?" Mom asks.

"When I have time."

"Anyone special?" She passes me the bowl of cucumbers and onions in vinegar.

"You're not using dating apps, are you, Jo?" Dad asks. "Those are bad news. Nothing more than creeps looking for sex, right?"

I say "no" in the same breath that Colten says "yes."

Tossing a hard scowl in his direction, I clear my throat before shifting my attention back to my dad. "It's a mixed bag. It's also about the only way to meet people these days. I've met a handful of decent guys, but I haven't met anyone with big enough balls to handle my profession."

"My point exactly, Jo. You need to find a friend who can get you a date with a decent guy." Dad takes a bite of his burger.

My phone vibrates in my back pocket, and I retrieve it.

Detective Mosley: My balls are huge.

I glance up at him across the table. He dips his chin to his plate to hide his grin while setting his phone on the table facedown.

Josie: Not really. I've seen a lot of testicles, so I would know.

He glances at his phone and smirks.

"Colten, I was so glad your mom called me. She seemed overjoyed that she got to spend time with Reagan while your ex-wife went on her honeymoon."

"Not ex-wife," I say. "He didn't marry her. He just impregnated her." I stab a potato with my fork and bring it to my mouth, pausing it at my lips when I realize all eyes are on me. "What?" I shrug. "He did."

Colten clears his throat. "For what it's worth, which isn't much at this point, I did propose to Reagan's mom, but we both knew our relationship wasn't there. We had feelings for each other, but not the kind that two people should have when they get married. It was the right call."

"That's mature of you. Is there anyone special in your life now?" Mom asks.

Colten chews a bite of food and looks right at me as I sip my water. "As a matter of fact, I am seeing someone who I think is pretty special."

I choke on my water.

"She's a doctor. Incredibly confident. Sometimes she's stubborn to a fault, but I like her feisty side."

Dad belly laughs. "Sounds like Jo. You should introduce them. They'd be best friends."

I stare at my half-empty plate.

"She's a little commitment phobic, so we don't go out much. I know she's not ready to meet my friends. She got burned years ago, and she's having a hard time getting over it even though it's been nearly two decades."

"I don't know, Colten. She sounds unstable," Mom adds. "You might be too good for her."

"I doubt it," I mumble before shoving a bite of food into my mouth.

Colten seems to be the only one who hears me, and he nudges my foot under the table. I return his gesture with a hard kick to his shin. He grunts, drawing concerned looks from my parents.

"You okay?" Dad asks.

Colten nods, reaching down to rub his leg. "Cramp. Long car ride."

"How's Benji?" I ask, opting for a change in conversation.

AFTER LUNCH, we get dressed for the funeral and load up in my mom's Camry. I stare out my window, hands tightly folded on my lap as we make our way to the service. Colten leaves his hand on the middle seat between us like he used to do when we were younger. I'd set my hand next to him, letting our pinkie fingers touch without my mom or dad noticing. It used to feel intimate and a little forbidden.

Things have changed. We can't be trusted to let any parts of our bodies touch.

However, the second we join the line of people filing into the church, Colten rests his hand on my lower back. I try to squeeze between my parents as soon as we enter the church, hoping to claim a seat between them instead of next to wandering hands Colten. Sadly, my dad reaches for my mom's hand, blocking my attempt. When we slide into the pew, I nestle right up to my mom, so much so that she shoots me a funny look that I ignore.

Colten unbuttons his suit jacket and stretches his arm behind me, resting it on the polished wooden edge, his fingers lightly teasing my hair. It makes me shiver, and I scold my body for such a weak reaction while he half grins in victory.

Mom shows me the picture of Vera on the front of the funeral program. It's a photo that my mom took of Vera at the Pella Tulip Festival.

"Denise asked me if I had any photos from our trip to Pella because she talked about it all the time," Mom whispers.

I nod, smile, and try harder to ignore Colten's close proximity.

The service begins, and I watch her family in the front pew. She had three children: Denise, Abby, and Phillip. Abby died of a rare brain tumor after she had her first child—Vera's first grandchild. Shortly after, her husband, Jerry, took his own life because he couldn't deal with the grief. I've only seen Denise once before today. She visited from DC with her two children the summer before my sophomore year. And I've never met Phillip.

As the service continues, I think about anything but the words flowing from the podium. It's my funeral trick. If I don't listen to the speakers, I won't get emotional and leave a blubbering mess. Sometimes, I take the clinical approach and imagine doing the autopsy where they are a stranger to me. What was the cause of death and how I discovered it.

Colten's arm around me disappears, jolting me from my alternative thoughts. He stands and wedges his way out of the pew and then walks to the front of the church.

"What is he doing?" I whisper to my mom.

She points to the funeral program, and his name next to the song "Ave Maria."

They asked him to play the piano? I shouldn't be surprised because Vera had a grand piano, and Colten loved to play it instead of his keyboard. Still, how many years has it been since he's seen her? Did she have it in her will? Did my mom suggest it to her family? Did he offer on his own when he heard the news?

The adult version of Colten Mosley in a sharp black suit, playing the piano ... it does things to me that should never happen at a funeral service.

"He has magical hands," Mom whispers, leaning closer to me.

I blush. God ... I hope she doesn't notice. I can't refute it. Colten's hands know what they're doing.

By the time he's finished, I think I'm the only one not crying. New funeral trick: imagine Colten doing magical things to me with his magical fingers.

When he returns to the pew, he eyes me with an expression I can't read. His arm returns to the back of the pew behind me while his lips touch my ear. "Hard-ass. Do forensic pathologists not cry at funerals?"

Before I can answer, Vera's son takes the podium. "That was beautiful. Thank you, Colten."

Colten gives him a tiny smile and an easy nod.

Phillip continues, "My mom moved to Des Moines years ago to be closer to her sister who was battling breast cancer. Denise and I were in college and our dad had ... passed on." He clears some emotion from his throat. "Denise and I were worried that she might feel lonely or overwhelmed with responsibility. But we quickly learned she had neighbors who adopted her as part of their family. And we heard so many stories about Colten and Josie." He laughs a little. "I'd never met them, but I felt like I knew them from all the stories Mom shared. She loved listening to Colten play the piano. And Josie ... are you here?"

A few people look around, and Mom nudges my arm.

I slowly raise my hand and smile.

Phillip gives me a nod. "Hi, Josie. Nice to finally meet you. My mom adored you. She said you were the most inquisitive child she had ever met. She said you devoured books like she did, and you questioned everything and everyone. And she just knew you would marry Colten. I guess she was right."

I stiffen.

My parents chuckle.

Colten plays it cool like ... WE'RE MARRIED.

Of course, Phillip thinks that because Colten has his arm behind me like I'm his property.

I return a constipated smile. Do I shake my head? Is it proper to correct a grieving son in the middle of his mother's funeral?

Phillip continues his gratitude for the people who graced Vera's life.

We make the slow drive to the burial. In my attempt to ignore Colten, I find myself listening to the minister say some final words about Vera.

I watch her kids console each other and her grandchildren.

Then I think back to my times with Vera.

"Colten has another girlfriend. Would it kill him to not have a girlfriend for ... two seconds?"

Vera laughed as we spread blackberry jam onto warm biscuits in her kitchen. Mom sent me over to return several mason jars, and Vera easily persuaded me to eat biscuits and jam with her.

"He's biding his time."

"What does that mean?" I asked.

"It means he's distracting himself with other girls until he can have the one he really wants."

"Who's that?"

She bopped my nose. "You, silly."

"Me?"

"Of course. He always has stars in his eyes when you're in the same room. I predict you will marry Colten Mosley someday. You'll be Josephine Mosley. No man will love you like Colten." She shrugged, swiping a finger through the jam on her biscuit. "That's just my prediction."

I didn't know Vera's track record with predictions, but I liked her, and I trusted her.

Colten hands me a folded tissue, bringing me back into the present. It takes me a few seconds of eyeing him suspiciously before I realize he's handing it to me because I have tears streaming down my cheeks. Only ... they're not because Vera died.

I'm crying because my dream ... my fate died.

CHAPTER
Twenty-Three

"She killed her family. Changed her name. And moved to the Midwest. She's the perfect serial killer. Sweet old lady who makes jam."

I didn't one hundred percent agree with Josie's assessment as we spied through the hedge bushes at Vera Hollinger crocheting in a wooden rocking chair on her front porch. Then again, at twelve, all we had to do on the weekend was make up stories about people, so I played along.

"I bet she has retractable claws."

Josie snorted.

"Are you two munchkins going to hang out in the bushes all day, or are you going to come here and offer me a proper introduction?" She didn't glance up for a second.

We froze, covering our mouths to hide our gasps.

After sharing several wide-eyed blinks, I let my hand slide from my face. "She might be nice," I whispered.

Josie's hand flopped to her side as disappointment stole her expression. "Fine," she mumbled, pushing through the bushes.

"Well, hello there. I'm Vera Hollinger. Who are you?"

Josie pushed me in front of her as we plodded through the yard to her porch steps.

"I'm Colten, and this is Josie. She lives there." I pointed to her house on the same side of the street. "And I live right across the street."

"It's a pleasure meeting you, Colten and Josie. Do your parents know where you are?"

"We're not babies. We can go wherever we want," Josie said. "My dad's the police chief."

A tiny grin wrinkled Vera's face. "I'm aware. I met your parents several days ago. They told me to expect two very inquisitive kids snooping around here."

"What are you making?" Josie nodded to the yellow ball of yarn on Vera's lap.

"I'm not sure yet. I think it might be a hat for my sister."

"It's summer," Josie stated the obvious.

"Indeed. But my sister has no hair, and she's often cold."

"What happened to her hair?" I asked.

"It probably fell out. Does she have cancer?" Josie decided to step in front of me like I was too stupid to ask the right questions, and I probably was.

Vera's gaze returned to the yard, then the crochet hook in her hands, and she nodded.

"Sorry," Josie and I said in unison.

"If she dies, Roland Tompkins will take good care of her."

"Josie," I gritted her name between my clenched teeth.

"I'm just saying ..." She shrugged.

"Who's Roland Tompkins?" Vera asked.

"He's the funeral home director. Josie has a weird obsession with death."

She elbowed me. "I do not. I just like to do things that are more interesting than hit a ball with a bat or play the piano."

Vera's hands paused, and she glanced up again. "I play the piano."

"Me too," I said.

"I don't. My dad thinks survival skills are the best hobbies to have," Josie said.

"Josie kills Bambi."

Again, she elbowed me. "I've never killed a deer, stupid."

"I'd love to hear you play the piano sometime. I have a beautiful piano that my husband bought me. I don't play it much anymore, but I can't bring myself to get rid of it either."

"I don't have a real piano, just a keyboard," I said.

"Oh ... then you'll love my piano. It's a shiny black Steinway & Sons. It was just tuned after I moved in. Would you like to see it?"

"Can't. I have to ask my mom," I said.

"I'll take a look," Josie said.

I rolled my eyes. She wasn't supposed to go into strangers' houses, and she knew it.

"Why don't you both check with your parents and we'll see it another time. I picked some of the blackberries from the bushes out back. Maybe you can come for biscuits and jam."

As all kids did at twelve, we lit up with excitement at the possibility of Vera making jam and biscuits for our next visit.

"We'd like that," Josie said. "Bye."

"See you later, munchkins."

We ran back to Josie's house, out back, and straight into the woods where we climbed our favorite tree.

"I should ask Vera to teach me how to crochet," Josie said.

"Why?"

"It's a useful skill, and I bet it's something that won't ..." She popped her lips several times. "What was the word my dad used ... oh! It won't *intimidate* boys like when I fish and hunt."

"What's that even mean?"

"Intimidate?"

I shook my head. "No. Why did he say it?"

"Because I don't have a lot of real friends besides you."

"Maybe it's the other girls who think you're weird."

"Who said anything about being weird?" She wrinkled her nose and squinted at me.

"I'm just saying—"

"You don't know what you're saying."

She wasn't wrong. It was possible other boys were intimidated by her because she sure intimidated me. As much as I jumped at opportunities to mock her or call her weird, I really wanted to live inside of her head. I'd never met anyone like her. Not another kid, not even an adult who looked at the world and life the way Josephine Watts did. Living in her world was like living in a movie.

A mystery.

An adventure.

Maybe even the beginning of a love story.

CHAPTER
Twenty-Four

T HE SUN SETS while Mom and I do dishes, and Colten has a beer on the deck with my dad.

"Did your mom make your dad help with dishes?" I ask her. "Because my mom used to make my dad do the dishes. This feels a little 1950s to me."

She laughs. "Your dad's back has been bothering him lately. Standing in one place for too long aggravates it."

"What's Colten's excuse?"

She gives me a hip-check as we stand at the sink. "What's your deal with Colten? You don't act like adults together. You act like the same two kids who used to terrorize the neighborhood. If I didn't know better, I'd say you're holding a grudge."

"What do you mean, 'if you didn't know better?'"

"You're thirty-five. So accomplished. Independent.

Brilliant. I can't imagine a mother who is prouder of their daughter than I am of you. It's not the 1950s. And you are a shining example of what it means to be a woman right now. You've never depended on a man. I haven't given up hope that you will one day find someone who complements your life and whose life you will complement as well. I think growing up with Colten next door taught you so much about relationships ... and eventually about letting go. To this day, I'm in awe of how gracefully you two parted ways after graduation."

I dry the colander so long the stainless-steel shines like new. If I look at her, she'll see the lie. All that motherly pride will spiral down the drain with the dirty dish water. When Colten abandoned me, I did an Oscar-worthy job of hiding the pain.

I perfected the brave face.

I regurgitated the "I'm happy for Colten" speech.

I touted my accomplishments ... my college acceptance letters.

Loving Colten Mosley came with a hefty price. I had to let my heart break in complete silence. It felt like someone asked me to keep living without breathing. Everyone except his mom thought I was sad about my "friend" enlisting.

"I think I'm going to take a walk before bed." I drape the towel over the dishwasher handle.

"What time are you leaving in the morning?"

"Early. Maybe six. So I won't be long."

"Okay. I'll make sure the coffee's ready."

"Thanks." I slip on my tennis shoes and exit the front door, making my way to the back of the house, hoping Colten and my dad are too busy talking to notice me.

To my delight, my tree is still there. Not as much to my delight, it's a little harder for my thirty-five-year-old self to climb it. But I manage to get to the first big branch, letting my feet dangle as the crickets and frogs sing the song of summer with barely a sliver of sun left at the horizon.

"You were quiet at dinner," Colten breaks my peaceful train of thought.

I glance down at him.

"It's been an emotional day," he says with a little grunt while he jumps to grab my branch, pulling himself up easier than he ever did as a kid. Figures ... life just got easier for him. "Did you know that Vera thought we would get married?" He chuckles. "She never told me that."

I want to shove him out of the tree and pray that he breaks both legs and a sharp stick impales his penis like skewering a kabob. "Would it have made a difference?"

Again, he chuckles. It's an insecure laugh. "You didn't want to marry me."

"I love how everyone seemed to know what I did or didn't want at the time. I love how everyone knew better than I did what was best for my life. It was such a relief to not have to busy my brain with making decisions for myself. Whoa!" I start to fall off the branch like I did the time I broke my arm.

"Can't work with broken bones, Dr. Watts," Colten says with his arm hooked around my waist, steadying me again.

One of my hands grips the branch while my other hand grips his leg. I catch my breath. I used to be fearless. Even when I did fall from the tree, I wasn't scared. Just in pain.

"I'm going inside." I nod for him to move out of my way so I can climb down.

Colten hops out of the tree with little effort. I, on the other hand, make the dismount look incredibly difficult. Yes. Things have changed. I have a healthy fear of breaking something.

"I've got ya." He grabs my ass as I ease down the trunk.

"I've got it, handsy." When my feet hit the ground, I turn and take a step away from him.

"Listen, I should not have let it get so far at your place. The attraction mixed with so many years of not seeing you ... mixed with your emotional fragility. It just all—"

"Wait." I narrow my eyes. "My *emotional fragility*? Are you kidding me? There was nothing emotionally fragile about me that night or any other night for that matter."

Colten shrugs before sliding his hands into his back pockets as the wind starts to pick up, bringing in the forecasted storms. "I assumed I caught you having a weak moment. Why else would you have sex with someone who you, in your words, 'hate?'"

It's a good question, but the answer is not emotional fragility. That sounds weak. I'm not weak. I'm ... well, I'm not sure, but we're going to find a more accurate word than "fragile" to use.

"Maybe I just wanted to get laid. And you ran my date off, so ... slim pickings."

A grin confiscates his entire face. "You had sex with me because I was your only choice? You're going with that story?"

I cross my arms over my chest and lift my chin. "A *true* story."

"Stop scraping your teeth over your bottom lip if you don't want me to kiss you."

I freeze and release my lip from my teeth. "Asshole."

"Stubborn overthinker." He steps toward me, hands making a play to grab my face and kiss me. That's what has always followed "stubborn overthinker."

I bob and weave once before running as the clouds open up and drop buckets of rain on us.

"Ahh!" I squeal, squinting against the rain as my shoes fail to grip the wet ground.

Colten grabs my arm, keeping me on my feet just seconds before I nearly land ass first in the mud. His hand slides from my upper arm to my hand.

Our fingers interlace, and he runs toward the house with me a few steps behind him.

We slip into the side garage door, me in his arms,

his lips inches from mine until my dad clears his throat.

I jump right out of Colten's hold and wipe the water from my face. "Hey ... uh ... we got caught in the rain."

Dad wipes his hands on a towel. He should be in bed with Mom, not out in the garage cleaning his guns. His silence makes me feel like a child getting caught.

"Go get dried off while I have a word with Colten."

"A word?" I chuckle. "No. I'm not twelve or fifteen. I don't live here. And you don't tell me what to do. If you need to have a word with Colten, then you'll have it in front of me."

"Fine." Dad cocks his head and eyes Colten. "Are you screwing my daughter?"

Well, shit ...

"Yes."

"What?" I whip around, jaw unhinged while Colten keeps his steady gaze on my dad. Not so much as a flinch. "We are not..." I turn back toward my dad "...we are *not* in a relationship."

"I didn't ask if you're in a relationship. I asked if you were screwing," Dad says.

I say "no" again as Colten says "yes" again.

"Jesus ..." I shake my head. "First, my sex life is none of your business. I'm thirty-five. But since Colten is being such an asshole about it ... yes, we had sex once. And it will never happen again."

"Is that correct?" Dad has the nerve to ask Colten for confirmation.

I'm ready to kill them both.

Colten slides his gaze from my dad to me. Face straight and unreadable.

I pivot and stomp my feet toward my dad, hands on my hips. "What is wrong with you? Why are you questioning me? Why are you questioning us? Why can't you be a normal dad who sees something that wasn't for your eyes and slithers out of the room in embarrassment because his daughter is a grown woman who has sex with whomever she pleases whenever she pleases?"

Immediately, I realize how bad that sounded. Still, I own it. Whatever. If I'm having sex with a new guy every night—which I would not do—that's my business, not his.

Dad frowns.

I blow out a long breath, losing my will to let this be a big deal when it's not. I'm leaving in the morning. What's the point? "I had an itch. Colten scratched it. End of story."

His frown deepens.

"I never would have cheated on her," Colten says.

"W-what?" Did I hear him right?

This has become a private conversation between my dad and Colten. Neither one will look at me. It's like I'm not here.

"Doesn't change anything." Dad lifts a shoulder.

"I know. I just need you to know it. Even if you made me doubt it then, I know better now. I'm not my father."

"Thank god for that. Everything turned out for the best. The past is the past." Dad nods several times.

"Did you ..." I can barely say the words because my brain's struggling to put the pieces together. I take a step closer to my dad. "Did you know?"

My parents never knew, or so I thought. Colten's mom promised to not say a word. And I respected Colten's desire to have my dad's respect since his dad was simply ... a terrible husband and father. I thought it would all work its way out.

We would graduate.

We would be adults.

And we'd tell my parents that we were in love.

He blows a long breath out his nose. "I wasn't stupid. Or blind. Or deaf. Did you really think you could sneak around behind my back without me knowing?"

My head eases side to side. "Why didn't you say anything?" I ask, just above a whisper.

"I did. I said something to Colten."

This shouldn't hurt. It's been too long. But it does. Seventeen years ago, Colten carved the most jagged hole into my heart. And all this time, I had no idea that my dad handed him the knife.

"How could you?" I turn around, facing Colten. "How could *you*?"

"Josie ..." Anguish spreads across Colten's face.

"You chose my dad over me? Is this some cruel joke?"

"I chose you," he says.

My head shakes over and over again.

"Your future."

"No," I snap. "You chose *your* future, and it didn't include me."

"Jo, it was nearly twenty years ago," Dad interrupts. "A childhood crush. Look at you now."

Look at me now. I'm so tired of hearing that everyone around me saved me. Nobody saved me. I saved myself. They have no fucking clue ... not a single one of them.

"You had a scholarship, Josie. I didn't. And I didn't have the money for college. I didn't have a clue what I was going to do. And when you said you wanted to take a year or two to decide if medical school was what you wanted ... I knew it was because of me." Colten runs his hands through his hair, face still distorted with those lines of anguish and desperation.

"Well, aren't you an arrogant asshole for assuming that. And a liar for not just saying that. You joined the fucking Marines just to get away from me. Were you willing to die for your country because of your heroic patriotism or because you *so* desperately wanted to please my dad and go someplace you knew I would never follow you?"

"Jo, it was infatuation. Lack of a better choice for both of you. Not love."

I knew my dad always wanted me to be a boy, but I never noticed all the ways he subtly belittled me and my feelings. Starting with my name. And I let him because I wanted to be the apple of his eye. I wanted to prove that I was just as good as any son. And I was different, so fitting in, if only in my dad's eyes, mattered to me.

"Not love …" I echo. Colten used those same words when he ended us.

There is nothing left to say to either man, so I brush past my dad and head into the house. Instead of taking a shower, which I need, I set my phone's alarm, change into a nightshirt, and crawl into bed. I don't want to risk seeing Colten or my parents again before I leave early in the morning.

CHAPTER
Twenty-Five

Josie watched me self-destruct, and I knew she'd be part of the wreckage. Still I didn't have the nerve, or maybe a true incentive, to stop it. Misery loved company. And I was miserable.

By our senior year, I'd found the one thing more toxic than misery and hate ... spite.

Doing the opposite of my father's wishes became my life's mission, even if it was at my own demise. He told me not to drink or do drugs.

I got a fake ID, drank every weekend, and scored some pot from a kid named Tyler Vogt.

My dad told me baseball players didn't need to bulk up. It might limit my swinging ability. I lived in the weight room.

Lived on protein.

Lived to disappoint him ... to spite him.

I deserved the World's Greatest Fuckup Award by the end of the year. I got my first DUI. Got suspended from playing baseball my senior year. Lost my chance for a scholarship. And nearly didn't graduate after starting a fight with Andy Miller because he took Josie to the prom (I was suspended from that too) and told everyone she sucked his dick in the parking lot. Of course, I didn't believe it was true, but it didn't matter. Either way, I was going to beat the living shit out of him because Josie was mine.

Until ... the perfect storm.

Two weeks before graduation, on the heels of the prom fiasco, I was going to tell Josie's parents about us. Despite my bad behavior, her dad liked me. He blamed my behavior on my father's poor example. I had no fucking clue what I was going to do with my life, but it involved Josie.

I'd go wherever she decided to go to college. She had more than one scholarship offer. Josie was the smartest person I knew and the only person who brought any sort of peace to my life. If I had to get a job at a hardware store or bagging groceries, I was prepared to do it. Anything to be with Josie.

If I let her take off to college without me, some smart, put-together guy would steal her. Of that, I had no doubt.

Just as I sped down the stairs, on my way to talk to the chief, my dad came in the front door.

"Where are you going?" he asked.

"What do you care?"

He grabbed my arm to stop me. By then I was so much bigger than him; it wouldn't have taken much for me to have put him on his ass.

"Your mom told me you've been secretly pining for the chief's daughter."

My parents' reconciliation pissed me off. I couldn't believe my mom took him back. And apparently that meant she was sharing everything with him again.

I jerked out of his hold. "Well, it's not going to be a secret much longer."

"She's the smartest decision you've ever made. I'm amazed you haven't screwed that up too. Josie's going to make something of herself. Maybe her work ethic will rub off on you." His approval of her stifled my plans. It sucked all the oxygen from my lungs. I managed to shut the door behind me and trek over to her house, but I no longer knew what I was going to say to the chief.

Spite … so much spite.

"Colten." He gave me his manly nod before spraying foam on his Chevelle's tires. "What's up?"

I had no words, just thoughts that never made it out of my mouth.

I love your daughter. I have since the moment we first shared cookies and milk. I didn't know those feelings I had way back then were love … but they were. I'm going to follow her to college and take care of her. I have no clue what I'm going to do with my life other than do right by her. Do I have your blessing?

I cleared my throat, but I couldn't clear my head.

The echo of my dad's words wouldn't stop whispering in my ear, prodding my conscience, and igniting my natural instinct to spite him. "Um ... I was going to talk to you about Josie and me, but it's not uh ..."

Chief Watts stood tall and drew in a breath so deep I think he took all of the oxygen from the garage. When he let it out, his mouth tipped into a disapproving frown. "I'm not blind or stupid. I know you have a little crush on my daughter. And I think she probably has some sort of feelings for you too. But it's a little late to be having this conversation with me, don't ya think?"

Think? I had no idea what to think. What conversation did he think I was going to have with him? A confession? A mission statement? An apology?

"Josie's going to medical school. We're all very proud of her, aren't we?" he asked.

I nodded slowly.

"I think you're lost, son. I think you need something that will give you direction again. Discipline. Life skills. A clean slate."

I agreed. I needed Josie. Did that mean I was agreeing with my father?

"I was a lot like you. I had a shitty father. Chip on my shoulder. A mile-long list of bad decisions. Then I enlisted in the Marines. It changed my life. Mentally. Physically. Emotionally. Other than marrying Savannah, it was the best decision of my life. It made me the man she wanted to marry."

The military?

My parents were anti-war. My dad scoffed at the idea that any young person would voluntarily sign up to risk their life for their country in what he called "endless wars."

"You think I should enlist?"

He rested his hand on my shoulder, giving it a firm squeeze. "I do. I think you should let Josie live her life, the life she's been earning through hard work and dedication. Don't be the person who pulls her heartstrings and derails her future over infatuation or a lack of a better choice. It's not love. Let her go. Wish her well. Then pack a bag and get some real-life skills for yourself. If you decide on college, it will be free. Or you might choose law enforcement like I did. Whatever you choose, it will be the right decision for *you*. Okay?"

He read my mind ... only not really. I had too many voices in my head drowning out my own. Too many emotions. Love. Hate. The desire to please. The pressure to do the right thing.

The right thing ... I had no clue what that looked like.

Josie was going to be a brilliant doctor. She'd probably cure cancer or some other awful disease. And I'd ... what? Bag groceries? Stock shelves?

Or ... defend my country, acquire life skills, serve my community.

I thought we could wait for each other. We could be together after reaching our full potential. Was that fair? What if I died? What if she passed up opportunities to find love while waiting for me ... and then I died?

"Yeah," I said with my heart in my throat.

"Hey, I never got a chance to ask you. What did Andy Miller do to earn your fist in his face a dozen times?"

"He started a rumor about Josie that wasn't true." I didn't know if it was true. I hadn't talked with Josie since the incident. She wasn't happy with me. But I had to believe it was just a rumor. That was the only thing that kept me from killing Andy.

"Just between us, thank you. I've always felt better knowing you've been looking out for Josie's best interest. I know she can be a handful, and maybe that's why she's never had a lot of friends. You've been like a big brother. I won't ever forget it." He glanced over my shoulder and nodded. "Speaking of my awesome daughter ..."

I turned my head as Josie pulled into the driveway. She climbed out of her red Civic and pulled off her sunglasses. It wasn't anything new to see me hanging out with her dad, but the distrust on her face leaked her emotions without saying a word.

"What are you two doing?"

Her dad returned his attention to the Chevelle. "Solving the world's problems."

She scoffed. "I highly doubt that. I'm going for a run."

"I'll go with you."

Josie's right eyebrow slid up her forehead. "You

don't run. You lift weights and try to intimidate innocent people." She eyed her dad as if to make sure he wasn't focusing on us.

My lips twisted. "I do run. Let me change my shoes."

She blew her hair out of her face and rolled her eyes. "Whatever. If you're not back in five minutes, I'm leaving without you."

By the time she finished her warning, I was already to the street. "I learned how to tie my shoes a long time ago," I hollered. "I'll be back in less than two minutes because I need to grab socks."

Minutes later, I beat her to the end of the driveway, but not by much. She wanted to leave me behind. The second she saw me, she started a fast-paced jog. I sped to catch up.

"How's Andy's face?" I asked.

"How was being expelled from school for two weeks and nearly not graduating?"

I grinned. "It was good. I spent most of my time with Vera, eating biscuits and jam and playing the piano. Slept in. Caught up on laundry ..."

"You're lucky Andy didn't press charges."

"He's lucky I didn't break his fucking nose."

When we reached the end of the street, she stopped, hands parked on her hips, black hair falling out of her ponytail. "I don't need you to defend my honor. If I decided to beat the shit out of every girl who talked about what you did or didn't do with her, I'd be in juvie."

"Should I be offended that you've never felt the need to defend my honor?"

"Pfft … you're not defending my honor. You haven't even asked me if it's true." Josie's dark eyes narrowed, daring me to ask her.

It didn't matter. Okay, it mattered, but I wasn't going to confess that. Either way, Andy deserved everything he got and then some. I shrugged. "It's a moot point." I started jogging again.

"Why?" Her feet slapped the pavement behind me.

"Because it's none of my business at this point. And when you leave for college, it won't be any of his business either. He'll be here, working for his dad. It will be hard to suck his dick remotely."

"And where will you be?"

"Basic training."

"What?"

I raced past her because I wasn't ready to have that conversation with her. I wasn't even sure if that's what I was planning on doing. It came out, and I felt the need to commit.

Commit to a direction.

Commit to a purpose.

Commit to letting her go.

And it fucking hurt.

"Jesus, would you stop and look at me?" She grabbed the back of my shirt.

I sighed and turned. "What?"

"You can't enlist."

"Why not?"

Her lips parted while her head swiveled in denial. "B-because … it makes no sense."

"It makes perfect sense. I fucked up my scholarship opportunities. I have no clue what I want to do with my life. My dad's an asshole, and my mom is pathetically gullible for taking him back. I have no reason to stay around here—"

"Me! You stay for me!" Panic infiltrated her words, and it took herculean strength to steady my emotions.

"You're not staying here. You're going off to college."

"Then you come with me. We talked about this so many times. I'm tired of our stupid hidden relationship. Part of me was relieved that time your mom caught us. I just wanted to have a normal relationship with you. This stupid facade is about to end. We tell my parents, and we don't give a fuck what they think. You don't need my dad's approval anymore. We don't need anyone's approval."

"It's not about approval, Josie. It's about our future. But *we* don't have a future right now. There's your future, and there's my future. One of us will have to sacrifice for the other, and that's ridiculous. We're too young to make rash decisions because of some…" I searched for the best word, but the only one that came to mind was her dad's word "…infatuation. Maybe we've felt a bond because of close proximity or simply lack of a better choice. That doesn't mean it's …" I sighed and lowered my voice, choking back my emotions and calming my frustration. "That doesn't mean it's love."

Tears filled her eyes. I'd only seen Josie cry a handful of times, and it usually involved a physical pain like falling out of a tree or cutting open her knee. She bit her quivering lower lip and wiped her tears the second they fell to her red cheeks. "Y-you don't l-love me?"

Yes. God ... I loved her more than any other human being. I loved her more than myself. I loved her more than God even if that was a sin. I loved her *so* much that I had to let her go. And that meant I had to lie to her. That hurt more than any physical pain *I* had ever experienced. "I care about you. You're my best friend."

Josie stopped wiping her tears; there were too many. Instead, she took off running.

Let her go. Just ... let her go.

I couldn't let her go. Not like that. If I couldn't tell her *the* truth, I wanted to tell her *a* truth. I let her run for a while, keeping a safe distance behind her. With each step, I imagined one day we'd find each other again, and the timing would be right. She would be a doctor, saving lives. And I would be something infinitely better than I was in that moment. I would be a man who didn't need to please a police chief or wreck my life to spite my father.

The more distance we covered, the more those words solidified in my mind. I would let her go to be that better man. Just ... not yet.

When she reached the batting cages, she continued to run to the field where we used to race each other, the field where we believed bad people lived, waiting to kidnap us. Josie stopped, bent over, and rested her hands on her legs while she gasped for air. Her shoulders shook, and her deep breaths morphed into howling sobs while she dropped to her knees, her body folding onto itself.

I kneeled in front of her and pulled her to me.

"No!" Her arms flailed as she tried to keep me from holding her.

I hugged her arms to her body and all of her to me. She wriggled and wriggled while crying more than I had ever seen her cry ... more than I had ever seen anyone cry. After a while, she stopped fighting me, and her sobs subsided into tiny hiccups while her hands fisted my shirt.

"Don't leave me," she whispered.

Gritting my teeth, I swallowed hard. Tears burned my eyes, but I couldn't set a single one free.

"It-it's us, C-Colten. It's a-always been u-us ..."

I kissed the top of her head. Said nothing. Felt *everything.*

"Tell me you l-love me."

I love you.

Tightening her grip on my shirt, she pounded my chest and glanced up at me with sad, red eyes. "Tell me," she croaked out the words.

I gritted my teeth harder and refused to blink.

She released my shirt and grabbed my face, moving to her knees again and kissing me with a punishing intensity. I kissed her back, memorizing the taste of her mouth, the feel of her tongue against mine, her soft hands on my whiskery face, the rise and fall of her chest brushing mine.

Did she know how many times I wanted to leave the world? Leave the pressure of my dad's expectations, the embarrassing shadow of his indiscretions, the cloud of depression that hung over our house for years. Did she know she was the reason I kept going? The promise of *us*?

I lived wholly, eternally, unequivocally for Josephine Watts.

Why didn't I tell her when it mattered the most?

I never thought I'd let her go.

I never thought I'd miss my opportunity to say all the things I kept inside for so many years.

Yet, there I was ... suffocating in a miserable bubble of unshed tears and unspoken emotions. My heart clogged my airway, throbbing, burning like my eyes. I wasn't sure I could live without her, but I had to try.

She pushed me away and stood, taking my hand and tugging it until I stood and followed her into the woods. We didn't make it far before she grabbed my shirt again and pulled me to her as she rested her back against a tree trunk. Sticks and winter's compost crushed beneath our feet as I pressed my body to hers.

Her fingers teased my abs beneath my shirt before she worked it up my torso. I broke our kiss and discarded my shirt as she did the same to hers.

Again we kissed. Never feeling her hands on my body again felt like its own torture. Would I die for my country? I didn't know yet. But I would have died for

Josephine Watts. I would have died in that moment had it meant I never had to let her go.

"I love you, Colten. I love you more than anything or anyone," she whispered as I kissed my way down her neck.

That lump in my throat doubled. It stung and pulsed. A monster of grief with a chokehold on me. I could barely breathe.

Her fingers teased the waistband of my jogging shorts. I moaned into her mouth. When her warm hand slid into my briefs, my hips jerked, and I broke the kiss, moaned louder, a growl of sorts, while my forehead rested on hers. "Josie ..." I whispered.

"I want this," she whispered while her hand tormented me. "I want this with *you*."

Pulling her hand from my cock, I took both of her hands and held them to my chest. And we remained idle, sharing each breath, saying everything without saying anything.

Again, her body vibrated with emotions, stifling new sobs while my nose rubbed against hers, while my lips ghosted along her face, while I pressed one last kiss to her lips.

Josie wasn't some girl in my life; she *was* my life. The sun. The air. Gravity. My whole world and reason for existing.

Did she feel it? Really *feel* it in her soul?

"Good luck, Josie. You're going to be a huge success."

When I took a step back, she squeezed her eyes

shut and covered her face with her hands, trembling with emotion. I grabbed my shirt, turned toward home, and didn't look back.

But I heard the two words she whispered, and they hit me so hard, my steps faltered under the weight of their real possibility.

"Don't die ..."

I had what I needed to get my diploma, so I did not go back to school. I skipped my graduation (another solid "fuck you" to Coach Mosley), and I never saw Josie Watts again, until seventeen years later.

Life never went as planned.

CHAPTER
Twenty-Six

I'VE NEVER HAD huge aspirations. No plans to cure cancer. No intentions of being the best at anything. I went to medical school because everyone thought I'd be a good doctor. And ... Colten Mosley left me half naked in the woods after rejecting me, after not saying those three words to me.

Here we are, seventeen years later, and he's once again following me.

"Are you really leaving without saying goodbye to your parents?" Colten asks as I get into my car a little after five in the morning.

He tosses his bag into the back of his vehicle and shuts the door.

"When did you become an early riser?" I mumble, sparing a tiny glance in his direction.

"Marines. Four a.m. every morning. We really

should have ridden together." He has the nerve to act like nothing happened last night, like I didn't discover the truth behind his cowardliness.

"No. We should never do anything together again."

"Never is a long time."

I grunt. "Tell me about it."

Before he can respond, I climb into my car and shut the door. For six hours, he follows me home, stopping once for gas and to use the restroom. He doesn't say anything; he hangs back like a cop tailing a suspect. A few miles before my exit, he goes right toward his house, and I take my first full breath in six hours.

An hour later, my phone rings and "Detective Mosley" illuminates my screen. I hop off my stationary bike and take a sip of water, thinking hard about not answering it. I've had enough of him for a few lifetimes.

"What is it?" I answer as clipped as possible.

"You're breathing hard. Are you having sex?"

I click *End* and toss my phone on the chair. Again, he calls me. I ignore it this time. Then it chimes with a text.

Detective Mosley: I've taken a bullet twice. I've been resuscitated once. Stitches more times than I can count. And none of that hurt like it did when I left you in the woods seventeen years ago. Just thought you should know.

I stare at his text and sip more water.

Another chime of a text.

Detective Mosley: Don't blame your dad. He made a suggestion, but it was my choice.

Grabbing my foot, I stretch my quads while rereading his texts.

Detective Mosley: I should have said it, but it wouldn't have changed what I did, so it felt cruel to say it.

I switch legs, feeling his words deeper than I want to feel them.

Detective Mosley: But I felt it, Josie. God … I felt it in my fucking soul.

"TEENAGER DROPPED off at the ER entrance. They didn't even stop the car." Dr. Cornwell waggles his eyebrows.

I shrug, feeling a little melancholy this morning which means I'll take whatever he gives me. After he assigns two more cases to me, I don my PPE and head to the autopsy suite.

"Morning." Detective Mosley smiles before masking as I brush past him, heading to the cold room.

The abandoned body is my first case this morning, and I assume, the reason Colten's here.

"Morning," several students say as I grab the microphone to dictate the external exam.

Ignoring Colten, I talk my way through the exam, occasionally quizzing the eager students.

"She's good," Colten murmurs to one of the students as I make my first cut.

The young woman nods several times. "She's the best … but don't tell Dr. Cornwell I said that."

I grin without looking away from the decedent, thankful that I'm masked and behind a face shield.

Twenty minutes later, when I'm solidly in my zone, Colten breaks his silence, but not with a question about the decedent. "What are you whistling?"

"I think it's 'Knocking on Heaven's Door,'" one of the young observers says.

"Do you always whistle?" Colten asks.

More than one of the students answers in unison, "Yes."

Colten chuckles. "You used to whistle when we'd do our homework together."

"You went to school with Dr. Watts?" The young woman who called me "the best" asks Colten.

"I did. She was my first love."

My hands pause and Alicia lets out an audible gasp that only I can hear. I hope only I hear her.

"For real?" the young woman asks.

"The realest," Colten says.

When I glance up at him, he winks.

"What happened?" she asks him.

"She became a brilliant doctor, and I joined the Marines."

"Are you married? Dr. Watts is single."

Who is this girl? Do I know her name? And how the hell does she know my marital status?

He chuckles.

Two hours later ... I've got nothing, and that frustrates me to no end.

"Nothing?" Colten asks.

I shrug. "We need to wait for toxicology."

"Did you miss something?"

I exit the suite to use the restroom. "Unlikely."

"Did you get my texts?"

I pause at the locker room door. "Yes." I push through it and use the restroom before donning new PPE. When I exit, my shadow awaits me.

"Have dinner with me tonight."

I breeze past him. "No."

He grabs the back of my gown where it's tied and tugs it to stop me. I sigh. Colten's never been so relentless—that was always my role. We have a silent standoff. I don't turn toward him, and he doesn't let me go. We've had more silent standoffs than I care to remember.

After a few seconds, he releases me, and I get back to work.

SUNDAY, I grab pho on my way home from errands and settle onto my sofa with the warm bowl of broth and noodles and a good book. While I slurp the last of it, there's a tap at my window facing the front yard. I make my way toward the noise, contemplating grabbing my gun, but then I see a white piece of paper pressed against it with black Sharpie writing.

I'M SORRY

I shake my head and return to the kitchen.

Tap. Tap. Tap.

Blowing out a long breath, I peek around the corner again.

I SHOULD

HAVE

SAID

IT

It takes time for his words to penetrate the scar tissue around my heart. Time for me to convince my feet to carry me to the front door. Time ... Has seventeen years been enough time for an eternal grudge?

"Let me say it, Josie," Colten says from the other side of the door. "Let me say it when I don't have to walk away. Let me say it when it doesn't have to be a consolation. A really shitty goodbye."

If I open the door, my heart wins, and my pride and conscience will never fully recover.

"I was just too fucking stupid to figure it out. I was too angry at my dad. I was too persuaded by your dad. I was lost. I was weak. And you deserved more, Josie. So much more."

I rest my palms and the side of my face on the door.

"And I remember thinking ... what if some day we find each other again and everything is just right? The time. The place. Just everything. And here we are, Josie. It's not fucking coincidence."

There's another pause, and I wonder if he's given up. I hope so because I can't take much more.

"You. I would have chosen you."

I narrow my eyes, the side of my face still pressed to the door.

"When we went to the batting cages and talked about being kidnapped, and we discussed who we'd choose if only one of us could live ... I would have chosen you to live because for so very long, you've been the only purpose to my life."

"Jesus ..." I whisper, blinking back the tears.

I wait. And wait. I wait until I hear nothing. I wait until my legs are tired of standing in one place. I wait until his confession no longer seems real. Then, I crack open the door, and he's still there.

"I'm not going anywhere because I. Love. You. Josephine Watts."

My lower lip gives me away with its uncontrolled trembling before I can curl my lips together to hide it.

Colten lets the white sheets of paper fall to the ground and takes one step toward me, hands on my face, fingers in my hair, lips claiming mine. I grip his arms to steady myself.

I let myself fall a little into him. I let myself fall a little for him.

I let myself feel something less than hatred. All that hatred because he made his mark on a nine-year-old girl's heart, and she ... *I* have never been the same.

I've always been his.

He kicks the door shut behind us and walks me backward, clueless to where he's guiding me, reckless as we nearly trip. Am I too old to be clueless and reckless with Colten Mosley? I hope not.

"Do you know where you're going?" I giggle while he kisses my neck, hands palming my ass.

"I'm a detective, Watts ... I'll figure it out." He does.

He finds my bedroom after we leave a trail of clothes in the hallway. When the back of my knees hit the bed, his hands ghost along my skin to unhook my bra. It slides down my arms, and my hard nipples brush his bare chest while his lips feather over mine, teasing me.

My breath morphs into a soft panting with every excruciatingly slow move he makes. His middle finger slides under the crotch of my panties, teasing my clit.

"J-jesus ... what are you doing to m-me?" My voice trembles when I press my lips to his sternum.

"I'm trying to make you weak in the knees."

When said knees start to buckle, I release a nervous chuckle. "Done." In the next blink, I suck in a sharp breath while he thrusts his middle finger inside of me, his other hand sliding into the back of my panties. He squeezes my ass, pulling me flush to his chest.

"Yeah?" He grins, millimeters from our lips touching.

I really, *really* like adult Colten Mosley. His confidence doesn't waver for a second. He could make me orgasm with nothing more than that look in his eyes. He eases his finger out of me and uses it to trace my bottom lip. The tiny grin on his face swells a fraction before he licks my lower lip, a slow swipe of his tongue. He bites it with a low growl vibrating his chest. Then he sucks on my lip like I'm the best thing he's ever tasted.

"I need more," he says between kisses while his grip on my ass stings, making me feel like a meal to a starving man.

It's a heady feeling as I close my eyes and whisper, "More what?"

He cups my breast for a breath before his hand dives down the front of my panties. "More of this."

An unfamiliar ring tone interrupts us. It's his phone.

"Fuck!" He sighs, removing his hand from my panties.

I bite my lips together and take a deep breath.

He traces his steps back to the hallway to find his jeans next to one of his sneakers. I inspect his perfect ass in those tight black briefs while I ease my ass onto the side of the bed.

"Mosley," he snaps.

I think I like grumpy Colten Mosley. I definitely like grumpy Colten Mosley half naked in my house.

"Yeah. Uh-huh ..." He turns toward me, and his brow knits together when his gaze lands between my spread legs like he's confused. "Okay," he says in a clipped tone, taking slow steps back to me while his eyes flit up my body to meet my gaze.

It's only then that I realize my hand has drifted down the front of my panties while gawking at him.

"I'll be right there." He tosses his phone onto the bed next to me. "Watts, what the fuck are you doing?"

"Are you leaving?" I inch my hand out of my panties. Maybe he didn't really notice. Maybe he thinks I had an itch.

Well, I do have an itch of sorts.

"Yes, I must go. I'm sorry." He kneels in front of me and drags my panties down my legs.

"What are you doing?"

He doesn't look at me.

"C-Colten!" I suck in a harsh breath when his face plants between my legs. I fall back onto one elbow while my other hand grips his hair.

"I'm saying goodbye," he mumbles.

"Col ... just ..." My head spins with each slurred word that fights past my lips. "God ... yesss ..." Just before I orgasm, I think I might lose consciousness. My knees squeeze inward, trapping his head when my pelvis jerks.

"I have to go," he says, wedging his head out from between my legs. I completely collapse back onto the bed.

On a satisfied sigh, I lift back onto my elbows and watch him get dressed. "I feel bad."

"About what?" he murmurs, zipping his jeans before tugging on his shirt.

"I'm rather satisfied at the moment, and you're leaving, well ... *not* satisfied. So I feel a little bad for you."

He shoves his feet into his sneakers and takes several long strides to get back to me.

I sit up, and he cups the back of my head and kisses me. Pulling back an inch, a half grin tugs at his lips, and he whispers, "I highly fucking doubt it."

I don't want to grin. I'm not sure I'm ready for him to fully know how ridiculously happy I am, but I can't help it.

"I'll see you later." He kisses my forehead before heading toward the front door.

He's gruff.

He's sexy as hell.

He's intimate and tender.

And I think he's finally ... mine.

CHAPTER
Twenty-Seven

By nine o'clock, I jump onto my stationary bike and sweat until close to ten. Then I shower for bed and give up on seeing Colten again tonight or even getting a text or phone call.

I arrive at work on Monday by seven.

Dr. Cornwell eyes me over his glasses. "Am I distracting you with work?"

"I have court this afternoon, and I'm meeting with a family in an hour. It wasn't an unusually slow night. You and Glasby can handle two cases. If it were me, I'd split it and each take one."

He rolls his eyes at me just as Glasby strolls into the conference room.

"What?" Glasby says.

"Nothing. Just a big day for you and Cornwell.

Good luck." I sip my coffee to hide my smirk while I head to my office.

As I review my notes in preparation to meet with the Harvey family about their daughter who committed suicide by running her car into a train, I keep a close eye on my phone. This is ridiculous.

I should call him or text him. I'm a grown woman. My days of stalking Colten Mosley are over. Yet I can't help myself. I'm on a physical high.

It's the sex.

I know what I've been missing for seventeen years, and now I'm pissed off at every woman who has had Colten's hands, mouth, or any other body part on them.

Eventually, I'll come down from the sex high and have to deal with the emotional reality that I'm still mad at him. I still have so many questions that he needs to answer.

By the time I get to court, I'm ready to crush my phone like it's my phone's fault that Colten has been ghosting me. I give in. I hate it, but I do it anyway.

Josie: Hi.

Yep. That's it. One word. Like "tag, you're it." A knock on his door. A nudge to see if he's paying attention.

I have to relinquish my phone to get through security at the courthouse. As I make my way to the courtroom, Dylan Paine, the most cutthroat attorney in town, calls my name. When I glance over at her, I see him, Mr. "He Hasn't Responded To My Text" Mosley.

"I've called your office at least a hundred times. I need the Kaylee Robinson report," Dylan says like she thinks I'm in charge of getting a report to her that I didn't write for an autopsy I didn't perform. She's always given me the impression she doesn't believe I'm a real doctor or part of the justice system.

I ignore her for obvious reasons.

"Oh ..." She leans into Colten and playfully nudges his arm. "Have you met Detective Mosley? Surely, you've run into each other by now."

Colten's grin grows in tiny increments. "We're actually old friends."

Friends. Is that what we are now?

"Oh? That's crazy. Small world. Aren't you originally from Iowa, Josephine?" She's never called me Dr. Watts, except when questioning me on the stand, and even then, she says it like it leaves a bad taste in her mouth.

"I am. So is Colten."

Dylan lifts her eyebrows. "Colten, huh?"

Yes, Dylan ... I'm on a first name basis with the detective because I orgasmed in his mouth yesterday, and I showed him my breasts before I even really had anything to show him.

"Well, I'm meeting with a client. Tell your office to call me back."

I give her a tight smile. I won't be telling "my office" anything.

"Call me sometime, Detective."

Last I knew, she was married. But her "call me" sounded personal, not professional.

"Should I tell her, or do you want to tell her that you don't call people?" I ask the second she saunters off toward the exit.

"New phone." He pulls said phone out of his pocket. "I haven't downloaded anything from the cloud yet, so I didn't have your number."

"And you forgot where I lived?"

He slips his phone back into the pocket of his suit jacket. Then he loosens his tie and unbuttons the top two buttons to his shirt. "I had a little trip to the ER last night." He shows me the bandaged area on his neck. "Seven stitches. Missed my artery. I brought a gun to a knife fight, but I was outnumbered."

I stare at his neck without saying anything.

"Don't gasp like that, Josie. I'm good. I'll be fine. Really, no need to overreact." He feigns when I *don't* react.

I smirk and lift my gaze to his. "You weren't on my table this morning, so I wasn't worried. Maybe I should teach you how to use your gun properly."

"Maybe I should put something in your mouth to shut you up."

Again, I let my amusement free with a small grin. "Small things are choking hazards."

"Fuck you," he says on a laugh.

"I thought you would, but you tried to get yourself killed instead."

Complete satisfaction lights up his face. I haven't forgotten how to verbally spar with him.

"I have a stack of paperwork. There's a slim chance that I get more than two hours of sleep tonight. But I want to take you to dinner this week."

I step closer to him, picking at the corner of his bandage and pulling it back just enough to see his stitches. Yes, whoever cut him missed his carotid, but just barely. After I replace the bandage, I button his shirt, basking in our little bubble as he watches me. I fix his tie and glance up at him, my hands still on his tie.

"Do you love me, Josephine Watts?"

My lips twist as I lift a shoulder, not ready to declare a single emotion because they're all so blurred. "I *something* you."

He returns an easy nod. "I have to get back to the station."

My gaze returns to his tie as I nod several times. "I figured. I have to get to court."

His hands take mine, pulling them away from his tie and interlacing our fingers while guiding our hands behind my back, forcing me to look up at him again. "Go set the record straight."

"I will."

My confidence pleases him. I can see it in his eyes. Can he also see that he's the weakest part of me?

I'm too busy looking at him to see anyone else, but I feel people's gazes as they pass us. Maybe people I know; maybe people he knows. They're wondering what we're doing, our intimacy on public display.

I don't care. I'm done hiding, and I think he is too.

"Are you going to—"

He doesn't let me finish before bending down. "Yeah, I am." He kisses me. It's soft and quick, too quick. "Bye," he whispers over my lips before releasing my hands and adjusting his tie.

I get one last smile from him and a sexy wink.

THAT EVENING, while making dinner, I get a call from him.

"Did you find my number in the cloud?"

He chuckles. It's deep and slow. "Not yet. I haven't had time to mess with the cloud, and by mess with the cloud, I mean have the IT dude do it for me. I got your number the old-fashioned way."

"By asking me and writing it down on a napkin or the back of a junk mail envelope? Because I don't recall that."

Again, he gives me that chuckle, and it reaches through the phone and touches me in a way that makes me miss him despite having seen him earlier today. "No, I pulled it from the internal database."

"Did you get a warrant?"

"I did. It was Sunday afternoon, which I know how hard it is to get a warrant on a Sunday, but I did. It was at your house. I had to get on my knees to do it, and it required some very particular lip service. Eventually, I was granted a solid 'yessss,' which I interpreted as permission to gather information on you in any way I deem necessary." He sighs. "I'm drowning in paperwork. I'm so fucking tired. My wound itches. And I just want to know what your bed feels like because I can't seem to make it there despite two solid attempts. How are you?"

I don't answer right away. Instead, I let his voice and his words echo in my head. He's the old Colten, using me as his safe place to let go of his day's frustrations. And he's the new Colten with different frustrations. But one thing hasn't changed ... not being with me still brings him down.

"I'm playing baseball twenty-four-seven. It sucks. I haven't seen you for more than two seconds while passing you in the hall at school. Just meet me outside for a few minutes."

I waved from my bedroom window. "Look. You're seeing me."

He grumbled. "Not the same."

"I was grounded all last week. I can't risk sneaking out at ten-thirty on a school night. Sorry."

"I'm good. Filleting fish. Want me to bring you dinner?"

I can hear the riffling of papers in the background. He has me on speaker, and he's working as we speak.

"I want *you*, Watts. I already had dinner."

"Takeout?"

"Food truck."

I laugh. "Same thing."

"Filleting fish, huh? You know you can buy fish already filleted. Don't you ever get tired of dissecting shit?"

"I usually find the cause and manner of death before I have to dissect too much shit. But to answer your question, no. I don't get tired of dissecting things. Are you having an affair with Dylan Paine?"

He coughs. "S-she's married."

"Hence the word *affair*."

"Do I come across as the guy who sleeps with another man's wife?"

"I'm getting to know the new Colten Mosley, so I'm not ready to make a judgment on that."

"I'm the Colten you knew seventeen years ago, just with more hair, more scars, and more—"

"Experience."

He hums. "I hope so."

"Who was your first?"

"My first what?"

"Sexual encounter."

"You, Josie."

"We didn't have sex."

"No, but we were sexual."

"Intercourse. Who was your first penetration?"

He coughs another laugh. "Jesus, Watts ... you're so clinical."

"I'm a doctor."

"Mindy."

"Mindy who?"

"I don't know," he says. "I met her at a bar the week before basic training. I was drunk. She was drunk. And we fucked. At least, I think there was penetration. The details are sketchy. It was in the back seat of her Chevy Malibu while we waited for her friend to come drive us home."

"Sounds romantic."

"It was. I thought about proposing, but not knowing her last name or literally anything else about her made finding her again difficult. Who was your first?"

Before I answer, I hear him whispering something to someone else.

"Are we talking about our first sexual encounters with an audience?"

"No," he says. "Rose just dropped another stack of files on my desk. She's gone. You were saying?"

"I'm going to let you get back to work." I toss my fillets into a bowl of marinade.

"You're not off the hook. You owe me the story of your first time."

"You owe me a lot more than that, but we'll save that for another conversation."

"Good night, Josie."

"Night."

CHAPTER
Twenty-Eight

THERE'S a mass shooting at a nightclub the following night which means Colten will live at work, especially since the shooter is still at large. I stay plenty busy with the bodies of the gunshot victims and my own reports to type up.

By Friday, they have the suspect in custody, and the community in mourning gets a tiny sigh of relief and hope for justice.

I leave work just before six and decide to visit Colten at the station.

"Hey, Dr. Watts. What's up?" Detective Rains glances up from his desk behind stacks of paperwork.

"I'm looking for Colten, uh ... Detective Mosley."

"I sent his tired ass home. I'm sure he'll be here again early in the morning, but he was running on fumes. Anything I can help you with?"

I shake my head and smile. "Nope. Have a good weekend. You should probably get some rest too."

He barks a laugh. "I have three kids at home, all under the age of ten. Work is my idea of rest."

"Fair enough. Good night."

"Good night, Dr. Watts."

I don't give it much thought before I steer my car in the direction of Colten's house. There doesn't appear to be a light on anywhere in his house. My finger moves toward his doorbell, but I stop just before pressing it.

With my foot, I nudge a planter to the side.

"No ..." I shake my head and laugh out loud. "You do not have a house key under your planter, *Detective Mosley.*" He's probably the make-my-day kind of guy who dares anyone to break into his house.

While I unlock his front door, I try to remember if I saw a security alarm. The door opens in silence, so I think I'm in the clear. I tiptoe upstairs to his bedroom. He's asleep on his back, arm cocked over his head. Removing my clothes down to my panties and bra, I slide into the other side of his bed. Opting to let him sleep, I keep my distance, staring at him until I fall asleep.

Early in the morning, a large, calloused hand splays along my belly, hooking me and turning me to face him. Our legs scissor, and I realize he sleeps in the nude.

He brushes some hair away from my face. "Did you break into my house?"

I grin. "I have a warrant."

"I'm going to need to see it."

I hold up my hand and wiggle my fingers.

He narrows his eyes.

My grin swells while said hand slides beneath the sheets and grips his erection, slowly stroking him.

He groans, eyes drifting shut, lips parting for a few breaths. "You're right. That definitely warrants breaking into my house."

I grin while kissing his bare chest. His hands tangle in my hair softly before clenching it and tipping my head back to kiss me with vigor.

It's a good kiss. Hard but slow like every move we make. We're a tight band of need yet controlled. Unhurried.

Colten releases my hair to unhook my bra. Then he pulls me on top of him, flinging my bra to the side while I kiss my way up his neck. He fists the backside of my panties and gruffly peels them from my body.

Everything is new but familiar.

He rocks his hips and pushes into me sitting astride him. His hands grip my hips to guide me at his pace.

"Touch yourself, Josie."

I open my eyes to his intense gaze and cup my breasts. He rocks his pelvis harder into me. The muscles in his jaw flex for a moment. His right hand releases my hip, clutching my wrist to pull my hand from my breast to his mouth. Like a lion savoring its prey, he licks my fingers several times. Then he guides my hand to my clit.

I touch myself for him. Desire builds in his eyes

while his tongue makes a slow swipe along his lips, and his gaze affixes to my hand.

"You're the most exquisite human I have ever known," he rasps.

We spend the early morning hours lost in the sheets. I haven't been looking for *a* warm body; I've been looking for *his* warm body.

Spooning naked with tangled legs and woven arms while he hugs me to him, he kisses the back of my shoulder. "Tell me about your first time."

I giggle. "I'm not telling you about my first time while we're like this."

"Fine. Tell me about your second time. Was it me a few weeks ago?"

"Mosley, you do realize I'm an expert in death. I know ten different ways to kill you that would look like an accident or suicide."

He squeezes my breast that's been cupped in his hand like a security blanket since we assumed this position. "I'm just going to stick with my original belief."

"And what was that?"

"That you kept your virginity for me."

"Sure. That's why you saw a guy leaving my place in the morning when you surprised me by bringing your mom for a visit. What do you think I did with that guy all night?"

"He looked like the loser kind who has a foot fetish. I assumed you slept, and he snuck photos of your feet.

They're probably all over the internet, and now hundreds of thousands of guys jerk off to your feet."

I wriggle my body around to face him, giving him the hairy eyeball.

His breast hand becomes an ass-squeezing hand as he pulls me closer. "I'm good to go again." He grins while his erection slides along my belly.

"Tough luck, Mr. Duck. I'm hungry."

His grin doubles. "That works too."

"Solid food." I roll my eyes.

"It's pretty solid."

"Colten."

"Josie," he mimics in a high-pitched voice.

We're nine years old all over again.

"Donuts?" he asks.

"Tell me you work in law enforcement without actually telling me you work in law enforcement." I laugh.

Colten rubs his lips together to hide his grin for a few seconds. He's irresistibly sexy with his dark, whiskery face and messy hair this morning. "The donuts are for you."

"You don't eat donuts?"

He moves his shoulders in a weird shrug. "I was planning on eating you while you eat a donut."

Damn, he's good.

I don't even try to hide my grin. "Donuts work for me."

CHAPTER
Twenty-Nine

Seventeen years.

I honestly started to think I'd never see Josephine Watts again. Here she is, back in my life, making a mess of her cinnamon and sugar donut while I sit across from her at a round table, sipping coffee.

It really is a goddamn miracle.

She licks her lips, glancing at another couple coming into the donut shop. I could stare at Josephine Watts all day. I still can't believe she's back in my life.

"I think you're the biggest disappointment of my life," she says as whimsically as one might say while suggesting a movie.

I study her for a second from behind my cup of coffee, waiting for her to elaborate.

She doesn't.

"That's not exactly something a guy likes to hear

after he drops seven dollars and fifty cents on coffee and a donut for a girl."

Josie blows the steam from her coffee and grins. "Let me elaborate."

"Please. I'd love to know where this is going."

"I've always been logical. Curious. Scientifically minded. I operate on facts. I easily detach from things, which is why I'm so good at my job."

"Wow, don't be so modest."

She chuckles. "I didn't say I'm the best, but I'm good at it. I imagine you're good at your job too. You've never done anything half-assed that I can remember."

I nod several times. "Carry on."

"You've been this unsolved mystery in my life. People in my line of work don't like checking that 'undetermined' box. It's frustrating. What did I miss? How did I miss it? Are there more questions to ask the family? To ask the investigators? I like things neat and tidy. Go through the process. Make a determination. Move on. But with you, I haven't been able to move on. It's easy to blame you for how we ended, but I, and I alone, have been the one in control of my reaction to what happened to us. And frankly ... I'm disappointed in myself for moving on all these years without really letting go. I'm disappointed in myself for carrying around this chip on my shoulder. I deserved better."

I let her words sink in; then I reach across the table and take her hand, turning it to expose her forearm and the tattoos on it. Leaves and vines like her other forearm. My thumb traces one of the vines. "I don't think you have these tattoos to cover track marks."

Josie's eyes narrow a fraction, studying her arm and the tattoos as if she hasn't seen them before, as if they're not hers. "Cutting. I did it before it was really popular." She grunts. "Maybe I was a trendsetter. It got me through my first year at college. Eventually, I got tired of wearing long-sleeve shirts all the time. I got tired of guys seeing them and thinking I was unstable. It just ..." Her sad gaze lifts to mine. "It took away the pain. Pain numbing pain."

My thumb continues to trace the scars underneath the black lines of ink. "Was I that pain?" I whisper.

She sits back, pulling her arm from my hand. "I didn't tell my parents about us. I didn't tell them how crushed I was the day you left me in the woods." She shakes her head and whispers, "I didn't tell anyone. Now, I realize my dad suspected something ... but he didn't know the depth of my feelings. Your mom knew, but I never let her see the extent of my pain."

"Was I the pain?" I repeat.

Josie keeps her gaze on her mug of coffee and nods. "Josie ..."

She holds out her arms. "I let another human crawl under my skin, like the sharp tip of a scalpel. That's disappointing. I should have known better. I should have done better." When she wraps her hands around her mug, her eyes blink up, giving me her attention and a hint of her beautiful smile. "I know why you left me. It took seventeen years, but I know. It might take seventeen more to fully understand why I didn't let go, why I let the ghost of our past drag me through so much pain and resentment for nearly two decades. It's ... disappointing."

"Life is really fucking hard."

Josie nods.

"Well, here we are for whatever reason. I say we seize the moment. We should move in together or ..."

Her eyes widen.

I shrug. "Or ... get married. You know ... something like that."

She's frozen in place except for intermittent slow blinks.

Scooting my chair forward, I reach beneath the table and grab her bare legs, giving them a squeeze. "Seventeen. Years. We've spent too much time apart. Let's just do it. Let's be together."

Josie shakes her head, lips parted. "N-no ... I'm not marrying you or moving in with you. I don't even know if I want to be married at this point in my life. And I like my living arrangements."

"I like you in my bed," I say.

"I was in your bed last night, and it didn't require a certificate of marriage or a change of address."

"You're as stubborn and as difficult as the day we met." I release her legs and lean back in my chair.

"For the record, Mosley, you had your chance to have all of me. I would have married you the day after graduation. But things have changed."

"What's changed?"

Her fingernails tap the side of her coffee mug. "I discovered my true self-worth. I realized I don't need you."

"Still here you are, the morning after spending the night with me."

She grins. "I said I don't need you. Doesn't mean I don't want you."

"What if I'm an all-or-nothing? A packaged deal? What if I don't want to be your boy toy?"

"You've been my boy toy since the day we met."

She's not wrong.

"What if I want a wife?"

She pushes back in her chair and stands, clutching her purse. "Then you should have married your daughter's mother."

I follow her to the door, digging my key fob out of my pocket. "Can we swap house keys?"

"Why do I need your house key when I found your top-secret location in less than ten seconds?"

I open the passenger door for her because I'm a gentleman (sorta). Before she gets in the vehicle, I pull her into my arms, forcing her to look up at me. "I love you, Josie."

She smiles, but damn my unlucky life to hell, if she doesn't reciprocate the sentiment.

"You used to love me," I say, but it sounds more like a growl.

"I did. Silly me."

"Love me again."

"I'll think about it."

"Like you're going to think about moving in with me? Like you're going to think about marrying me?"

"Disclaimer: I'm not going to marry you. But let's say you had the slightest chance of marrying me." She curls two fingers into quotes and lowers her voice like mine. "I say we seize the moment. We should move in together or get married. You know ... something like that." She ends her quote and gives me a tight smile. "That's not the way to go about it. In fact, it might be the worst proposal in the history of proposals. So now I'm starting to really question your side of the story regarding Katy and the proposal. Did she say no to your proposal because you didn't love her? Or did you give her a multiple-choice question with marriage as one of the possible answers?"

I don't give a shit that she's busting my balls at every turn. She's in my life, in my arms. Last night she was in my bed. If she made this easy for me, I'd be shocked. Josephine Watts has always been a marathon of mind-games and emotions. I'd be disappointed if she didn't make me work for it.

I grin. "Do you want to A: go back into the donut shop so I can bend you over the bathroom sink and fuck you before we grab a few more donuts for later? B: stop by the grocery store with me on the way back to my place because I'm out of food? C: marry me? D: move in with me?"

After a few seconds of no reaction, she twists her lips. It thrills me that she's playing along. We're going to the grocery store. That's fine. I don't expect a miracle today. Then ... she gives me a miracle. Just ... uh ... not at all the one I expect.

Wriggling out of my arms, she sashays back to the donut shop. "Listen, Mosley, if we get arrested for public indecency, you'd better be ready to call in a favor."

CHAPTER
Thirty

I CAN'T HELP but wonder what my life would have been like had Colten not ended us. Would we have gotten married? Would he have gone into law enforcement? Would I be dissecting bodies? Would we even still be together?

"You're glowing today, Dr. Watts," Colten says as we stroll through the aisles of the grocery store. "Pink cheeks. Swollen lips. Ruffled hair."

"Two decades ago, you knew better than to gloat," I say, tossing food into the cart that's not for my kitchen. "I liked that Colten better."

"Nonsense. That pimple-faced kid tripped over his words and fumbled his dick." He grabs the box of salt-free crackers from my hand and returns it to the shelf before I get it into the cart.

"He was endearing."

"Embarrassing," Colten grumbles.

"When do you see Reagan again?"

He tosses a bag of potato chips into the cart. "Hopefully for her birthday in two weeks. It's a party. You should come with me."

"Hmm ... I'll check my schedule. I might have a date that weekend."

"Speaking of that pimple-faced, dick-fumbling kid," he says, "the one who sat idle while you dated other guys? Yeah, I'm not him. I'm much closer to the version you knew right before we graduated ... the one who beat the shit out of what's his face who took you to prom."

"Andy?"

"Sure whatever." Just the mention of Andy's name seems to irritate Colten. It's kind of cute.

"I think you're too mature for that."

"Try me."

I grin, finding a unique satisfaction in this conversation.

"Did you?" he asks.

"Did I what?"

"Suck his dick?"

An elderly lady passes us, and from her scowl, I'd say her hearing is pretty good, and she's not a fan of sucking dick.

"Is it a little sadistic that it brings me joy knowing that question has sat unanswered in the corner of your mind all these years?"

"I wouldn't call it unanswered. More like uncon-firmed. I'm pretty sure I already know the answer."

"I did it."

Colten doesn't say anything, but his body stiffens, and he takes a hard swallow, teeth clenched.

"I didn't want to start college with so little experience."

I'm fairly certain he just flinched, but he won't look at me. He picks up the pace and throws items in the cart that I'm not sure he even wants.

In the checkout lane, he ignores me. When I reach for one of the bags, he grabs it first, carrying all the bags while taking long strides toward his car.

His poor bread takes the brunt of his anger before he slams the back door and climbs into the driver's seat. I can barely keep a straight face while my ego gobbles up his brooding attitude. Just as he reaches for his seat belt, I lean across the center console. He cocks his arm, giving me his elbow to stop my motions.

I cup his chin, forcing him to look at me while I grin. "I asked you to take my virginity. You passed on that opportunity. Why did I owe you my mouth around your dick?"

It's too perfect. I'm not sure anything can make up for what he did to me, but I deserve every little morsel I can steal.

"I didn't suck Andy's cock," I whisper before sucking on his lower lip and teasing it with my teeth while my other hand tugs on the button to his jeans.

"But I'm going to suck yours." I release him from his briefs.

"Josie ..." My name falls from his lips with a little anguish. He's conflicted.

A little mad.

A lot turned-on.

Which one will win?

His hands gather my hair while he lets out a groan as my answer.

We've managed to channel our inner horny teenaged selves where every look and every conversation leads to something sexual. My dad isn't here to ground me. My mom isn't here to tell me how playing hard to get is the smart choice.

I'm not ready to share an address with Colten or marry him. But this orgasm high we've been on ... always chasing the next one ... well, it's pretty spectacular.

"Jo-s-sie ... fuck ... you."

I release him from my mouth and turn my head, glancing up at him with raised eyebrows.

He grips my hair tighter and bites back his grin. "If you stop, I will fucking die."

I lick it. "Oh, Andy ..."

"Josie ..." he growls my name and grips the side of his seat, his hips making a tiny thrust toward my mouth.

I giggle, collecting more of those morsels of torture. Then I finish the job because that's what detailed oriented people do.

"F-fuuuck ..."

I sit up and grin, licking the corner of my mouth just as the old lady from the store walks past the front of his car. He blows out a long breath while his body slumps like his spine evaporated with his orgasm. His hands work to tuck, zip, and button.

I fasten my seat belt and reach down by my feet, retrieving the small box from the floor. After pulling out a donut, I take a bite and grin. "Palate cleanser," I mumble.

If a look for the love child of adoration and mystification exists, it's residing on Colten Mosley's face. "I knew you loved me." He smirks, starting the car and shifting it into drive.

I snort, slowly shaking my head. Blow job equals love through the eyes of a man. Figures.

Before we get his groceries put away, his phone rings. He listens, frowns, nods, and says three words. "On my way."

"Call me later?"

Colten shrugs. "You could come with me. I know a guy with a badge. Ever seen a real crime scene?" He slips his phone into his pocket and pushes me up against the counter.

I rest my hands on the edge of the counter and chuckle. "I have my own badge."

Pressing his lips to my neck, he grins before kissing me. "Might as well come get a preview of your work for tomorrow."

"Who died?"

He lifts his head and takes my hand. "That's what we're going to find out."

The second we get out of the car, Colten flashes his badge, and I dig through my purse for mine. By the time I get it, he's twenty yards ahead of me, huddled with the crime scene unit near the end of the pier.

He's no longer Colten, my reunited childhood crush; he's a detective and I am a forensic pathologist. Richard Claiborne, the medicolegal investigator, gives me an extended glance when he looks up from the body on the pier.

I answer his unspoken question. "I was in the area."

He nods.

I meet with the coroner who pronounced the time of death.

Scene briefing.

Walk through.

Preliminary examination.

The decedent's abdomen has been mutilated.

"Look what we have here." In the sand a few feet from the body, there's a tied latex glove finger. "He's a mule," the officer says.

I walk farther down the pier toward the other body. A shock wave of whip-like snaps drowns out all other noise.

Gunfire.

I start to turn, then ...

CHAPTER
Thirty-One

It's an unnerving sonic boom of deadly projectiles moving through the air. Guns are drawn. Chaos ensues.

I immediately search for Josie, but I can't move. There's too much gunfire. Too many bodies falling to the ground. The crime scene turns into a war zone.

Josie. Josie. Josie …

I fire at the armed insurgents clad in black vests, a circle of them firing at us while several others grab the bodies. They're robbing our fucking crime scene, but I don't care. Take the bodies. Where is Josie?

For some reason, Beethoven's *Moonlight Sonata* plays in my head. It's what I played when life felt out of control as a teenager. It's what soothed me during my time in the war zone. Today, it's a preamble to death.

Josie. Josie. Josie …

As quickly as they appeared, the armed men fire their way toward a moving van, load the bodies, and speed off as my team, those who aren't wounded, climb into squad cars in pursuit of them.

I hear my name, but it's a mere echo. Beethoven's too loud, drowning out everything while I run toward the pier—the last place I saw Josie.

Her bag's near the edge, halfway between the location of the two missing bodies. I follow the blood. Her blood? I don't know, but it leads me to the side of the pier. Diving into the water, I frantically search the cloudy abyss for any sign of her.

Josie!

I swim toward her body, seemingly suspended in the water. Her shirt's caught on a piece of scrap metal lodged in the sand and rock. Blood swirls in the water around her. As my lungs begin to burn, I free her and drag her to the surface.

"Help!" I yell on a gasp. "HELP!" I swim toward the shore, but no one's running to help us because *everyone* needs help. They took two bodies and left a smattering of new ones.

Just as I get her out of the water, an officer and a paramedic help me, taking over.

She's gone.

I've seen enough bodies to know ... she's gone. Still, I listen to Beethoven and remain unmoving as they work on her. She's been shot. And she's not breathing.

"She's gone," I whisper, but no one is listening to me.

I shouldn't have left her. Seventeen years ago, I shouldn't have left her. I should have followed my fucking heart. It might have changed the course of our lives forever. Maybe she wouldn't have been a medical examiner, and maybe I wouldn't have gone into law enforcement.

We'd be married with two unruly kids she never imagined wanting. But finding *the one* changes everything. Our house would be small, but our hearts would be full ... and beating.

Josie's heart is not beating, and mine feels incredibly purposeless. I think about Reagan's exuberant smile and the way she squeals "Daddy," and it's the most beautiful sound in the world. The sonata's tempo picks up. Reagan needs me. I have to keep breathing, keep living. I made it seventeen years without Josephine Watts in my life. What's eternity?

I didn't deserve her anyway, and we both knew it.

The paramedics transport her to the ambulance. My feet trudge through the sand under the weight of my drenched clothes and the gruesome cloud of gravity.

Bodies ... there are bodies everywhere with one less medical examiner to autopsy the ones that won't make it.

I shoulder my way past the paramedics, grabbing her hand as they try to push me away. "I should have said it." The words rip from my chest as I hold her limp hand. "Josie ... fuck ..." I can barely breathe past the pain gripping my throat like a noose. "I should have ...

said it." I lose her hand when she's lifted into the ambulance. My fingers thread through my hair as my eyes burn and my head inches side to side. "I love you ... I love you."

The back doors to the ambulance slam shut, lights flashing, people swarming all around me. And Beethoven fades along with the ambulance lights. I hate that I know I can't follow her body. I'm hardwired to step over dead bodies to save the living. Bravery doesn't take time to mourn until the battle is over.

Josie's killers are on the run. The battle is not over.

———

By the time I catch up to the rest of my team, they're calling for air assistance as the shooters fly off in a helicopter.

"FUCK!" I slam my car door and kick the toe of my black boot through the dirt.

"We'll get 'em." Rains holsters his weapon before resting his hand on my shoulder. "Where were you?"

I shake my head, finding it nearly impossible to speak. Gritting my teeth, I clear my throat. "Josie ... Jos ... Dr. Watts ... she ..."

Rains wrinkles his face. "Oh fuck."

I nod and glance up at the sky.

"I'll meet you back at the station," he says.

"I have a stop to make first."

When I arrive at the hospital, it feels like the bones in my legs are splintering, refusing to carry me toward her body. I have to see her to know … for it to feel real because reality evaporated hours ago, replaced with hell on earth.

What will I tell her parents?

"Where's Josephine Watts?" I ask the nurse and shake my head. "Dr. Watts. She was brought in several hours ago."

The nurse checks her computer.

"Has next of kin been notified?" I ask.

"I'll check." She shakes her head. "Dr. Watts is still in surgery."

"What?" She's mistaken.

"Are you family?"

I pull out my badge.

"You can wait in the waiting room, or I can call you when she's out of surgery."

She's alive …

For nearly three hours … I've thought she was dead. My heart pounds, aching from the brutal fists of reality striking it over and over today. Even this new sliver of hope cuts into all four chambers because she still might not make it. Sometimes hope is the evilest bearer of bad news.

I sit in the waiting room when I know I should be writing up reports or checking with Rains to see if they caught the shooters. After a rancid cup of coffee, I call her parents, but it will take them a while to get here. Will she wait for them, or will they show up just to wait for some other medical examiner to complete the autopsy and release the body to them for the funeral?

She should have stayed at my place or gone home to pack her shit and move in with me. Literally anything that would have kept her far away from the evils of humanity. This is on me. I invited her. I was selfish for wanting more time with her.

Hours later, Josie's out of surgery and in the ICU in critical condition.

"If she makes it through the night, then she has a good chance of waking up," the doctor says.

I nod. Then I sit and wait some more.

CHAPTER
Thirty-Two

MOM.

She smiles, but I don't trust it. My dreams have been too vivid.

Dad.

He's in my dream too, but they're not doing anything except staring at me. Mom has tears in her eyes.

My gaze circumnavigates the room. It's not my bedroom. It's a hospital room. Great ... one of these dreams again. In a few more blinks, I'll be autopsying myself. This is a crazy, reoccurring dream that I have at least once a month. Last time I found cancer; the time before that, it was asphyxiation.

"Josephine, I'm Dr. Panchak. Can you hear me?"

"Yes," I rasp. Jesus, my throat hurts. The pain in this dream is more vivid than others have been.

I squint when he shines a light in my eyes. I jump when he presses a stethoscope to my chest.

He chuckles. "Sorry, it's a little cold."

This is *so* real.

Dad brings his phone to his ear, but I can't make out what he's saying as he slides his gaze to me every few seconds.

"You had a gunshot wound," Dr. Panchak says. "Do you remember that?"

"No," I whisper.

This doesn't feel real. Is it real?

"Do you know the year?"

"Twenty-twenty-two." I reach for my throat as the words cut like razor blades.

"Good. Do you know the two people standing behind me?"

"My parents."

"Excellent. You were pulled from the water, resuscitated, and we removed the bullet from your small bowel and repaired it. We're keeping you for a few days, but I expect a full recovery. You were very lucky someone pulled you out of the water when they did."

"Did they find him?" I whisper.

"The shooters? I'm not sure. We can check on that for you."

"N-no ... there was no gun," I say.

My parents give the doctors a look. I've seen that look before. It's the look you give someone when you're in the presence of a crazy person. But I'm not crazy.

"Josie ..." My mom grabs my hand when the doctor

steps aside, tapping his tablet while my dad sidles next to me, opposite my mom. "Colten pulled you from the water. Your dad just called him. He'll be here soon. He's been here for days. We told him to go home and shower."

"There were two. They were about five and eight."

"Two what?" Dad asks, his brows furrowed.

"Two girls. He buried their bodies in the cemetery."

Mom squeezes my hand. "You need to rest. We're so glad you're going to be okay. I'm sure things are a little confusing now. You've been unconscious for two days. I think you need to give your brain a chance to recoup and catch up. We'll talk about what happened later. Okay?"

Later? What about the families? Have they notified the families? They're going to be equal parts devastated and relieved. Closure is incredibly bittersweet. I'll ask Colten when he gets here.

Within the hour, Colten arrives. He rests his hand on mine and clenches his teeth while swallowing. "Hey," he says as if he's the one with a sore throat.

"Hey. Did they get him?"

He shakes his head. "You mean them? And no. They crossed the Mexican border and took out several border patrol officers in the process."

"What are you talking about?" I cough and point toward the glass and pitcher of water the nurse brought in for me.

Colten pours me some water and holds it to my mouth so I can sip it from the straw.

"I'm talking about the remains of the two girls at the cemetery. You know, the long hair tied to the oak tree branches at the church?" The sicko shaved their heads.

Colten's nose scrunches, eyes squinted. "Josie, you've been unconscious for two days. They're going to run some more tests before you're discharged, but I think you're a little confused right now. Maybe you're recalling autopsies you've performed."

"The church was in Nashville."

"We're going to grab something from the cafeteria," Mom says.

Colten glances back at her and nods once before offering me a sympathetic smile. "I'll look into those bodies and get back to you."

I start to protest. This is urgent. But I can see from the look on his face that my pleas will not be expedited. "Thanks."

When my parents exit the room, he brings my hand to his mouth and presses his lips to it while closing his eyes. "Fuck, Josie ... I thought you died. You weren't breathing." He opens his eyes, and that one look is filled with so much anguish it makes my heart ache.

"I heard you saved me. Thank you."

His Adam's apple bobs, and he nods. There's a storm of emotion in his eyes. I don't know what to say. I never get to say something was "a little touch and go," but a family's loved one will be okay. They'll pull through. Nope. Never. That's not part of my job.

Josephine Watts died of hypovolemia due to major vessel injuries from an abdominal GSW.

Or maybe I'm not out of the woods yet. Maybe my ending could change.

Josephine Watts died of septicemia following an abdominal GSW.

"Now can you see if they found the girls' bodies?" I ask.

Colten offers me a tiny headshake. "Josie, you're confused right now. I don't know what girls you're talking about."

"Then why did you say you'd check on it?" It's so vivid in my head. Is it a dream? Who dreams of something so morbid? My fascination with death has never led me down the road of imagining such horrid homicides.

"Because you need a chance to physically and mentally heal. And I didn't want to upset you. Can you give it a few days, and then we'll revisit what's bothering you if it's still bothering you?"

"I suppose," I whisper. "What happened to me?"

"I was called to investigate a double homicide at the pier, and we were ambushed because the bodies were mules and they wanted their drugs. You were on the pier, fell into the water after you were shot. And I pulled you out." His voice shakes with those last five words. "I'm ... so fucking sorry. You shouldn't have been there."

He thought I was dead.

I'd say this is karma for what he did to me right

before graduation because there were many days I wondered if he was alive. But I don't believe in karma, so this is nothing more than a tragedy. A close call that no human deserves to experience.

I WAKE up in the middle of the night, and I can't breathe. My mom calls for a nurse.

"There's m-more."

"Shh ..." Mom tries to soothe me by stroking my hair. "It's just a dream."

My abdomen screams with pain, and the nurse gives me something for it ... something that knocks me out until morning.

The next day, I see a neurologist. The exam and all the scans come back normal. Then I see a psychiatrist. They think I'm mentally unwell. If I don't shut up, they'll have me on the kinds of medications that will leave me with very little pain and barely coherent. So I shut up about the girls. For now ...

"What's going on between you and Colten?" Mom asks while I take tiny bites of mashed potatoes.

I'm hoping to go home today.

Dad doesn't move from the chair by the window. He's on his second nap of the day. I'd nap, but when I close my eyes, I see things. Things that make me mentally unstable according to everyone else. So I don't sleep without heavy drugs that shut off my mind.

"We're ... something." Just as I say those words, I

have a flashback of us in a car doing something that's frowned upon in public. It makes me smile, the kind that warms my cheeks.

"What's that look about?" Mom asks. "Is it something romantic?"

It's something sexual. I think. At this point, I don't trust my thoughts. Reality is blurred. Maybe I dreamed it. Lord knows I've had a plethora of inappropriate dreams in my lifetime about Colten Mosley.

"Maybe. It's new."

Mom nods slowly, rubbing her lips together. "I see. I always wondered if you two would end up together."

Speaking of …

Colten pops his head in the room, doing his usual late day check-in.

"Hey, beautiful." His smile makes me feel beautiful, but only for a few seconds. I've caught a glimpse of my knotted hair in the bathroom mirror. It's not beautiful.

Dad stirs, peeling open his eyes and stretching his arms over his head on a big yawn. "Looks like our shift is up for now."

Mom rolls her eyes before kissing my head. "I'm not sure what your 'shift' is aside from watching TV and napping. But yes, we can go to dinner now. We'll see you later, sweetie."

"They're discharging me," I say.

She gives me a frown as Colten sits on the edge of my bed. "I fear it won't be until tomorrow now."

I shake my head. "I'm leaving today."

My parents try to appease me with fake smiles before exiting the room.

"Missed you today," Colten says, leaning in for a kiss.

"Have I given you a blow job lately?"

He stops an inch before my lips, blinks several times, and clears his throat before releasing a soft chuckle. "Why do you ask?" He pecks my mouth and sits up straight, loosening his tie.

"Because it popped into my head. We were in your car."

He fails at suppressing his grin. "The day of the shooting. We uh ... did a lot that day."

My memories around that day are sketchy at best. "A lot?"

"Let's just say it was a good day ... until it wasn't."

"My mom asked about us. Have you not said anything to them?"

"It hasn't come up. It's hard to fit 'I'm in love with your daughter' into conversations about drugs, mass shootings, and a GSW to their daughter's abdomen that caused her to nearly drown."

"Was it a good blow job?"

"Jesus Christ ..." Colten rubs his face, trying to wipe off that grin.

It was a good blow job. I figured. Blow jobs make me less crazy than talking about dead girls and the whereabouts of their bodies. I really need out of here. I need my computer and some time alone.

"When we do disclose our relationship status to your parents, let's not start with the blow job. Okay?"

"What is our relationship status?"

Colten opens his mouth to speak then pauses for a few seconds. "We're getting married."

My face scrunches. "What?"

"Yeah. It's probably part of that day's events that you don't remember. I proposed over donuts and coffee. You said yes. Then we went grocery shopping and home to discuss ... wedding plans." His grin doubles. "And then I was called to the pier, and you came with me."

I really need my memory of that day to come back. "You proposed without asking my dad first? He's awfully old-fashioned. I don't know how he's going to feel about it. And I'm surprised I said yes."

"Oh? Why is that?" He cants his head to the side.

"Because I can't imagine wanting to get married."

Gazing out the window for a few breaths, he twists his lips. "You didn't say yes. You said no. And then I asked you to move in with me, and you shot me down again." He cringes, returning his attention to me. "Sorry, bad choice of words."

I grin. "That sounds more accurate."

"But now that you've danced with death, I'm sure your outlook on life has shifted." He kisses the inside of my forearm over my tattoos that cover another great shift in my life.

"Rains? Is he okay?"

Colten nods. His drooping expression squeezes my heart. "But we lost two others, and three were injured."

"Are you okay?" I cup his cheek, and he leans into my touch.

"I didn't get shot."

The pad of my thumb tracks his lower lip. "Are you okay?"

His gaze makes a slow assent to mine.

"I didn't die," I whisper.

He nods and takes a hard swallow before wedging his large body in bed with me, burying his face in my neck on a long exhale. "I think a part of *me* did," he mutters.

The gravity of all the things I can't remember from that day settles on my chest, leaving a dull ache. I wish I remembered. I wish I could take away Colten's pain.

I wish I knew why I can't stop thinking about these girls.

CHAPTER
Thirty-Three

"I'm in love with your daughter, but she won't marry me or even move in with me," Colten spews out his confession over dinner—his belated birthday dinner— a week after I'm released from the hospital. He doesn't even glance up from his plate.

My mom smirks. Yeah, she knew.

Dad? Not so much. He's waking up from his ignorance-is-bliss state. And now he looks sorely hungover with the news.

"And since you're leaving tomorrow..." Colten blots his mouth with a napkin and risks a glance in my parents' direction "...Josie's going to move in with me so I can take care of her."

"I'm not," I blurt.

He clears his throat and smiles, but not at me. It's like I'm not here. It's reminiscent of the hospital when everyone talked about me while my eyes were closed, but I could still hear them.

"What I meant to say is I'm going to stay with her at her place ... because she's comfortable there ... until she gets better, which realistically could take several months if not longer. So you both can feel rest assured that she'll have all of her needs met."

This is a coup. I'm being ambushed again!

I think Mom's going to cry.

Dad? Nope. No tears in his eyes. He clears his throat and eases his fork onto his plate. "Colten, I'm sure you have good intentions, but ..."

"I love her. I've loved her nearly my whole life. And I'm sorry that you're just now finding out, but it doesn't change the fact that ..." He shrugs. "I love her."

Mom wipes a tear. I don't know how to react. I'm mad. And touched. And ... something.

Dad eyes me for confirmation. I don't know what to say, so I say the obvious. "He loves me."

"And do you love him?"

Damn you, Dad!

The room shrinks with all eyes on me, a tiny specimen under a microscope. I give my attention to Colten, the perpetrator.

I'm not marrying you. I'm not moving in with you. I will not be manipulated. I will not give you anymore blow jobs. I'm mad as hell right now!

"Yes. I love him."

It's a lottery-winning smile that engulfs Colten's handsome face. I'm sure it feels amazing to have someone say those three words when you need them the most. He didn't show me the same consideration seventeen years ago, but ... whatever. I have to let that shit go.

Dad torments Colten with his silence and unreadable expression. But this man who loves me reaches under the table and squeezes my leg as if to let me know my dad's feelings about us no longer matter. Where was this Colten when I felt the need to cut my skin?

Dad stands. All eyes shift to him and his stony expression. "I can't think of a better man for my daughter. You have my blessing." He slaps Colten's shoulder and squeezes it.

His blessing?

No. No blessing required. This isn't a marriage. It's not even cohabitation. It's temporary in-home nursing.

I'm fine. I can walk to the end of the street and back. I can walk upstairs, albeit rather slowly. And despite Dr. Cornwell's insistence that I take a minimum of twelve weeks off work, I'm going back in two ... maybe three.

"You're restricted from lifting more than ten pounds for eight weeks. How are you going to lift and reposition dead bodies?"

AFTER MY PARENTS leave the following day, and I'm no longer being monitored twenty-four-seven, I grab my computer. I have four to five hours before Colten will be off work and here with his things, a changing of the guard.

Hair hanging from trees at churches.

Remains of girls' bodies buried in cemeteries.

My fingers furiously type in different searches, but they all come up with the same results.

Winston Jeffries. 1892 to 1901 reign of terror.

Long hair tied to tree branches in Nashville, Tennessee, churchyards.

Young girls. Shaved heads.

Nearly a decade of kidnappings.

The bodies were never found.

NEVER. FOUND.

Jeffries was convicted of thirty-seven counts of first-degree murder and hanged in Owensboro, Kentucky, on February 10, 1902.

I search for Winston Jeffries copycats.

I search for literally everything I can think of that might make sense of what's in my head. Before I realize it, the day passes. I've not taken my required walks. I've not eaten. And I've not touched my pain meds.

"Honey, I'm home," Colten announces as he traipses into my living room, depositing a big duffle bag in the hallway first.

Shutting my laptop, I smile. "Hi."

His forehead wrinkles. "What are you doing?"

"Nothing. Why?"

"Because you look guilty."

I shake my head. "No. Guilty of what?"

"What were you looking at on your computer?"

"Nothing much."

"Porn?"

I hesitate for a few seconds.

"Seriously? Are you seriously watching porn?"

I give him a tight smile and lift a shoulder.

The priceless look on his face is exactly what I need after a long day of not figuring out a damn thing.

"Bullshit," he says, kneeling on the floor in front of me, wedging his body between my legs and nuzzling my neck. "I missed your lying ass today."

I giggle when he bites my neck. Then I hiss because laughing doesn't feel good after surgery.

He sits back, a cringe stealing his face. "Sorry."

I have to quell the urge to ask him to look into the missing girls for me. I need peace of mind. I can't focus on anything else, yet I can't keep pushing this subject when no one takes me seriously. They say it's confusion since the accident, but it's not.

"What do you want me to heat up for dinner?"

I grin. "My mom really went overboard. We have meals and cookies for weeks."

He sighs. "I'm good with that." Bending forward, he rests his head on my lap.

I slide my fingers through his hair.

He hums like a cat, purring with each stroke. When we're like this, I don't feel those missing seventeen years. I just feel him.

My best friend.

My lover.

My Colten.

"Long day?"

Again, he hums. "So long. I have a pile of paper-work on my desk, but I left it for tomorrow because I needed this."

"Your hair stroked?"

"You."

Feeling needed in this kind of way is indescribable.

"I should take a walk. Want to go with me? Then we can warm up dinner. Shower. And eat cookies in bed while watching a show. I love my parents, but I was also so happy to see them go home this morning. Is that terrible?"

"No," he murmurs like he's half asleep already.

"We can skip the walk. You're too tired."

"Nope." He sits up and scrubs his hands over his face. "Rehab. Rehab. Rehab. You need to walk. And I'm your guy."

My guy ...

Colten stands and offers me his hand to help me to my feet even though I can do it by myself, even if I'm still a little slow. His arms snake around my waist. "The shower part ... was that an invite to shower with you? I mean, I need a shower. And you know ... global warming and lakes drying up ..."

Of course, I want him to shower with me, but I don't give it away without making him squirm a bit.

"No funny business. I promise."

I laugh. "Does anyone call it 'funny business' anymore?"

"Somewhere, I'm sure." He kisses me.

I grab his shirt, keeping his lips to mine. When we kiss, I don't think about the bodies of girls with shaved heads. When we kiss, I don't think about the pain.

He pulls away and shakes his head while licking his lips. "Not fair. I just declared no funny business, and you kiss me like that?"

"Like what?"

"Like you want me to have a fucking hard-on all night." He adjusts himself.

"Or that I missed you today."

He grumbles. "That was more than a missing me kiss. Let's go for that walk."

"STOP!" I scream, jackknifing to sitting. "Ouch! Fuck ..." My hand goes to my incision while Colten sits up and wraps me in his arms.

"I've got you," he whispers. "It was just a bad dream. Just a bad dream ..." He hugs me with a gentle rocking motion.

Tears make hot tracks down my face. I don't know if I'm crying because of the dream or because my body did something it was not ready to do.

"Josie ..." he kisses my face, claiming all of my tears. "Was it about that day?"

It was about a day, but not the day he's implying. The same thing happened ... only the girls were different girls. A different church. Different tree. It was so real. I tried to stop him, but I couldn't because I couldn't see him. I've never seen him. Just the girls.

"Yeah," I say in a shaky voice. I want to tell him more. I *need* to tell him ... tell someone before this gets worse.

"Did you take your pain meds?"

I shake my head.

"Why not?" His fingers ghost along my arms.

I shudder. "Because I don't like how they make me feel."

"Isn't that the point? To *not* feel?"

"Hand me the pills," I say just before swallowing back a little bile. I don't have a weak stomach, but this is different. It's not what I see in my dreams. It's what I feel.

Colten hands me a pill and a glass of water from the nightstand. "It won't last forever. You need to sleep. You've been restless for hours."

I nod and hand the glass back to him.

With my heart still racing, he spoons me. I wish I could find his arms in my dreams ... my nightmares.

"I've got you. Just rest." He kisses my head.

I try to focus on the warmth of his body against mine. His skin pressed to mine like a shield. His arms an impenetrable armor. Still, I'm afraid to close my eyes.

CHAPTER
Thirty-Four

The problem with having an unforgivable asshole for a father was the embarrassment that came with people finding out about his indiscretions. Yes, plural.

"Is it true your dad grazed Holly Gill's breast during study hall?" Anne Perez asked at a party a week before the end of our junior year.

For the record, his first affair was with a woman who cut his hair. Thankfully, and I used that word lightly, she was of legal age. The school had no real grounds to fire him. However, Holly was seventeen, days shy of her eighteenth birthday, and a senior when my dad was filling in for the study hall supervisor and allegedly grazed her breast with his nose.

Yep, his fucking nose.

She was walking through the cafeteria during study hall, running late to her next class, and my dad stopped her because she had both of her shoes untied. She also had a jammed finger from volleyball and said she couldn't tie her shoes because her fingers were buddy taped.

Good ole Coach Mosley helped her out. Tied both shoes and *allegedly* slowly stood via his nose touching her breast. There were rumors that he did, in fact, inhale, but he denied it. Apparently, he went to stand, lost his balance, and fell into her. Nose to breast. And the alleged inhale was a gasp on his part.

Shock and embarrassment.

After years of reconciliation, my dad betrayed my mom's newly earned trust.

"I think it's true that Holly Gill manages to shove her tits in everyone's face. And most guys have been a victim of her being a slut," I yelled over the music, taking a long swig of my fourth or fifth beer.

"I heard he could be fired." Anne took my beer and helped herself to a sip.

"She's not even the one who filed the complaint." I tried to roll my inebriated eyes.

Some other kid in study hall made the anonymous complaint. When asked about it, Holly shrugged it off and said she didn't remember, which was not an actual denial that it didn't happen. My dad flat-out denied it.

"Didn't your dad cheat on your mom?" Anne continued to feed my desire to drink more beer.

"I don't know, Anne. Did your mom try to suck my dad's dick?"

She gasped as I tipped back my beer again, a little

unstable on my feet and unaware of my surroundings, mainly, the staircase right behind me.

Thunk. Clunk. Thunk. Clunk.

I ate it with one step backward.

No one called an ambulance because we were all underaged kids drinking at Tanner Collier's house while his parents were out of town. I could have died all in the name of keeping everyone else out of trouble. Tammy, one of the not-so-drunk girls at the party, called my "emergency contact," aka Josephine Watts. She knew Josie was my friend of sorts and figured she'd know a way to make sure I didn't die and everyone else didn't get in trouble since her dad was the police chief, and he liked me.

Everything blurred from that moment on until I cracked open my eyes, completely clueless as to my whereabouts or how I got there. A warm body was pressed to my back, and gentle fingers caressed my hair.

"I'm gonna be sick," I said before rolling out of bed to the floor. That was when I realized I was in my bedroom. I did something like a half walk, half crawl to the toilet and vomited over and over.

Josie was there, rubbing my back.

Josie was there with a glass of water.

Josie was there with her kind eyes.

Josie didn't say a word … she was simply there.

As I sat on the cold linoleum floor, sipping the water, my other hand wiped the sweat from my forehead, only … it wasn't sweat.

"You cut your forehead when you fell down the stairs," Josie said. "I couldn't find any bandages, and I didn't want to leave you alone to run to my house for them because I'm worried you might be dying of a brain bleed, and I don't want you to die alone." She was kidding.

I thought. Actually, I didn't know. After all, it was Josephine Watts. I could usually read her, but I was too drunk that night.

"Chad's asleep. Your dad's not home. And I think your mom took some sleeping pills and passed out on the sofa. Don't worry. It's not an overdose; I counted them."

My dad was probably off accidentally boning Holly Gill. One of those freak accidents where he tripped, and his dick landed inside of her. No wonder my mom needed pills to sleep, and I wouldn't have blamed her had she taken the whole damn bottle.

I handed Josie the glass of water and slumped to the side. Dying of a concussion felt like a welcomed opportunity compared to the pain. "I fucking hurt everywhere," I groaned.

"You fell down a flight of stairs." She chuckled, positioned herself behind me again, and again, held me to her, caressing me, while whispering, "I've got you," in my ear.

The next morning, we were back in my bed. I had no recollection of going from the bathroom floor to my bed, but I must have at least crawled because there was no way little Josie carried me.

"My mouth tastes like ass," I rasped while opening my eyes.

Oh my fucking head ...

It pounded.

Josie was tucked under my arm on her side, hugging my torso. I didn't want to move, but I had to take a leak before I sprang a leak in the bed.

"Your dad's going to kill me, gut me like one of his trophies, when he finds out where you are."

She nuzzled my neck. I didn't want her nuzzling my neck. Well, I did, but not when I smelled like vomit and ... ass.

"My dad thinks I'm at a friend's house. And your mom is on her morning walk."

I peeled her arm from my torso and groaned while shifting to sitting. "I'm going to shower. Thanks for ... everything."

After I made it two steps toward my bedroom door, Josie cleared her throat. "Need help?"

I glanced over my shoulder, eyes squinted.

She chewed on her lower lip, struggling to maintain eye contact with me. God, I loved her so fucking much. It was then I realized she wasn't wearing anything but a T-shirt of mine and striped cotton panties in shades of pink. Her dark hair hung over her shoulders and fell partway over her face, hiding some of her nervousness.

Did I want Josie to help me shower? The answer was as simple as the question: did I have a dick?

But ... where was Chad? When would my mom be

home from her walk? What if Chief Watts discovered Josie was at my house instead of at a friend's house? Since I managed to survive near alcohol poisoning and a tumble down a flight of stairs, I decided to call it while I was still ahead.

"I can manage."

She averted her gaze and nodded.

I was a stupid fuck. I was just too stupid and young to see it.

"Wait for me?" I asked.

She nodded again, picking at a string hanging from the hem of my T-shirt.

After I showered, brushed my teeth, and gargled twice to get rid of the ass taste, I peeked my head out of the bathroom and listened for my mom or Chad.

Nothing.

With a towel around my waist, I took two long strides to my room and closed the door behind me. When I turned toward Josie, her eyes were huge. She tucked her knees toward her chest under my tee and leaned against the wall at the head of my bed. Her unblinking eyes drifted south to my towel and back up my body.

"F-feel better?" she croaked before clearing her throat.

"Yeah." I felt marginally better. Cleaner. But my whole body ached, especially my head. It was hard to say if the ache in my head was from the alcohol or the fall.

"I uh ... see you found a bandage?"

I nodded, touching my head.

Her gaze roved along my torso. "You're bruised."

Glancing down, I tried to see where her eyes had landed.

"There." She motioned with her head.

I inspected my ribs and abs while she crawled off the bed and padded her bare feet to me.

"Here." She feathered her fingertips along the red area on my hipbone just above the towel.

I shuddered from her touch, and that made her glance up at me. We stood idle and silent for several seconds. I needed to get dressed, but she was in my room. I should've taken my clothes into the bathroom with me, but I wasn't thinking straight. Instead, I had a growing erection behind my towel because Josie touched a bruise on my hip.

And she was in my T-shirt.

And I'd gotten a glimpse of her panties before I showered.

And I'd considered rubbing one off in the shower while thinking of her in her pink panties, but I didn't because I didn't want to take the extra time.

I should have taken the extra time.

Instead, there I was, adjusting my towel and tucking my abs, anything to hide it from her.

"Kiss me, Colten," she whispered, taking a step closer.

Jesus ... don't get any closer!

"Um ..." I tried to speak past the thick desire clogging my throat and stifling all coherent words. I took a step backward, my back hitting the door.

Josie lifted onto her toes, slid her hands behind my neck, and pulled me to her mouth. It was a slow kiss.

I clutched the front of my towel, holding on for dear life. Her warm tongue teased the seam of my mouth, and I opened for her. Our tongues touched, tentative at first, like we'd done so many times before; then our mouths fused with more need, also like we'd done in the past.

This time was different. I didn't have underwear and pants with a zipper and button keeping my dick under control.

She hummed, and I swore I was going to spew just from the kiss and the graze of the towel over the head of my erection. I told my other hand to remain fisted at my side.

Don't touch her!

It didn't listen.

It went straight to the hem of her shirt (my shirt) and worked its way up to her bare breast. Had God really existed, she would have been wearing a bra, a barrier that might have tripped my thoughts long enough to come to my senses.

No bra.

No God.

Her nipple was so fucking hard, hard like my erection. I cupped her breast and she moaned, making her tongue reach deeper into my mouth. When the pad of my thumb rubbed her nipple, our kiss faltered. Her chin dropped a fraction, and her lips pressed to my neck. I backed her to my bed. My towel hand started to weaken, but I kept it fisted.

Josie's overly curious fingers tugged at my towel.

"Uh-uh ..." I held strong. Sorta strong. My resistance weakened; and to be honest, it was downright flimsy at that point.

The only person in the world, who I gave more than two fucks about, wanted me in a way that made me feel like I didn't need the alcohol. Like my loser dad didn't exist. Like I had a purpose. And my purpose in that moment was to touch Josephine Watts.

Ever since the piano bench incident, the tension between us had been high. Either she hated me, or she was torturing me. Really, one and the same.

And when she wasn't firsthand torturing me, she was kissing some other guy which made me see every shade of red.

With one hand, I couldn't do everything I wanted to do to her, so ... I had to let the towel go.

She paused, taking a long breath to eye my erection bouncing between us. I grabbed her face and kissed her again. She started to lose her balance, so I guided her onto the bed and covered her body with mine as we kissed.

Her hands tentatively teased my bare back, easing their way down to my ass while spreading her legs to accommodate my torso. I didn't have a condom, not that we were going to have sex. We weren't. I was ... ninety percent sure of that. All I had to do to keep from going all the way with her was think of her dad killing me.

Unfortunately, that thought wasn't enough to make me completely stop.

"Colten ... don't stop."

And that right there was the reason I reserved that ten percent chance of having sex with her. Josephine was the worst temptation. She would have given me her virginity on so many occasions. I was a fucking saint.

Kinda ...

I shoved the T-shirt up her torso, and she grabbed it, taking it over her head. That was not what I was going for. Without the shirt, the only thing keeping us from doing something incredibly stupid, something that could get her pregnant and me killed, was her cotton panties. I might as well have wrapped a one-ply tissue around my dick and said a prayer to a god I knew wasn't going to do me any favors at that point.

"Do..." she panted "...you have ... a condom?"

I sucked her nipples and cupped her perky tits with my hands. "No," I murmured. "I'm ... not going ... to go ... that far."

Her fingers found their favorite place in my hair as she continued to writhe beneath me. Arching her back then planting her feet and lifting her pelvis toward me.

She wanted it.

I wanted it.

Why did *it* have to be so wrong?

Why did *it* come with so many possible conse-quences?

Damn ... why did working up to *it* feel so good?

"How far are you going to go?" she asked on a harsh breath.

Good question. I had no clue. And I certainly didn't want to stop.

I just knew that every time she lifted her hips, rubbing herself against my abs, I drove my cock into the mattress a few inches below her spread legs.

"You feel so ... g-good." She found her rhythm against me, and I kept telling myself I'd stop after a few more seconds.

And a few more.

More.

More.

More ...

I was well on my way to drilling a hole in the mattress.

"Colten? Are you awake?" Mom called from what sounded like a partial ascent up the stairs.

Major boner-killer.

Josie shoved my chest.

"Getting dressed, Mom. Be down in a bit."

Flying off the bed, Josie searched the floor for her clothes, putting them on in a matter of seconds.

I dressed a little slower, watching her to see if she was watching me.

She was.

"Oh my god ..." Josie whispered when we made eye contact.

"It's fine. She knows nothing." I rubbed my temples. Without Josie's naked body distracting me from my hangover, my head started to throb again. I think the erection and near ejaculation drew the blood and pain away from my head.

"You go downstairs and distract her while I sneak out," she said, shoving her feet into her shoes.

"Why'd you come?" I had to ask.

She stood up straight, cheeks red. "I didn't. I was close, though."

I shook my head. "I mean, why did you come get me from the party last night?"

Josie blinked. "You're my best friend. Wouldn't you have done the same thing for me?"

Stupid question.

There was nothing I wouldn't have done for Josie. I just wasn't sure she felt the same since I'd taken to drinking so much and being a dick at times because of the hatred I had toward my dad. I took out my frustration on too many people.

My mom.

My brother.

And sometimes Josie.

"I don't deserve your friendship, Josie."

She gave me a sad smile that I couldn't quite figure out.

"I'll go distract my mom."

She nodded.

I headed to my door.

"Colten?"

"Yeah?" I turned.

"I wanted you to ..." She pressed her lips together for several seconds. "I wanted you to go all the way with me."

Me. Fucking. Too.

I didn't respond with more than a tiny nod because I wasn't sure how I felt knowing that it was all up to me to keep us from going too far.

CHAPTER
Thirty-Five

"Wʜᴀᴛ ᴀʀᴇ ʏᴏᴜ ᴅᴏɪɴɢ ʜᴇʀᴇ, Jᴏsᴇᴘʜɪɴᴇ?" Dr. Cornwell asks the second I enter the autopsy suite.

It's been four weeks. I'm in full PPE, so he shouldn't complain, but he's going to anyway. I can tell by the disapproving tone of his voice.

"No *Dr. Watts* today?"

He chuckles. "Dr. Watts is on medical leave. *Josephine* has decided to make rounds today for some unknown reason."

"I missed you," I say.

He makes a gruff grunting sound as do several other ME's. "You're supposed to be home healing. My guess is you're not supposed to be driving yet."

"I didn't. I took a cab."

"You took a cab here because you missed me?" he asked, using pruning shears to clip the decedent's ribs before lifting the breastplate to expose the pleural cavities and pericardium.

"Green fluid. Probably pneumonia," I say.

He shoots me a look.

I grin behind my mask.

When he returns his attention to the pericardial sac, carefully opening it with his scalpel, I get to my real reason for my visit. "Have you heard of Winston Jeffries?"

"Do I look *that* old?"

"So yes. You've heard of him."

He chuckles. "He was a bit before my time, but yes, I've heard of him. He preyed on little girls with long hair, abducted them, shaved off their hair, and hung the locks from churchyard trees."

One of the students observing him gasps.

"Do you know of any copycats since him?"

"No. But I haven't watched the news in a day or two. Should I be preparing for hairless girls to flood my schedule tomorrow?"

"I hope not. Just … curious."

"You paid for a cab because of a sudden curiosity about a man who was executed over a century ago. Exactly what pain meds did they give you?"

"I can't find anything that says for sure if the bodies were ever found. I don't think they were. Everything I've read says they weren't."

"Have you tried Wordle? I hear it's all the rage. Really, Josephine, what are you up to?"

I need to tell someone. And I think I could tell Dr.

Cornwell if he weren't surrounded by students, and if there weren't two other bodies being autopsied by my colleagues who would jump at the chance to accuse me of losing my fucking mind.

"Wordle, huh?" I ask.

"Or Netflix. I'd go for a rom-com. A chick flick. No medical shows. No horror movies."

I nod. "Got it. Well, thanks for your help." I head toward the door.

"Did I help?"

"No. Not really."

While I exit the building, my phone rings. It's Colten.

"Hi," I answer.

"Hey. I was in the neighborhood, and I decided to check in on you, but you're not here."

"See? That's why you're such a brilliant detective." I put him on speaker to order a ride.

"Where are you?"

"I brought some cookies to work." It's not a lie. I did intend on bringing cookies, but I forgot to grab them from the freezer last night to thaw out.

"And how did you get to work?"

I roll my eyes. "I take back my comment. You're not a very good detective. It's called a cab, Detective Mosley. Uber and Lyft were solid options too. And before you try to scold me for leaving the house, it's been four weeks, and I'm feeling better."

My wound is feeling better. Beyond that, I'm either sleep deprived if I skip my meds or walking around in a fog that makes it impossible to focus if I do take them to sleep.

"You didn't sleep well again last night. You should be napping."

I didn't sleep well because I had another dream. More girls with shaved heads. More bodies buried in a cemetery just above bodies that were buried earlier in the day.

"You are more than welcome to start sleeping at your own place so my restlessness doesn't rouse you from your beauty sleep."

"What place? I sold my house when we decided to move in together."

I smirk as the car pulls up to the curb. "Nice try."

"You'd miss me if I weren't there."

"I wouldn't."

I would. I'd miss him terribly because I've grown accustomed to the sound of him coming home (*home* ...) and collapsing on the sofa before resting his head on my lap while releasing a long day's sigh, like being with me is his first real breath of the day.

"I love you too," Colten says.

I grin and shake my head. "Gotta go. See ya later." I end the call and give the driver my next stop. Dr. Terrance Byrd.

Terrance went to medical school with me, and we saw each other about six months ago at the courthouse. He's a psychiatrist.

"Can I help you?" his receptionist asks when I close the office door behind me.

"I'm here to see Dr. Byrd. I don't have an appointment, but I was hoping he could squeeze me in for a few minutes between appointments. I'm Dr. Watts from the medical examiner's office." That has nothing to do with my visit, but I know it's her job to screen all visitors who are not on his schedule for the day.

"He'll be occupied for another forty-five minutes with his current appointment. I can take your number and have him call you if you don't want to wait."

I take a seat, gingerly bending my torso, and smile stiffly. "I've got time."

Right on the nose, Terrance emerges from his office after his patient exits. He smiles. "Josie. How are you?" Giving me a slow once-over, he frowns. "I was sorry to hear about your accident. Thank God for miracles."

I grin. "Miracle indeed. I'm healing quite well. Do you happen to have a few minutes I can steal?"

He glances over at his receptionist. "Can you move my one o'clock to one-thirty?"

She nods.

"Come on in." He gestures with a snap of his head.

It's a dinky office but calming and neutral with wood wall art and deco planters full of succulents.

"Have a seat wherever you're comfortable. Can I get you something to drink? A snack?"

"I'm good. Thanks." I take a seat in a chair by the window.

He grabs an apple and sits on the leather sofa. I think I took his chair.

"So what brings you by?" He takes a bite of his apple, probably his lunch.

"Have you ever had anyone have a near-death experience who then had visions or dreams of things that are not related to the near-death experience or anything in real life at all? *But* they feel real. And each dream builds on the other dream, becomes more real, more detailed."

He chews a big bite for several seconds. "Not in those exact words. But I wouldn't say any two near-death experiences are exactly alike. What did you see?"

I thought I was ready to have this conversation with someone, but now that I have the opportunity to share it with someone who is trained to deal with this, I find it really hard to say the words. It's not like I saw Colten's dad or my grandparents.

"Josephine?"

I drag my gaze away from the narrow succulent garden on the windowsill behind him. "I saw long locks of hair from little girls' shaved heads tied to tree branches in a churchyard. Then I saw where the bodies were buried, but I didn't see who did it."

I'll hand it to Dr. Terrance Byrd. He's perfected controlling his reaction. And I thought I was an expert at suppressing emotional responses.

"Where are the bodies buried?"

"In a cemetery. They were buried on top of caskets that were recently buried so that no one would get suspicious and look there for the bodies."

"How do you know that?"

"Know what?"

He stares at his apple for a few seconds. "How do you know that's why they were supposedly buried there?"

I shrug. "It's the most logical explanation."

Terrance nods slowly. "Have you recently had a girl with a shaved head on your table?"

"No."

"Read books about shaved heads?"

"Not recently."

"This started after your heart stopped?"

"Yes. I have dreams ... well, nightmares, but only if I don't take medication for the pain or to help me sleep. Sometimes I wake up screaming. It's so real. And I remember every little detail from the nightmare. And they're not all the same. Each time they are different girls, and their hair is tied to different trees in different churchyards. So I looked it up, thinking maybe it's an actual thing that has recently happened. But I can't find anything except a serial killer who did this exact same thing in the late 1800s, early 1900s."

Terrance takes another bite of his apple, studying me or maybe just absorbing my words. "Had you read or heard about this killer before your accident?"

"No."

His eyebrows draw together while he stares at his half-eaten apple again. "Your scans came back normal?"

"Yes."

"Did you have a concussion?"

"No."

"How long were you out? No pulse?"

"I don't know."

"Have you had any dreams like this before? Or even just lucid dreams?"

"No."

He sighs slowly. "What's your inclination? What's your gut tell you that you should do about it?"

I laugh. "My gut's telling me to go to Tennessee."

"What do you expect to find in Tennessee?"

"I don't know. Maybe an old cemetery that matches one from my dreams. Maybe ..." I twist my lips. "Is it possible that my near-death experience didn't put these visions in my head? What if it took away other memories that would give the images context? What if I studied Winston Jeffries when I was a child, and those are the memories I lost?"

"What are the chances that, as a child, you would have studied a late nineteenth century serial killer?"

My nose scrunches into a guilty expression. "I sorta had a thing with death. So if I'm being honest, it's not wildly impossible or even all that unlikely. Dahmer. Bundy. DeAngelo. I was curious."

"Well, trauma can cause selective memory loss. And you're right, losing parts of our memory can make it difficult to understand some of the memories that do exist. Context is everything."

Chewing on the inside of my lip, I flit my attention back to him. "We took a trip to Nashville when I was eleven or twelve. I don't remember everything we saw, but I wouldn't be surprised if we walked through a few cemeteries."

He shrugs. "When you're feeling better, check it out. See what you find. It might help put your mind at ease. Maybe something will trigger other memories and put everything into context."

I nod slowly. "Maybe."

"Don't do anything extreme like dig up graves."

With a tight grin, I roll my eyes. It's a preposterous idea … if it were anyone else but me.

"Let me know what you find out. Now you've piqued my curiosity."

I hum. "Mine too."

CHAPTER
Thirty-Six

"I THINK YOU SHOULD SEE SOMEONE," Colten says, waltzing down the hallway Saturday morning in a pair of shorts, no shirt.

"Congratulations," I say, pouring him a cup of coffee instead of entertaining his topic of conversation which has to do with my nightmares. "I heard you caught your killer. Did you find the saw? I have to know ... was the cord six feet? When did you get home last night?"

"Slow down ..." He chuckles. "After two in the morning. And we have our *alleged* killer. We don't actually know yet. And if you must know, we have a saw and the cord is indeed six feet, but the handle is not red."

I nod slowly. "Interesting. Tell me what you've got on him. I'll tell you if you're going to get a conviction."

He takes the coffee and kisses me. "Good morning. Let's not get off topic. About last night ..."

"I'll take the sleeping pills. Or you can sleep in the guest room. Or go home. You need your sleep."

"Josie, it's not about my sleep." He sips his coffee before taking a seat at the counter and pulling a cinnamon raisin bagel from the bag. "It's about your nightmares. Were you having them before the accident? You didn't the night before the accident when you stayed at my place."

"We were having sex all night. I'm not sure I had the chance to dream. But no. I wasn't having these particular nightmares."

He sighs, setting his mug on the counter with one hand while rubbing the back of his neck with his other hand. His palpable frustration makes the air between us thick with unspoken words. "Is this about the shooting or are you still thinking about the girls or hair or ... whatever?"

I know he thinks my mental status is on shaky ground, and he doesn't want to hear it. "It's uh ..." I stare into my coffee mug. "The girls."

Colten sighs. "Tell me about the nightmares."

I glance up, hesitating with my response until I know he's really ready to listen. "It's always a church-yard. Always long hair tied to the branches. Sometimes I see the girls with their shaved heads. They look terri-fied one minute and dead the next. But it's so magni-fied in my mind's eye that I can't make out a location. I'd say their ages are anywhere from eight to eleven.

All white. The bodies are always buried in cemeteries in recently excavated plots. It might have something to do with Winston Jeffries."

"Who is Winston Jeffries?"

"An infamous serial killer who did this in the late 1800s."

He nods slowly. "I'll look into it. See if there's been any recent copycats."

I pause my coffee mug at my lips. "You will?"

Colten takes a bite of his bagel. "You're a dog with a bone. You always have been. If looking into this helps you let it go, then I'll do whatever it takes. I don't want to spend our entire married life dealing with your dreams."

I sip my coffee and mosey in his direction. "You won't."

Turning to the side, he widens his knees on the stool and pulls me into his body, hands resting on my ass as if it was made for that very reason.

"We're not getting married, so there is a zero percent chance of you spending time *dealing with my dreams* because there is a zero percent chance of me marrying you."

His lips twist as his mind searches for the perfect comeback. "Is it just me? Would you marry some other guy?"

"Tell me why you want to marry me."

"To make it hard for you to get away," he replies without a second's hesitation.

I hug my belly with one hand as I chuckle. It's a lot better, but laughter still gives me a little zing.

Colten takes my coffee from my other hand and sets it next to his before helping me (unnecessarily) onto the stool next to him so that our legs are scissored. I love that he likes to be close, always a part of his body touching mine. And now it makes more sense if he's afraid I'm going to "get away."

"Women have typically received the unfair label of 'ball and chain.' Colten Mosley ... are you saying that you want to be my ball and chain?"

"You've always been a little slippery." He takes another bite of bagel, but it doesn't completely hide his smirk.

"Slippery?"

He nods while swallowing. "One day I was your boyfriend. The next day I wasn't. The second I got another girlfriend, you stalked me, tempted me, pissed off every other girlfriend I attempted to have. You said jump. I asked how high?"

"I never said jump."

His hands slide along my bare legs, just under my nightie, thumbs teasing my inner thighs. "It was a look you gave me. I think it was even the very *first* look you gave me. It said jump, and I was a goner. Did you not see the way *I* looked at you? Every fucking look asked 'how high?' It still does. I don't think it's physically possible for me to walk this earth without gravitating toward you."

Seventeen years ... and not a day's passed that I

haven't thought about Colten, not a day that my thoughts haven't gravitated to my memories of him.

That smile, the one hijacking his lips and gleaming in his eyes ... it's everything. He leans in a few inches from my lips. "Every woman who has asked me if I loved her has received an extended pause for an answer. As long as there is a Josephine Watts walking this earth, I am incapable of loving another woman." He tips his chin and rests his forehead on my collarbone. "You're it. Always have been. Always will be."

"I'll marry you," I whisper.

Colten lifts his head slowly, confusion etched into his face. "What?"

I shrug a shoulder. "I'll marry you, *if* ... you take me to Tennessee."

The confusion deepens. "What's in Tennessee?"

"Sightseeing."

He searches my eyes for a few breaths before grinning. "I'll take you anywhere."

I can't help but mirror his smile. I've loved this boy nearly my whole life.

Colten's lips press to mine. It's slow—lazy Saturday slow. I know he needs to go into work, but he doesn't seem to be in a rush.

Did I really just agree to marry him?

His words have always played me with the ease his fingers drift along ivory keys. He effortlessly makes me want him ... need him.

Ghosting his lips from my mouth to my ear, eliciting a flurry of goose bumps along my skin, he whispers, "How are you feeling this morning?"

"G-good ..." My fingers tease the nape of his neck while my tongue fumbles my words. My heart works a little harder to accommodate all the sensations Colten elicits.

"Want to feel even better?" He sucks the skin below my ear, his hand inching between my legs.

No panties.

Nothing to slow him down.

His finger makes an easy swipe, stopping at my clit, circling, torturing.

I swallow the pooling saliva in my mouth before I end up drooling all over him. My legs spread another inch. He grins just before kissing me again.

The soft satin of my nighty teases my hard nipples, and all I want is to feel his naked body pressed to mine.

He slips two fingers inside of me, fucking me with his hand between my legs and his tongue in my mouth.

My fingers dig into his back as he stands, hunched over me.

Kissing me.

Fingering me.

Rubbing the heel of his hand against my clit while his other hand cups the back of my head, deepening the kiss.

A tiny tug grips my abdominal muscles, but I can't register any discomfort because all I feel is the build up to my orgasm.

Col-colten ... Colten ... oh god ...

He stills his hand and slows the kiss while my body stiffens for a few seconds before melting into a limp state. It pulls a grin from him against my mouth. Of course, he's proud. In a matter of minutes, he's expertly manipulated my mind and my body. Josephine Watts's puppeteer.

Now who's the one asking how high without saying the actual words?

But just to make sure, I frame his face with my hands. "Do you love me, Colten?" I selfishly want one last confirmation. I want what he couldn't give any other woman.

"Yes," he says without hesitation. A wide grin acting as an exclamation point.

I tingle from the aftereffects of the orgasm *and* reality sinking into my conscience. Emotions burn my eyes, but I keep them in check. "I love you too," I whisper, dragging the pad of my thumb over his lip before kissing him again.

CHAPTER
Thirty-Seven

Colten goes into work for a few hours while I do more research. I suppose I should call a bunch of people to tell them I'm engaged, but I really don't care if I'm married to Colten. It's for him, not me.

I won't take his last name.

I won't give him more babies.

I won't do his laundry.

He gets a piece of paper that says I'm legally his wife.

And I get to go to Tennessee with him.

It's a fair exchange.

I do more research on Winston Jeffries, but I can't find anywhere that says the bodies were found.

They're in the cemeteries.

Frustrated, I move on to near-death experiences and get lost in vlogs and YouTube videos. Just when

I'm ready to call it quits for the day, I find a vlog on the fourth search page. No one goes to the fourth search page unless they feel desperate.

Hello. My name is Desperate.

It's a simple vlog about a woman's near-death experience, not at all like mine. She struggled to deal with voices in her head. I don't have voices, just visions. At the end of her vlog, she has a link: *For More Help.*

I click the link.

It takes me to a webpage that's all black except for a tiny light in the middle of the screen and an email in the upper right corner. Clicking on the email link, I send a message:

> *Hello,*
>
> *I came across your information while searching online for near-death experiences. I recently had an experience that has left me with visions that I don't understand. Would we be able to chat sometime?*
>
> *Regards,*
> *Josephine Watts*

"There's my fiancée," Colten says, loosening his tie as he rounds the corner to the living room.

"We're not using those terms." I shoot him a quick look before closing my browser and my computer.

"No?" He scratches his stubbly chin, cocking his head to the side.

"No." I reach for my glass of water on the coffee table, gulping it down until I emerge out of breath.

"Girlfriend?"

My nose wrinkles while I shake my head, returning the glass to the coffee table. "Sounds a little immature."

"Lover?"

"Not a word I'd want you using in public."

"My woman?"

"Caveman."

"Sex toy?"

I snort.

Colten smirks. "Bingo. Sex toy it is. I can't wait to introduce my new sex toy to my friends. Do you, Colten Mosley, take Josephine Watts to be your sex toy for better or worse in sickness and in health until death do you part? Why yes ... yes I do."

I stand, grabbing his loosened tie and pulling him to me. "Last chance to get it right."

His face explodes into amusement while he feathers his knuckles along my cheeks. "You're my Artemis."

He remembers.

My lips twitch, even if I want to act like I don't know what he's talking about.

"She was fiercely protective of those who were considered weak. Reclusive but passionately defensive. A champion of purity ... the virgin kind. I have it on good authority that you are no longer a virgin, but I think the rest still applies. Oh ... and we must not forget her lack of mercy and an overabundance of pride."

"I've caved to your ridiculous need to be my husband, so clearly I've lost a little pride."

"Ouch ..." He stumbles back a step, but I don't let go of his tie. "You wound me, Artemis."

"Stop." I giggle. "Artemis is not going to work. Let's stick with Josie or Dr. Watts."

"I knew you before your titties filled out a bra. And I know they didn't fill out a bra because you showed them to me before you wore a bra. So I don't think I can call you Dr. Watts and keep a straight face."

"Do women still show you their tits for half a Twix? Or now that you're all grown up, do you have to work a little harder for a sneak peek?"

"The question is ... what on earth do your dating app pricks get for a six-course meal if you flashed me for half a Twix?"

"Why are they pricks?"

"Because you're mine."

I shorten my grip on his tie, forcing him a little closer to me. "I wasn't yours when I dated them."

His lips corkscrew, eyes narrowed. "Hmm ... you sure about that?" He's so damn playful. "Do you think it's possible..." his head ducks, relieving the tension on his tie, coming inches from my lips "...that the reason I'm single and so are you is because I've always been yours and you've always been mine?"

I slowly shake my head. "What are you doing?"

His gaze sweeps over my face, the way someone takes in a breathtaking view. I feel it everywhere.

Lifting on to my toes, I rub my nose against his. "I already said yes. You don't have to chase me anymore."

"You deserve to be chased. Pursued. I fell in love with the girl I knew I could never contain. Let me chase you forever because I love that moment when you look back at me and grin. That moment when I know you love knowing that I always have your back."

Jesus ...

I think he broke my heart so easily seventeen years ago because I knew I would never meet another Colten Mosley. He's my once-in-a-lifetime.

"Tell me about Tennessee. What are we doing in Tennessee? You threw that into the conversation this morning like asking me for my wallet while undressing."

I release his tie and head to the kitchen to browse the fridge for dinner options.

"Have a seat. I'll start something," he says.

"I'm fine." I open the fridge and pull out a few bowls of leftovers.

"What's in Tennessee?"

I set the bowls on the counter and turn toward him. It's not that I'm afraid to tell him ... okay, I'm a little afraid. "It's where Winston Jeffries killed all those girls in the late 1800s."

Colten covers his face with one hand, hiding his frustration behind it before letting it fall to his side. "Josie—"

"You said you'd take me anywhere if I agreed to marry you. No stipulations. If you're going to try to talk me out of going, then I'm going to renege on saying yes to your proposal."

The muscles in his jaw flex. He can gnash his teeth all he wants. It won't change anything. He pinches the bridge of his nose. "And what are we going to do there? Get permission to exhume the dead bodies so you can study them?"

"We can't get permission to exhume bodies that haven't been found."

"You said they were buried in a cemetery."

"Yes, but to my knowledge, no one else knows that."

"Jesus, Josie ..." He shakes his head. "Do you hear yourself?"

"You didn't experience what I did."

Colten eyes me with a mix of pain and frustration. "Are we going to every cemetery we can find? Most that probably weren't there in the early 1900s? Are we going to churchyards that weren't churchyards when this Winston guy killed these girls? Are we going to—"

"I don't know!" I turn, feeling the same level of regret that's on Colten's face for pushing me this far. "I don't know," I whisper.

He sighs. "I just don't want to feed your ..."

"My? My what? My craziness? My insanity?"

He glances at the ceiling for a few seconds. "I want you to get better, not worse. I feel like ..." Returning his gaze to me, he frowns. "I feel like you're chasing the boogieman. A year ago, Reagan was so afraid of the boogieman. Well, I think she just called it a monster. So when I had her with me, I promised to stay up all night, standing guard at the end of her bed. After she fell asleep, I went to bed. I woke early the next morning to return to the end of her bed before she woke up. But she was three. You're thirty-five."

I'm hurt that he doesn't believe me. At the same time, I don't know what I expect him to believe because I don't know what's happening to me. "What if during my near-death experience, I was shown a ... vision. A premonition. What if this is not something that has already happened, but is about to happen? Some people have very accurately predicted events in the future. What if I can stop something terrible from happening?"

Colten curls his lips between his teeth while drawing in a long breath. "Do you know how many anonymous tips we get about premonitions? Do you know how many of them come to fruition?"

"How many of them come from people who have had a near-death experience?"

"Josie ..."

I hate the sympathetic expression on his face. It's pure pity.

"For the record, I saw a psychiatrist, and he suggested I go to Tennessee. So even if you think I'm insane, going to Tennessee is not the insane part."

"The psychiatrist you saw right after the accident?"

"No. I saw one the afternoon you called looking for me. The day I took cookies into work."

"Why didn't you tell me?"

"I just did."

He frowns. "Josie ..."

"I didn't tell you that day for the same reason I'm already regretting telling you now. I hate that look on your face."

"Listen, there are several other people I know from the day of the shooting who weren't physically injured, but they're struggling with some PTSD. Not all PTSD is the same. The mind can do weird things after something so stressful. And if you keep having visions in your sleep, maybe you should see a sleep specialist."

"Wow, Dr. Mosley. Did they teach you that in medical school? If only I would have gone to medical school, then I would be smart like you. And an expert on the human brain."

"Josie, don't do this."

I pull a plate from the microwave and hand it to him. "I'll go by myself."

"You're not going to Tennessee by yourself."

I put the other plate in the microwave. "I think we established my age and the ridiculousness of unnecessary fear. Let's stay with that theme and not get overprotective about me going to Tennessee by myself. Believe it or not, before you came back into my life, I did a lot of things by myself, including live by myself."

Colten glances over at me while he fills a glass from the fridge's water dispenser. "You want me to leave?"

"I don't care."

"Well, try. Try to care, Josie. I'm done with the games. They were fun for a while, but I'm not really going to let you pity marry me. If you don't want to marry me, we won't get married. If you don't want me living here, I'll leave." He sets the glass on the counter next to his plate and sits on the barstool.

"By all means, Colten. Whatever you want … whatever you need. I'll try to care, like you cared the day you obliterated my heart seventeen years ago." I hold out my wrists. "I cared then. I care now. So back the fuck up and tell me who doesn't care?"

Colten stares at my arms.

I drop them to my sides. "I don't blame you," I whisper.

"I do," he whispers back to me.

I blink back my tears. "I've wanted one thing since I was a nine-year-old girl trying to win my dad's heart, trying to make friends, trying to find my place in this world."

Colten's gaze lifts to mine. "What?"

Swallowing past the lump of vulnerability in my throat, I ease my head side to side. How can he not know? "You." My hand quickly bats away a tear. "I've hated you so much for so long. Do you have any idea how hard it is to hate someone for that long?"

His Adam's apple bobs as his gaze shifts again, unable to keep it locked to mine.

"It takes *so* much love, the kind of love that relentlessly aches, eating away at your soul. And here we are. You want to live with me, marry me, do all the things that other people do. But I've never been 'other people.' I want you, Colten. Any way I can get you. However, I feel like you want me the way … you want me. I've never been normal. If something really fucked-up is going to happen to someone after a near-death experience, it's going to be me. If that's too much for the adult version of Colten Mosley, then you can have a pass. No hard feelings."

He flinches, shaking his head.

I measure my next words carefully. "The reason my job exists is because not everything in life is what it seems. So even when you show up to a crime scene and find a body that has a bullet hole in the head, you can't definitively say the person died from that gunshot wound. Maybe they died of a drug overdose first, and someone shot them in the head anyway. *I* am the person who goes through the proper steps to make that determination. I deal with facts in my job. I don't write death certificates based on speculation. There is a process. So I'm going to Tennessee because I think it's part of the process. And you can stay here and wait for the chance to say, 'See, I told you it was the bullet to the head.' But I won't care if you're right. It's not about ego. It's about following a process. Facts matter. Sometimes being right is just dumb fucking luck."

Colten blinks a few times and murmurs, "I don't want a pass. Not ever. I'll go with you to Tennessee. You lead. I follow. That's just what we do."

CHAPTER
Thirty-Eight

Thirteen.

Officially teenagers.

I didn't feel a new level of confidence, nor did turning thirteen prompt my parents to give me more freedom.

The very day Josie turned thirteen, she was ready to demand full adulthood freedom. Chief Watts chose that very day to tighten the reins on her.

"Oh my god! My parents gave me a curfew. I mean ... they've always given me a time to be home, but it's not the same time. It's always been dependent on the situation. But now I have to be home by nine on school nights and ten on the weekends. It's ridiculous!" She nearly fell out of the tree from her animated ranting.

"Did you ask them why?"

Josie huffed, blowing the hair away from her eyes.

"They said I'm at the age where I'm more likely to get into trouble or be influenced by other kids. As if I'd do something stupid because someone else told me to do it."

I had a mile-long list of stupid things I had done because someone else told me to do them, and by someone else ... it was Josie.

"You don't have a curfew. I have one because I'm a girl. That's not fair. If my dad is going to call me 'Jo' and dress me in camouflage on the weekends to go hunting, then he needs to give me a boy curfew."

"What's a boy curfew?" I asked, swinging my legs to the same rhythm as hers.

"It's *no* curfew. Gah! Haven't you been listening?"

Listening? Sure, I was listening. I just wasn't focusing on everything. Josie had the best rants. You could tell she was well-read because her vocabulary and ability to build a strong case for her demands far exceeded my abilities or anyone else's who was our age.

"Listen, I heard a group of kids are going to sneak out and spend the night at the cemetery. I think we should go," she said.

"I don't think it's a good idea."

"You don't think anything is a good idea if it involves risk."

"I don't think something is a good idea if the risk involves your dad killing me for not stopping you."

"Fine, I'll go by myself. You stay home and have your mommy read you a bedtime story."

She never played fairly. I always felt coerced by her questioning my bravery. Later, I realized it was a challenge to my masculinity. How masculine did she expect me to be at thirteen? I had like ... four hairs in my armpits and maybe double that in pubic hairs. Nothing on my chest. Nothing on my face.

I sighed and grumbled. "What time are we sneaking out?"

Josie nudged my arm. "I knew you'd come around. My parents should be asleep by eleven. Let's meet out front at eleven-thirty just to play it safe."

She led ... I followed. That was us.

That weekend, I learned a lot about Josephine Watts. Mainly, what I learned was I had underestimated her creepy side.

While kids several years older than us jumped at every sound, freaked out, and ran home early, Josie didn't flinch. She moseyed from headstone to headstone making up stories for what killed each person.

"Beatrice died of a broken heart after her beloved Henry died a year earlier." She traced each name with her finger. "Calvin died when his wife found out he was cheating on her. She murdered him in his sleep, took their two kids, and fled to Canada."

I sat with my back against Beatrice's headstone, her story seemed less haunting. "You've scared everyone off."

Josie shrugged. "The zombie apocalypse isn't real. I don't know why everyone is afraid of dead people. I mean ... they're dead. Just empty bodies."

"Do you believe in Heaven?"

"No. But don't tell my parents. It's funny ... they thought it was okay for me to believe in Santa Claus and the Easter Bunny because they thought it was fun and cute. But them believing in God is even more ridiculous because they're adults. They should know better than to believe in something you can't prove. Right?"

She was asking the wrong person. I believed in God. There had to be a god and a Heaven so that there could be the devil and a Hell. My dad was going to Hell for cheating on my mom, the way Calvin's soul was probably in Hell for cheating on his wife in Josie's made-up world.

"Can you imagine being buried alive?" I asked.

"That doesn't happen very often. Instead of putting bells on the corpse's toes like they used to do, they use machines to see if the heart is working. That's what Roland Tompkins told us. Don't you remember? You were there too."

I spaced off during Josie's long conversations with the undertaker. Mostly, I thought about my next meal, but occasionally I'd imagine what songs would be played on the organ. Probably Schubert's *Ave Maria* or Handel's one about feeding his flock.

"When I die, I'm going to donate my body to science. After, of course, I donate my organs. Well, I suppose it will be my family donating my organs, if I have a family. My parents might be dead by then. I'm not getting married or having kids, so I won't have them to make that decision. Maybe Benji will do it for me. What do you want done with your body, Colten?"

"I want to be buried in a cemetery so my family can visit me."

"That's selfish. You should save lives by donating your organs. And help medical students by donating the remains of your body to science. When they're done with your body, your family will get the ashes. I don't know … maybe they can bury the ashes, and you can still have a headstone. We'll ask Roland when we see him again."

"Why are you not getting married? Who's going to love you when your parents are dead?"

"Benji."

"What if your parents got in a car accident with Benji, and they all died, leaving you with no family except grandparents who will probably die before you? Then what?"

Josie traced the name on another headstone. I couldn't see it; we were too far away, and the closest streetlight flickered off. "Then you'll have to love me. That's what friends do, right?"

"No. Friends like each other; they don't love each other."

She scoffed. "You can love a friend without it being … you know … more than friends. And we've kissed, so we're sometimes more than friends."

"Well, I'm going to get married. I bet you do too. My mom always tells me the future is unpredictable.

Whatever I'm thinking now probably won't be what actually happens to me."

"BOO!"

I nearly pooped my pants when Josie sneaked up behind Beatrice's headstone.

"Ha! Scared you." She plopped down beside me.

"D-did not," I insisted despite my hammering heart and stuttered words.

She rested her head on my shoulder. "Colten?"

"Hmm?"

"If nobody else wants my ashes, will you take them?"

I had no idea what I was going to do with them, but she seemed sincere, so I nodded. "Sure."

CHAPTER
Thirty-Nine

A WEEK before our scheduled trip to Tennessee, Colten makes arrangements for Reagan to come for the weekend. I use it as an excuse to send him home for a bit. I know I'm keeping him awake at night. It's undeniable in his tired eyes and incessant yawning.

Since our argument two weeks ago, we haven't discussed the marriage. He didn't want a pity marriage, and I didn't say anything to correct him. Now, it's awkward. I really don't know where we stand. It's like the fight didn't happen, but it's also like he didn't propose, and I didn't say yes. I've been too preoccupied with my nonstop research to focus on where we stand.

After taking Reagan out for pizza Friday night, we watch a movie at his place. Reagan makes herself comfy in the big recliner with at least three blankets while Colten and I take the sofa.

I feel his eyes on me more than the TV, and I suppress the urge to ask him why he's doing it.

"Bedtime, Button," he says to Reagan as soon as the movie ends.

"Will you read me a story?"

He folds her three blankets. "Of course."

"Will Josie read one too?"

I smile. "Uh ... sure."

"Why don't you head upstairs with Josie. Get your teeth brushed and pick out a story. I'm going to do a few things in the kitchen, and then I'll be up."

Reagan heads upstairs as I stand from the sofa.

"Coming, Josie?" she yells from the top of the stairs.

Colten grins. "She adores you."

I roll my eyes. She hasn't known me long enough to adore me. "I'm coming."

While Reagan brushes her teeth, I wait in her bedroom. It's an explosion of pink paint, a mural of a white cat, and a dozen or so stuffed animals covering the single bed. I remove the stuffed animals and flip through the books on the shelf by her bed.

"Ready!" Reagan flies into the bedroom and leaps onto the bed. "Oh, my ponytail." She tugs at the elastic, and it gets tangled. "Help, please."

I work her hair out of the knot, freeing the elastic. Then I slowly run my fingers through her long hair. Winston Jeffries would have loved Reagan's hair. As soon as that awful thought enters my head, I pull my hand away from her head. "So ... what story are we reading tonight?"

"That one. *Magic Treehouse.*" She points to a book on the top shelf. "Chapter four."

"You remember what chapter you were on?" I laugh, grabbing the book.

"Yep." Reagan settles under the covers after grabbing a stuffed penguin from the floor and hugging it.

"That's a cool cat on your wall. I wonder who painted it."

"My daddy."

I chuckle, but Reagan is dead serious.

"Wow ... I had no idea your dad could paint."

"Grandma Mosley said Daddy can do everything."

I don't doubt that.

By the time I'm done reading a chapter, she's asleep. I put the bookmark in the book, slide it back on the shelf, and take a minute to stare at her in a peaceful slumber. Her dark hair framing her face. Her long eyelashes resting on her pink cheeks. Her flawless skin. I imagine she's what an angel would look like.

This little girl is part of Colten. He willingly (even if unknowingly) gave a piece of himself to another woman, and they created a life together. I think Reagan is special. Delightful. All the things an innocent child should be. So why don't I wish she was mine? Why don't I wish it was me who made a life with Colten?

The lack of those feelings makes me feel broken inside as a human. There are many people in the world who have no desire to procreate. I'm sure they don't feel broken. Maybe they made that decision later in life, as adults. They assessed their life, their careers, and their aspirations, and they decided parenthood wasn't for them.

Not me. I've *never* wanted children. I never played with stuffed animals or baby dolls and pretended to be their mommy. I have no maternal feelings. No ticking biological clock.

After shutting off the light, I gently pull her door partially closed just as Colten climbs the stairs.

"She asleep?" he whispers.

I nod.

"Thanks for reading to her." He stops on his way to her room, takes my face in his hands, and gives me a soft kiss, ending with a smile. "Be right back. I need to kiss her goodnight."

Of course, he's kissing her goodnight. That's what he does. He pulls dying women from the water. Kisses his daughter goodnight. And paints murals of cats. He's a normal human with normal instincts and feelings.

"You're leaving?" he asks on his way down the stairs.

I slide my feet into my sandals. "I am."

"You're allowed to stay here." He pulls me into his arms, my back to his chest.

I grin when he buries his face in the crook of my neck. "You paint, Colten? You painted that cat?"

"She asked. I said I'd give it a go."

"Give it a go ..." I laugh. "Are you bad at anything?"

"Apparently, I'm bad at convincing you to stay the night. I think I've been bad at convincing you to do anything ... ever. You always leave me guessing where I stand in your life."

I turn in his arms, sliding my hands into his back pockets. "I said I'd marry you. What more do you want?"

"I want you to *want* to marry me." He gathers my hair and pulls it off my shoulders, giving it a playful tug.

Lifting onto my toes, I press a soft kiss to the corner of his mouth. Taking several steps backward toward the front door, I shake my head and turn the handle. "Colten Mosley, you should know me better by now." I turn and head toward my car without shutting the front door. "I would never do anything I didn't want to do."

Just as I unlock my car, he calls, "So you *want* to marry me?"

"So it would seem."

"Fine. Stop begging. I'll marry you, Josephine Watts."

HOURS LATER, I wake in a sweat, heart ready to burst from my chest and a clawing panic eating me alive. Something is so very wrong with me. For the first time, I question if I was supposed to live. Maybe Colten made a mistake by saving me. These are not dreams. They are fragments of reality. Whose reality? I don't know.

Is this a warning? Has the future been given to me? My mind doesn't work this way. I thrive on reason and explanation. Science. Testing. Solid data.

There are so many girls. So many bodies.

Grabbing my computer from my nightstand, I open it and start searching for answers. Two unsuccessful hours later, a new email chimes, and I open it.

It's from the parapsychologist I messaged in desperation a while back.

Namaste, Josephine.

    I have a feeling you've come to the right place. I can see you on the 14th.

    3:00 p.m.

    Athelinda

She left her address—in Berkeley, California.

I'm not flying to California. Even thinking about it makes me want to commit myself to a mental institution. I might have considered a day drive, but there's no way I can justify airfare to meet with a person I found from a fourth page internet search.

Dear Athelinda,

    Thank you for replying to my message. However, I live in Illinois. I will continue to look for help closer to me.

    Regards,

    Josephine

I stare at the time on my computer. 3:25 a.m.

Again, my email chimes. It's Athelinda. I realize she's on West Coast time, but it's still the middle of the night there.

Josephine,

It's two weeks out. If you're experiencing what I feel you're experiencing, it will not get better. It will get more intense. I'll save the date and time for you.

Athelinda

What she "feels" I'm experiencing? I've sent her two brief emails. How can she possibly have any sort of feeling about me or my situation?

I don't respond. It would seem like I'm arguing with her. There's no sense in engaging her anymore. I'm not going.

Sighing, I close my computer and rub my eyes before nestling back under the covers. My hand stretches across the bed to the empty spot.

I miss him.

I've missed him for seventeen years.

Colten wants to know where he stands in my life? In the middle. He's always in the middle of my thoughts with every other thought tripping over him.

Do I want to get married? No.

Do I want to be a wife? No.

Those are basic facts. Always have been.

Do I want to marry Colten? Do I want to be his wife?

Those are different questions. He's the exception to everything. He's always been the exception.

I've never liked carrot cake, but I love his mom's carrot cake. It's the exception. I don't know why. Is there a secret ingredient?

What's Colten's secret ingredient? I don't think I'll ever know. It's just *something*.

CHAPTER
Forty

Colten has a busy week preparing to be away from work for a few days for our trip to Nashville, so I don't see him.

I fall into the black hole of the internet. Every time I get lost there, I emerge with two possible conclusions: I either have a legitimate mental illness, or I have a brain tumor that the neurologist missed.

Reading someone else's mind is a distant third, but I don't like that one because I don't believe that's possible, and therefore it makes me feel mentally ill. Also, it imparts a responsibility to figure out whose mind I'm reading before they follow through with these murders.

On Thursday, Alicia stops by with tacos and a sinful chocolate cake.

"You look so good. Are you feeling as good as you

look?" she asks when I take the cake from her and close the front door.

"Mentally or physically?"

"Uh ..." She chuckles. "Both."

"Physically, I'm doing really well. I'm ready for work."

"Are you lifting heavy stuff?"

"Not yet." I grab plates while she pulls the containers of tacos from the sack.

"There's no way Cornwell will let you come back to work before you can lift heavy things. Last week, we had a four-hundred-pound man whom we nearly flipped onto the floor while trying to turn him."

"I'll lift with my legs."

"Pfft." Alicia rolls her eyes as we take a seat on the sofa with our plates of tacos. "How are you doing mentally? Any PTSD?"

"That's a really complicated question." I lean forward, biting into the soft shell fish taco.

"How so?"

I press a paper napkin to my lips and swallow. "I see things."

"Vision issues? Floaters?"

"No. I saw something; I had a vision, when I was unconscious or when my heart stopped."

"What did you see?" she mumbles over a mouthful of food.

I stare at her while she stares at her next bite of taco. Is she ready for this? "I saw long locks of hair hanging from trees in churchyards. I saw young girls having their heads shaved. I saw their bodies being buried on top of other dead bodies in cemeteries."

Alicia's taco drops from her hand back to her plate, eyes unblinking, lips parted with a little sauce smudged on the side of her mouth. After a few seconds, she swallows hard and licks the sauce. "That's uh ... weird. I mean ... probably not unheard of for people in our line of work. Is it related to a case you worked on? Is it the serial killer you were asking Cornwell about?"

"Maybe. I'm not sure anymore. If it would have been just once, I would not be thinking about it. I see disturbing things all the time. I don't have an issue letting them go. But I keep seeing things. The hair. The girls. The graves. I see them when I sleep, but the visions are equally as clear when I'm awake. So tomorrow, I'm going to Tennessee because I feel this clawing need to go there since the only thing I can find online that matches my visions is Jeffries. He was a serial killer who was executed in the early 1900s. He shaved the girls' heads. Tied their hair to churchyard trees. And buried the bodies in cemeteries over preexisting bodies. And since I can't find anywhere that says the bodies were ever found ... well, I just need to know." My words come out in a long trail, building momentum and leaving me breathless.

Alicia waits to respond. What's there to say? I'm mentally struggling. It's not a side she's seen of me because it didn't exist before now.

"I don't think it's a good idea for you to go to Tennessee by yourself."

"I'm not." I take a bite of my food. Then another bite. And another bite.

Alicia waits.

I chew, avoiding eye contact with her.

"So ... who's going with you?"

"Colten," I mumble.

"Detective Mosley?"

I nod.

"Are you on good terms with him again? I thought you held some animosity from the past. Are you friends again?"

"I think we're getting married."

"WHAT?"

Glancing over at her, I give her a sheepish grin. It's all I have to offer.

"Why?" she asks.

It's a valid question.

"I think the love part of our love-hate relationship might be more powerful than the hate."

She coughs a laugh. "Oh my gosh ... you're serious?"

"I think so. Right now, I have bigger things occupying my mind, so—"

"Where's the ring?"

"What?" I ask before taking a drink.

"The engagement ring. He didn't propose without a ring, did he?"

I stare at my left hand for a split second. "Oh, no ring. It wasn't that kind of proposal."

"Um ... what does that mean? I didn't know there were different kinds of proposals."

I wave my hand as though I can brush off the skepticism in her words. "It was spontaneous. Which is really more romantic, right? And I wasn't keen on the idea since I've never wanted to get married. But Colten has been the exception in my life for just about everything. Then, one day, he said some incredibly nice and heartfelt things to me, and I realized being married to him wouldn't be the worst thing ever. So I agreed to marry him."

Then he fingered me until I nearly fell off the kitchen stool. And they lived happily ever after. The end.

"That's ..." She grapples for words.

I point to the last bite of my taco. "These are the best tacos. Why haven't we had these before?"

"You see dead people and you're marrying Detective Mosley. And you want to talk about the tacos?"

"They're *really* good."

Alicia shakes her head a half dozen times. "When's the wedding? Did you tell Cornwell? Have you told your parents? What are you going to do in Tennessee? Dig up graves?" She sets her plate onto the coffee table and runs her hands through her hair. "Shit ... what are you going to do if you find the bodies? They'll arrest you. Quarantine you. Torture you with tests and experiments and then dissect your brain."

"That's a little extreme." I roll my eyes. If I'm honest, I've thought of all of that, even worse.

"Colten. Fucking. Mosley." She shakes her head and grins.

I chuckle. "Yep. I've said those three words just like that so many times."

"Is your family excited? They have to be. What about his family?"

My lips corkscrew. I haven't told anyone besides Alicia. And I assume Colten hasn't either, but I'm not sure. "We haven't shared the news. And maybe you should keep it to yourself until we do. Okay?"

Alicia's grin swells. "Aw ... I feel so special."

"That was my goal." I give her a toothy grin.

She laughs.

CHAPTER
Forty-One

Colten and I don't converse much on the flight to Nashville. It's not a romantic weekend getaway. We're not visiting family. It's not even a funeral.

"Where to first?" Colten asks when we get into our rental car.

"Just … drive," I say, feeling a little off. The visions in my head becoming clearer.

"Okey dokey." He drives.

I scan the area for a few miles. "Turn right up here."

Colten gives me a quick sidelong glance then turns on his turning signal. A mile or so down that road, I whisper, "Next right."

He turns.

We take a left and one more right outside of the city.

"Stop!"

Colten slows and pulls onto the shoulder. I don't wait for him to completely stop before I jump out and jog toward a house on some acreage.

"Josie!" Colten chases after me.

The property has a wood fence corralling several horses in a lush pasture that leads to a barn and a sprawling house. A mansion, really.

"Jesus, Josie ... you're trespassing. And running. You're not supposed to be running." He grabs my arm.

I rip it from his hold and continue running in the same direction, stopping under a large oak tree.

Breathless.

A little scared.

And tingly all over.

"This is the tree. The first tree I saw," I say between labored breaths. "The day of the shooting."

"How do you know? How can you possibly know this?"

"I just ... do."

I see the hair flowing in the wind, all tied to the same branch. Two shades of brown and the longest locks in a nearly white blond. The barn stands where the church used to be. A tiny brick church with a steeple-covered bell.

I run my fingers along the rough bark. "This tree has been here for generations," I whisper. "Like every body that ends up on my table ... it has a story to tell."

"What's the story?"

I ease my head side to side. "I'm not sure, but I feel it. I'm going to know."

Colten walks around the tree, glancing up at the branches and flickering leaves. "When will you know?"

I close my eyes, letting my fingers slide down the trunk. "Soon."

"Josie, we need to go."

I open my eyes, following the sound of gravel crunching beneath tires. A white extended-cab truck rolls to a stop. A bearded man in jeans and a black button-down climbs out. He reaches behind the seat and retrieves a rifle.

Colten steps in front of me, putting himself between me and the man.

"This is private property," the man says in a gruff voice while taking slow but long strides toward us, gripping the gun with both hands across his body.

"Our apologies. We were just leav—"

I shoulder my way past Colten. "Is this the tree?"

"I said it's private property. It's not open to sightsee-ing." His grip tightens on the gun as the distance between us fades.

"Did Winston Jeffries tie young girls' hair to this tree?"

The man slowly peels off his sunglasses, revealing his dark squinted eyes and leathery crow's feet.

"Josie, let's go." Colten's hand cuffs my wrist.

"Who wants to know?" the man asks.

"I do," I say.

"Why?" He stops eight feet from us.

"Peace of mind."

He chuckles, coughing several times. A smoker's cough, wheezing and cackling. "Why on earth would knowing such a thing give you peace of mind?"

"Because I died eight weeks ago, and before they resuscitated me, I saw this exact tree."

He slides his sunglasses back onto his stony face. "I'll give you ten seconds to get the hell off my property, you crazy bitch."

"Thank you for your time. We are leaving right now." Colten grips both of my arms and guides me toward the fence and our rental car. "I think you've had your gunshot wound quota met for the year or, for that matter, this lifetime. Wouldn't you agree?"

"It's the tree. He all but said it. Did you catch that? It's the tree, Colten." I knew I was right from the second I saw it. I knew how to get to the tree without knowing where it lived. I feel vindicated and completely terrified.

Colten helps me over the fence and opens the car door. He doesn't say a word on the way to our hotel. He stops by a burger joint and orders food, but he doesn't ask me what I want. Maybe he thinks not talking about it will make it go away. I wish that were true.

I sip my drink without touching my food while he eats, occasionally glancing out the hotel room window. We each sit on our respective beds for nearly an hour, backs parked against the headboard, legs stretched out long.

"Josie," he exhales, breaking the droning rhythm in

my ears of the air conditioner, "how do you know that? Did you see it online? I know you've researched this ad nauseam. You must have seen images. Videos. Something. It's the *only* explanation. I know it. And if you really think about it, you know it too."

If I really think about it.

I've thought of nothing else.

"What if the bodies are there?" I whisper.

"Where?"

Sliding my legs off the side of the bed, I tip my chin and stare at my bare feet. "The place we're going tonight."

"THIS IS a class C felony punishable by up to ten years in prison and up to a ten thousand dollar fine," Colten says as I choose my shovel in the aisle of the home improvement store.

"Then we'll just get one shovel, and you'll wait in the car. Isn't being an accessory to a crime a little more forgivable in the eyes of the law?"

"I'll lose my badge."

Satisfied with the yellow shovel with a black handle, I head toward the checkout. "Then I'll take you back to the hotel first."

He mumbles something I can't quite decipher. When I get to the checkout and set down my shovel, a second shovel slides in next to mine along with two pairs of leather gloves Colten grabs from a checkout display. I meet his gaze, and he shrugs.

When she gives us our total, I reach for my credit card, but Colten hands her cash and gives me a look.

Okay. No tracking this purchase.

As we maneuver the shovels into the back of the vehicle, I ask, "Why?"

He shuts the hatchback and shrugs. "You give a new meaning to doggedly chasing your dreams. And I'm your ..." He sighs, sliding his hands along my face, fingers into my hair.

"You're my ride-or-die?"

He nods slowly.

Swallowing past the lump in my throat, I pull away and climb into the vehicle.

"Where are we going?" he asks, fastening his seat belt.

"Just drive."

Again, without further questions, he drives. I give him directions. I don't know where they came from, but they're in my head. Every right and left come out of my mouth on instinct until we stop at an old cemetery.

I'm eerily calm given the fact that I could be in jail by the end of the night. Colten follows my lead as we carry our shovels through the graveyard to the far corner, using the lights on our phones to guide our way. It's a magnetic feeling. The closer we get to the spot, the stronger the feeling gets.

I drop my phone and the shovel, squeezing my eyes

shut and pressing the heels of my hands to my eyes. "N-no ... No. No. No."

"Josie." Colten drops his shovel and pulls me into his arms. "What is it?"

Panic slices through my nerves, acid in my throat, a hundred pounds on my chest. I'm not asleep, but I can see it so clearly.

Elizabeth Allen

"They're close ... so close." I crack, choking on a sob as I see two girls, one halfway covering the other. Both facedown. Both with their heads shaven.

Dead.

"The dirt is ... f-freshly tilled." I grip Colten's shirt. I don't want to take a step closer, but I can't force myself to go backward either.

"Josie, tell me what to do. We can go home. Let's just go home." He alternates between stroking my hair and kissing my head.

"I ... can't." I want to. I so badly want to turn around and go home, but I can't run from what's in my head. It won't let me hide.

Taking a step back, I wipe my face. "Look for Elizabeth Allen," I whisper.

Colten picks up my phone and hands it to me. With the light of it between us, I see the horror on his face. He's not afraid of what we're about to find because he doesn't believe there's anything to find. That look is heartbreak. He loves a woman who is no longer the woman he remembers. Colten thinks he's slowly losing me. I think I'm slowly losing me too.

"Elizabeth Allen," I repeat taking back my phone.

He nods once, turning left while I go right because I'm being pulled right, each move no longer mine. Every decision is made before my consciousness has a chance to give it a second thought.

The rays of light from my phone drift from one headstone to the next until landing on Elizabeth Allen. Covering my mouth with my free hand, I stifle another sob. I've *never* wanted to be so wrong as what I want to be right now.

Why am I right?

Why do I know this?

How do I know this?

"Jesus ..." Colten whispers at my back. "How ... how did you know that name?"

I don't answer because I don't have the answer. I only have these terrible visions and the growing pain that comes with them. He's inches from me, yet ... I've never felt so incredibly alone. "Where's my shovel?" I mumble.

"You shouldn't be shoveling. You're not healed." He stabs his shovel into the ground. It brings a new round of tears to my eyes. He's risking everything for me.

I hold the light while he unearths the vision that's been haunting me for nearly two months. He's unearthing every night of stolen sleep. He's unearthing the unimaginable.

The dirt piles up next to me, the hole hollowing by the second. It's starting to feel as hollow as my soul.

"Stop," I whisper.

He doesn't hear me.

"Stop!"

Colten wipes his sweaty brow. I feel his questioning gaze on me, but I can't tear my eyes off the hole he dug. He climbs out of the hole.

"Josie!"

I jump into the hole. Falling to my knees, I claw at the cold dirt until my fingertips graze the brittle remains. Feeling tortured into submission, my mind stretches past its limits, grasping for truth, for reason. An explanation.

Pulling the last layer of dirt toward me, the human remains come into view.

"Josie, get out of the hole."

I start to cry again, but this time, I can't stifle it.

"Josie, don't touch anything else. Get out of the hole." When Colten's hand slides around my arm, pulling me to my feet, I try to find my legs, but I can't. He drags my limp body out of the hole like I imagine he pulled me out of the water after I died.

"I have to call this in. Josie, do you hear me?"

"C-Colten ..."

He cradles my tear drenched face while my lower lip quivers.

My gaze makes a painful ascent to his as my mind finds that explanation that's been just beyond reach until now. "I'm still in that hole."

"What are you talking about?" His face scrunches into confusion, his breathing as labored as mine.

"I think I was one of those girls Winston Jeffries murdered." My gaze averts to the grave again before quickly returning to Colten. "I found ... myself."

After a few breaths, he takes a step back and brings his phone to his ear.

CHAPTER
Forty-Two

THIS TRIP to Nashville was supposed to be closure, the end to Josie's wandering thoughts. This trip was supposed to give her mind a sense of relief so she could sleep.

Heal.

Work.

Marry me.

As suspicious and downright eerie as the journey to the oak tree felt, the owner gave us nothing definitive, and that allowed me to keep things in perspective, even if it only fed Josie's obsession.

Purchasing shovels? Fine. It wasn't a crime … yet.

Letting her guide me to the cemetery? Suspicious, but possible. After all, she's done so much online research.

Even as I felt my career crumbling with each shovelful of dirt, I clung to a hope for closure. If I dug long enough, I would reach Elizabeth Allen's casket. I knew it in my gut.

Now, while officials arrive at the scene, while I watch them tape off the area, call in more experts, do all the things I've done so many times ... reality finds its way into my head. A brain worm infesting every inch of space.

"Tell the truth, Josie. No matter what they ask you, tell *your* truth. Tell them about your accident. The visions. The sleepless nights. The tree. Tell them about the unrelenting need to come here. Because if those remains belong to girls who were murdered well over a century ago, then you're not the killer. Tell them the truth, and let them deal with the rest."

She says nothing.

We reach the road, and they escort us to the back of a police cruiser. They have questions to ask, and we'll give them answers, even if they aren't going to like said answers. They will despise Josie's explanation, but they won't be able to formulate a better one. The unexplainable, sometimes "other-worldly" explanation for an event is something that haunts every investigator. We can't solve crimes without tangible proof, an eyewitness, or a confession that matches the crime.

On the way to the station, I reach for her hand and squeeze it, but she doesn't squeeze mine back. When we're questioned, she tells her truth, void of all emotion, and I tell mine. We're looked upon with skepticism because, after all, I'm a homicide detective from

Chicago, and she's a medical examiner. We came a long way to dig up the unsolved mystery from a crime that was committed way before anyone alive today was even born.

"Josie, you're going to have to talk to me," I say when we reach the hotel after being told to not leave town until they can question us more tomorrow.

She shuffles her feet into the room and stands at the window, staring out into the night. "What do you want to talk about?"

I don't know.

I have all the same questions as the police asked us tonight. I have all the same questions that they'll ask us tomorrow. She's not insane ... I mean, she found remains of bodies that were not in a casket. I don't know if they'll be able to identify the bodies, but they need to find an explanation better than Josie's for why the remains were there if we're not to believe her.

"I don't think you're mentally ill, insane, crazy ... whatever fucking word you want to use. I think this situation is what's crazy. It doesn't make sense in a way that my brain can comprehend."

"I know," she whispers.

I take a few more steps, standing behind her for several breaths before wrapping my arms around her, dipping my head to bring my lips close to her ear. "I love you, Josephine Watts."

With those words, she sucks in a breath and lets it out in a shaky exhale while wiping a few tears.

"Why do you think you were one of those girls? Does it feel like the only explanation?"

She eases her head side to side. "Because I felt it."

"Felt what?"

"The straight blade along my scalp. And ... the fear."

MEMORIES OF A LIFE
COLTEN & JOSIE: PART TWO

CHAPTER
One

"Colten messages me hourly. Does he really think I want to know what he had for lunch? Does he need to know our dinner plans at ten in the morning? Do I care that a friend of a friend is pregnant with triplets?"

Dr. Byrd rests an ankle on his opposing knee, wearing an expression of deep thought.

I continue, "He bought new black boots for work. His mom is taking water aerobics. A funny TikTok. Detective Rains has a hangnail." I roll my eyes. "Okay, not that one, but nearly as ridiculous. He sends all these messages when what he really wants to say is, 'Are you doing okay? Have you thought about that girl, the one you think you were? Have you made an appointment with your psychiatrist? Are you still planning on marrying me? Have you told anyone else about your theory?'"

"Have you?" Dr. Byrd asks.

"Listen … it's not a theory. I haven't been wrong once since the day I woke from my near-death experience. I want to be wrong. This isn't the kind of 'right' anyone would find satisfying. But no, I haven't told anyone except the Nashville police. If I didn't have the credentials that I do, there's little doubt that I would have been committed by now."

"Do you believe in reincarnation?" he asks.

"I think I've reached the point of 'if it walks like a duck and talks like a duck.' Tomorrow the clouds could part and angels could descend from heaven. If that happens, even the most headstrong atheists will take a moment to rethink their beliefs. So … yeah. I'm inclined to believe in reincarnation since I have such inexplicable things in my head from a time way before the existence of Josephine Watts from Des Moines, Iowa."

"Tell me about the girl."

"The one I was in another life?"

He nods.

I shake my head. "I don't know. I just remember the feeling. Feeling scared. Feeling the edge of the straight blade against my scalp. It cut me. He told me to hold still."

"Who told you?"

"Winston Jeffries."

"Are you sure?"

I glance up at Dr. Byrd. "Who else would it be?"

"I don't know. I just want to know if you're sure it

was him or if you might be deducing it from the information you've gathered online coupled with the visions in your head."

"No. I mean ..." I rub my temples. "I don't know. I just want to forget. Whatever's in my head, I want to forget it. I felt a responsibility to follow through and figure it out. Now that I have, I just want to forget about it. It wasn't a premonition. I don't feel the urgency to prevent these girls from dying."

"Are you back to work?"

"Two weeks." I blow out a long breath. "I need work. I need my mind to find its place again."

"And the engagement? Are you making wedding plans?"

I laugh. "No. I haven't told my parents yet."

"Why?"

"Because ..." I shake my head. "I don't know if I can be that girl he murdered *and* be a bridezilla."

"Has Colten told his family?"

"I don't know."

"You haven't asked him?"

"He's ... I don't know. He's okay, yet not okay. Colten and I have always danced around the truth. For as long as I can remember, we've made our own reality. We've had front row seats to watching the rest of the world and acting like it doesn't affect us if we don't let it."

"How has that worked for you?"

"It's amazing, until it's catastrophically heartbreaking."

Dr. Byrd gives me a slow nod. He's clueless. I don't

mean it disrespectfully. I'm his "undetermined." Undetermined sucks.

We wind up our session with me feeling none the better. If I'm not going to let him medicate me, he's helpless. I don't think patients with near-death experiences comprise a large percentage of his clientele.

When I get home, I scroll through my emails to find the parapsychologist in Berkeley. I missed my appointment. It's time to reschedule.

CHAPTER
Two

Two students dressed in trench coats went on a shooting spree at Columbine High in Littleton, Colorado.

Colten's mom refused to let him watch the news. She wanted to protect him and his brother from such evil. We were twelve, so it wasn't out of line with good parenting.

"Let's talk about this," Dad said to me a few nights after the horrific massacre. He and Mom sat me down at the kitchen table, and we discussed the events. It's not that my parents weren't "good" parents; they just had a different definition of good parenting.

"We don't want you to be afraid to go to school," Mom said, setting a plate of cookies and a glass of milk next to me.

"I'm not."

"That's good, but if you have questions—"

"Someone said they were bullied in school, and that's why they did it," I said.

"Well, we might never know since they're no longer alive." Dad leaned back a fraction and crossed his thick arms.

"What if they weren't bullied?"

"What do you mean?" he asks.

"What if they just wanted to kill people because ... they liked it?"

Rarely were my parents speechless, but that night, they had nothing. Not one word.

Finally, Mom cleared her throat. "Why do you think anyone would kill other humans for ... fun?"

I shrugged. "I overheard one of my teachers talking to another teacher in the hallway. She said the boys were psychopaths. So I stopped by the library on my way home from school and looked up psychopath."

"Um ... Jo, you're twelve. I don't think it's a good idea for a twelve-year-old to study psychopaths." Dad's face wrinkled. "It's a lot for your immature brain."

"Nothing is wrong with my brain. You've always said I'm too smart for my own good."

They laughed, but it was an uneasy laugh.

"If they were bullied, it would mean they hated the kids they killed. But psychopaths don't have feelings like that. They think they are better than everyone else. They don't feel bad about the things they do. They don't think about what other people are feeling when they do bad things to them. They don't have any regrets. Can you imagine doing bad things and not feeling guilty? You don't feel guilty when you shoot a deer, do you, Dad? Or if you have to shoot a bank robber, right?"

Dad coughed, bringing his fist to his mouth and easing his head side to side. "That's ... that's different, Jo. I'm not a psychopath. I would never hurt innocent people, and if I did by accident, I would feel terrible. Remorseful. Pained."

I roll my eyes. "I wasn't calling you a psychopath. I'm just saying, maybe those two boys had something wrong with them that made them not feel bad about killing other humans the way you don't feel bad about the deer. Dustin Santi told me people eat dogs in other countries the way we eat cows or chickens here. So what I think is kinda weird and gross is not weird and gross to other people. I bet those two boys who killed those kids would have eaten dogs. Don't you think?"

For the second time that night, I left my parents speechless.

While other kids at my school were lined up at the door to the guidance counselor's office to discuss how scared they were by the Columbine shooting, I was eating cookies and milk with my parents while discussing psychopaths and other cultures eating puppy dogs.

"Listen, sweetie, maybe don't talk about this with other kids ... or even other adults for that matter," Mom said.

"About psychopaths or about eating puppy dogs?" I

dipped my last bite of cookie into the milk.

My parents shared a look. "Both," Mom said.

"Why?"

"Because it's not just kids who are in shock and scared; it's adults too. Parents are having a hard time sending their kids to school because they're worried it could happen to them."

"I've been going to school. Are you worried about me?"

"We love you. And of course we'd be devastated if anything happened to you, but the chances of it happening to you at your school are really, really slim. You have a better chance of dying in a car accident," Mom said.

"Or getting hit by lightning," Dad added.

Mom shot him a scowl.

He lifted a shoulder. "What? It's true."

"I'm going to Colten's." I stood, taking my glass to the sink.

"Don't talk about it with Colten either. Okay?" Mom stressed.

I nodded, giving her a stiff smile before shoving my feet into my sneakers, pulling on a hoodie, and running across the street.

"Hey, Josie." Becca smiled, opening the front door. "Colten's upstairs, practicing piano."

I stepped inside, toeing off my shoes.

"How are you doing, hon?" she asked with an ugly, concerned look on her face.

"Fine. Why?"

"Have your parents talked with you about Columbine?"

"Uh-huh. They said not to discuss it with anyone … and I mean anyone."

Her pink lips parted, and she gave me a single slow nod. "Of course."

"I'm going to see if Colten's about done."

"O-okay." She seemed a little off as I zipped past her, straight up the stairs.

My momentum came to a screeching halt when I reached Colten's bedroom door. His fingers played the saddest song I had ever heard. I tiptoed a little closer. His body moved with the music like the metronome on Vera's piano.

Colten was only one of three boys who I knew that played the piano. He was also the best. I wasn't the best at anything. I wasn't liked by everyone like Colten. My "uniqueness" never felt special, just different. Not Colten. He was special. He could do everything. And most days I felt certain the only reason he was my friend was because my dad was police chief. Sure, I was smart. Who really cared about that yet? No twelve-year-olds talked about honor roll or scholarships. They couldn't pronounce valedictorian let alone care about it.

"Josie, you're such a creeper," Colten mumbled without stopping his fingers.

I sighed and sat next to him on the piano bench, facing away from the keys. "Why are you playing such a sad song?"

"Why is it sad?"

"Because it's slow. It's funeral music."

"Have you been to a funeral?" He stopped playing and angled his body toward mine.

"No." I frowned. "Not yet anyway. Nobody I know will die."

His head jutted backward. "That's mean. You sound like you want someone to die so you can go to their funeral."

"I'm curious. That's all. I don't want someone to die. Not like those boys in Colorado, who killed the kids at their school."

Oops ... I may have broken my promise to my parents.

"My mom said they were sick. Not like a cold. Like something was wrong with their brains," Colten said.

"Psychopaths. I stopped by the library and looked it up. Don't worry. You're not a psychopath."

"I know I'm not. But ... how would you know?"

"Because you say sorry a lot, and you mean it. I say sorry too, but I don't always mean it. But if you died, I would be sad. So I know I'm not a psychopath either. But I've been thinking a lot about it. Do you think Richie Gregg is one? He's mean to everyone. When he gets in trouble, he doesn't care. And his dad smokes in the car when he picks Richie up from school. My dad said parents who smoke in the car with their kids don't care about their health. So if Richie's dad doesn't care about his son, he probably doesn't care about other people either, which means Richie might be like his dad."

And just like that ... I equated smoking to being a psychopath. Sure, some days I was too smart for my own good, but at twelve, I think I was, more times than not, too dumb for my own good.

"My grandpa smokes around Chad and me, but he's never killed anyone," Colten said.

"Not all psychopaths are killers. But my dad said secondhand smoke can kill you, so it's possible your grandpa could kill you by accident. I don't think they'd arrest him. My dad said a woman accidentally backed over her daughter while pulling out of the garage. The girl died, but the mom didn't get arrested because it was an accident."

"Did you finish your homework?"

I frown. "I don't have homework."

"What about your report on an American president?"

"I did it yesterday after school."

"You finished it in one day?"

I nodded. "Are you done?"

"No. I have to finish it tonight."

"I thought we'd go to the park."

"Can't. I have to finish my paper."

"I'll finish it. Who's it on?"

Colten's face soured. "You can't write my paper for me."

"Why not?"

"Because we could get in trouble."

"Who's going to know?"

Colten's lips twisted. "It's Taft."

"Taft? Why did you choose Taft? Because he was the only president to serve both as President and as Chief Justice?"

Colten blinked several times. "No. Because I like his mustache."

I snorted. "Are you serious?"

He shrugged.

"Fine. Show me your three sources. I'll write it, and then we can go to the park."

"I think this is wrong."

"Wrong is what those boys in Colorado did. This is no big deal."

"Why do you keep talking about those boys?" He opened his backpack and pulled out a black three-ring binder.

"Because it's interesting."

"It's awful."

"Awful things can be interesting. Why do you think they make us study wars in history?"

"Because they're interesting?"

I took his binder and grinned. "No. Nice try. We study bad things, so we don't repeat history. You don't listen in class, do you?"

Colten frowned. "History is boring. Nobody listens."

I listened, but I didn't have time to explain my school habits. I had a report to write so Colten could go to the park with me. There wasn't much I wouldn't do for the boy next door.

CHAPTER
Three

My FUTURE of marital bliss is off to a great start. I lied to Colten. He thinks I'm meeting with a specialist at the university. A specialist in reincarnation. If he were here to see the run-down strip mall in front of me, he'd lose his shit.

The door reads: Psychic. Walk-ins welcome. Estimated wait time is eternity.

I pull on the handle, but it's locked.

"Come in."

I glance up at a camera mounted in the corner just as the lock to the door clicks and buzzes.

Oof ...

The pungent smell of incense just about knocks me over.

"Welcome, Josephine." An older woman with witchy silver hair takes a bow. When she stands erect, her lips part into a slight smile. They're dry lips sticking to brown-stained teeth. Her cough isn't that of a smoker's. It's more of a death rattle.

"Thanks." I glance around the room. There's a black ceiling dotted in stars and moons hanging from fishing lines. Two round velvet pillows reside in the middle of the wood-floored room. White painted clouds cover the baby blue walls.

"I am Athelinda. Please remove your socks and shoes."

I glance down at my feet then at her feet. Calloused heels, bunions, crooked toes, and thick yellow nails.

"I encourage you, if it's in your zone of comfort, to remove all of your clothes and slip on a loose gown like mine." She nods to the hooks on the wall and the sheer white gowns hanging from them. "We don't want anything restricting your energy."

I can see basically everything through her gown, but I nod once anyway, shuffle my feet to the wall, and remove my clothes. Coworkers have seen me naked in the locker room at work. I'm not modest.

After I pull the gown over my head, I meet her in the middle of the room and sit on the pillow opposite her, both of us in lotus pose.

"Let's close our eyes, take a few deep breaths ... in through your nose for four seconds and out through your nose for four seconds. Keep your eyes closed as we go through a few questions."

I close my eyes, and when I do, I see the girls with

the shaved heads. The hair hanging from the tree. The cemetery.

In for four … out for four.

I repeat this until she speaks.

"How long were you under the water?"

My eyes pop open.

"Close your eyes."

Her eyes are closed. How does she know mine are open?

"How do you know about the water?"

"Your date of birth. You were born on a Friday in October. An autumn child born on a Friday will resurrect previous lives if submerged during their final breath."

This is weird, dare I say crazy? I can see how people would bolt out of here with her logic, but I'm here because I'm struggling with my own brand of crazy.

"I don't know how long I was submerged."

"What did you see?"

"Long hair tied to tree branches in a churchyard. Then I saw girls with shaved heads being buried in existing graves."

"Who buried them? What did that person look like?"

"I don't know. I never see that person."

When I hear her wrestling around with something, I open my eyes. Her shaky twig fingers retrieve a big book from beneath her pillow as she leans to the side. It's weathered and mottled in shades of brown and says

"I AM ..." The binding whines in protest as she opens it.

"I see a lot of people with gifts. They don't feel like gifts at the time, but they are powerful privileges that come with a second chance at life." She flips through the delicate pages that look as fragile as an onion peel. "You, however, have not been granted a gift or any sort of privilege, I fear."

I frown. This was not a good idea.

She stops on a page and moves her finger beneath the lines of script, mumbling to herself.

"I know what it means. I just need help getting rid of the memories."

Athelinda glances up at me, yellow eyes narrowed into tiny slips. "What do you think it means?"

"I was one of the girls buried in the cemetery."

"Why do you think that?"

"Because I remember the feeling of fear and my head being shaved. I know where the bodies were buried."

"Was all the hair hanging from the same tree?"

I shake my head. "But all the trees were in church-yards in Tennessee."

She clears her throat. "And were all of the bodies buried in the same cemetery?"

Another headshake. "But all of the cemeteries are in Tennessee."

"So you've seen many girls and many locks of hair tied to various trees?"

"Yes."

"You've seen more than one cemetery?"

I nod.

"If you were one of the girls, how did you see more than one cemetery?"

I shrug. "Maybe I witnessed other deaths before mine. Maybe it was its own form of torture. If the killer was a psychopath, he enjoyed watching me suffer."

"I'm very sorry, Josephine. But you were not one of those girls."

"How do you know?"

"Because your element is water. You point west. Sunset. Autumn. Waning moon. Water. That's why your spirit attempted to leave when you were in the water. And where you came from is how you died in the life you resurrected. We come from the opposite of where we are now. You came from air. Your spirit in that life left this world in air, not earth. These girls were buried in *earth*. They were not hung from air. That was symbolic of something else, not the manner in which they died."

"They were dead before they were buried in earth. Their death might have been air." I don't know why I'm arguing with her. I'm not equipped with enough knowledge of elements and their symbolism.

"If they were dead before they were buried, and you were one of those girls, then you wouldn't have visions of a cemetery. Visions of previous lives are from moments when we were actually alive. I've died many times. Trust me, I know." She closes the book. "I can assure you; you weren't one of the girls."

"Then the visions don't make sense."

Her gaze drops to the book, her pointed fingernails tapping the cover. "As I was saying earlier, this is not a gift. I'm sorry this is happening to you. I wish there were more I could do."

"What is *this*? What are you referring to?"

"Vita Atonement." She brings her attention back to me.

I study her for a few moments before nodding. "Life reparation?"

Her thick brows slide up her forehead a fraction. "Exactly. This life is your chance to make up for the life you remember. Vita atonement lives are never easy. The souls trapped in a body during this kind of life cycle are often unsettled. They don't fit in well. They're often battling between *what is* and *what was* without realizing it. And it's incredibly rare to have what you have."

"What do I have?"

"Recollection. You now have the missing piece. You now know why you've struggled to find your place, to fit in, to submit to what is 'normal.' Atonement won't be easy for you, but you have a better chance than most who navigate Vita Atonement without recollection."

I shake my head. "I ... I don't have recollection if you're telling me I wasn't one of those girls."

"Josephine, you know. Your brain is trying so hard to protect you. It's why the brain blocks certain memories like trauma. It's why you don't recall the day you died, how long you were underwater, how your lungs felt when they needed oxygen but none was there to be had."

"What …" I continue to shake my head. "What are you saying?"

"You know."

I continue to shake my head.

"You can't forget it until you let it in, atone it, and bury it for good."

"Atone what?"

"You know, Josephine. Close your eyes and let it in."

I don't want to close my eyes. I want her to stop being so cryptic. "Just tell me."

"I don't have to," she whispers. "You already know."

This is worse than the images.

This is worse than the feeling I had the night Colten unearthed the bodies.

This is … unimaginable.

"No …" I stumble getting to my feet.

"Let it in."

"N-no …" I sway while my legs attempt to carry me to my clothes. Is this what it feels like to be drunk? To have no control over your body and your mind?

"You have to make this right in the universe."

"STOP IT!" I rip off the gown and grab my hair, fingers digging into my scalp. My knees buckle, sending me to the floor in a naked ball of despair. I want to pull out my hair and rip off my skin. Plunge a knife into my chest and cut out my own heart.

You weren't one of the girls … you were Winston Jeffries.

CHAPTER
Four

"Time's up. You ready to talk yet?" Rains asks as I stare at my computer a little before ten p.m.

"What?" I glance up from my desk littered with paperwork and empty coffee cups. I've messaged Josie a dozen times and called her at least that many.

"Can we talk?"

I sigh, running a hand through my hair. "Yeah, sure. What's up?"

"I dug your ass out of trouble in Nashville. I'm still getting calls about Dr. Watts. I don't find out you were childhood friends until the two of you raid a cemetery in another state. You begged me to give you some time to 'deal' with her before explaining everything to me. Well … times up." He sits on the edge of my desk and crosses his arms.

"We were neighbors, inseparable until I left her to

go into the Marines. I was messed up because my dad was an asshole. Things didn't end well with Josie. I don't see or hear from her for seventeen years, then boom! I run into her at a restaurant while she's on a date, then I see her at work. What are the chances, right?"

Rains nods slowly, brow pinched tightly.

"She hated me, still kind of hates me, but I think she loves me more. Just like I think we're getting married because I vomited some half-ass proposal to her out of nowhere. Then the shooting at the pier. Then these memories from her near-death experience. The next thing I knew, we were on a plane to Tennessee to dig up dead bodies all because she's had visions related to a serial killer who was executed over a century ago. I mean ..." I shake my head. "I couldn't make up this shit if I wanted to. Everything we told the Nashville police was true. Well, it was Josie's truth. Fuck if I know what's true right now because I don't have a better explanation for how she knew about those bodies, yet ... I can't quite swallow the idea that she was one of the victims in another life."

Rains twists his lips. "That's ..."

"Fucked-up. One hundred percent." I lean back in my chair and scrub my hands over my face. "I appreciate all your help getting the chief to dig my ass out of trouble in Nashville."

"You're lucky you still have your badge."

I nod.

"Do you believe her?"

I ask myself this question every day. "I don't know, man. I just don't know."

"She's the most intelligent, laser-focused person I know," Rains says. "She's methodical and a perfectionist when it comes to details. But even the most put-together people can lose a piece of their mind after something like what happened at the pier."

"Still doesn't explain how she knew about the bodies." I'm not trying to be argumentative with him, but there is no explanation for her knowledge of those bodies, and my mind keeps circling around to that one very important detail.

Rains nods slowly. "Sure doesn't." He inspects me with an unreadable expression. "So ... when were you going to tell me that you've been screwing the ME?"

I have no humor inside of me at the moment, yet his question pulls a chuckle from me anyway. "I'm not sure. Maybe a few days before the wedding. Josie and I have never had a normal relationship. I'm not sure why I think we can have one now. Clearly, we're off to a great start."

Rains smirks.

"She's never wanted to get married. Never wanted to have children. She's never been in the range of normal."

"So why ask her to marry you?"

Again, I chuckle, glancing at my phone, waiting for her to contact me. "I don't know. I think I want her to be with me, like really, officially be with me. And I want to tell the world that she's mine and I'm hers. God … I sound like a pussy, but I've loved her since … hell, I don't know. Before I really knew what I felt had a name."

"And now she sees dead people. And she doesn't want kids, but you have a daughter."

"And she's in California supposedly visiting some expert on near-death experiences, but she won't answer my calls or my texts."

"Do you follow her location?"

I shake my head.

"I'm not sure she's really going to marry you if she won't let you track her location."

"I haven't asked her."

"Why?"

I shrug a shoulder.

"You're afraid of her."

"Pfft … I'm not afraid of her."

"She dissects dead people all day, and at night, she sees more dead people. She knows where lost bodies were buried. Fuck, man … not gonna lie … I'm a little afraid of her."

"You don't know her like I know her."

"Then you know she's okay. And you trust that she'll check in when she's ready. She disarmed a guy with a single shot to his leg, and she didn't take a day to even second-guess it. Did that surprise you?"

I watch the cleaning crew shuffle into the office area with their roller carts of supplies.

"Maybe she's not the same Josie you remember."

Just as I consider the truth to his words, my phone chimes.

Josie: Sorry. Busy day. I'm home.
Me: You're home? Thought you were coming home tomorrow?
Josie: I need you.

I scoot back in my chair. "I'm going home."

"That her?"

I nod while grabbing my suit jacket from the back of the chair.

"Tell her hi."

I don't answer him with more than a mumbled "okay" before taking the stairs to the exit.

I TRY to call her on the drive to her house, but she doesn't answer. I nearly forget to lock my car before running to her front door. It's unlocked, and I frown at her carelessness while opening the door and flipping the deadbolt behind me.

"Josie?" I toe off my shoes before tossing my jacket onto the back of the sofa on my way down the hall. The only light that's on in the whole house is the one to her bathroom. I ease open the door.

"I need you."

Those three words have haunted me since she sent the text and refused to answer her phone.

"Josie ..." I sigh when I see her in the bathtub filled with water and bubbles. "Why are you home early, baby?" I toss my tie onto the floor and unbutton my shirt.

When she turns her head toward me, I'm struck in the chest with the saddest smile I've ever seen. "You've never called me that," she whispers.

"Called you what?" I kneel next to the bathtub and press my lips to the side of her wet head, closing my eyes for a second to inhale her faint floral scent.

"Baby."

"Sorry. Do you not like it?" I sit back on my heels.

She tries for a genuine smile, but it's as if her face won't let her. "I do. It makes me feel..." her gaze drifts to the bubbles as she smooths the top of them with her hand "...innocent."

Innocent?

This has to be about the girl. The innocent girl she claims to have been.

As I open my mouth to ask about her trip, she abruptly stands, water and suds clinging to her naked body. "Do I look innocent?" Her voice barely a whisper.

I question if I'm hearing her exact words. My gaze roves along her body. "Baby, that's a loaded question with you standing in front of me looking like you do after weeks of not touching you like..." my gaze lifts to her "...like I want to touch you."

"Touch me," she whispers, her hands reaching for my shoulders. She snakes them around my neck.

"You're wet."

"I know." She kisses me, leaning into me, forcing me to wrap my arms around her body to keep us from falling.

Her legs wrap around my waist when I lift her from the bathtub. Her lips move against mine with urgency.

"Are you ... o-okay to do this?" I fight to get my words out between kisses. My dick is ready to break through my pants. It's hating me for questioning what's happening.

"Mosley ... just fuck me."

She wins. So does my dick. My conscience will deal with the rest later.

"W-what are you d-doing?" she murmurs against my mouth when I rest her backside on the vanity.

"I'm doing as you asked." I rip off my shirt and shove down my pants.

"Coltennn!" One of her hands flies to the edge of the sink when I plunge into her. The other hand rakes down my chest.

"Tell me you're okay," I whisper against her ear while my hands grip her ass. I want to move. I *need* to move. But I refuse to hurt her.

"Don't stop," she says on a harsh breath, her legs wrapping around my waist.

She looks like my Josephine. She *feels* like my Josephine.

Her touch.

Her voice in my ear.

The beat of her heart so close to mine.

But something is missing. Just ... something.

"Harder, Colten ..." Her fingers curl into my flesh, pulling me closer.

I drive into her over and over.

"Harder!" she demands.

"Jesus, Josie ..." I can't go any harder without breaking her. So I go faster. I grip her ass harder with one hand and grab her breast with my other hand, pinching her nipple *hard*.

"Hard—"

I kiss her, cutting her off, reaching my tongue to her fucking tonsils. Her long moan touches every inch of my skin when we find our release while every muscle contracts.

Josie wriggles out of my hold. I take a step back, breathless. She lowers to her knees and wraps her lips around my cock.

"Fuck ... J-Josie ..." I don't know what she's doing. It's ... not necessary. It's so damn unexpected. I should tell her to stop. One hand reaches for the wall while my other hand finds her head, my fingers threading through her hair. I'm going to tell her to stop in just ... a second.

Fuck me ... that feels good.

She releases me and kisses her way up my body, her hand on my cock, replacing her mouth. Her teeth tease my nipples, firmly biting each one, making my body jerk. I feel her grin against my skin while her lips ghost their way to my ear. "Fuck me again, Mosley. Only this time ... *harder*."

CHAPTER
Five

I SLIP out of bed a little before 3:00 a.m., leaving Colten naked on his stomach and dead to the world.

The pain is numbing. I *need* to feel something real, something in this life. Something human ... something humane.

Colten could have broken every bone in my body, ripped me apart with his teeth like an animal, and it still wouldn't have been enough.

Hugging myself, I sit in the corner of the sofa and stare out the window while my fingernails dig into the flesh on the back of my arms. It's been years since I've had long nails, but I've had other things on my mind that didn't involve grooming habits.

My mind races back to California where I threw cash at Athelinda, ran out of her building, and I didn't look back. My wobbly legs picked up speed until horns honked and tires screeched. I stopped in the middle of the street while drivers swerved to keep from hitting me.

Even now, I feel breathless.

Wordless.

Lost.

Whatever life this is, I don't want it. If I am *him* ... I can't do it.

Why did Colten save me? Why couldn't he have waited just a minute longer? Maybe even ten ... twenty seconds would have made the difference between death and near death.

My poor parents. They spent my whole childhood trying to make me feel special and unique, when in reality, I was a demon in the body of their little girl. What could they have possibly done wrong to deserve me?

When the sun starts to make its way into the morning sky, I brew a cup of coffee. As soon as I take a sip, I spit it back into the cup. It's hot and tasteless. I bring my nose close to the steam and take a whiff. It has no aroma. What is wrong with me? Am I in purgatory here on Earth? Is that what Athelinda meant?

"Good morning."

I turn toward Colten's sleepy voice. His messy hair and big yawn stand a few feet behind me with a blanket tied around his waist.

"Colten ..." I whisper. "I'm so very sorry." My gaze affixes to his chest. He looks like a cat attacked him. A big, mean cat. Deep scratches. Speckled areas of dried blood. I curl my fingers and inspect my nails. They're dark with dried blood as well. When I hug my chest, I feel the rough patches on the back of my arms that probably look like a raked garden as well.

He doesn't make a single glance at his chest. Instead, he shrugs. "It's fine." He takes a step forward.

I stiffen as he kisses the corner of my mouth.

"Colten ..."

"My love," he says adoringly, almost playfully while making his own cup of coffee.

I flinch when he turns his back to me. It matches his chest. I did that. I hurt him. Marked him. And I did it all in the name of *feeling*. Only ... I didn't feel it. But I'm sure he did because he's a normal person with real feelings.

"Colten ..." I gently splay my palms and my cheek against his back. Closing my eyes, I whisper, "I'm *unwell*. You have to protect yourself ... protect your daughter."

"Hey, no." He turns, framing my face in his strong, protective, *loving* hands.

What did he do to deserve me? Wasn't having an awful dad enough?

"Baby, what are you talking about? It's a few marks. They'll heal. I'm okay. Do you hear me?" Colten shakes his head. "And what are you talking about protecting Reagan? Protect her from what?"

Me.

"Josie, what happened in California?"

I lean into his touch and close my eyes. "I have to

tell you something," I whisper. "And it's going to change *everything*. And I need you to promise me that you will walk away like you did seventeen years ago."

"Josie—"

I open my eyes. "Promise me you'll remember that your life has so much purpose and meaning. You have a beautiful daughter. And your mom and brother. A job you love. You have everything, Colten. And you had it without me."

"No." He shakes his head, eyes narrowing while his grip on my face tightens. "I'm not promising you anything of the sort. What the hell happened?"

His anger pulls a few tears from my eyes. I welcome them. I welcome any sign of human emotion. "The visions, the memories ... they're not from one of the girls."

Colten nods. "Okay."

"I was him." I bite my shaky lower lip. The ugliness of the truth burns in my chest ... in my soul. My fucking awful soul.

"Who?"

"Winston Jeffries."

Colten blinks a few times before his hands drop to his sides. In an unexpected twist, he laughs.

Laughs!

Fist at his mouth, hand over his belly laugh. "No." He snorts. "That's an interesting take on all of this, but ... no."

"I don't want to believe it either, but—"

"Good." He grabs my shoulders and lowers his face

level with mine. "Whoever put that shit in your head is mental. You absolutely should *not* believe them. Josephine Watts, you are way too smart to do anything short of what I'm doing." He laughs some more. "It's beyond ridiculous. It's laughable. You see that, right?"

I can't laugh. It's not in me. No smiles either. I find none of this amusing.

"I never see the person who did it because I'm seeing it through his eyes. I wouldn't have memories of him burying *my* dead body. I wouldn't have memories of times that he buried other bodies at different cemeteries, but I do, Colten. The *only* explanation is that I was him. A ..."

A serial killer.

I can't say the words. I don't know if I'll ever be able to say them.

Colten's head stays on an endless swivel like it's running on batteries. Back and forth. He can shake his head until it breaks from his neck. It won't change anything. God, I wish it could.

"I need you to let me be Dr. Josephine Watts, Medical Examiner. Our paths will cross with work. That's it. I can't marry you. I can't be your friend. I can't be anything to you."

His gaze shifts from me to the window, and he squints just as the sun catches his eyes. "I think we should have a small family-only ceremony in January. After the holidays. We'll take a week and honeymoon in Costa Rica or Ecuador. We'll rent a little place near a beach. Sun. Tropical food. Lazy mornings in bed. I'll book us massages and maybe a rainforest tour. It will be perfect." The only thing that's perfect is his smile. It's perfectly heartbreaking.

"Also, did I mention we found the motherlode of evidence for your favorite chainsaw killer? We had enough for an arrest, but the conviction will be a slam dunk now. He had an underground storm shelter. We must have passed it a hundred times because it was covered in brush and grass. Then Rains heard something squeak under him. I don't think we would have otherwise found it. Isn't that crazy? The saw we confiscated before the arrest wasn't on his property, but it had his prints. Before he lawyered up, he said he found it in a dumpster—he does work for a sanitation company, so it wasn't implausible. But there was blood all over it, so why would he salvage it and put it in the back of his truck?"

I wait for him to return his attention to me, and I offer a sad smile. "Colten."

He deflates when I don't take part in his distraction. Then he shrugs a shoulder, neutral expression. "It's my turn."

I chuckle, shaking my head. "Your turn to be the bossy one, huh?"

Stupid childhood promise.

"After you broke your arm, you said I could be the bossy one in approximately twenty years. It's been twenty-one years since you promised me control. It's past due."

Colten nods. He's wearing such a serious expression. It's a brave one.

"There was an asterisk with fine print. Did you read it when I made that promise to you? I think it said the agreement was null and void if it was discovered that either one of us was a murderer in another life."

"Reagan will be our flower girl." The hint of a smile pulls at his lips. "She'll be ecstatic. Katy said she loved being a flower girl at her wedding."

He has no idea how thin the thread holding me together is. I'm not sure how many more mornings I will be able to justify waking up, breathing in and out, and existing in this "Vita Atonement." I can't plan this wedding. I can't find an ounce of enthusiasm for his storm shelter discovery.

"I took little girls like Reagan, shaved their heads, and I killed them."

Colten winces. "Shut up. Just ... don't ever say that again."

"Look at you," I whisper, refocusing on his chest. "You couldn't fuck me hard enough last night. I felt nothing while shredding your skin." I slowly turn so he can see the back of my arms. "I didn't feel this either. I'm dead inside. I've always been dead inside." I turn back around. "All this time, I've been pretending. I even fooled myself into thinking that I could be a little normal, a little humane."

"I'm not walking away."

"I'm not giving you a choice." I tip my chin up, jaw set.

He grunts a laugh and pivots. "I have to work."

I don't move. Maybe I can't. Or maybe my idleness

is symbolic of standing my ground. Really shaky ground.

Minutes later, Colten emerges from the bedroom with his white shirt untucked and partially buttoned and his tie in hand. He's the sexiest man I have ever seen. I think his presence in my life is the biggest catalyst for my life reparation. I took what mattered most to other people in that other life, and in this one, I will have to give up what matters most to me.

"I love you," he says. "And I'll see you later." He bends to kiss me.

I take a step backward, averting my gaze to the floor.

He releases a soft sigh. "I'm never leaving you again."

I know this. I believe him. I will be the one to leave him.

After my front door clicks shut behind him, I pad my way to it and flip the deadbolt. Colten Mosely will not step foot in my house again unless it's to remove my lifeless body from it.

CHAPTER
Six

"I can't be your boyfriend ever again," I said the day after Josie got her cast.

She handed me a Sharpie to sign it and rolled her eyes while we sat at the kitchen table. Her mom was putting Benji down for a nap, and her dad was still at work. "Because I broke my arm?"

I signed her cast. The first signature. "No. Because your dad said I can't ever kiss you again, and what's the point of being your boyfriend if I can't kiss you?"

She snorted. "You're not seriously listening to my dad."

"I am. I am very seriously listening to your dad." I capped the marker and handed it back to her. "He's going to talk to my dad about teaching me to use a rifle."

"Your mom is never going to let you use a gun. She hates guns."

"No, she doesn't."

Josie eyes me. "Um ... yeah, she does."

"How do you know that?"

"Because of Columbine. She still talks to my mom about it. And I overheard her saying to my mom that she hates guns. She used those exact words."

"Your dad is the chief of police. I think she'll let him teach me."

"She won't." Josie shrugged like her two words ended our discussion.

"I'm still asking her."

"Go ahead." She hopped off the stool and grabbed the Tupperware container of cookies, hugging it to her while peeling off the lid with her good hand before offering me one.

"I could have opened that for you."

"I'm not helpless." She wasn't. Never had been, never would be.

"If I broke my arm, I'd let you do everything for me. Do my homework. Feed me. Tie my shoes. Carry my schoolbag ..."

Josie's pouty lips turned downward. I responded with a huge, chocolate-chip-cookie grin. I had no shame in my game.

"My grandma said she'd rather die than have people take care of her. She's really smart, and she thinks I'm just like her." Josie twisted her lips. "It's weird to think that death is better than letting someone help you. But if I am like her, then maybe someday I'll choose death over someone feeling sorry for me and doing stuff for me. My other grandma got sick, and she has to wear adult diapers. My grandpa helps her change them. It's really nice of him, but still … I bet she feels embarrassed."

"He's her husband. That's probably what a good husband should do. My dad wouldn't do it for my mom, but we both know he's an asshole."

"Colten, don't say that."

"I'm going to be a better husband than him."

"You'd change your wife's adult diaper?"

My nose wrinkled. I couldn't imagine that. I had never changed a diaper before. "I mean … maybe. If I loved her."

"Don't marry her if you don't love her." Josie rolled her eyes and laughed.

I grabbed a second cookie. "You know what I mean."

"Yeah. I know. I hope I don't need anyone's help. I want to be like my other grandma. After my grandpa died, she did everything. Mowed the lawn. Fixed a leaky toilet. She's pretty awesome."

Sometimes I wanted to be Josie. She had a great family and so much confidence.

Me?

I had an asshole dad. A stupid brother. And a mother who loved me, but she was emotionally whacked out because of my dad.

"I promised my parents I would never ask you this,

but ..." I eased into a question I'd been meaning to ask her for a long time but never got the nerve.

"Ask me what?"

She set the lid on the container of cookies, and I pressed it down before she had the chance to *not* ask me.

"Did your mom cheat on your dad?"

"What?" Her head whipped backward.

"Not recently. I mean years ago. You said your mom had sex with another guy, and that's why your skin color is a little darker. Did she cheat on him?"

"No." Her face wrinkles.

"Then why do you have a different dad?"

She stares at her cookie for several seconds. "I don't. My dad is my dad. He's not my biological dad, but he's real."

"Is that what your parents told you?"

"Yes."

"And you didn't ask any more questions?"

"Of course I did, but they said it wasn't important until I get older."

"That's weird. How old?"

"They said when I'm an adult it will make sense."

I had a million questions. My biggest question was how she could be fine with them not telling her the truth until she was an adult. I hated when my parents lied to me. Josie, however, wasn't like me or anyone else for that matter. One minute she was too curious for her own good, on the verge of getting in trouble, and the next minute, she seemed to not care about something as interesting, and maybe a little crazy, like the fact that the chief wasn't her real—*biological*—dad, yet her mom supposedly didn't have an affair.

Josephine Watts processed everything in life a little differently than other kids—and maybe most other humans.

CHAPTER
Seven

"Josie ..." My mom's eyebrows jump up her forehead after she unlocks and opens her front door. Her gaze shifts to the small suitcase at my side. "What are you doing here?" She steps aside to let me into the entry.

"I needed to get away." I slip off my shoes and set my suitcase by the stairs.

"Away from what?" She eyes me suspiciously.

"Colten."

"Trouble in paradise?" She heads into the kitchen to get food. That's how she has always greeted guests. A drink and something sweet like cookies, brownies, or lemon bars if she's feeling generous toward my dad.

I get two steps into the kitchen and stop. A six-hour drive in silence, my phone shut off to keep from hearing the chime of his texts and calls, no recollection of anything specific that I saw, heard, or thought for those six hours ... and now it hits me.

It. Hits. Me.

Tears sting my eyes while everything from my throat to the pit of my stomach seizes up into a tight knot of despair. I turn away from her and swallow hard, pinching the corners of my eyes to keep control.

I lost him ... I lost the boy next door.

"Are you still having visions and dreams?"

I clear my throat and take a deep breath while finding my way to the kitchen table before my knees give out on me. I haven't felt this hopeless and devastated since ... well, forever. "I am."

"How did your trip to California go?"

I clear my throat, fighting for every last morsel of composure. "How do you know about that?"

Mom sets a tray of brownies next to me along with a cherry-lime sparkling water. "Well, it would have been nice to have heard it from you." She gives me a little scowl. "But I had to hear it from Becca. We've been keeping in touch, and Colten told her. I guess he shares stuff with his mom."

Some stuff. Mom's not lecturing me on not telling her that I accepted his proposal a while back, so he must not have told his mom either. Smart. He sensed the wedding might not happen.

"Remember that time you and dad were in New Orleans right before you got married? You told me you had your palm read by a psychic. Dad thought it was ridiculous, but you believed her, and since then, everything has come to fruition?"

She nods, cupping her tea in her hands. "The good and the bad," she whispers.

"The good and the bad," I echo. Bad ... there was something so very bad.

There still is.

"I found a psychic of sorts who specializes in interpreting near-death experiences. She's a parapsychologist. Colten thinks I saw a 'specialist' at the university. This woman is..." I shake my head "...a very different breed."

"What did she tell you? Did she confirm that you were one of the victims?"

My head eases side to side while I pick at the brownie.

"Then what did she say?"

Again, my emotions rush to the surface, desperate to release.

I lost him.

"Will you tell me the truth?" The words squeak past my throat.

"About what, Josie?"

"I know I'm your daughter, and you're a good mom." I glance up with a shaky smile. "If I wanted to be a mom, I'd want to be you. Not grandma, even though she said I'm like her. Not Vera. Not anyone I've known or can even imagine. I'd want to be you."

Her eyes gloss over with tears, and she smiles. "Thank you, Josie. That's..." she wipes the corners of her eyes "...that's the kindest, most loving thing anyone has ever said to me."

For a breath, for the briefest of moments, I feel human. I *feel* something that's truly of this lifetime. "My point is I know you're hardwired to love me unconditionally. I know you're hardwired to see the best in me. To see nothing 'wrong' with me. But I know I've never fit into the range of normal in so many ways. Have you..." I force my gaze from my brownie back to hers "...have you ever wondered if my soul is not a good one because of my biological father?"

She winces. "No. Not once. Your soul? Are you kidding me? Josie, you are one of the kindest souls I know. You are *the* kindest soul I know. That's what makes you special, or as you have said for years, ... different."

"You've never wondered why I don't want to be a wife or a mom? You've never wondered why I brought home every dead thing I happened upon? You never wondered why I spent so much time with Roland Tompkins? You never wondered why I spent an unhealthy amount of time studying mass shootings starting with Columbine? Does my choice of profession not give you pause for a tiny second? Did you know that I'm really good at what I do? Does that all seem like something a kind person with a good soul would do?"

More tears collect in her eyes. "What did she say to you?" she whispers. "What did she do to my baby?"

I open my mouth to speak, but the thick and suffocating words lodge in my throat. All I hear is the truth. All I see is the pain in my mom's eyes. I don't want to bring it all back to her, but I am. I'm unearthing her past like I unearthed those bodies, and I can't undo it.

Then I think of Colten, and all the tears release.

Mom covers her mouth to hold back her sob as she shakes her head. "Tell me what she said."

I hate myself. I've harmed myself, but I've never truly hated myself until now. Rubbing my quivering lips together, I wipe as many tears as I can. "She said I wasn't one of the girls he killed. I was …"

"Him," she whispers while her face contorts into anguish while her eyes fill with more tears.

I hold my breath to keep from sobbing. Clench my teeth. I don't breathe a single breath while returning a slow nod.

Mom tries to stifle her own sob, and I don't know who should be consoling who. It feels like this shared burden. Like we're carrying something heavy, and we don't know who will give out first.

Who will stumble?

Who will surrender under the weight of truth?

I feel guilty for sharing this with her, but at the same time, I feel seen. Even if I don't have a mother's love in my soul, I recognize it as the realest, most undeniably perfect part of human existence. Not all mothers are good ones, but I believe the ability to nurture without expecting anything in return is what makes women the sole reason humanity still exists.

They are the peacekeepers.

The givers of life.

The healers of hearts.

And there is me. I am an imposter. An undeserving punishment to anyone who has let me touch their life.

And ... I hate myself.

"I'm sorry," I say, wiping the tears from my face.

Mom shakes her head. "No. God no ..." She's out of her chair and wrapping her arms around me from behind my chair. "Don't you ever apologize for anything. This will not define your life. *I* am the one who is sorry that you have to experience this."

"You did n-nothing." I lay my hands over hers on my shoulders.

"I should have known," she sobs in my ear, hugging me harder.

"No, Mom." I wriggle my way out of her hold to turn toward her. Standing, I pull her into my arms.

We cry, clinging to each other until the back door opens, and my dad steps inside, removing his boots while eyeing us. "Jo, what are you doing here? What happened?"

I take a step away from my mom and wipe my eyes. "Um ..."

"She and Colten are having issues."

He rolls his eyes. "I'll call him. He should know better."

"What? No." I shake my head.

Mom grabs my hand and gives it a squeeze. "Cool your jets, Isaac. They'll work it out on their own."

We haven't talked about Colten. I don't know how

to read my mom. Does she not want my dad to know? Will he not believe me the way he didn't believe anything the psychic in New Orleans said to them years earlier?

"Have you stopped having those crazy dreams? That's probably your problem. You need to let that crap go, Jo."

Let it go.

Chin up, Jo.

Dust off your knees, Jo.

Don't you dare cry, Jo.

How would he feel if he knew and actually believed I was a man (the boy he wanted) in another life? And I didn't cry over skinned knees. I killed little girls. Would that version of me be better than the daughter who didn't live up to his expectations less than five percent of the time? And that five percent was my lack of a penis. An impossible standard at the time.

"Isaac ..." Mom wipes her face and gives him a warning.

"It was a long drive. I'm going to take a bath." I jab my thumb over my shoulder.

Dad continues to eye me. Beneath his gruff comments about my dreams, I sense his genuine concern. We've spent so much time together over the years, hunting and fishing. I count on him not only as my *real* father in life, but as a friend too. However, he can't fix this for me, and that will eat him alive. It's not that he'll believe me, just that he can't "fix" my messed-up mind.

Oh, how I wish it were as simple as weekly counseling and a magic pill.

Mom grabs her phone from the counter and holds up the screen.

Colten.

She hands it to me. I try to resist taking it, but she shoves it into my chest. "Don't shut him out."

I don't have a choice.

"Really? My mom's phone?" I answer it, climbing the stairs, feeling exhausted and full of despair.

"I'm not walking away, Josie."

"I know. That's why I'm doing it." I close the bathroom door and turn on the water to the tub. "Why did you call my mom?"

"Looking for you. I'm sitting in your living room, and you're not here. Your toothbrush is gone. I assumed; I *hoped* you went home."

"Because my parents like you and you think they'll put in a good word for you? Sorry to disappoint you, Detective Mosley, this isn't about you."

"I disagree. If it's about you, it's about me."

"I'm not marrying you."

There's a pause on the line. I grab a towel and check the water temperature. Have I upset him? Hurt him? It's not a lie. This isn't about him.

"I'll take you however I can have you."

I put him on speaker and set it on the counter while I undress. "Maybe you can have me in another life. But not this one."

"What if I'm not asking?"

"Then you don't know me at all." I move the phone to the ledge of the tub and step into the water.

"What's that sound?"

"The bathtub. I'm five seconds from ending this call. I'd appreciate it if you'd leave my house."

"Josephine ..." He sighs as I slide into the water and close my eyes. "Do you have any idea how many times you kept me from drowning? How many times your hand reached for mine like a goddamn lifeline? When everything around me felt so heavy and impossibly ugly, there you were. When I pushed you away, you kept running back to me over and over again. Even when you knew you couldn't solve my problems ... You. Held. My. Hand. Something so simple as the delicate hand of a friend is what carried me through some really tough times. Did you know that? Did you know that you carried me with one fucking hand?"

I blink, letting my tears disappear into the water. I hug my fisted hands to my heart while my body shakes with silent sobs. This is different. He had a terrible father. *I* was a killer. I killed little girls.

"So that's one ... one life saved by Josephine Watts. I know you're counting. You're thinking about the lives taken by *him*. Don't let him win. He's not here, but you are. Make it right. Do good. Be kind. Love unconditionally. If this is true, if we get more than one life, then this is your chance to be everything he wasn't."

My eyes continue to burn with endless tears. Not a single word can squeak past the emotion in my throat. It's not that Colten says the right thing at the right time. It's that he believes me, or at least, he believes *in* me. My ride-or-die. It's gut-wrenching to be loved like this and not feel worthy.

It would be so easy to take his proffered hand and pull him under with me, but it's not just him. He has Reagan. And for her, I press *End*.

CHAPTER *Eight*

"Daddy!" Reagan runs into my arms as Katy follows her up my driveway, carrying her bag.

"What's your magic potion?" Katy asks, giving me a half grin. "She's never this excited to see me after spending time with you."

I kiss Reagan's cheek and set her down. She runs into the house. "I need a snack," she says.

"I have good snacks. That's my secret."

"Junk food." Katy rolls her eyes and hands me Reagan's bag.

"Raisins."

"Covered in chocolate?"

"Is there any other way?" I smirk.

"Colten ..." Katy shakes her head and turns, taking a few steps.

"Have fun."

She laughs. "It's a conference. I'm certain that's the definition of anti-fun. Oh ..." Turning back toward me, she twists her lips for a second. "Is it safe for me to ask about Josie?"

"Safe?"

"Reagan's mentioned her name several times. She said Josie got hurt, but she's doing better. She said Josie read her a bedtime story, and she's your friend from a long time ago. Am I being too nosey asking about her?"

"I've known Josie since the fourth grade. We were neighbors. She's an assistant medical examiner, so our professions cross occasionally. Before I moved here, it had been seventeen years since I'd seen her. There. Now you know about Josie."

"So ... she read our daughter a bedtime story. Is she *more* than an old friend?"

I press my lips together, contemplating my answer. "Since you're a happily married newlywed, can I be honest with you?"

"Yeah ..." she says slowly.

"Josie is the reason we never got married."

Katy grunts a laugh. "And here I thought me saying no was the reason we never got married."

I slide my hands into my front pockets. "You said no because I hesitated when you asked if I loved you. I hesitated because you weren't ..." I take a deep breath. It hurts to talk about her when I feel like I'm losing her.

"I wasn't Josie," she murmurs.

I nod.

Katy stares out at the street. "Well, I certainly hope you don't let her get away this time if she's the only woman you're capable of loving." She continues toward her car.

"Did you really love me?"

Katy rests her chin on her shoulder, her gaze not quite finding me. "Yeah. I loved you. And I love Sean. I guess my heart's bigger than yours." She gets into her car and pulls out of my driveway.

I turn, slowly shaking my head. Maybe she does have a bigger heart or maybe Josephine Watts is larger than life.

"Are you eating all the chocolate raisins, Button?" I nuzzle my face into Reagan's neck.

She giggles. "No."

I eat the one pinched between her two fingers.

"Daddy!"

This girl ... she's the only thing keeping me from losing my mind while Josie tries to distance herself from me. I'm not letting her go again. I won't abandon her. And I'm not giving her a choice in the matter. I will save her.

"Is Josie coming over?"

I sit next to her at the table and grab a handful of raisins from the box. "You won't see Josie this time. Sorry."

"Is she still sick?"

"She's better, but she's not here. She went back to Iowa to visit her parents."

Reagan shrugs. "Okay."

I smile. It is okay. Everything will be okay. It has to be.

CHAPTER
Nine

Shortly after Josie turned seventeen, she did a genealogy project for history. I asked her to a movie with me and some other friends, but she needed to work on her project by asking her mom about her biological dad.

Six of us went to the movie without Josie. Less than an hour into it, an employee interrupted the movie, calling my name. I was a little embarrassed and a little freaked out. It had to be an emergency.

Did something happen to my mom or Chad?

Funny ... I didn't spare a thought for my dad.

I followed the employee to the entrance where Josie stood. Her eyes looked like red spider webs. She'd been crying.

"Josie, what happened?"

She hugged me and started crying again. I didn't

know what to do, so I held her for what seemed like forever.

"Let's get out of here, okay?" I said, shifting my body so she was hugged to my side.

We climbed into my old truck, and everything went silent. Josie no longer cried. She stared out the window, holding completely still. Eerily still.

I did the only thing I knew to do ... the thing I knew she'd do. I reached my hand across the console and laced my fingers together with hers. It drew a shaky breath from her. And it scared me. I had never seen Josie like that.

"My father," she whispered. "My biological father ... he..." she swallowed hard "...raped my mother. She was on her way to her car. It was late and dark after her class. My dad was waiting for her at home. It was their anniversary, and he had a candlelit dinner waiting for her. But she never came home that night. One of his officer friends came to the house and told him someone found her on the ground next to her car. They called for help. She was at the hospital. Battered ... but not broken."

I squeezed her hand, at a loss for words.

She laughed, but it was far from a happy laugh. "Want to know why they kept me instead of aborting me?"

All I had was a slow nod.

"Because it was their anniversary, and they didn't want it to forever be a reminder of something awful. So now ... it's the anniversary of ..." She laughed a little more. That time it sounded slightly maniacal. "My conception. My fucking conception. How messed up is that?"

It was all very messed up.

"I have half the DNA of a rapist. Didn't expect to find that out when I sat down to discuss my project with my mom. I have evil running through my veins, and there is nothing I can do about it."

I squeezed her hand again, and she squeezed mine back while turning her head toward me.

"I didn't ask her, but I kinda read between the lines. If it had been a day earlier or a day later, I might not exist."

Clearing the thickness from my throat, I found my voice. "Well, that would be tragic."

She smiled. It made me feel like a king. I liked doing or saying anything to make Josie smile. It was the most tangible thing I never held in my hands, but god ... I felt it everywhere.

"Drive, Colten."

"Where are we going?"

She fastened her seat belt and stared out her window, releasing a soft sigh. "Anywhere."

We drove out of town until we hit no other option but gravel roads and miles of corn fields. I pulled to a stop when the road I chose dead ended at a dirt circle drive, an old barn, and the remnants of a silo.

"I have a blanket in the back seat. We could get in the bed of the truck."

Josie nodded. "Yeah." She opened her door while I retrieved the blanket.

Before I made it to the back, she had the tailgate down and hopped into the bed. I jumped in behind her and spread out the blanket. When I sat with my back to the window, she nestled between my bent knees with her back to my chest. I hugged her to me, inhaling her sweet shampoo, absorbing her warmth, and imagining how awful life would be without her ... fighting with feeling oddly thankful that someone raped her mom. It was confusing.

"Where do you think we'll be in ten years?" she asked. "Together, right?"

My arms hugged her tighter. I liked that plan, not that it was much of a plan. "Yeah."

"Or at least friends. You might want things I don't want. A wife. Children. A normal life." She laughed. "You're going to be the best dad. Nothing like your dad. And you're going to let your kids do and be whatever they want. And you're never going to cheat on your wife. You're never going to rape a stranger and leave her on the ground in a parking lot."

I grunted a painful laugh. "Uh ... I certainly hope I'm not a rapist. Maybe we should elevate my life's goals to something greater than the simple lack of being a rapist and a cheater."

"I said you'd have a wife and kids. That's good, right? I mean ... you want that, don't you?"

I wanted *her* ... however I could have her. That seemed like a long shot at best. My life was slowly unraveling. My grades. My desire to be anything more than "not my dad."

It didn't matter how Josie came into the world; she was going to do great things and make it a better place. Josie made everything better.

"What do you want?" I asked without answering her question.

She rested her head back onto my shoulder, staring at the starry sky while the screeching of crickets and katydids filled the air. "I think I want to be a doctor. I don't know what area of specialty, but something that's ... I don't know. Something hard or something that most doctors don't want to do."

"Like a butt doctor?"

Josie giggled. "A proctologist? Maybe. Or maybe a podiatrist. Stare at feet all day."

"At least a gynecologist gets to see babies."

Again, she giggled. "Yeah, nothing good comes out of the butt or hides between toes. And when I'm not doing gross stuff, I'll come watch you play baseball. Maybe I'll be best friends with your wife."

I had no answer to that. It was hard to imagine that our sneaking around, hiding our relationship from friends and her parents, was going to end in just ... friendship.

"But you don't have a wife yet." She turned her head and grinned at me.

"Not that I know of." I grinned back at her.

"Do you still want to kiss me now that you know I have evil in my blood?"

"You have evil in your blood. I have asshole in mine. Maybe we were made for each other."

Her smile swelled. "Maybe," she whispered.

I kissed her. After a while, we repositioned, lying on the blanket.

Kissing.

Our legs scissored.

And our future uncertain at best.

CHAPTER
Ten

"I WAS A TERRIBLE DAUGHTER," I said to my mom after my dad left for work. We sat on the deck in our robes, sipping coffee, watching pedestrians pass on the trail that used to be dirt. It's now a beautiful green space, and my tree is still there.

"What are you talking about?"

I blow at the steam. "My junior year, when you told me about the rape, I was so self-absorbed, thinking only about myself. I felt so angry and betrayed. And just … lost. I felt sorry for myself. For *myself*. And you were the one who was raped." I shake my head. "That was really terrible of me. But that's who I am. I'm a terrible person."

"Stop it." She reaches over, resting her hand on my leg and squeezing it. "Look at me."

I lift my gaze to hers. The same question swirls in my head.

What did she ever do to deserve me?

"If I told you dandelions are taking over the neighborhood, and you took a walk, all you'd focus on are the dandelions. It wouldn't matter if there were ten or ten million. That's all your eyes would see because I planted the idea in your mind. It's a distorted reality. You never thought you had bad blood before I told you about the night you were conceived. You never thought you were a serial killer until some psychic told you. The fact is you were a child conceived from rape. And maybe … just maybe your soul carries a piece of a man who did awful things over a hundred years ago. But that's not who you are."

I don't know who I am. My mind won't shut off and let me go back to the woman I was before the shooting. It took years for me to accept what happened to my mom and what that meant for me.

"Sometimes, I feel like it's too much. It's exhausting waking up every morning with a hangover from my dreams. My head hurts, and the anxiety is like nothing I have ever experienced. I don't want to eat pills for the rest of my life to keep from *feeling*. I don't want to spend every waking hour second-guessing my choices, wondering if I've just had a bad day or if I'm in a bad mood because I'm a bad person. And I can't un-read what I've already read. If reincarnation is a real thing, then it explains why a five-year-old can sit down at a piano and play Mozart without having ever taken a lesson or without having ever heard Mozart. So then the question I have is ... what happens when I do something without realizing what or why I'm doing it?"

What happens when I do something bad because in another life I was a psychopath? What if that's my hidden talent?

It would explain why I'm so good at what I do.

Clinical.

Precise.

Emotionless.

"Don't answer that." I stand. "I'm going to head home. I just needed to tell you. I guess I needed someone to share the burden with me. And ..." I puff my cheeks before blowing out a long breath. "Once again, I'm a terrible daughter. I've handed you an impossible situation to solve. And I know by nature, you feel the need to solve all of my problems."

She stands, setting her coffee on the side table. "You're right. I wish I could solve all your problems. While I'm at it, I'd like to solve all the world's problems. But I can't. And I know this." She presses her hands to my cheeks. "But it's not going to stop me from trying. I love you as much as one human can possibly love another human." She bites her lips together for a beat as emotions fill her eyes. "It was my choice to bring you into this world. You are *not* allowed to leave it while I'm still alive. Do you hear me?"

My jaw clenches as if not breathing, not blinking, not moving will keep me from falling apart. I nod. No mother should have to say those words to her child. It's a fucking suicide speech. And I showed up less than twenty-four hours ago, laying out all the reasons my mom might need to convince me it's not okay to exit this world yet.

"Josephine, do. You. Hear. Me?"

I nod.

"Now, go make things right with Colten."

I can't. I just ... can't.

WHEN I GET HOME, there's a note on my pillow.

All those girls I kissed when we were kids ... I closed my eyes and thought of you.

I hold the note to my chest and close my eyes ... and I think of Colten.

After a restless night of more images of dead girls' bodies, I wake at four and start making notes of the number of bodies at each location and the names on the headstones. I don't think this is Vita Atonement, but I feel like it's the only visible road to take right now.

I snap a photo of my notes and send it to the lead detective who interrogated me in Nashville.

I meet with my physical therapist a final time before going back to work. Then I stop by the grocery store. When I get home, I put my groceries away and decide it's time to get back on my stationary bike per my therapist's suggestion. When I go into the bedroom and toss my shirt onto my bed, there's another note.

Detective Mosley is a trespasser.

I loved it when you sat next to me while I played the piano ... but I loved it more when you'd lie on my bed, making my pillow smell like you. Before I left this note, I rubbed myself all over your pillow. I hope you like it. I hope you like me.

Without thinking, I find myself hugging that note too, against my chest, closing my eyes ... and thinking of Colten.

Over the next two weeks, Colten dabbles in breaking and entering every time I leave my house. I'm not sure how he gets any work done. Chicago has way too much crime for him to leave daily notes on my pillow.

Remember that time you found a dead frog by your favorite tree? I found him near the pond by the batting cages, and I left him by your tree as a gift to you. I'll never forget how excited you were. I'll never forget how I felt like nobody knew you like I did. I'm still loving knowing that no other human will ever know you like I do.

Colten gave me a dead frog. It makes me laugh out loud. I remember that day, but he never said a word, never let on that it was him.

Another day ...

The week I mowed your lawn while your family went on vacation, I spent hours under the tree in the front yard, lying in the grass in your favorite reading spot. I liked the world through your eyes. I still do.

Another day ...

The last time Reagan stayed with me, I told her about Artemis. Then I told her you were my Artemis.

Another day ...

The greatest day of my life, aside from the birth of Reagan: the day Jo Watts turned out to be the neighbor girl instead of the neighbor boy.

"You're with me today, Dr. Watts," Dr. Cornwell says the second I walk into the conference room on my first day back to work.

My colleagues give me a few smiles and kind "welcome backs." They're not looking at me like someone who got shot in the line of duty. I'm not sure how to read their expressions.

"You're quite the local celebrity." Cornwell holds up a physical newspaper.

I snatch it from him.

Assistant medical examiner believes she was a murder victim from over a century ago. Helps officials find victims' bodies in Nashville.

"Is it true?" Cornwell asks.

"Which part?" I hand the newspaper back to him without reading past the headline.

"Any of it? All of it?"

I glance around the room, all eyes on me. "Listen, I'm just going to tell you what I've told everyone else. I had a near-death experience after the shooting. Since then, I've had visions and dreams about Winston Jeffries's victims. Everyone in the room knows me well enough to know that I don't believe in this kind of lunacy. Yet, here I am, experiencing it firsthand. I have no explanation."

That's not totally true anymore, but it was for a while, so it's all they're getting. I have no plans of telling the police that I was wrong about my role.

"And why am I with you today?" I shoot Cornwell a look.

"My, my … aren't you a little chippy today. Anyone else would find it an honor to be with me for the day."

"I feel like you don't trust me. Like you're demoting me."

"I'm observing you for one day. Just one short day, Dr. Watts. It's the responsible thing to do. I need to make sure you're physically and emotionally up to the task."

"You're just observing?"

He nods, holding up his hands. "I won't touch a thing."

I take a seat at the table and remain obediently quiet while Dr. Cornwell goes over the cases for the day.

When I get to the autopsy suite, Alicia has my first case on the table waiting for me. "Josie, good to see you back."

"Thanks."

Alicia eyes Dr. Cornwell. I ignore every ounce of skepticism in the room, which is hard to do because it's thick today.

Will I stumble?

Hesitate?

Miss something?

Mess something up?

Will Dr. Cornwell have to jump in and save the day? Save my ass?

Not a chance.

My brain is good at multitasking. It can be fucked ten ways to Sunday from the near-death experience yet not miss a step or a shred of evidence over the next two hours. I don't give Dr. Cornwell a single glance nor do I acknowledge the other critics who should be focused on their own cases.

"Next," I say, leaving Alicia to close up while I take a restroom break, strutting out of the autopsy suite with confidence. I rip off my PPE and speed walk down one long hallway and then another, finding refuge on the other side of a vending machine.

On a gasp, I hunch over, resting my hands on my thighs.

Breathe ... breathe ... breathe ...

I'm a killer. I don't deserve the trust of these victim's families or Dr. Cornwell or all of Cook County. I am a fraud. An imposter. And I can't fucking find a breath.

A hand touches my shoulder, making me jump. The second my gaze lifts, I see him.

Colten.

He says nothing. Nothing is exactly what I need because I can't breathe or talk. I'm scared that I might start crying if I'm forced to do either.

I need a minute. A minute of silence.

I slowly stand up, and he pulls me to him, my face

against his chest while his hand cups the back of my head.

Weeks of breaking into my house.

Weeks of leaving me notes.

Weeks of silence from me.

And he says nothing.

God ... I love this man.

When I feel a vibration, I step back. Colten pulls his phone from the inside pocket of his jacket and answers it. "Mosley."

My gaze affixes to his chest because now things feel awkward. The silence no longer fits. I glance at my hand while he takes it in his.

When I look up at him with his phone to his ear, he gives me a tiny smile that says all that it's always said.

I've got you. You're not alone. This will pass.

He squeezes my hand before releasing it, turning, and pushing through the door to the stairway. I get my butt into the locker room, use the toilet, and gown-up for my next case.

CHAPTER
Eleven

"This is unprofessional," Dr. Byrd says, taking a seat across from me at a Mediterranean restaurant a few blocks from his office. "You're my patient."

"I'm not, Terrance." I take a sip of water. "I'm just an old friend buying you dinner."

"I'm married." He gives me a lifted eyebrow while placing his napkin on his lap.

"Good thing I'm okay with buying you dinner without the promise of sex."

"I'm ordering the most expensive thing on the menu *and* dessert. Maybe even a few drinks. You'll also pay for my cab home, correct?" He gives me a challenging expression. "I feel like this 'friends having dinner' is just your way of not paying for my services."

"Or ... I want to talk to you in an environment where you can leave your professionalism at the door and be completely honest with me." I draw lines in the condensation on my water glass.

"What makes you think I've been anything less than honest with you?"

"Because I can tell you're out of your comfort zone with my issues. And when I tell you what I found out in California, you're going to want to tell me I'm batshit crazy. I need your *honest* expertise. Nothing sugar-coated. Not like when I tell a family their loved one probably didn't suffer, but I know that probability is slim at best."

Terrance eyes me just before the waiter takes our order. As soon as it's just us again, he blows out a long breath. "Tell me. And I'll give you my honest opinion."

I glance around the restaurant to see how close the nearest table and set of ears are to us. "I saw a psychic who knows a lot about near-death experiences."

"You lost me at psychic. I'm already silently judging you."

I chuckle. "I'm judging me too. And that's not accurate. She's a parapsychologist. Just hear me out. She said I wasn't one of the victims."

"Never mind. I like her after all."

"Wow. You won't let me finish. You must really have to force yourself to hold back your reaction when you're on the clock."

He smirks. "You have no idea."

I give him the stink eye. "As I was saying ... she pointed out all the reasons I wasn't one of the girls he killed. And it made sense, well, most of it. Then she nudged me until my brain stretched just far enough to see what I had been missing."

Terrance presses his lips together, biting his tongue, I'm sure.

"I was Winston Jeffries."

He doesn't let anything leak. No reaction whatsoever.

Running my hands through my hair, I frown. "I killed thirty-seven little girls in another life. I was a psychopath. And while I didn't want to believe it; now, I see it's the only thing that fits. God ... it fits so many parts of my life before the shooting."

He blinks once, maybe twice.

"You can speak now."

Nodding slowly, he scratches his chin. "You're batshit crazy."

I nod several times. "I know. Except ... I'm not. Not really. I know what I see. And I've sent other locations to the Nashville police, and they've found more bodies right where I told them they would be. One girl ... one girl that he killed wouldn't know all the locations of thirty-seven bodies. Did you not see today's paper?"

"I don't believe everything that gets printed."

"Well, believe it. Open your mouth. Chew it up. Then swallow it. After you digest it, tell me what it means if it doesn't mean that I was Winston Jeffries."

Resting one arm and his opposing elbow on the table, he props his chin on his fist in a thinker's pose. "Out-of-body or near-death experiences are not well studied for obvious reasons, but I'm sure you already know this. Death is not a specific moment, even if a qualified professional marks a time of death. It's a potentially reversible process. Not everyone who goes into cardiac arrest dies. Again, you know this. So the question is, what happens in that small space of time when the heart, lungs, and brain cease to function? Understanding of the human brain is still in its infancy despite great strides over the years. I think there are some brilliant minds who are making good guesses at what these NDEs mean. I'm just not one of them. And I don't know who your psychic friend is, but I'd be happy to refer you to a professor I know. He's written a few papers on neurophenomenology of near-death experiences. I know he's worked with other doctors using high-density ECG during an induced NDE-like state, but to my knowledge they've had little success. However, if I'm being completely honest, Josie, I'm inclined to ask what your endgame is with this? Let's take liberty and just say you are right. You were Winston Jeffries. Now what? You can't undo the past. You can't be held accountable for something that happened over a century ago. You're not a serial killer in this life. What is the endgame? Do you just need someone to say they believe you? If that's the case, I'll do that. I have no explanation for the bodies. The bodies sell it for me."

"I don't need to be believed. Or right. Or anything ego-driven. I need to forget it. All of it. It's poison in my brain. Imagine waking up every day after a long night of seeing dead children in your dreams. Then imagine feeling responsible for their deaths. This is what I'm living with right now. And it's not just when I sleep. Right now, I can see the graves. The dead girls. There's not a pill strong enough to get rid of these visions. And it makes me question my entire existence. I don't understand what my purpose is. And I'm so scared of some switch getting flipped and losing it. I don't trust myself."

"You're afraid you're going to hurt someone or yourself?"

I nod.

"Which one?"

"Both," I whisper as our food arrives.

After we eat for a few minutes without speaking, Terrance glances up at me, wiping his mouth. "How are you and Colten?"

"Over."

"Why?"

I give him a look. He can't be that stupid.

"Did he end it, or did you?"

"I ended it."

"Why?"

"Terry, you can't really be asking me this."

"I am. You've always talked fondly of Colten. The love of your life. Your best friend since the fourth grade. I wouldn't normally advocate anyone using another person to give them purpose or reason for their existence. But in your case, I'm inclined to make an exception. Maybe instead of distancing yourself, you should..." he twists his lips "...lean in a bit."

"Lean in a bit?" I narrow my eyes. "That's your brilliant, a-decade-of-medical-school advice to me. Lean in?"

He offers a half shrug before taking a bite of his food. "Let him help you through this. You trust him. He might be the perfect person to get you through the rough patch."

"The rough patch? You are definitely not getting dessert out of this. I think about dead girls all day and all night. It's not a rough patch. It's unimaginable mental anguish."

"Maybe consider changing your profession or taking more time off. Give yourself more opportunities to not see or think about the deceased. Memories, real or not, are imperfect. They fade whether we want them to or not. Time is your friend."

"I'm not changing professions. I love my job."

"Then lean into that. Are you back to work?"

I nod. "Today was my first day back."

"And it went well?"

My gaze shifts to my plate. "It went ... fine."

"What's that pause about?"

On a sigh, I glance up at him. "The chief ME hovered over me all day, making sure I was okay to be back at work. And I was. I did everything right. I didn't need any help. But ..."

"But?"

"Mid-morning, I had a mini breakdown or panic attack. I couldn't get Winston Jeffries out of my mind. And then I started questioning if I should be back at work yet ... or ever. I started to feel like a fraud. What would people think of me if they knew my secret?"

"This doesn't have to be something you're hiding. That implies you have accountability. This is something you're working through. It's nobody's business but yours. No accountability. No need to feel like a fraud."

I consider his words.

At the same time, I see naked girls, heads shaved, in a pile awaiting burial.

I was one sick fuck ...

After dinner, I get Terry a cab, but I can't go home.

How did I survive seventeen years without *him?*

When life hits an impasse, when the air gets too thick, when I can't find my way, I navigate to *him.*

CHAPTER
Twelve

Josie's car is in my driveway when I get home just before ten-thirty at night. I make a slow trek to the door, wondering what's brought her here. It's been a long fucking day thinking about our silent interaction at the county medical examiner's office. I was a little surprised to see her during my quick visit with one of the other MEs. I thought she had one more week before returning to work.

Has she read my notes? Kept them? Ripped them apart? Lit them on fire?

The door opens to silence. There's a light on over the kitchen sink, but she's nowhere in sight. When I reach the top of the stairs while loosening my tie, I see her curled into a ball on my bed, hugging my pillow.

I skipped dinner, and now I'm starving. I could use a shower, and my teeth need to be brushed and flossed.

But I can't make it past the bed. The floor creaks beneath me when I take a step closer, and Josie jumps.

Her tired eyes blink open after she sits up and rubs them several times. "Hi," she whispers.

"Hi." I sit on the edge of the bed, angling slightly toward her.

"My uh ... psychiatrist ..." She crawls toward me.

I grab her hips as she straddles my lap, dark hair stuck to her face that she doesn't bother to address. She's so fucking beautiful it hurts to look at her when I know she's not well.

"He told me to lean in."

I nod slowly. "Lean in, huh?"

"Yeah," she whispers, brushing her hands over the back of mine and interlacing our fingers while bringing my palms to her face. "Can I lean into you?" Her head tips to the side, *leaning in* to my touch.

My lips find hers, kissing her slowly. Her hands slide to my tie, removing it and letting it drop to the floor before working the buttons to my shirt. Our kiss grows stronger as she pushes my shirt over my shoulders.

One by one, our clothes get tossed aside until it's just us, the sheets, and the rest of the night.

She leans into me.

And I lean into her.

This isn't the body of a serial killer. My hands, followed by my lips, trace every soft curve. She makes the sexiest sound when I slide my tongue between her spread legs. Her fingers dig into my back, finding old scars and making new ones while I move inside of her.

The bedsprings offer a slight protest, syncing with our labored breaths and the occasional whisper of my name ... of her name ... of a god whose existence feels less likely every day.

I wish we could stay like this forever because it feels like the *us* we've been searching for since the day we met. When she collapses on top of me, gasping for her next breath, I roll us to the side. Pulling the sheets over our naked, entwined bodies, I drift off to sleep with the first girl who felt like the sun. The air. Gravity. And my whole world and reason for existing.

MY ALARM GOES off at five.

No Josie.

But my sheets smell like flowers and spring rain ... and maybe a hint of formaldehyde, so it's a damn good morning.

I hope.

I slip on jogging shorts and a hoodie and grab my tennis shoes before heading downstairs. Josie's not in the family room or the kitchen, but there's a note by my coffeemaker.

Pilates. Shower. Breakfast. Work. Thanks for letting me lean in. XO ~J

CHAPTER
Thirteen

"I CAN GO," Dr. Cornwell says at the morning meeting.

"If you don't quit coddling me, I'm going to lose it." It's too late. I can't walk back those words. *Lose it like Winston Jeffries?* I sigh. "I did fine yesterday."

Not counting the breakdown by the vending machine.

"It was my case. I wrote the report. I can testify in court. I'm fine. Really."

He slides his reading glasses up his nose. "Very well then. Off you go." He gives me a shooing motion with his hand.

After I get to the courthouse, wait forever to get through security, use the restroom, and make my way toward the courtroom, I run into Dylan Paine.

"I'm surprised to see you here," she says, applying lip gloss before going into the courtroom.

"I'm testifying."

"I know." She pauses her motions and gives her lips a light tap together. "I'm just surprised."

"Why? Because you don't think I'm a real doctor?"

Dylan grins. "I've never said that. I just think you're young, not as experienced as Dr. Cornwell."

"Funny … I have a long list of people who I think are more experienced than you, but I don't feel the need to remind you."

She draws her head back a few inches. I'm a little punchy today. Just as she starts to speak, the elevator dings, and the doors open.

Dylan smiles, and I glance over my shoulder at Colten. Chicago's too big, and so is this courthouse to find myself stuck in this same threesome again. It has to be part of my atonement.

"Detective Mosely. It's always nice to see you." Dylan bats her fake eyelashes.

Maybe she and her husband have an open marriage, but I doubt it. I think she's nothing more than a disingenuous whore.

Wow, Josie … who are you?

Colten gives her a tiny smile and walks toward me, stopping with a good three feet between us. "Morning," he says.

Just as Dylan opens her mouth to speak, I take two steps closer to him. Way closer than colleagues or even friends would stand. Through the corner of my eye, I see her mouth clamp shut, choking on her unspoken words. I couldn't care less about her. She needs to get her ass into the courtroom and start making her case before the DA puts me on the stand to obliterate every shred of evidence she thinks she has to exonerate her client.

"You look…" the corner of Colten's mouth curls a fraction "…pretty today."

My grin doesn't hold back, especially when Dylan makes a tiny huffing noise and clicks her heels into the courtroom. "Do you remember the first time you called me pretty?"

Colten presses his lips together for a few seconds. "That's a hard one because I thought it so many times. When did I get the nerve to say it?"

"The first time you saw me trying on fly fishing waders in the garage. You weren't saying it as a compliment."

His barely detectable smirk morphs into a full-on shit-eating grin. "Yes, I was absolutely complimenting you. I hid most of my compliments behind sarcasm because it was the only way I could say them to you without you making fun of me."

I roll my eyes. "So your game was to make fun of me before I made fun of you?"

"My game was to give you the *illusion* that I was making fun of you, when in reality, I was a lovesick boy."

I wet my lips because they are not glossed like Dylan's—and because I want Colten to kiss me.

"I'm still that same lovesick boy," he whispers before answering my silent request with a soft kiss.

I grin against his lips. "When are we going to talk about you breaking into my house?"

He stands erect. "Says the woman who broke into mine last night."

"I used the key," I cup my hands at my mouth and whisper yell, "under your planter."

"Well, I used the key on my keychain." He pulls his keys out of his pocket and shows me a key, presumably my house key.

"Where did you get that?"

"Your dad made me a copy shortly after the shooting."

"My dad has a key to my house?"

"So it would seem." He pockets his keys.

"And he's making copies and giving them out to ... just anyone?"

"Just anyone? Is that my new rank?"

I start to return a snarky reply, but it dies on my tongue. I'm all out of snark this morning. "Listen, last night—"

"Don't." He shakes his head. "I don't want to be another burden in that mind of yours. I'm not a problem you need to figure out and solve. I'm not giving up on you or on us. Nor am I pushing you for anything you're not ready to give."

"What if I'm never ready?"

He shrugs. "Maybe lovesick boy is my destiny."

Ouch ...

"Destiny can suck."

"Tell me about it." He winks before bending forward and pressing his lips next to my ear.

It makes me shiver every time.

"I love you, Josephine Watts," he whispers.

"That sucks for you too," I mumble.

Colten deposits the lightest kiss to my cheek.

Another shiver.

"You're mine. Not his." He sidesteps me and makes his way to the courtroom past me without one glance back.

When I'm called in to testify, I state the facts. I'm then subjected to a slew of ridiculous what-ifs from Dylan Paine.

She ends her questioning with the most ridiculous one. "How often do you conclude an undetermined cause of death?"

"As often as the cause is unable to be determined."

She frowns at me squashing her attempt to make me look incompetent in front of the jury.

"Would you say more often than your superiors?"

"Objection," the DA says. "Irrelevant."

"Sustained," Judge Adelman says. He knows I'm extremely qualified to be on this stand and often superior to my superiors.

"Doctor Watts, were you recently injured in the line of duty?"

"Objection," Dan, the DA, is not happy with Mrs. Paine In The Ass. "Irrelevant."

"Sustained."

"Is it true that you had a near-death experience, and now you see dead people?"

"Objection! Badgering the witness."

"Sustained. Counsel, approach the bench."

I watch both attorneys approach the bench; then I scan the jury. Dylan needs to discredit me because she's losing her case. And I'll hand it to the douchebag, she's managed to sow a little doubt into their minds. I can tell from the looks on some of their faces.

The attorneys leave the bench.

"No further questions, Your Honor," Dylan says with her back to the judge.

Dan faces me. "Doctor Watts, did you graduate at the top of your class in medical school?"

"Yes."

"Did the chief medical examiner himself pursue you, encourage you to leave general surgery, and make the glowing recommendation for your forensic pathology fellowship?"

"Yes."

"Have you published nearly forty peer-reviewed papers?"

"Yes."

"Have you had hands-on teaching with medical students?"

"Yes."

"Have you been cleared to work since you took a bullet in the line of duty?"

"Yes."

"No further questions, Your Honor."

The judge dismisses me. When I walk past Dylan's table, I give her a wink. It's a good luck wink. She's going to need it.

When I exit the courtroom, Detective Mosley's leaning against the opposing wall with his head bowed to his phone. He glances up, and much like yesterday, he says exactly what I need to hear without saying anything. Pushing off the wall, he slips his phone into his pocket with one hand while taking my hand in his other. We wordlessly make our way out of the courthouse and down the stairs where we stop, and he turns toward me.

I grab his lapels, staring at his chest while taking in a deep breath. I wasn't expecting Dylan to cross that line. I was angry, but I didn't show it. Still, I imagined shaving her long blond locks from her head, and that's messed-up. So messed-up.

"Lean in," Colten says, interrupting my thoughts.

I don't look up at him; I tighten my grip on his lapels ... and lean in, resting my forehead on his shirt over his heart. I *hate* feeling so unworthy of him. It's uniquely hollowing.

I am a bad person loved by a good man.

"I believe you," he says. "I just don't know how to fight demons that lived in another century. And as much as I want to crawl into your head and occupy every inch of space in your brain, I can't. I also can't let you walk away. I *trust* you, Josie. You have to let that be enough."

Tipping my chin up to look him in the eyes, I give him a sad smile. "What if I don't trust myself?"

Colten inches his head side to side and repeats himself from earlier. "You're mine. Not his."

Colten's, not Winston's.

I can't separate it quite like that.

CHAPTER
Fourteen

"I HEARD my parents talking about your mom," Josie said as we were biking to the pool the summer before sixth grade.

"What were they saying?"

"That your mom is ... hmm, what was the word? Struggling? Yeah, I think that was the word. They said she needs to get help."

"Help doing what?"

"I think it's because she cries a lot, and my mom said she's sometimes in her robe all day. She gets the mail in her robe, and she takes you to piano lessons in her robe."

"She's sad because my dad's living in a trailer."

"If it were me, I'd be sad because my husband cheated on me. No ... not sad. I'd be mad. I'd probably hurt him."

I laughed as we locked our bikes to the rack by the pool entrance. "What would you do?"

"Blunt trauma to his testicles."

"What?" I didn't hear her right. Did I?

"My mom said I should never kick a boy in the testicles because it can cause serious damage. I looked it up. Pain. Swelling. Even a rupture with lots of blood in your scrotum."

"My what?"

"Scrotum. It's the part of you that looks like a turkey and holds your testicles, letting them hang low from your body to keep cool. If they get too warm, your sperm die."

"Shh ..." My cheeks filled with hot embarrassment when the teenaged girl checking our pool passes gave us a weird look. She must have heard Josie say testicles *and* sperm.

I veered right near the boys' locker rooms, and Josie went left toward the girls'. Meeting on the other side, we searched for a place to keep our towels and bags.

"If I had a husband, and he cheated on me, I'd kick him hard in the balls with my boots. My mom said it could cause a guy to not be able to make children someday. And that seems like a fair punishment for cheating, don't you think?"

I'd been kicked in the balls on more than one occasion, usually an accident. Just talking about it made my stomach hurt. "I don't think my mom will kick my dad in the nuts. She says she still loves him."

"I'd kick him in the testicles, but I think my parents would ground me."

"Don't call them testicles." I dropped my bag next to the fence.

"That's what they're called."

"You sound like a doctor."

"Maybe someday I'll be a doctor, so it's a good idea for me to keep calling them testicles instead of nuts or balls."

I never thought she had a loud voice until we were in public talking about testicles. Then it felt like she was using a megaphone, and everyone could hear her.

"The one exception to kicking someone in the testicles ..."

Here we go again.

"... is if someone is trying to kidnap you or touch your genitals. A kidnapper or a pedophile. Or it could be the same person, right?"

I had no idea what a pedophile was, and I wasn't going to ask her until we were someplace private for fear that she'd use the word *genitals* ten times in her loudest voice.

"If a pedophile kidnapped you, they could tie you up and touch you whenever they wanted to. I suppose that would be easier than stalking kids outside of schools. Right?"

I gathered that a pedophile was a pervert. That's what my mom called adults who touched kids' privates. I felt certain Josie's dad talked with her a lot about pedophiles or perverts. Josie was eleven going on thirty.

"Do you want a grape ice pop?" I asked her, desperately wanting to change the subject.

"Orange."

I nodded, escaping to the concession stand before she could talk about ... anything. The second I returned with the ice pop, she started up again.

"I think I'm going to start spending time with your mom like when you're at baseball practice. Chad spends all of his time playing video games. And you guys don't have a dog or any other family pet, so I'll spend time with her. Then maybe she'll not be so sad. Maybe she'll get dressed."

Even at eleven, I knew there was something special about Josephine Watts. She wasn't trying to be anything more than the girl who treated other people the way she wanted to be treated. Of course, I didn't tell her that, but maybe I should have.

"You can be our pet." I laughed at my own joke.

Josie attempted to give me a sneer, but she started giggling. "I won't even pee on the carpet. My dad said we can't get a dog because they pee on the carpet, and then you have to pay a carpet cleaner to suck up the mess, and they charge you a whole bunch of money for every visit. He said we can't afford a dog because they can barely afford Benji and me. I know they really mean him, not me, because the only time they call the carpet cleaner is when Benji makes a mess."

"We had a dog in Texas, but my dad ran him over with the car."

Josie's nose wrinkles. "Did he die right away?"

"No. His back legs were broken, and he was going to need a cart with little wheels. And something was wrong with his insides too. We were going to have to push on his belly to help him go pee. So my dad had the vet kill him."

"Put him down." Josie rolled her eyes. "Not kill him."

"The vet gave him something so his heart would stop beating. He killed him."

Josie finished the last of her ice pop and nodded. "Yeah, I think so too." Then she shrugged. "My dad and I kill animals. Maybe I should be a vet someday."

We tossed our wrappers into the trash and headed straight to the line for the waterslide. From that day on, Josie made a point to visit my mom almost every day until my dad moved back home. Josie was a lot of things, but first and foremost, she was a good person.

CHAPTER
Fifteen

I WAKE from a restless sleep with a gasp, jackknifing to sitting. Heart racing. Chest burning. Sweat beading along my brow and trickling down my back. He took the girls from family gatherings. *I* took the girls from family gatherings.

After a 2 a.m. shower, I pull on a pair of black sweatpants and a white tank top and gulp down a glass of water. It clinks when I set it in the sink while closing my eyes. Young girls with long hair, ribbons, and giggles of innocence.

For hours, I stare out the window, nestled under a blanket on the sofa, waiting for sleep. I manage two hours of no dreams and wake when I hear the alarm in my bedroom. While shuffling my feet down the hall-way, there's a knock at my door. I continue to the bedroom to shut off my alarm first. As I get closer to the door, the deadbolt turns. I jump to the side, squatting down and retrieving my gun from my purse on the floor. When Colten's head peeks around the corner, I blow out a sigh with the gun still aimed at him.

"Morning," he says with his eyebrows raised, and his gaze glued to my gun.

"You have to stop breaking into my house." I lower my gun and return it to my purse.

He holds up his key. "Remember? I'm not breaking into your house."

I stand. "What are you doing here? It's five o'clock."

"I got called just after midnight. A woman's body was found in a suitcase at the airport. I was on my way home and decided I needed to see you."

"I know where you live. My house isn't between the airport and your house. Nor is it between the police station and your house."

"I didn't say *you* were on my way home. I said I was on my way home and wanted to see you."

"I'm not much of a sight at the moment."

"You didn't sleep well?"

I yawn. "I haven't slept well since you made the terrible decision to save me."

Colten follows me to my bathroom. "It wasn't a decision or a choice. It's instinctual. I need you in this life."

"Liar." I comb through my slightly damp hair.

He frowns at my reflection. "Remember that period when you visited with my mom nearly every day until my dad moved back home?"

I give him a single nod.

"It was the nicest thing I had ever seen anyone do for another human. At the time, I couldn't figure out why you would do it. She wasn't your mom. And nobody told you to do it. I was too immature to see it."

"See what?" I pull my hair into a tight bun.

"See that you were a good person. It's who you are. You don't have to try. No one tells you to be a good person. It's *who* you are."

I squeeze a glob of toothpaste onto my toothbrush and eye him in the mirror.

"I trust you." His hands find my waist while his lips press to the back of my neck.

I spit and rinse. "I abducted the girls from big events like weddings and funerals. Anywhere there was a crowd of people who were too distracted to properly watch the kids. Good people don't do that." I turn toward him, resting my hands on the edge of the sink. "It's only a matter of time before I see how they died. And I don't know if I'm emotionally equipped to deal with that. I've seen some truly grotesque things. I've dealt with liquid human remains. I've autopsied decapitated heads, no bodies. I've seen children who have been violently raped before being killed. I've put unborn babies in jars. It's a job. It's what I do, not who I am. But those girls ..."

Colten's hands slide around my neck, his thumbs brushing my cheeks. "What can I do?"

I deflate. I was ready for him to scold me for saying *I* instead of *he*. I was ready for him to give me part two of the you're-a-good-person pep talk. "Just be you," I whisper, snaking my arms around his waist.

"Who am I?"

I close my eyes, feeling exhausted. "Everything."

"Call in. Don't go to work today," he says.

I peer up at him. My gut reaction is to roll my eyes at the ridiculous suggestion. I don't skip work. That's not me. I also don't ignore my gut reactions. For some reason, I find myself nodding.

"I'm tired. Can we crawl into your bed and sleep until noon? I have to write up some reports, but I can do that later."

Again, I nod. Then I text Dr. Cornwell before sliding into bed next to Colten. He pulls me to his warm body and kisses my forehead.

Maybe it's Colten's embrace or maybe it's sheer exhaustion, but I sleep until eleven-thirty without a single vision or dream. I wake before him, but I don't move. His face is so close to mine; I can't help but inspect every tiny detail from the little scar by his eyebrow to the gray working its way into his five o'clock shadow. Long eyelashes. Full, downturned lips.

God ... it's always been him.

Colten's Josie *is* kind. Colten's Josie wouldn't harm anyone. Colten's Josie is confident and smart. Colten's Josie doesn't run from fear. I like Colten's Josie.

As if the spinning thoughts in my head are making actual sounds, Colten blinks open his eyes.

"I'm going to need help because self-doubt is a pernicious bitch. Your job is to get me there. Get the job done. And remind me every day that I'm your Artemis. Okay?"

Colten blinks slowly. "What did I miss?" he asks in a sleepy voice. "Get you where? Get what job done?"

"Get me to the altar. Make sure I'm wearing white, but I don't look ridiculous. Don't take no for an answer. Then just ... hold on to me."

It takes a few seconds for things to register, but when they do, his grin swells, engulfing his entire face.

It's a glorious smile. Spectacular. Just like him.

I give him my best smile as well, but it hurts. Everything inside my chest hurts. It hurts to stay. It hurts to walk away. Life hurts. I just think it could hurt a little less with Colten in it. And ... I hurt because I'm scared out of my mind that this is a terrible idea. But ... he trusts me. And ... I trust him.

CHAPTER
Sixteen

"WANT TO TALK ABOUT IT?" Dr. Cornwell asks when I arrive in the conference room.

"About?" I fill a cup with coffee while everyone else takes a seat at the table.

Dr. Cornwell pours a generous dose of creamer into his coffee. "You took a personal day yesterday."

"And?"

"It's your first personal day."

I smile. "Well, that's not true. I took a lot of days off after I died."

Stirring his coffee, he eyes me. I half expect him to laugh, but he doesn't. Not even a smile. "I can only imagine what you must be going through. Has it gotten any better?"

Better? He thinks I believe I was a young girl

murdered by Winston Jeffries. I can only imagine what he would think if he knew the truth.

The truth …

Is it true?

Truth is ascribed to things representing reality. I've never felt so out of touch with reality. How could I possibly know what's true?

"I'm getting married." That's my brilliant answer. If I just believe hard enough, marrying the boy I've loved for as long as I can remember might be the answer to … something.

Dr. Cornwell's bushy, gray eyebrows jump up his forehead. "I didn't know you were seeing anyone."

Gotta hand it to Alicia, she keeps our talks a secret.

"Colten Mosley."

Those bushy brows take a dive into a sharp V of confusion.

"Detective Mosley."

"Oh. How am I just now hearing about this?"

"The engagement?"

"All of it. I had no idea he was courting you."

For a second time, he makes me smile. It feels like something a normal human would do. I've never felt perfectly normal, but it was far better than not feeling human.

"How long has this courting been taking place?"

I chuckle. Now he's doing it to get a reaction from me. "Since we were nine."

"Oh good lord … that's some stamina."

I can't help myself. "Yes. Colten has a lot of stamina." I smirk.

Dr. Cornwell glances down at his coffee mug; then his gaze jumps back up to mine. He just got it. "Well..." he clears his throat, and I swear he's blushing a bit "...I suppose congratulations are in order."

"Thanks." I really need to call my parents. They should have found out before my boss. I glance past him to the rest of the MEs at the table. "Can we keep it between us for a few days? I haven't told all of my family."

Any. I haven't told anyone.

He makes a lock and key motion at his lips.

I take a seat at the table, and Dr. Cornwell introduces the cases for the day. He only gets a few words in before the most cringe-worthy sound blasts from my phone at full volume.

First, I silence my phone in the morning before I shower.

Second, I don't have songs for ringtones.

Third, I'm going to kill Colten.

It's his name on my screen with a goofy picture of his face, like a mug shot, that I did not take. And he has the ringtone set to The Dixie Cups' "Chapel of Love."

Fumbling with my phone, I mute the call and send it to voicemail.

"I guess the cat's out of the bag now." Cornwell grins.

Heat fills my cheeks, all eyes on me ... the blushing bride.

As an early wedding gift, Cornwell gives me the

five-year-old girl who was found dead in her family's swimming pool. He leads the students around the autopsy suite, spending extra time at my table. I ignore the look in his eyes, the test he's given me.

Am I okay with a drowning victim?

Am I okay with a young girl?

Am *I* okay?

"What is the mechanism in acute drownings?" Cornwell asks.

"Hypoxemia and irreversible cerebral anoxia," one of the students says as I make my Y incision.

"Good. What are the five stages of drowning?"

"Water infiltrates the airway—"

"Nope. Anyone else?" Cornwell prods.

His abrupt interruption of the first student keeps everyone else silent.

"Surprise and panic," I say. "Then water enters the lungs. You involuntarily hold your breath. Next ... lights out. In as little as thirty seconds, you're unconscious. Respiratory arrest. You start to sink. Turn blue. Possible convulsions. Cerebral hypoxia and ... death."

"I don't think everyone counts the last one," one of the students says. "Because when you're dead, you're no longer drowning."

I glance up at her. "What if you're not dead?"

Her gaze darts around at the other students, but no one jumps in to save her.

After a few seconds, she clears her throat and eyes me again. "You mean if you're not biologically dead?"

I nod, pausing my scalpel.

"You have three minutes."

"Then what?"

"Well, your brain cells die, and your chances are kinda ... non-existent."

"Dr. Watts drowned with a gunshot wound to her abdomen," Dr. Cornwell announces. "But she's a freak of nature. We don't know how long she was submerged, but it seems likely it was longer than three minutes. We'll never know. Anyway ... here she is with enough living brain cells to do her job flawlessly."

He emphasizes the "flawlessly". It's his nod of approval. Another test I've managed to pass.

"Touch my phone again, and I will remove both of your hands, Mosley."

Colten glances up from his desk, a little before seven. There are only a few people left on the floor. He pushes back in his chair and stands while wearing a champion's grin. "You won't."

I set my bag on his desk and let him pull me into his body. "Try me." I tilt my head back to look at him.

"You like what my hands do to you. I'd only have my tongue, and while we both enjoy what I can do with it, I think you'd miss these magical digits." He holds up his hands and wiggles his fingers.

I glance around to see if anyone's paying attention to us. "Everyone at work knows, yet ... I haven't told my parents."

"They're thrilled. Your mom screamed, and your dad did his long 'hmm' as if he wasn't sure, but then he said I was the only man for you."

"You told my parents!" I grab his shirt and jerk it.

"I'm making it happen, baby. You told me to get you to the altar. Step one: tell our family."

Our family.

Not families.

We have a village. My parents love him, and his mom loves me. We are one family. My fingers release his shirt, and I press my hands flat to his chest. "Were they really happy?" All anger disappears.

Something about his expression softens. "You're okay with me telling them?"

I shrug before lifting onto my toes and brushing my lips over his. "Get me to the altar, and I'll say I do." I kiss him.

His hands cup my face. When the kiss ends, he narrows his eyes a fraction, and he takes a seat in his chair, scratching his chin. I ease my backside onto the edge of his desk.

"I fucking love you so much."

I smile, unsure of what to say back to him. All of my emotions clog my throat. I love him too. But it doesn't take away my fear. Trusting him is all I can do.

Resting his elbows on the chair's arms, he rubs his lips together before grinning. "I didn't tell your parents. I just wanted to get you worked up, but you only gave me ten seconds of satisfaction."

With a slight eye roll, I shake my head. "My parents

adore you. Really, you could have told them."

"My par—" Colten pauses. "My mom adores you, but you know that."

"You were going to say parents."

His brow furrows while he gives me a slow nod. "My dad liked you." He lowers his gaze.

"Why do you make it sound like that was a bad thing?"

"Because it was," he mumbles.

"I don't understand." I nudge his leg with mine, forcing his gaze back to me.

He frowns. "I was on my way to your house to tell your dad about us. To tell him that I loved you. And I wanted to go wherever you went after graduation."

I slowly shake my head.

"Just as I was walking out the door, my dad came home. He made some snide remark about me secretly pining for the chief's daughter. I said it wasn't going to be a secret much longer." Colten rubs his forehead. "Then my dad said you were the smartest decision I had ever made. And he was amazed I hadn't screwed it up yet. He thought your good work ethic would rub off on me. And ... well ... that rubbed me the wrong way. It triggered my toxic need to do the exact opposite of what he wanted." He shakes his head. "I ... I was so damn self-destructive. I didn't want to please him. I didn't want to *be* him. So I didn't tell your dad that I loved you. I did the opposite. And when your dad suggested the Marines, I knew my dad would hate that idea. So ..."

He glances up at me again.

I don't know what to say. This hurts.

Colten rakes his hands through his hair, leaving it a mess. "Have you ever wanted so badly to not become something or someone, that you're willing to destroy your own world to prevent it? You're willing to destroy everyone around you too?"

After a few breaths, I get misty eyed, and recognition flickers in Colten's eyes. I start to speak, but I can't, so I swallow back some of the suffocating emotion.

On a slow exhale, he closes his eyes for a beat. "Of course you know," he whispers.

I let seventeen years pass. I held a grudge for *seventeen years*. I hated Colten Mosley because ... I *loved* Colten Mosley. That wasn't hate. I had no idea what true hate felt like until Athelinda shattered my existence into so many unrecognizable pieces that I can't imagine ever feeling whole again. Still, I'm trying.

My job.

My family.

My friends.

Colten.

They're pieces I recognize. They belong to Josephine Watts. I need all the pieces of her I can get.

I wipe the corner of my eyes. "Did you tell your mom?"

"Not yet, but she'll be elated." He leans forward in his chair and takes my hands, brushing his thumbs along my knuckles. "I think we should set a date."

This fear is borderline paralyzing. I still have the

urge to go hide. Sometimes I have the urge to inflict pain upon myself. The guilt ... it fills my lungs like I'm in a constant second stage of drowning. Then there's the other shoe waiting to drop, the next horrific, century-old vision.

How did I murder those girls?

"Bring up a calendar." I smile despite the knots in my stomach. I never thought the day would come that I'd have to psych myself up just to be a functioning human being.

Colten's whole face comes to life. "Yeah?"

I give him the why-not shrug.

He releases my hands and snatches his phone from his desk. "I was originally thinking right after the holidays. I know they're right around the corner, but ..." Giving me a quick glance, his nose wrinkles a bit. He's bracing for me to object or return some sort of apprehension.

"Perfect," I say, feigning my best calm confidence. My pulse has to be close to one-forty. Maybe January is too far away. Maybe we should elope immediately. Will it really happen if we wait for me to go out of my mind?

"How about the seventh?"

"The seventh it is." I have to remind myself not to grit my teeth or clench my fists. I'm getting married on January seventh. Normal, non-serial killers do that sort of stuff. *Josephine Watts* deserves this. I really, really want to be her.

He taps his phone screen, adding an event to his calendar on that date:

Marrying the girl of my dreams.

"Listen," he says, head still bowed to his phone screen. "When we tell my mom and she asks about your engagement ring, tell her it's being sized."

"I don't have an engagement ring, probably because I proposed to you."

"Whoa ... what?" His head snaps up. "Not true. Not true at all. I proposed to you at the donut shop."

"Oh? Was that really a proposal?" My lips twist to the side. "Maybe, but I broke off our engagement after I got back from California. Two nights ago, I proposed to you."

Tiny wrinkles line his forehead. "You thought 'Get me to the altar. Make sure I'm wearing white but I don't look ridiculous. Don't take no for an answer. Then just ... hold on to me,' was a proposal?"

Pushing off his desk, I step between his legs and lace my hands through his hair while his hands grip the back of my legs. "It was an epic proposal. The kind only one's soulmate would give. It wasn't predictable. It wasn't a cliche. It was all heart. It was twenty-six years of friendship finally taking that next ... beautiful ... step."

Colten's gaze locks with mine. It, too, is beautiful. "Just to be really clear, in case you missed it a few minutes earlier ... I fucking love you so much."

I make the slow descent to his mouth. "You, my future husband, are something to behold. And I fucking love you so much too."

CHAPTER
Seventeen

My parents react to our engagement news just as Colten predicts: he's perfect, I'm perfect, we are even more perfect together.

Becca will find out soon. It's been a week since telling my parents and swearing them to secrecy. My mom is dying to plan this wedding with Becca. I've booked another session with Dr. Byrd. I'm not sure if that makes me responsible, proactive with my mental health, or if I'm admitting that I'm mentally slipping.

"I'll stay in the car," I say when Colten pulls up to Katy's house to pick up Reagan for the big surprise.

"You should meet Katy. She'll want to meet you since you're now a big part of Reagan's life."

I'm a thirty-five-year-old woman who dissects dead bodies. I'm marrying the love of my life despite not caring about marriage. I don't want kids of my own. Oh

… and I was a serial killer in a past life. Just the kind of person a mother would want to be a *big* part of her daughter's life.

Colten struts his way to the front door of the white with red brick two-story while I lag three steps behind him.

When he reaches the steps to the stoop, he glances back at me and holds out his hand. "Come here."

I take it and drag my feet up the stairs.

"Is she hot?" I ask before he knocks on the door.

"What?" He gives me a funny look.

I shrug. "You always went for the hottest girls in school. I'm just curious if you continued that trend."

It takes him a second to speak or even blink. "You're right." He smirks. "I went for you, Josie, and you were by far the hottest girl in school."

I scoff. "I was not. And you know what I'm talking about. We were never officially anything."

"You're right again." He squeezes my hand while his other hand knocks on the storm door. "We were everything."

The door opens.

Yep. Katy is a hottie.

"Hey! Reagan is finishing her snack. Come in." Katy smiles at me; then her gaze goes to my hand in Colten's.

"Katy, this is Josie Watts. Josie, this is Katy."

"Nice to meet you." Katy smiles. I think it's genuine, but I've always struggled to read hot girls correctly.

"You as well," I say.

"What time does your mom's flight get in?" Katy asks Colten.

"In an hour."

"Well, I haven't told Reagan since you said it's a surprise. Is she coming for anything special or just a visit?"

"Josie's mom is coming tomorrow, and the four of them are going to go wedding dress shopping."

Katy's eyes widen. "Oh ... is your mom getting remarried?"

Colten chuckles. "No."

Katy's attention shifts to me.

"January seventh." I grin, and I fear it looks as goofy as it feels. "Mark your calendar." *Well, shit. Did I just invite Colten's baby mama to our wedding?*

"Wow! Congratulations." Katy shakes her head at Colten. "Never thought I'd live to see the day."

Me neither.

"Reagan?" Colten calls her name. His thumb rubs my finger, a little fidgety and anxious to get out of here.

"Daddy!" She tears around the corner and flies into his arms, forcing him to release my hand.

"What's this?" He kisses her cheek, and she squeals when he licks something from the corner of her mouth. "Mmm ... strawberries." He sets her down. "Grab your bag. We have to get going. I have a surprise for you."

Katy eyes me again after Reagan runs upstairs. Was I supposed to give Reagan a big hug and exuberant greeting as well? I didn't even say hi.

What's wrong with me? I helped watch Benji. I even changed a few diapers. I should have a few motherly instincts or nurturing tendencies embedded in me somewhere.

"Is this your first marriage," Katy asks.

"Yes."

"Kids?"

I shake my head and offer a stiff grin.

"Oh, well, I guess it's a race to see who gives Reagan a sibling first," she says.

Colten laughs. It's a nervous laugh, and his equally nervous thumb is about to wear through the skin on my finger.

"You'll win. We're never having kids," I say with confidence.

"Oh." Katy looks at Colten for confirmation.

No confirmation needed. There is a zero percent chance of us having kids.

"Well..." Colten shoots me a sidelong glance "... never is a long time. Anything could happen."

Nope. Not anything.

"Ready!" Reagan barrels down the stairs, dragging her duffel bag behind her.

Colten takes the bag and Reagan's hand. "See you Wednesday."

"Bye." Katy leans down and kisses Reagan's head. "Love you, sweetie."

Reagan talks our ears off on the way to the airport.

"See the plane?" Colten points to the sky as we exit toward the terminal.

"Are we going in an airplane?" she asks, bursting with excitement.

I hope Becca can live up to the high expectation of a trip on a plane.

"No, Button. It's something else."

We park and head toward the gate. By the time we get there, Becca's coming down the elevator.

"Grandma!" Reagan races toward her.

Apparently, Grandma is better than airplanes.

Colten steps behind me and wraps his arms around my waist, kissing my head. While Reagan has Becca preoccupied fifteen feet away from us, I turn in his arms because I have to get this off of my chest.

"I had a tubal ligation before I started med school. No babies."

He frowns. "You had your tubes tied?"

"Yes."

"Why?"

"Because I don't want children."

He shakes his head slowly. "But how could you know for certain at such a young age?"

"Colten, I've known this for as long as I can recall. I told you this when we were kids."

"But that's just it; we were kids."

"And now I'm in my mid-thirties, and I still don't want kids."

I can't read his expression, but it doesn't give me a good feeling.

"Before we tell your mom and Reagan, you need to

decide right now if Reagan is it for you. I will not be giving you a child. Not ever."

"I choose you." No hesitation. He says it so quickly, so confidently, it punches a hole in my gut. He's giving me the kind of love most women only dream of. And I feel unworthy. "It's you. No question."

I nod just as he glances over my shoulder.

"What are you two up to?" Becca says, holding her arms out for Colten.

He hugs her before picking up Reagan, hiking her onto his hip. "I asked Josie to marry me, and she said yes."

Incorrect. But I don't squabble over the details.

Becca's eyes fill with tears while she pulls me in for a hug. "Finally," she whispers.

"I want to be the flower girl!" Reagan claps her hands together several times.

"Of course, Button."

When Becca releases me, her palms press to my cheeks. "You've always been my daughter. I can't believe my boy is finally making it official."

I smile. "My mom's coming tomorrow. How do you feel about shopping for a wedding dress?"

"Ah, perfect!" Her hands drop from my face and go straight to my left hand. "Where's your ring?"

"It's being fitted," Colten says before I have a chance to answer. "Let's get going. Parking is expensive."

CHAPTER
Eighteen

MY MOM ARRIVES Saturday morning in time for the four of us girls to have lunch before shopping for dresses. While my mom chatters nonstop, Becca sips her post lunch coffee and strokes the back of Regan's long, dark hair while she plays on her iPad.

I'm mesmerized by it, fixating on it. I can see it hanging from a tree in a cemetery. The silky strands whipping in the breeze. I can imagine what she'd look like without her hair. I know exactly what she would look like without a pulse. Without a breath. No reflexes. No pupillary constriction. Her skin would sag, making her prominent joints become pronounced. Her sphincters would relax, passing feces and urine. All the blood would drain from smaller veins. She'd be pallid. Pallor mortis. As hours pass, her body temperature would drop to the air temperature around it. Without a heartbeat, blood would pool from gravity. Livor mortis. More time would pass, and her muscles might stiffen. Children don't always follow the same pattern as adults. Rigor mortis might spread from her jaw and neck to her chest, abdomen, and extremities. A lifeless body. The end of innocence.

"Where are you?" Mom rests her hand on my arm, tearing my gaze away from Reagan.

I feel warm. Too warm. And my heart's racing fast. Too fast. "No ... nowhere. I ... um ..." I scoot back in my chair. "I need to use the restroom. Please excuse me." When I get to the ladies' room, I splash water on my face and press several hand towels to it. Using the same towels, I shove them inside of my blouse and blot the sweat from my cleavage and armpits.

"She's fine," I whisper. "She's fine." I didn't hurt Reagan. I would never hurt Reagan.

Right?

While I run my fingers through my hair, I curl them into fists and tug ... tug more ... harder ... harder ...

The door opens to my right, letting the chattering from the restaurant seep inside. I release my hair and fix it while a lady closes the stall door behind me.

"Everything okay?" Becca asks when I return to the table.

"Absolutely." I smile, sitting in my chair just as the waitress sets the bill on the table. I grab it before anyone else can.

"No. I've got this, Josie." Mom tries to argue with me.

I shove my credit card into the black check presenter, and the waitress scoops it up two seconds later.

"Sorry. Too late." I wink at her. I've gone from trying to pull my hair out of my head to a version of chipper that makes me cringe.

In the cool fall air, we stroll down the busy street toward the bridal boutique and pass a hair salon.

"Mind if we stop in here to see if they have an opening?" I ask.

Mom and Becca share looks of confusion.

"I've been so busy with work that I've totally neglected my hair. And I'd love to have it looking nice before I try on gowns."

They nod and offer agreeable smiles.

"Great. Uh ..." I gesture to the opposite side of the street. "There's a toy store if you want to walk around it with Reagan until I'm done."

Again, they return slow nods. "Text me when you're done?" Mom asks.

"Sounds good."

I'm in luck. They have an opening.

An hour later, I meet them outside of the toy store. The door opens, and they emerge, glancing around for me. They look right past me the first time.

"There she is!" Reagan spots me.

I smile, making my way to them. Mom's and Becca's jaws drop.

"Do you like it?" I wrinkle my nose and rub my hand over the back of my head and my short pixie cut.

"I like it," Reagan finally says when my mom and Becca don't answer.

"D-do you like it?" My mom breaks her silence.

"Yeah. It will be way better for work. I can sleep in later because it will take me two seconds to do my hair. Less drying time after I shower. And on my wedding day, I won't have to fuss over flyaways."

"Flyaways," my mom whispers, losing some color from her cheeks.

"It's refreshing." Becca smiles. "Shall we try on dresses?"

"Let's do it." I take Reagan's hand. With a new bounce in my step, feeling so much lighter, I lead them to the bridal boutique.

For the nearly two hours we're here, trying on dresses, my mom keeps looking at me. She looks brokenhearted.

When I try on dress number fifteen, I smile at her in the mirror. "It's just hair, Mom."

With a forced smile, she nods.

"This is the one," I declare, turning in a slow circle. It's a simple, long-sleeved off-the-shoulder, white dress. An elegant sheath dress. Perfect for a January wedding in the Midwest.

"It's stunning," Mom says, seeming to snap out of her shock. Finally.

"Colten is going to bawl his eyes out," Becca says.

Everyone laughs.

I don't see Colten crying on our wedding day.

Four dress orders later, we head to Colten's house, grabbing pizza on the way.

"Looks like he's home," Becca says when she sees his car.

Reagan sprints into the house. "Daddy! We got dresses!" Seconds later, she trots down the stairs just as we're shutting the door behind us, carrying the pizza and drinks to the kitchen. "He said he needs a shower."

"Well, we'll start eating. He won't care," Becca says, opening the pizza boxes on the table.

My mom sits in a chair and sighs. "Oh my achy feet."

"Right?" Becca plops down and passes a plate to my mom.

"I'll be right back," I mumble, but I don't think they hear me over their aching moans and rumbling stomachs.

As I ascend the stairs, I run a hand through my short hair. From the moment I told the guy at the salon to chop it off, right up until this very moment, I felt confident and empowered. I clearly have hair issues. I thought this would help. Now, I don't know.

I can't stop thinking about Colten's reaction. He loves (loved) my hair. Running his hands through it. Burying his nose into it before taking a long inhale. Stroking it after sex.

I open the door to his bedroom then the door to his bathroom. His naked backside is to me as he washes his hair in the shower, the glass covered in condensation. When the door clicks shut behind me, he glances over his shoulder, wiping suds from his face.

I fold my hands behind me and lean against the door. I've never felt so naked.

He pushes open the glass door, eyeing me with an unreadable expression. Maybe it's the steam or maybe it's the memories of what I survived today and how out of control I felt this afternoon, but I can't look him in the eye.

"Rough day, baby?"

I nod slowly, keeping my gaze on the deep blue bathmat.

Wet feet step out onto it. Another step. And another step. His hands cup my face, forcing me to look at him as he drips water all around us, on my blouse and jeans. "You look pretty." He grins. "Like ... really pretty."

All the emotions from the day pool in my eyes a breath before his mouth covers mine. He reaches behind me and locks the door before his hands make quick work of unbuttoning my blouse, removing my bra, and ridding me of everything from the waist down. Then he kisses me again, guiding me into the shower, closing the door behind us.

His hands caress my scalp like they did before I cut my hair, like he's running his fingers through invisible locks. I draw a low groan from his chest when my hand wraps around his cock.

I used to love that Colten Mosley saw everything about me. He had X-ray vision to my emotions. Now, it's painfully embarrassing. After seventeen years, I reappear in his life only to completely fall apart. Who signs up for this?

His lips brush along my neck while his hand cups my breast. "Stop thinking so hard, Watts." I feel his grin along my skin. "I love you. You love me. Don't complicate it." He kisses my shoulder. "Let us be the one part of your life that's easy."

My eyes drift shut, and my head lulls back slowly with every inch he journeys down my body.

"Colten ..." I whisper, one hand flat on the tile to my side, my other hand in his hair while his tongue flicks between my legs.

"Hmm?" he hums, making my next breath stumble from my chest.

"Why do you love me?"

He doesn't answer right away. Maybe he didn't hear me over the water. Maybe he didn't hear me because my words came out as nothing more than a mumble. With his mouth between my legs and his hands on my ass, I manage to stay solely in this moment. My mind likes this moment ... so much.

I love you. You love me. Don't complicate it.

My orgasm rips through every cell in my body until I think I might pass out. Colten kisses his way back up my body.

My breasts.

My neck.

My ear.

And he whispers, "I love you because I'm incapable

of *not* loving you. It's involuntary. It's a deeply woven thread in my fucking soul." His right hand grabs my leg, pulling it up as he pushes into me.

I suck in a breath, each thrust harder than the one before. He takes me all the way up again, blows my mind, and catches me when I start to fall, when my knees give out, when I just want to let him carry me forever. His hand moves from my breast to my hand on the tile wall, and his fingers lace with mine, squeezing hard.

"I love you ..." I whisper while my lips brush his cheek. "I love you more than life."

We kiss, our lips the only thing moving while the loop of pleasure spins out of control, his release warm inside of me ... everything's warm, yet a little shivery, like we're floating. This cocktail of sensations holds my mind completely captive in this moment.

When I find my legs again, we share nothing but smiles, the kind we used to share as two mischievous kids. Then we quickly dress and head toward the stairs.

"Oh, wait." Colten turns around, retreating to his bedroom.

I follow him, poking my head around the corner while he disappears into the closet for a few seconds, returning with something in his hand.

"It's been *resized.*" He winks, holding a ring pinched between his finger and thumb. "Can you pretend that you're not seeing it for the first time? Can you pretend that I had this the day I proposed to you in the donut shop? Can you pretend that you said yes in that very moment?"

It's not a diamond. I don't think. It has fern-like specks in the stone.

"It's dendritic quartz. In honor of Artemis. A reminder of the forest she loved." He slides the stone set in platinum onto my ring finger.

It's a perfect fit. I don't know how he did it.

"I'm glad it's back." I lift my gaze from the ring to him. "I missed it."

Colten returns a slow nod, his expression a little more serious. "I know the feeling."

Me ...

He means me.

He wraps me in his arms, presses his hand to the back of my head, lowers his nose, and inhales like nothing has changed.

CHAPTER
Nineteen

Two weeks before I turned eleven, I decided to trim my hair since my mom was too busy with Benji to take me to get my hair cut. Having no patience to wait until my dad could take me or watch Benji, I decided to figure it out on my own with my mom's sewing scissors. My bangs were too long, so I cut them. They were crooked, so I cut them more … and more, and suddenly they were way too short. So I cut the rest of my hair, hoping it would even out the look, make it so my bangs didn't look so short. Every cut led to another cut to even and straighten, but I had no luck getting anything to look even or straight … just butchered all to hell. And bangs about six millimeters long.

"Oh my god, Josephine Eleanor Watts!" My mom gasped after putting Benji down for his nap.

I stared at her reflection in the mirror. She

surveyed the pile of hair in the bathroom sink and all over the floor before returning her attention to my reflection.

"It got away from me," I mumbled.

With one hand cupped over her mouth, she nodded. "I told you I'd take you next week," she said, her hand drifting from her mouth to my hair, barely touching it like it could break.

"I know." I frowned.

"Sweetie, your bangs ..." Her fingertips grazed the spiky ends of my barely existent bangs. The stubble on my dad's face after three days was longer than my bangs.

"I can't go to school." Tears filled my eyes. "They won't let me wear a hat. And everyone will make fun of me. I can't. I won't."

"Shh ..." she hugged me and caressed my butchered hair. "We'll figure something out."

Something indeed.

After working her magic on what was left of my hair, I ended up with a layered bob that reached no farther than my earlobes, and my new best friend was a headband. Mom combed hair forward from the crown of my head and secured it with a headband. Viola! Fake bangs.

"They're gonna know," I murmured the next morning at breakfast.

"Not if you leave your headband in place."

"They'll make fun of the headband because I never wear a headband."

"You have a new hairstyle. They'll clearly see that it's short, so the headband will just be part of your new, shorter hairstyle." She set a glass of orange juice by my bowl of cereal.

"Ugh!" I grumbled. "I'm not even hungry." Pushing back my chair, I ran upstairs and spent the next ten minutes staring at my teary-eyed reflection in the mirror before I had to catch the bus.

"Wait up!" Colten called.

"Go away. Not today," I said, but he couldn't hear me.

"Did you get your hair cut?"

"Duh," I said halting at the bus stop.

He jumped in front of me, inspecting me.

I kept glancing away. "Could you stop staring so much?"

"What? Don't you like it?"

I laughed. "Of course, I like it."

I hated it.

"Don't you?" I forced myself to look him in the eye.

Colten nodded slowly. "You look pretty. Like ... really pretty."

I hadn't known him all that long, but I'd known him long enough to know he meant it. Colten Mosley thought I looked pretty.

At school, several teachers complimented me on my new hairdo. None of my friends said much, but that was okay. I wasn't keeping it that way for long. The sooner it grew back out, the better.

Nearly making it through my first fake-bangs day,

the last recess came along to ruin it. Toby Tyler, meanest boy in school, thought it would be funny to steal my headband and run to the ball diamond with it.

"TOBY!" I pressed my palm to my super short bangs and chased him. "STOP!" Catching up to him, I jumped for my headband while he held it just out of reach.

"Oh my gosh, you freak. What happened to your hair?" Toby laughed and so did two of his buddies.

In the process of trying to get the headband, I revealed my spiky bangs. A putting green.

Tears filled my eyes, but there was no way I was letting a single one go, not in front of Toby.

"Give it back, Toby."

I glanced behind me at Colten strutting his way toward us.

"She's a freak, Colten. Your little girlfriend is a freak," Toby taunted.

Colten grabbed Toby's shirt and shoved him onto the ground.

"What the heck?" Toby had the audacity to look shocked, but Colten had two inches on him, and everyone knew it was no competition.

"Get out of here, and don't touch her again." Colten grabbed my headband.

Toby growled something before stomping away with his friends.

I turned my back to Colten and quickly blotted my eyes before facing him again. "Thanks," I murmured, taking the headband and tipping my chin while trying to put it back on my head with the fake bangs pulled forward.

"What happened?" Colten asked.

"Toby took my headband because he's a jerk."

"No. I mean, what happened to your hair in front?"

"I cut it too short. And now I can't fix it." I ripped the headband back off my head and threw it on the ground.

Colten picked it up and shook the dirt from it.

"My mom took hair from back here and pulled it forward, so it looked like bangs, but ..." Again, I got emotional and had to fight the tears.

Colten slipped the headband onto my head and pulled it forward while tucking hair from the back of my head toward my forehead under the band, just like my mom had done. "There. It's fine. I'll tell Toby to keep his mouth shut, or I'll punch him in the face."

"Don't do that." I glanced up at Colten, patting my head to check my hair.

"I won't. I'm just going to tell him that so he doesn't tell everyone that ..." He wrinkled his nose, gaze inspecting my hair again.

"That I'm ugly?"

"No. You're not ugly. I told you this morning that you look pretty ... very pretty."

I didn't need or want a Prince Charming, but had I been in search of one, it would have been Colten Mosley.

Chapter Twenty

"I DIDN'T THINK I'd see you again," Dr. Byrd says.

"That makes two of us."

"Nice haircut, by the way. I bet it's a breeze to do in the morning."

I walk around his office, inspecting his succulents while he remains at his desk. "Tell me how you really feel about my hair? Ask me why I did it?"

"Why did you do it?"

I turn. "I don't know. You tell me. You're the expert."

Pressing his lips together, Terrance lifts his chin and dips it into a sharp nod.

"Oh, and I'm engaged again. You said to lean in, so I'm leaning all in." I touch one of the thick leaves, and it snaps off. Figures. I'm not to be trusted.

"Are you angry?"

"What makes you say that?" I toss the broken leaf onto his desk and plop into the chair.

"You didn't answer my question," he says.

"You didn't answer mine."

He grins. "Okay. I sense you're angry because you paced my office for ten minutes before sitting down. You announced your engagement with no enthusiasm. And you're picking a hole in the arm of that chair."

I stop my fidgeting and frown at the tiny hole I made. "I had lunch with my mom, Colten's mom, and his daughter. And while Colten's mom stroked his daughter's long hair, I imagined what she would look like without that hair. Then, I imagined what she would look like dead. So yeah ... that has me a little agitated."

"And that's the reason for the new hairdo?"

My lips twist. "No. I did that because I tried to pull my hair out while I was in the bathroom failing miserably at composing myself."

"Are you having more visions or dreams?"

"Yes."

"Do you want to share them?"

"Last night, I woke up after seeing one of the girls foaming at the mouth. I poisoned the girls."

He squints. "Are you sure?"

"Sure? No. I'm clearly not sure about anything. But it fits. I was a chemist. That's what I found on the internet. Most poisons come from soil, and the parapsychologist insists the girls died from earth."

"What if we keep a separation? Refer to him as Winston Jeffries instead of you."

"Now, you sound like Colten."

"I'm trying to keep things straight because we are discussing two lives. Winston Jeffries and Josephine Watts. I need to know that when you're saying I, you're referring to something in this life. That's all. Okay?"

I nod, folding my hands on my lap so they don't destroy anything else today.

"Cyanide?" he asks.

"Perhaps. Or Strychnine."

"It's another piece to the puzzle you can share with the authorities."

"I'm sure they're working hard on this century-old crime." I roll my eyes.

"Then let's address your fears."

"What am I afraid of?"

"Maybe hurting someone? Hurting Colten's daughter? But you must remember that thoughts are just that … thoughts. You imagined things about her, but did you actively want those things to happen to her?"

"What? Of course not."

"Then let's talk about ways for you to practice self-awareness and mindfulness. You've already identified your negative thoughts. Now let's work on replacing them with something that is true or realistic. What makes you feel good?"

"Sex with Colten."

Terrance gives me a small nod but averts his gaze to his notebook.

"When these awful thoughts come into my head, I should replace them with thoughts about having sex with Colten?"

"Sure." He clears his throat. "If it's appropriate. If you're with friends or family or at work, it might not be the appropriate redirect. Maybe think of your favorite food."

"Colten's cock."

Terrance eyes me.

I return a toothy grin. "Kidding."

"Fuck you, Josie."

I bark a laugh. This laugh alone is worth every penny of our session. "Are you allowed to say that to a patient?"

He pours himself a glass of water. "Every case is different. Sometimes I have to be unconventional."

"And there's nothing conventional about me?"

He sips his water. "You already know the answer to that."

"Okay. So think happy thoughts. That's what you've got for me today?"

"Replace negative thoughts. I'm not saying you have to think happy thoughts all day. We have thousands of thoughts go through our mind every day; most of them are neither happy nor sad. Think of all the thoughts we have about mundane tasks that we do. I also don't want you thought-stopping."

"What's that?"

"It's looking for negative thoughts so you can stop them. It means you're subjecting yourself to anxiety by anticipating negative thoughts. Deal with them only when they happen. Don't anticipate them happening. But when they do, redirect your thinking to—"

"Sex with Colten. Got it."

Terrance blows a breath out of his nose. No smile. "The goal is to make this automatic. And eventually, you might notice less and less of these negative thoughts. You can also try guided meditation at night. Or you can take a dopamine blocker."

"I'm not taking antipsychotic drugs again."

He nods. "I understand." He glances at his watch. "Time's up."

ON MY WAY HOME, Colten calls me.

"How was therapy?"

"How did you know I was at therapy?"

"I'm tracking your phone. I set that up when I set up your ringtone. I can't get you to the altar if I can't find you."

"Mmm ... I don't know if I buy that."

"So what did Dr. Birdie say?"

"Dr. Byrd. And he said I need to have more sex and think about it as often as possible. I realize you have a demanding job, so I might have to recruit some help."

"I'm not laughing."

"Me neither. I hate those dating apps, but if I just stick to random hookups and don't fret over meeting for dinner first, it will be easier."

"Still not laughing."

"Really? That one was a little funny. Where are you?"

"I just got home."

"Helping your mom make dinner?"

"My mom took Reagan to a movie."

"My mom left this morning."

"Uh-huh." He seems a little distracted.

"You're not inviting me over?"

"I'm working on my car."

"Which one?"

"Samantha."

I laugh. "Samantha?"

"I named my cars after the first woman I fucked in them."

What the hell?

"How original." I skip my exit. "Well, I'll see you around."

"Okay. Night." He disconnects the call.

I floor it, speeding past my exit. Who says that to their fiancée? I have no desire to get into any of his cars ever again. Who the hell did he fuck in my dad's Chevelle? He's a grown adult. Why is he screwing women in his cars?

As soon as I pull into his driveway, I march to his garage, opening the access door and slamming it behind me.

"Watts," he says from the pit under his car, country music blaring from the speaker. He peeks his head out, his blue tee clinging to his chest, grease on his face and arms. "Didn't think I'd be seeing you tonight."

"What's the Chevelle's name? What's your work car's name? Do you have names for each of the rooms in your house?" I park my hands on my hips.

He hops out of the pit and grabs a towel, wiping his hands. "Are you hooking up on dating apps?"

I roll my eyes. "Of course not."

"You're losing your edge. Not gonna lie … I'm a little disappointed." Tossing the towel aside, he takes a swig of cola from the can on his workbench.

"Are you bullshitting me? Did you *lie* to me about naming your cars after skanks?"

"Skanks?" He coughs after taking a swig. "Why do the women I date have to be skanks?"

"If grown women are fucking you in your cars, then they're skanks."

"I love you, Josephine Watts. I've loved you for as long as I can remember." He saunters toward me. "But if you joke about hooking up with men from your stupid little dating apps, then I'm going to get even. Now, we're even." His black boots hit the toes of my white sneakers.

"Your Corvette's name isn't Samantha." It's not a question. It's … a confession of my gullibility.

He smirks.

I nod slowly, looking just past his shoulder as I unbutton my jeans.

"What are you doing?"

After toeing off my shoes, I shimmy out of the jeans

and shrug off my tee, standing in front of him in my bra and panties. "I want you to name her Josie."

Excitement spreads along his face as his smirk explodes into a full, ear-reaching smile. "Which one?"

My hands twist behind my back to unhook my bra. "All of them."

"You're a temptress. The devil in disguise." He leans down to kiss me.

"You're the devil! Murderer!"

I lean to the side, holding my hand up to stop him while pinching my eyes shut.

"What is it?" he asks.

I shake my head. "It's ..."

A voice. It's the first time I've heard a voice in my head. So clear. So close. No vision. Just a voice. A girl screaming those words. A young girl.

"You're the devil! Murderer!"

It's so loud I can't hear Colten. His lips move, but I can't hear him. Again, I close my eyes. My hands press to the side of my head over my ears.

He cuffs my wrists, pulling my hands away from my face. "Josie!"

And then it's silent in my head.

"Baby, look at me." It's barely an echo, but I hear Colten. "Tell me what's happening."

I shake my head.

"No. Don't do that. Tell. Me. Tell me what you saw."

I continue to shake my head. "I ... I didn't see. I ... I heard a voice."

"Whose voice?"

My gaze flits around the garage; I can't focus. It's nauseating. The voice. The young girl. What she screamed ... it's all nauseating.

"A girl," I whisper, fisting my hands and hugging them to my chest so he doesn't see me shaking.

Colten kisses my forehead. "It's okay. Everything's okay." He retrieves my clothes from the floor and proceeds to dress me. I feel like a child. "What did the girl say?"

"S-she ..." I shake my head. "She screamed. She called ... she ... she called me the devil." Forcing my gaze to stay on his, I choke on my next words. "She called me a murderer."

Colten's brows draw tight, a smudge of grease on his cheek, pain in his eyes. "Him. Not you."

I blink.

"Him. Not you," he repeats.

I think of Dr. Byrd asking me not to say "I" when referring to him. But ... it's getting harder to separate the two in my mind since that life wants to infiltrate this one.

"Do you hear me?"

I nod.

"Him. Not you."

I start to turn, but he hooks his arm around my waist, pulling my back to his chest while he buries his face into my neck. My bare neck ... because I had my hair chopped off ... because I'm slowly losing touch with reality.

"We'll figure this out," he whispers. "But you're not

alone." His right hand slides from my stomach to my chest, his palm over my heart.

I cover his hand with mine. "I'm scared," I whisper.

He hugs me so tightly I swear my bones bend. "Not on my watch ... not ever again." His words settle along my skin, slowly sinking beneath the surface. Does he feel guilty that I got shot on his watch? And how can he protect me from ... myself?

CHAPTER
Twenty-One

I can't lose her again.

The problem is ... I have no fucking clue what to do.

Josie sits on my workbench while I finish messing with my car for the night. She's wearing a brave face as if I'm the one who needs reassurance.

"I think I'm going to go back to California," she says.

"Negatory."

"Negatory? What do you mean by that?"

I chuckle. "Well, the last time you went to California, you tried to dump me."

"Let you go."

"When we were seniors, did you feel dumped or let go?"

"Fine, dumped. But—"

"I'll go with you," I say, reaching for my socket wrench and glancing up at her.

Her lips twist. "Um … no. Not a good idea."

"Well, then you aren't going either." I crank the socket a few times and poke my head out of the pit. "Why is it not a good idea for me to go with you?"

"Because I don't want to deal with your reaction to Athelinda."

"Ath what?"

"Athelinda. She's the *specialist*."

I refocus on the bolt. "And what reaction will I have? She's a doctor. I'm sure she knows more than I do about this stuff."

"She's not a doctor."

"Professor … whatever."

"She's not a professor."

"You said she works at the university. If she's not a doctor or a professor, what is she?"

She remains silent.

Again, I poke my head out. "Josie?"

Her nose wrinkles. "I stretched the truth a bit."

"You lied?"

"That sounds so bad."

"How should it sound?"

"I don't know." She hugs her arms to herself and shrugs. I hate seeing her like this. The girl I knew … the woman I heard behind me at the restaurant … the doctor in her element … is not this Josephine Watts. The shorthaired woman before me has a fragility I never imagined possible. Since the accident, I've only had tiny glimpses of her where I haven't seen deep worry in her dark eyes.

Will the day come when my mind fully wraps around this? I wake every morning thinking *this* will be the day Josie realizes she wasn't a serial killer. I go to sleep every night praying for a simple explanation.

There is none.

"There's nothing you can't tell me," I say, climbing out of the pit and wiping my hands. "You know that, right?"

Her gaze lifts from her lap to meet my gaze. "I saw a parapsychologist. And she wasn't at the university."

I nod, continuing to work the grease off my hands.

"Her name means one who guards and is immortal. She's a little eccentric. And she's died a few times too."

I cough, tossing the towel aside. "A few times? How is that even possible?" I don't mean to sound skeptical, but surviving one death is statistically very unlikely, but a few?

Another shrug from her. "How did I know about the buried bodies? And by all means, I'm genuinely asking you because I'd happily jump at another explanation."

Wedging myself between her dangling legs, I rest my hands on her thighs. "Why do you want to see her again? Because you heard a voice?"

"Because she gave me the impression that she felt sorry for me like a stage four cancer diagnosis. I want to know how to get rid of the visions and the voices. There has to be something."

"You didn't ask her about this the first time?"

She shakes her head. "When I realized that I wasn't one of the victims, I had to get out of there."

I nod slowly.

"Daddy! We're back!" Reagan flies through the garage door.

"I'm greasy, Button. Easy. How was the movie?"

"Reagan!" My mom reaches the garage door, breathless. "Oh, thank god."

With narrowed eyes, I inspect my mom and her visible relief.

She presses her hand to her chest. "I was worried you two were ... well ... I just wanted to make sure everyone was *decent.*"

I press my lips together and nod once, taking Reagan's shoulders and pointing her toward my mom.

Josie hops off the workbench and manages to force a smile for my mom and Reagan.

"Let's head into the house," I say as Reagan skips toward the door and my mom nods in relief.

"I'm going to head home," Josie says behind me.

"Come inside, just for a little bit." I take her hand, and she doesn't argue. "I'm going to grab a quick shower. Mom made brownies earlier. Go eat one, and wait for me."

Mom and Reagan head straight to the kitchen, probably for brownies.

"I'll be upstairs if you need me. I'll hurry." I drop a quick kiss on her lips. "Will you be okay?"

Josie blinks a few times as if she's deep in thought before nodding once.

I take the fastest shower I have ever taken. No shaving. I'm not sure I got off all the grease. If Josie has another *moment*, I don't want it to be when she's alone with my mom and Reagan. When I get to the kitchen, Mom's putting the lid on the brownie pan, Reagan's at the kitchen table coloring, and Josie's standing behind her, braiding her hair.

It's normal. I think. I've never seen Josie braid hair, but clearly she can. It seems a little motherly of her, but she's not the motherly type. Maybe Reagan asked her to, but I kind of doubt it. When my gaze shifts from Josie's hands in my daughter's hair to Josie's face, she's eyeing me with more focus than she's had in the past hour.

I smile. It feels real, but maybe I'm missing the mark. She frowns and slowly undoes the braid before clearing her throat. "Thanks for the brownie. I need to get home."

"Well, give me a hug in case I don't see you again before my flight." Mom hugs Josie, and Josie lightly rests her hands on my mom's arms. Even her hug is off.

"Bye, Reagan." Josie's hand starts to move toward Reagan's head like she's going to rest it there while saying goodbye, but she stops inches from the crown of her head and balls her hand into a fist, returning it to her side.

"Colten, I'm ... unwell. You have to protect yourself ... protect your daughter."

Reagan mumbles a soft goodbye.

I follow Josie to the front door. "Stay," I whisper just as she reaches for the handle.

She turns. "You looked mortified when you saw me braiding her hair."

I shake my head. "I didn't know you could braid hair. That's all."

With a headshake, she frowns. "That wasn't a look of wonder or surprise. That was the look of a protective father."

Again, my head eases side to side. "You're wrong."

"I have to work in the morning. I don't have anything here."

"Stay anyway."

She attempts a smile. "We have the rest of our lives, right?"

"I'm more of a seize the moment kind of guy."

Opening the door, she chuckles. "No. You're not. Seventeen years ago, you could have seized the moment, but you didn't. And since then, you've had roughly one hundred forty-eight thousand, nine hundred and twenty hours to seize the moment. To find me. You didn't. And Reagan is one of the reasons. That's okay. You are now and always will be a father first." The corner of her mouth curls a little. "When I went hunting with my dad, he once told me that he didn't know what kind of man he was until he became a father. You're a good father, Colten, and a good man."

I let her get two steps out the door before I follow

her to her car. "Wait until you see what kind of husband I'm going to be."

At the driver's door, she turns, hands sliding up my chest and around my neck. She's right; Reagan is my world. I can't change that nor would I ever want to. But Josephine Watts owns some serious real estate behind my ribcage.

"Everything has fine print," she says, staring at my chest while her fingers play along the nape of my neck. "Reagan is your fine print. If we don't make it to the altar, she's the fine print. I know it. You know it. Don't pretend we don't."

"That little firecracker in there? I'm still trying to figure her out. It's only been five years. But you ... I know you. The best parts. And I laid claim to them many years ago. I don't need fine print."

I'm ready, completely anticipating a rebuttal.

Nothing.

She lifts onto her toes and pulls me toward her, giving me a slow kiss. Despite the air of melancholy around us, I kiss her, wrapping my future in my arms. Fuck the fine print or what she thought I was thinking earlier. I am *not* losing her again.

CHAPTER
Twenty-Two

"DON'T INTERRUPT. Just listen. And don't judge. She'll be wearing a very thin gown, and you'll see everything beneath it. I'll change into a gown as well, just be cool. And if by some chance she asks you to wear one, take off all your clothes and just do it. No questions asked," I say to Colten before we get out of the rental car parked in a spot out front of Athelinda's.

"I feel blindsided and a little pre-violated. You had two weeks and a four-hour flight to tell me this, but I'm just now being told?"

When I don't respond to his humor, he reaches for my hand and squeezes it. "Josie, I feel like aliens landed, and I didn't believe in them, but now they're here and there's no denying it. I'm trying to figure out how to adjust my thoughts to include aliens."

I nod several times while opening the door. "You

should have let me die. Living with aliens sucks." Before he can open his mouth, I get out of the car and take long strides toward the door.

"Josie—"

I hold up my hand to stop him from saying another word while I wait for Athelinda to buzz us in.

"Peace to you, beautiful friends. Please, take everything off and slip on a gown. We have much work to do." Athelinda presses her palms together at her chest and takes a small bow.

"This is Colten. He's my—"

"Yes, of course, my dear Josephine. No time for formalities. Clothes off."

After removing my socks and shoes, I head over to the wall with the gowns on hooks, unbuttoning my blouse on the way.

Jeans.

Bra.

Panties.

After I slip on the gown, I turn. Colten offers me a look that I can't decipher.

His face softens. "Josie," he whispers. He's still bothered by our last discussion.

"Put on a gown," I say.

He glances over his shoulder at Athelinda perched on her pillow, yellowish eyes on us. When he returns his attention to me, I give him one look. No words. Not even a blink.

Keeping his gaze on me, he shrugs off his shirt. He pauses for a few seconds before tugging the button to his jeans. When those have been removed, he partakes in another short stare off before glancing back at Athelinda again. She watches him with a straight face as well.

On a long inhale, he removes his briefs and stands straight with every ounce of confidence in his body.

I hand him a gown and brush past him toward Athelinda. When I sit on a pillow, she leans toward me and presses her cold hands to my face.

"You're exhausted." She frowns.

I swallow hard because she sees me, really sees me, and it has nothing to do with my threadbare gown.

Colten takes a seat on the pillow between us as we sit at 12:00, 3:00, and 6:00. He pulls his legs into a criss-cross and folds his hands over his junk.

"What do you see?" she asks me.

"I poisoned them. They foamed at the mouth."

Athelinda nods, pressing her dry lips together. She's okay with me referring to *him* as *I*.

I feel Colten's gaze on me. I didn't tell him that part. "I want to know how to get rid of the memories. I don't need to solve anything else. I don't need to recollect the moment I killed them or how they resisted when I tried to abduct them. I don't want to know if I did depraved things to them. I just want to forget every-thing before it gets worse. Or before I ..."

Colten stiffens. He's focused on a marriage; I'm focused on not taking my own life every time I see or hear something in my head. Cake samples would be so much easier.

"I'm afraid you will have to live with this," she says.

"Well, I wasn't living with it before the shooting."

She nods. "Perhaps you'll get some form of dementia as you age."

"Dementia? That's my best hope? What about a brain injury?" I'm being sarcastic.

Athelinda lifts a bony shoulder into a small shrug. "That could do it too."

"Jesus ..." Colten scrubs his hands over his face.

"How do I make things right?"

"That's a discovery you'll encounter on your life's journey. I can't say because no two are ever the same."

"And what am I supposed to do when I'm at a low point? When Colten's watching me stroke his daughter's hair, and I know what he's thinking—"

"I wasn't thinking anything," he says.

I ignore him, keeping my expectant gaze on Athelinda.

"You think WWJD."

"What if I don't believe in Jesus?"

She smirks. "That would be tragic. Jesus is one of my favorites. Long hair. Abs for days. Water into wine. Feeding five thousand. Healing a paralyzed man. The blind. The deaf. The resurrection? Seriously, the resurrection! Has there ever been a more perfect man?"

Colten readjusts on his pillow.

"What Would Josie Do?" she corrects. "When you feel overwhelmed. When you wake from these visions or hear voices in your head, think about Josephine Watts. What would she do?"

My head eases side to side. "I ... I don't know anymore. I've spent too much time analyzing my personality, my interests, my choices in life and comparing them to those of a psychopath." I stare at the floor between us. "My mom was raped. I am the child of rape. The perfect portal for evil. Oh my god ... think about it. JW. WJ. Josephine Watts. Winston Jeffries. That means something, right?"

"Josie ..." Colten rests his hand on my leg.

It feels like the temperature of the room drops ten degrees. Athelinda offers me a sad smile and nods. "Maybe."

My gaze lifts to the ceiling, focusing on stars.

"This life is a blink. And you know without a doubt, now, that we don't end when our hearts stop beating. If you weren't in this life..." she glances over at Colten "...you'd be missed. Your absence would leave emotional holes. But those holes are nothing compared to what you're experiencing now ... or what you'll experience as these visions multiply. Only you know. Only you can see your purpose. Only you can choose your direction. Only you will know if it becomes too much."

"What?" Colten shakes his head. "What the fuck are you talking about? Are you ... are you giving her permission to die? To kill herself? What the fuck is wrong with you?"

I don't feel his anger and rage. I feel empowered.

"Get up. Get dressed. We're leaving." Colten grabs my arm while he stands.

I shake my head.

He squats beside me. "Look at me." His hands frame my face. "I will not let anything happen to you. We are stronger than this. Do you hear me?" His words bleed with desperation, and it's heartbreaking.

"You have to make peace with her decision, whatever it may be," Athelinda says.

Colten ignores her, keeping his gaze on me. "She doesn't know you. *I* know you. I love you. We will get through this."

"How?" I whisper.

He swallows hard while lines dig into his forehead. "Together."

Oh, Colten …

I let him help me to my feet. Athelinda's sad smile makes an encore performance. I mirror her expression. Colten can be sympathetic. Agreeable. Sacrificial. He can be a million things, but he can't be me. He can't truly understand what this is like for me.

He tears off his gown, no longer caring about Athelinda's eyes on him. I dress a little slower.

"There is one …"

My gaze slides to her as she starts to speak.

Her teeth scrape along her dry lower lip. "One other possibility."

"Let's go." Colten ties his shoes.

"What?" I ask.

She leans to the side and retrieves her *I AM …* book. While flipping through the pages, she hums. "The odds would not be in your favor." Her finger traces with lines of script on the page. "They'd be so much not in your favor that I'm not sure I'd even call them odds."

"Just tell me."

Lifting her head slowly, she draws in a quick breath and releases it with one big whoosh. "If you have another near-death experience, it could erase these memories."

"No. Fuck no. Let's go, Josie." Colten's hand encircles my wrist, but I pull against his tug.

"It can't be worse than the other option," I say, opting to not say the actual words.

Suicide. Taking my own life. Checking out.

"Actually, it could. Dying instead of coming back to life is the least of my concerns for you." She glances down at the book again. "You could experience something just as bad or worse. It's foolish to assume this is only your second life. You could have brain damage. You could be in a coma, on a ventilator, which would mean your loved ones would have to make an awful decision."

"Or it could work," I whisper.

"Josephine, I am a rare exception to any rule. Most people don't come back from death once, let alone more than once. Your chances of winning the lottery might be better."

I shake my head. "My heart stops and we start it back up. I'll take those chances over the lottery."

"Jesus, Josie ..." Colten tugs on my wrist again. "No. We're leaving."

"No. That's not how it works," Athelinda says. "For you to have even a remote chance of losing the past-life memories, your heart has to stop beating for longer than it did last time. When it's not beating, your soul shifts through its many lifecycles. It won't release the one in your head until its time has expired. For that to happen, it has to be longer."

Colten grabs my purse and my shoes. "We're out of here."

This time, I don't fight him. My gaze locks with Athelinda's while he pulls me to the door.

She presses her palms together again and bows. "May you find your way in this life ... or another life."

When we get into the rental car, Colten doesn't start it. He grips the steering wheel and stares straight ahead. "Thanksgiving is next week. Christmas is the following month. Then we're getting married. I need..." He clears his throat.

I ease my head to the side. His eyes are red, jaw set.

"I *need* you to be there. I..." he pinches the bridge of his nose "...I need you to be in my life."

If I died, he'd grieve. My family would mourn my death. Then everyone would slowly move on. That's how it works in life. There's a process that follows death. Maybe not everyone follows the process in a particular order or at the same pace, but there's a process.

This is worse. It's limbo. This level of uncertainty is torture.

As long as I'm alive with Winston Jeffries in my

head, it's going to feel impossible for Colten to ... live. He'll always wonder if I'm okay. He'll not sleep well ever again. He'll never fully concentrate at work. He'll live in this limbo and pretend that everything's okay because I'm alive and in his life.

I don't want to be in his life like this. However, I don't know that I'm ready to leave. Instead, I have to trust that I'll know. When the time comes, I'll just ... know.

My hand slides across the console to his leg. "I'm here. I'll make turkey. I'll find the perfect tree. I'll meet you at the altar."

That's it. That's as far as I can go, but he doesn't need to know that. The relief on his face means too much. It means everything right now.

"I fucking love you. You know that, right?" He takes my hand and kisses it over and over before pressing it to his cheek, closing his eyes for a brief second.

"I know," I whisper. "I ... know."

CHAPTER
Twenty-Three

CHAD DIDN'T MEAN to start the neighbor's house on fire, but he did.

"Is Dad taking us to watch the fireworks?" he asked Mom the morning of July fourth. Our first Fourth of July since our parents separated.

I didn't care if he came home to take us to watch fireworks. I didn't care if he ever came home.

"Sorry, hon. He has other plans." Mom offered us a sad smile while she served us patriotic pancakes. Blueberries, strawberries, and bananas.

"What other plans?"

"I don't know."

"Well, call him," Chad insisted.

"It's none of my business, hon."

"You're not divorced. Call him." Chad was relentless. He was either fixated on his games and oblivious to the rest of the world or fixated on something else and relentless to the person whom he thought was responsible for granting his new wish. There was absolutely no in-between with him.

"Josie's dad said you could do better." I wasn't sure if anyone wanted my two cents, but I gave it anyway.

Mom stood up straight, set the spatula on the counter like it was a bomb ready to explode. Taking a deep breath, she turned toward the table and wiped her hands on a towel. "He is your father. And you need a father. Despite what Isaac said, I'm not looking for a replacement. I'm not looking to do better. I'm simply trying to raise two boys, take care of a house on my own, and keep myself from crying all day long. Maybe ... maybe your father doesn't deserve me. Maybe I can do better. But I still love him. Even if I'm angry with him. Even if some days I feel like I hate him for what he did to our family ... I still love him. Falling in love is the biggest risk your heart will ever take. You can't fall in love if your heart is not available, and the only way to make it available is by allowing it to be vulnerable. I hope you never have your hearts broken, but not taking the risk would be far more tragic."

Only in hindsight did I realize what an epic speech my mom gave to two clueless boys. Only in hindsight did I realize how honest and *vulnerable* she allowed her heart to be just to give us a peek into the world of relationships and heartbreak.

Sadly, neither Chad nor I had the emotional maturity to gain a single ounce of wisdom from that speech.

"If you're not going to call Dad, then I'm going to do it." Good old Chad. Dog with a bone.

"You will eat your breakfast. Brush your teeth. And help me with the dishes I need to make to take over to the Watts's house later."

"No. I won't." Chad poked the bear so hard I couldn't help but cringe.

Mom was patient, but she wasn't Jesus. "GO. TO. YOUR. ROOM!" She jabbed a finger in the direction of the stairs.

Chad, being the stubborn and belligerent little fuck that he was, threw a pancake at my mom, smacking her in the face. Her whole head turned red like the strawberries while syrup and whipped topping dripped from her jaw.

She stomped toward him. I had never seen her look so feral. Apparently, neither had Chad because he jolted out of his chair and sprinted up the stairs. When she turned back toward me, I tucked my chin and shoveled down my breakfast. Then, I cleaned up the kitchen without being asked and checked in on my mom. She was face down on her bed crying.

"Come on, twerp," Chad said, poking his head in the bathroom while I brushed my teeth.

"Where?" I asked.

"To get fireworks."

"They're illegal."

"They're in the garage."

I squinted at him before spitting.

"Dad bought them in Missouri the summer that we

moved. But then he found out that we lived next door to the chief of police, so he never set them off."

I jogged down the stairs behind Chad. "We still live across the street from the chief of police."

"He just pulled out of his driveway. We can set a few off before he gets back."

"I don't think it's a good idea. Mom doesn't even let me use a lighter for candles."

"Listen, pussy, sometimes you have to do fun stuff because it's fun, not because your mommy says it's okay." Chad pulled out the ladder and set it up right in the middle of the stall where Dad used to park. Retrieving a box from the boards along the rafters, Chad dropped it to the ground with a big *thunk*.

I lifted one of the flaps like something might jump out at me.

"Right there. Let's set off that rocket." Chad grabbed the big one from the top. "Now ..." he glanced around the garage. "Where's a lighter?"

I knew there was a lighter in the top drawer of dad's tool bench. He had very few tools, but he had a tool bench. He bought it after we moved to Des Moines. I think it happened shortly after Chief Watts asked him if he had a certain tool because the chief couldn't find his. My dad had a hammer and maybe two screw-drivers. I think it embarrassed him because, two days later, he bought the tool bench and several hundred dollars' worth of tools.

"It might be in the top drawer," I murmured. I

wasn't going to get it. This was all on Chad. At the same time, I was a little curious about the rocket.

Chad opened the top drawer, and sure enough, it was there. He plucked it from its spot. His fingerprints, not mine.

"Come on ..." He scuffed his sneakers along the ground to the backyard.

"What if you catch a tree on fire?" I asked.

"The trees are too green to catch on fire. God ... you're so stupid."

He was right. I was stupid. I was stupid to worry about the trees instead of the houses around us.

"Are you sure this is a good idea?" I asked as he set the rocket on the pad of concrete, literally feet from our house.

"Colten, shut up. You're such a baby." He lit the fuse, and we skittered back a few more feet as the flame quickly worked its way to the rocket.

Whoosh!

There it went. I had a full two seconds of retreat. For those two seconds, I felt like a baby. A mama's boy who was too afraid to have a little fun. After all, wasn't that what boys did? Break a few rules all in the name of fun?

Then ... it crashed into the neighbor's window. The Burmeisters. It was the first time I said the word "fuck" aloud.

"Go! Go! Go!" Chad shoved me toward the garage, and I ran as fast as I could.

"There's no phone in here!" I said in a panic.

"Shh!" Chad grabbed the box of fireworks and nearly fell off the ladder trying to heave them back into their spot.

"Chad! Their house is on fire! We have to call 9-1-1."

"So we get into trouble?" He glanced down at me like I was crazy. "Let them call. What's it matter?"

"What if they're not home? Mrs. Burmeister is really old. What if she can't get out of the house? What if the rocket hit her? Oh my god! She could be dead!"

"Shh!" He jumped off the ladder.

"I'm not being quiet. I'm calling for help." I started toward the door, but Chad grabbed the back of my shirt.

"You can't."

Something snapped. This urgency filled my veins, and my fists pounded against my brother until he released me. Then I sprinted inside and called 9-1-1. "Our neighbor's house is on fire. Come quick!"

"What's going on?" Mom ran down the stairs.

"Chad set the neighbor's house on fire! I have to see if Josie's dad is back home." I dropped the phone while the 9-1-1 operator was still talking to me.

Just as I crossed the street, Chief Watts pulled into their driveway. He opened his door and stepped out, holding two bags of ice. "Hey, Colten. What's—"

"The Burmeister's house is on fire. I ... I called 9-1-1."

He dropped the bags of ice and jogged across the street, past our driveway and through our backyard, hopping the short fence into the Burmeister's yard as smoke billowed from the broken window.

Chief Watts tried the handle. Then, he broke the window next to the door, kicked the jagged shards of glass with his boot, and slipped into the house. Minutes later, he emerged, coughing a little, and carrying Humphrey, their white cat, just as firetrucks arrived.

"They're gone."

My hand covered my mouth.

We killed the Burmeisters. I didn't do it, but I knew I would get blamed along with Chad. What would happen to us? Did they send young kids to prison?

Chief rested his hand on my shoulder for a second. He must have read my expression. "They're out of town for the holiday. Josie's supposed to be feeding their cat."

I nodded several times. I thought Josie did mention that, but I'd forgotten.

"Take the cat to my house." He handed Humphrey to me and headed around to the front of the house toward the firetrucks.

"Whoa! What happened?" As I turned around, Josie ran up behind me, mouth agape, eyes on the smoke coming from the window.

I handed her the cat. "Take him. I have to do something."

"Colten?"

I ignored her as I ran into the garage.

"What is wrong with you?" Mom screamed at

Chad. The garage door was open. He was sitting in the driver's seat of her car. "Why would you do this? Tell me why?" She stopped screaming and fell to her knees with her head on his lap.

He stared straight ahead, tears streaming down his face.

"I love you," she whispered. "No matter what … I. Love. You."

CHAPTER
Twenty-Four

WE STAY the night in California. Josie doesn't eat a bite of her dinner, and when I talk, she plasters on the fakest smile and nods.

"Would you like to take this to go?" the waiter asks her while depositing the bill onto the table.

She shakes her head.

"My dad killed himself."

Josie glances up at me, a hint of confusion in her expression.

"Two weeks after my parents separated, my mom took a whole bottle of pills."

Josie's expression falls flat. She didn't know that.

My gaze wanders around the restaurant. "We were at school. Luckily, my dad came home late that morning to pack up a few more of his belongings. I remember my mom being in the hospital for several days. Dad told us she had kidney stones."

Josie nods and whispers, "I remember that."

"Do you remember when Chad set the neighbor's house on fire on the Fourth of July?"

She nods again.

I let my gaze land on hers and stay there. "My mom found my brother in the garage. In her car. The car was running."

More confusion lines her face.

I tap the table a few times. "The garage doors were down."

Josie flinches. "Colten ..."

I chuckle and shake my head. "People in my life try to kill themselves." Reaching across the table, I take her hand. "I'd like it to stop."

Her gaze falls to her lap, chin down. When I squeeze her hand, tears race down her cheeks. She releases a quick sob and holds her breath. I'm not trying to hurt her or guilt her. I'm trying to save her, and I'm trying to stop this epic streak of tragedy in my life.

I place money on the table, slide out of the booth, and tuck her next to me as we exit the restaurant.

When we get to the hotel, she doesn't say a word and neither do I. We kiss. Discard our clothes. And make love like it's the last time we're ever going to do it.

"Why didn't you ever tell me about your brother?" she whispers, her back spooned to my chest a little after midnight.

"It took me a while to figure it out. And when I did, when I overheard my parents talking months later, discussing Chad's punishment and his therapy ... I got the nerve to ask my mom what they were talking about. My dad told her not to tell me, but she did anyway. And she made me promise not to tell anyone, even you. And for some reason, that felt like a secret I needed to keep because she cried the whole time she told me about Chad. I still have that image of them in the garage."

I kiss her head. "I wanted to tell you. I wanted to tell you when you told me about your mom being raped. I felt guilty for keeping something from you when you told me everything. But I didn't think Chad's attempted suicide was going to brighten your day after the news your parents gave you."

Josie laughs a little, her foot stroking mine. After a few minutes of silence, she maneuvers her body so that she's facing me. "I feel like I have cancer, and I need to promise everyone that I'm not going to die. At the same time, I feel like the cancer is spreading, and I can't stop it." Her fingertips ghost along my lips, tracing them. "I feel like I need to tell adult Colten that I'm going to be fine. But ... I think I could have told seventeen-year-old Colten that I'm really fucking scared of the cancer. And I feel like I'm going to disappoint everyone around."

I kiss the pads of her fingers. "For the record, seventeen-year-old Colten wanted to save you from the unfair and cruel things in his life. He was just too stupid and scared to figure out how to do it."

"And now?" she whispers.

"And now ..." I close my eyes as if I can hide from the truth.

"Say it, Colten. Saying it doesn't make it any more real. It doesn't make you a coward. It shows your strength. Don't ever run from the truth. The truth *always* wins."

I open my eyes. "I'm terrified. I feel responsible. I feel out of control. So damn helpless."

"Responsible? For the shooting?"

I think about that. "Maybe," I murmur.

"Or do you feel responsible for saving me?"

This is so messed-up. Why should one feel guilty for saving another life? Maybe because I feel like she blames me.

"What would you have done? Had it been me?"

She blinks several times before giggling and rolling onto her back, tossing an arm over her face to hide it. "I would have saved you. I would have done absolutely anything to save you. Risked my own life. Cut the beating heart out of an innocent bystander to give it to you. I would have slayed all the dragons and lit the whole world on fire to save you."

I can't help my grin. "And if it were me experiencing what you're experiencing, what would you do? WWJD?"

"I don't know," she whispers. "I've never known

how to let you go. But you ...” She rolls back toward me. All the laughter has died. Vanished smiles. “You let me go—”

“Josie—”

“Shh ...” She presses her finger to my lips. “I know why you did it. The point is you did it. And you survived. I hope I don't have to ever ask you to live without me, but you *can*.”

She's so wrong. Maybe then, but not now. For seventeen years, I had hope, even if only a sliver. Living without her—truly without her—without even a sliver of hope, it would kill me.

“Are you going to catch a wild turkey for Thanksgiving?”

It takes a few seconds, but she grins. “Well, we know *you're* not going to catch one. And you don't catch them. They can actually run quite fast. I'd suggest a shotgun, muzzleloader, or if you're feeling really confident, you can use a bow.”

This grin on my face feels good. I like our new conversation, and I like having a glimpse of my childhood friend again. So filled with facts about random things.

“Why do you have that smile on your face?”

“Because.” I peck at her lips.

“Because isn't an answer. I just told you I feel like I have an incurable cancer and you're grinning?”

“This is it, baby. All we have is now. This very moment. And in this very moment, you are with me.

We are gloriously naked. And we're discussing the best ways to hunt wild turkeys."

"But in the next moment, I could—"

"Nope." I kiss her again, biting her bottom lip and giving it a playful tug. "This moment. Not the one before, not the one after. Be present with me."

"This moment," she echoes.

I roll so she's under me, so I'm nestled between her sexy legs. So I'm inside her. My eyes close while my lips press to her shoulder. "This one right here ... it might be the very best moment."

Josie kisses my ear and teases the nape of my neck.

Fuck cancer ...

CHAPTER
Twenty-Five

Oncologists give cancer patients an idea, a possible timeline for the progression of their cancer. Odds of survival with treatment versus without treatment. Even the foremost experts in the field acknowledge there are so many variables that can change that timeline. Change *everything*.

I have no timeline. I'm not sure if it's a blessing or a curse.

We celebrate Thanksgiving with my parents in Des Moines and make plans to spend Christmas with Becca and Reagan here in Chicago so he can have Reagan Christmas Eve at his house. Plans are good. I like plans.

I work.

Colten works.

We put a *For Sale* sign in my yard. It makes more sense for me to live with him since Reagan has a room there with a fantastic white cat mural.

The images continue to flesh out in my dreams. More voices. More everything. The cancer is spreading.

I give Colten his moments, the good ones. And I swallow the bad ones. I suffer in silence as much as possible.

Like cancer patients, I have my good days and my bad days.

Today is a flat-out awful day.

"She was a cancer patient," Cornwell says as I glance at my tablet and my first case of the morning. "The dad said he found her dead in bed. Her oncologist isn't as confident in that explanation."

I nod, reading through notes from law enforcement at the scene.

"Dr. Watts?"

I glance up at Cornwell. "I can take her," he says.

I shake my head, eyes narrowed. "Why?"

"She's eleven. And she has no hair from chemo."

My gaze returns to the tablet, but my eyes no longer follow the words. "So?"

"Josephine, look at me."

Taking in a slow, controlled breath, I lift my gaze to his.

"It's been months since your accident, and while you're doing your job well, I've noticed you take a little longer to do it. You take a little longer to respond to questions from me. You take longer to write up your reports.”

“Is it a race? Is it affecting anyone else?”

“No, but I worry about you. Are you still in therapy?”

“No.”

“Do you think it might help?”

“Help what?”

He frowns.

I roll my eyes. “Fine. I’m still not sleeping well. It might be affecting my speed, but that’s it. And I can handle a cancer patient. Hair or no hair. Now, anything else?”

He inspects me for several seconds over his glasses before shaking his head.

Forty-five minutes later, I’m in full PPE, staring at the girl with no hair.

“Dr. Watts?”

I close my eyes.

“If you don’t hold still, I’m going to rip every lock of hair from your head.”

“It hurts!”

“Then you should have taken better care of yourself. I have to deal with your sister’s hair; I shouldn’t be bothered with yours as well. I feel like I have two daughters.”

“Ouch!”

“ENOUGH! Sit. Down! Don’t move. I’m going to take care of this once and for all.”

“Don’t ... p-please ... what are you d-doing? I’m s-sorry ... Please stop!”

"Dr. Watts? Josephine!"

I open my eyes.

Alicia offers me a sad smile. "Are you okay?"

I nod.

"Are you sure?"

Glancing around the autopsy suite, I search for anyone else eyeing me. "I'm sure."

It takes me an hour longer than it should to complete the autopsy.

"Let's talk," Cornwell says, stepping into my office and shutting the door behind him.

I glance up for a quick second before finishing the last line on my report. "*You're* coming to my office *and* shutting the door behind you. Should I be worried?"

He takes a seat in the chair opposite me, crossing his legs and folding his hands on his lap. "I'm not one to invoke unnecessary worry. However, I think a little worry might be appropriate. You're not you. You're doing an admirable job of pretending to be you. However, as admirable as it is, it's painful for me to watch you struggle. It's painful to see a feigned confidence instead of the real deal. When I'm in the same room as you, I swear I can feel your demons, but I can't see them, and I don't know what they're saying."

Leaning back in my chair, I study him for a few seconds. I've always thought I could confide in him. Not because I think he's experienced what I'm experiencing, it's because he's seen so much in his life. He's dissected the unimaginable. He's given a voice to the dead. And right now, I feel like I am *a* voice of the dead.

"Do you want the whole story?"

Cornwell's eyes narrow for a beat before he nods. While I proceed to tell him everything, he doesn't move, aside from the occasional blink. Not a nod. Not a smile. Not a grimace. The words fly out of my mouth while I have the courage to say them. And when I finish, he still says nothing.

"Dr. Cornwell?"

This time when he blinks, his gaze falls to his lap. "Josie ..."

He never calls me Josie. I don't like the way he says it.

"I think you are talented beyond words. I've never worked with someone like you. But you know this." He returns his attention to me, something quite grave in his eyes. "I feel honored that you trusted me enough to share this with me. However, as your superior, I must make decisions based on what's right for the job in which you've been appointed to do. I'm going to recommend that you take a leave of absence, your return contingent on a psychiatric evaluation and completion of any recommended treatment."

I'm ... blindsided.

How did I get this wrong?

"I had an evaluation after the accident."

"You need another one."

"I'm seeing a psychiatrist." My voice escalates.

"For an evaluation or to talk through your issues?"

"Talk through my issues. I already had—"

"So you're admitting you have issues?"

"Goddammit, Cornwell!" I stand resting my fists on my desk. "I took off more time for my injury than you did for your double hernia repair. I've seen two psychiatrists. I'm back to work. Who gives a flying fuck if I'm a little slower? I'm just as sharp. I'm completing my tasks, writing up reports, testifying in court. I died! What the hell do you expect? I'm still better at my job than every other ME in this building ... including you and your old ass. When you die and come back to life, then we'll have this conversation. When you figure out the mysteries of the universe and become a foremost expert on near-death experiences, then we'll have this conversation. But until then, I am not going to let you fucking fire me!"

He won't even look at me. Instead, he presses his hands to the arms of the chair and stands. "Take the leave of absence and get your shit together or empty your desk. I'm sorry." Turning, like the coward he is, he exits my office.

OUT OF ALL THE nights I wish Reagan were with her mom, it's this one. I'm not that lucky today.

Colten: Could you pick Reagan up on your way home?

He must not have checked my location because I'm already home. At my house.

I pedal faster on my stationary bike, staring at his

message. I barely made it home without running my car into a tree; I don't think transporting children is a good idea.

Avoiding the actual messenger app so he won't know that I saw his message, I turn off my location. I need time to figure out what I'm doing and if it's even worth doing ... if anything in this life is still worth doing.

After cycling, I do Pilates. Drink a half gallon of water. Clean every inch of my house with music blaring. And finally take a shower.

"Why the hell did you turn off your location?"

I shut off the water and pivot toward Colten. Eyeing him without a reply, I retrieve my towel and dry my body.

"Are you going to answer me? Did you see my text? I had to pick up Reagan and take her to work with me and have someone watch her while I interrogated a suspect."

I wrap my towel around my body. "She's not my responsibility. Sorry."

"Yes, I realize that. I thought we were getting married, and you knew she was part of the deal. You picked her up the week after Thanksgiving."

"And you're welcome, but as a rule, I'd say ... don't count on me for ... anything." I step out of the shower and rub the hand towel over the steamy mirror.

"What's wrong?"

I drop my head and stare at the sink. "I lost my job."

"You what?"

"I SAID—"

Colten cups his hand over my mouth. "Reagan is sitting on the sofa in your living room, just down the hallway."

I jerk my head away from his hold and take a seat on the toilet, pressing a hand to my head and fisting what little hair I can. "Go home. Take your daughter home. I just ..." My hand drops to my leg. "I need space. If I'm truly losing my fucking mind, I don't want to do it in front of Reagan."

Colten hunches in front of me, resting his hands on my legs. He looks like he's had a long day too. His hair is nearly as messy as mine. Tie loose and crooked. Tired eyes. "Why were you fired?"

Any other man would leave. They'd either give me the middle finger and find someone less messed-up ... or they'd stick their tail between their legs and skitter off. Sometimes I wish Colten would be that man. Instead, he ignores all boundaries and climbs all the walls I build. We have too much history. He helped write the book on Josephine Watts.

"I told Cornwell."

"Told him what?"

"Everything."

"Why?"

"Because I needed to tell someone."

"You have me."

I shake my head. "It's not the same. You've said it yourself. You're hardwired to love me. So are my parents. My therapist is trained to..." I shrug "...I don't even know. Alicia is my friend. But Cornwell has always pushed me. He's been a mentor. He has a lot of insight and years of experience. I feel like he's probably heard everything by this point in his career and his life in general. I thought he'd give me perspective in a way that no one else has been able to do."

Colten bows his head and mumbles, "But he didn't."

"No. He did. He not so gently reminded me that if this were happening to anyone else and I were an outsider looking in, I'd think that person was crazy. He didn't say those words, but that's what I took from it. And he's not wrong. He said to get help or clean out my desk."

"And what did you do?"

"No one can help me. So I cleaned out my ..." I haven't cried since I left work. I've been too angry. But now ... I'm just incredibly sad and hopeless. So with a blink, my tears break free. "I c-cleaned out my d-desk," I whisper past the lump in my throat.

Being a medical examiner is my life. It's the reason I've been single with no kids. I know my love for the man before me is indescribable, but he can't be my job. It's not a void that a person can fill. Losing my job— and my mind—feels like my soul has been stripped and is no longer recognizable. I don't recognize my reflection in the mirror.

I've lost my identity, and I don't know if I will ever find it again.

Colten catches my tears. He's caught so many tears, he could have his own personal Josephine Watts Ocean. "We've got this."

Damn you, Colten ...

We. Ride or die.

Only, he can't die. He has a beautiful little girl. And I know he loves her more than he has loved anyone, including me. And that makes me love him even more. It also makes me hate myself for allowing him back into my life. Maybe seventeen years ago he had it right. We should have ended our story on a sad note—on a moonlight sonata. I fear all that's left of our story is a tragic ending. I can't slow it down. I can't change its course. I think the ending has already been written. It was written the day I came into this world as Josephine Watts, another innocent victim of Winston Jeffries' wrath.

"Take Reagan home," I say, just above a whisper.

He rests his forehead against mine, easing it side to side. "I can't. I won't leave you. The night I fell down the stairs at that party, you got me home. You stayed with me because you wanted to make sure I was okay. That I wasn't going to ..."

Die.

I stayed with him to make sure he didn't stop breathing, that he didn't die from a concussion.

"Go."

He cups my face, forcing me to look at him. "Tell me you're not going to take your life."

Jesus ...

It's jarring. I don't know why it is. It just is. He's not saying anything that hasn't passed through my mind more than once a day, every day, since the accident. Spoken words give life and meaning. They take thoughts and ignite them, sending them into the world to burn. They can fizzle out. Or they can destroy everything.

You can only dance around the truth if it's unspoken. The elephant can't stay in the room once it's been acknowledged. And Colten can't turn back time and unsay those words.

"Say it," he says, teeth gritted, emotion choking his words. "Promise me on my life, on Reagan's life, on your family's life … promise me you will crawl into bed and fight every last nightmare, wake up in the morning, and continue to fight because you are stronger than this. You are so much fucking stronger than *him*."

I blink more tears.

"And if you can't promise me that…" he kisses every inch of my cheeks "…then I can't leave you."

When he looks at me, I search for words. For answers. For promises.

Before I can speak, he stands, opens the door, and heads straight to my closet.

"What are you doing?" I say at the threshold while he shoves clothes into a bag.

"You hesitated. You've lectured me on hesitation. The truth lies in those painful breaths of silence. So…" he pulls the towel from my body and proceeds to dress me in sweats and a hoodie "...you're coming with me. I'll arrange for my mom to fly in tomorrow, and I'll ask your parents to drive here first thing in the morning." He zips my bag and pulls the hood onto my wet head. For a second, he pauses.

Maybe he's daring me to protest, cross my arms, stomp my feet, beg him to trust me.

I. Have. Nothing.

No job.

No purpose.

No identity.

A hollow body filled with horrible visions.

He doesn't need to call anyone. He needs to drop me off at the hospital and admit me to the psych ward. If I tell them the truth, every last gruesome bit of it, they will conclude that I am unwell. And maybe Colten needs to have someone tell him that so he can save himself, so he can have permission to walk away and focus on what matters most.

Taking my hand, he leads me toward the front door. "Let's go, Button. Josie's feeling a little under the weather, so we'll get her put into bed, and I'll read you all the books you want."

I can't even look at Reagan, so I keep my chin tucked and let Colten lead us to his car, drive us to his house, and guide me upstairs while sending Reagan into the bathroom to brush her teeth for bed.

Just as he gets me settled under the covers, Reagan pokes her head into the room. "I'm ready."

"Grab your books and bring them here."

Christ ... he's afraid to cross the hall to her room and leave me alone.

"These!" She jumps onto the bed, letting her books scatter at the foot of it while crawling toward me. Colten looks in on us from his bathroom while brushing his teeth. "Josie, I'm sorry you're sick. Maybe you'll feel better tomorrow." She kisses my forehead. "Nope. No fever."

The already suffocating lump in my throat doubles as my eyes burn with more tears. I close them before any escape.

"Okay, Button, let Josie sleep. Get on my side and pick your first story," Colten mumbles over his toothbrush.

That's all I remember because I'm so very tired. Everything goes dark behind my eyelids. Quiet. Peaceful. And then ...

I hear a voice.

"Little girls. Little girls everywhere. Oh ... what's that? You lost your hair? Well, that's what you get for being better than your brother. That's what you get for making him look bad. Just ask sweet little Beth with her strawberry locks ... oh ... that's right. She's dead."

"NOOOOO! I KILLED HER. I KILLEDHER. IKILLEDHER!" I jackknife to sitting.

"Daddy ..." Reagan's voice. She's crying. "W-what's wrong with J-josie?"

"Shh ... I've got you," his voice fades, and the door shuts.

Her cries muffle. His footsteps fade. The door to her room clicks shut. And I'm alone with a cold sweat along my brow, a pounding heart, and the realization that I, Winston Jeffries, killed my sister Bethany. I poisoned her. I shaved her head. And I buried her body in a cemetery. Then I cried. I grieved. I did all the things my parents expected me to do while everyone searched for her. They searched for her until my mom took her own life with the same straight blade she used to shave my head. Then my dad drank himself into a coma every evening, waking up in the middle of the night to puke and do things to me that no dad should do to his son. I can smell the mix of putrid stomach contents laced with alcohol.

I can smell it from over a century ago. And that is why ... Josephine Watts has never consumed a drop of alcohol.

Puzzles start out slow, but as more pieces are found, it comes together faster and faster. This puzzle is coming together in bigger chunks. Not a piece at a time anymore. Ten pieces. Twenty pieces. And the picture it's creating just keeps getting more unbearable.

Throwing off the covers, I find my feet under shaky legs. When my heart starts to slow, I can hear Reagan's soft sobs. How does a five-year-old, who was once afraid of the boogieman, process someone leaping out of their sleep and screaming, "I KILLED HER!"

Dizzy with the faint residual echo of his voice in my head, I ease open the bedroom door and navigate the stairs by gripping the railing to steady my swaying gait.

I shove my feet into my sneakers at the entry and stumble into the cold December air, light flurries peppering the night skies, blurring my vision, and making me even more dizzy while my faltering steps take me toward the street.

"Josie!"

I walk down the middle of the street.

"JOSIE!"

I mentally go through my own autopsy. Blunt force trauma.

When people get hit by cars, it shatters their skeletons and their organs rupture. It can be unsightly. And it's usually not autopsied. But sometimes bodies are found after a hit and run, and we have to determine if a vehicle ran over a dead body or if it was the cause of death.

"STOP!" Colten wraps his arms around my whole body, like he could tackle me to the ground, only we don't fall. He drags me to the sidewalk as a horn screeches in our ears and taillights beam bright red in the distance a few seconds later.

He scoops me up in his arms like a child and carries me to the house.

"You have to stop saving me," I whisper.

When he gets me back into bed, Reagan comes into the room and crawls in next to me under the covers. "I have bad dreams too," she whispers. "Daddy will keep you safe. He keeps me safe."

Colten shuts off the light and slides in next to me so that I'm sandwiched between them. His arms snake around my waist, and his lips press to my ear while he whispers, "I'll stop saving you when you stop trying to die. But I'll never stop loving you, *needing you*, so tough luck, Mr. Duck."

CHAPTER
Twenty-Six

"This isn't your regular time," Dr. Byrd says, when I have a seat by the window, this time opting for the rocking chair. He has a solid mix of seating choices.

"I lost my job, so my schedule suddenly opened up. And since I've been entertaining the idea of suicide, I thought a quick check-in might be a good idea. You know … before I check out."

He eyes me without sharing my jovial sense of humor, probably because it's hard to figure out where the humor lies in my current situation.

"How often are you having these thoughts?"

"Daily."

"These thoughts … how intense are they … on a scale of one to ten?"

"Eight. Nine must be actively acquiring a weapon, drugs, rope, or unfastening my seat belt while approaching a tree at ninety miles per hour. Correct? And ten means dead or a failed attempt? Eight. I'm going with eight."

"How serious are you about following through?"

"Is this a checklist of questions you learned in school? It is. Isn't it? Next are you going to ask me if I've given any thought as to how I would do it?"

"Have you?"

"I'm a medical examiner. I know all the ways to die. It doesn't require much thought."

He nods. He's having self-doubt. No amount of training can prepare one to talk another human down from the ledge.

"Maybe we can talk about my job."

Dr. Byrd nods again. "What happened?"

"I was fired."

He frowns.

"Well, that's not fair. I wasn't outright fired. It was more of an ultimatum. Get a psychiatric evaluation. Get help. Or clean out my desk. I cleaned out my desk."

"Why?"

"Why are you asking questions you know the answers to? This isn't PTSD. This isn't going away. If I let you medicate me to the point that I no longer recall my past life, then I'll be close to comatose and unable to do my job anyway."

"Why did your superior give you the ultimatum? What tipped him off?"

"I'm a little slower than I used to be. Still capable. Still doing solid work. Just slower."

And I told him I was a murderer.

"Why are you slower?"

"Do you have kids, Terry?"

"Two."

I nod. "Imagine trying to do your job with your kids here. Chattering. Getting into trouble. Shaving each other's heads. Threatening to kill someone. Just … stuff like that. Would you run behind? Would it take you longer to do your job?"

"Of course."

I shrug. "Well, now you know. I have to cut through the voices, the images, the reminders of that life while trying to do my job, and sometimes it slows me down. But I do, in fact, get my job done. Well, not anymore because I don't have a job. And that's what brings me here. Without my job, I have nothing."

"You have family. Friends. You're getting married."

"Let me rephrase. Without my job, I *am* nothing. No purpose. No identity."

Dr. Byrd stares out the window for a second. It's unusual for him. I'm used to his laser focus. "Sometimes, our identities and purpose in life change."

"Terry, I won't make it. I won't make it another forty … sixty years with Winston Jeffries in my head. I don't know if I'll make it four to six months. Four to six weeks. You know this is a torture, not so different than ways that POWs are treated. And now I don't have a purpose. *Wife* is not my purpose, even if it becomes part of my identity. I don't believe it's my purpose."

Dr. Byrd stares out the window again. Even the "expert" has no solution.

And so ... we're done.

When I exit his office, Mom smiles at me. Mom, my babysitter for the day. Mom, my driver. I'm never alone.

"Would you be up for some shopping?" she asks. "I have a few gifts left to get."

"Sure." I search for a smile and find one that seems to appease her.

Over the next two hours, we file in and out of stores.

"What are you getting for Reagan?" she asks.

"I don't know. What do young girls like?"

Mom chuckles while flipping through a rack of men's shirts. "Need I remind you that you were once a five-year-old girl?"

"Need I remind you that I wasn't a normal five-year-old girl? And now we know why. I doubt Reagan is into dead things, but I suppose we can see if there's a zombie Barbie or a mortician Barbie." I laugh. Then I laugh some more. "Mortician Barbie comes with a casket and a dead body."

"Shh ..." Mom glances around the store.

I press my lips together to compose myself, but in the next breath, I have a memory, but it's not Winston's life.

"I had Barbies and a few other dolls."

Mom moves to another rack, but she doesn't look at me.

"I cut off their hair. All of it."

She ignores me.

"Mom, I cut off their hair. You knew this, but you didn't remind me?"

"What would have been the point? I think your dad would like this one. Red is his color. What do you think?"

"I think when I'm dead, everyone will look back at so many things in my life and find it to be a goddamn miracle that I made it as long as I did."

"Josephine Eleanor Watts ..."

We have a silent standoff. What does she expect me to say?

"I'm getting your dad this shirt." She turns and heads toward the checkout.

When we get in the car, she exhales and glances over at me. "I've talked with Colten. And we're both in similar situations with you."

"How so?" I stare out my window at the throng of people loaded down with gifts, congesting the sidewalks and gazing at the storefront displays.

"I chose to have you instead of aborting you. He chose to save you. You are so loved. And we hate what you're experiencing. Even if we try to imagine, I'm sure it doesn't even come close. I try to imagine what it would be like to relive the rape repeatedly. Or imagine what it would be like to watch him do the same thing to other women. And even if I could fathom that, I know it doesn't come close to what you're experiencing." She reaches for my hand and squeezes it.

I glance at our hands before lifting my gaze to hers filled with tears. "I can't undo your life," she says. "I can't undo my choice to bring you into this world. And I can't unlove you. Neither can Colten, your dad, your brother, your friends. We can't imagine this life without you. And maybe it's selfish on our part if you are miserable every day and every night..." she wipes several tears that spring free "...but you can't ask us to let you die." With her next blink, all the tears escape.

I'm not a mother. I never will be a mother. So I can't really understand how she's feeling. But I remember how I felt when I lost Colten. I remember that feeling led to self-harm, compelled to cut myself by the debilitating pain.

And he wasn't really gone.

He wasn't gone, yet I thought about him every day for seventeen years. What if that day he broke up with me was the day he died? What if one of the times he felt his world crumbling around him, he would have decided to end his life, like his father did years later?

What would have happened to me? Would I have grieved him and moved on, knowing he wasn't in the world? Would the absence of hope have been the closure I needed? Or would I have spiraled out of control and taken my own life? Romeo and Juliet.

"Reagan loves books. I'm going to get her books. Maybe a Kindle. Maybe a fun reading light or a cute book bag to take to the library. Katy dropped her off, a few weeks ago, with some new library books in a plastic grocery bag." I nod ahead. "Let's stop by the bookstore on the way home. I know a good one."

Mom wipes the rest of her tears and sniffles. Then she nods.

Books.

All I can give her is books.

She seems content with that.

After we get a slew of gifts for Reagan at the bookstore, she drives me to Colten's. His car is in the driveway. My parents are staying at my house, and his mom is staying with him. Everyone is here for me ... and Christmas, but mostly me.

Suicide watch is a full-time job.

"Want me to take Reagan's gifts to your house and wrap them so she doesn't see them?"

"She's at Katy's, but yeah, that would be great. Thanks." I open the door.

"I love you, Josephine."

I glance back at her before climbing completely out of the car. "I love you too, Mom. That will never change."

She nods slowly, but I see sadness resurrecting in her eyes. I see the pain and worry over the promise I can't make. "Night."

"Night." I close the door, but she doesn't pull out until I'm at Colten's door and he's in her line of sight.

Nobody trusts me.

"Good day?" he asks.

"Sure." I hug him.

His arms wrap around my waist. Lately, he's been hugging me a little tighter, a little longer, and I let him because I need it too. The world is a livable place when I'm in his arms. I can breathe a little easier, and hope doesn't feel like a dream out of reach.

When he does release me, he takes my coat and hangs it in the entry closet.

"Where's your mom?" I ask.

"In her bedroom. She had a slight headache, so she went to bed shortly after I got home."

I follow him to the kitchen.

"Hungry?"

I shrug. "We had a late lunch, so I'm not starving."

Colten opens a drawer by the fridge. "I'll give you half if you show me your tits." He tears open a Twix.

I don't look at the candy bar; I look at him and smile. "I saw you. Sometimes when I glanced at your window, I saw you looking at me. But you jumped behind the curtain. You always made me feel interesting in a good way. You always made me feel special. Sometimes I wondered ... if we wouldn't have been neighbors, would you have given me a second look? The time of day?" I reach for his proffered candy bar. "Half of your Twix?"

He takes a bite of his candy bar and scoots a chair close to mine so, when he sits, my knees are between his. "Probably not because you intimidated the hell out of me."

I roll my eyes.

He shrugs, taking another bite of his Twix. "True story."

"Why?"

"Because you were so smart and confident. And pretty ... god you were so pretty. And your dad wouldn't have been the neighbor who took me under his wing. He simply would have been the police chief, and you would have been the police chief's daughter aka off-limits."

I break off a piece of the Twix, stretching the caramel until it breaks then popping it into my mouth.

"When I was in the shower this morning, I thought back to the times when my dad would let me jump off his fishing boat into the lake. I'd go under and hold my breath until I just couldn't go another second. Until my cheeks hurt from holding the air in them, until my lungs burned. Once, my dad jumped in after me because he thought something had happened to me." I chuckle. "He was so mad. I just liked seeing how long I could hold my breath. Then I thought about Winston Jeffries, and I remembered something."

"What was that?"

I shake my head, setting the rest of my uneaten candy bar on the table. "I think someone tried to drown him or strangle him. I just remember so clearly the feeling of not being able to breathe, like someone was holding me under water or wrapping their hands around my neck."

Colten rests his hands on my knees.

"And then this afternoon, I remembered something I did to my Barbie dolls ... all of my dolls."

"You tried to drown them?" he says jokingly.

"No. I cut off all of their hair."

Colten's grin falls off his face.

"People can have tics and not know it until someone brings it to their attention. I dated a guy in college who would finish his sentence and then repeat the last few words of the sentence in a whisper, like an echo. He had no idea he did it until I mentioned it. To his knowledge, he didn't have a condition that would cause it. Maybe it was stress or sleep deprivation, or maybe it was genetic. It's just interesting that one can do something like that and not realize it. That's how I feel. I feel like I've had something that I didn't recognize until now. And the pieces now fit where they didn't fit before. Winston Jeffries has been popping into my life for ... well, maybe forever. And I'm only now starting to make the connections."

"You're not him, Josie. And you're not the only person who has cut their baby doll's or Barbie's hair. You're not the first person to see how long you can hold your breath underwater. You're not the only person who has been curious about death. And while I will concede that you have been and always will be a unique person, it has nothing to do with Winston Jeffries."

What do I say when he says all the right things? I wish I could love my way through this. Why can't love be enough? Why can't love conquer all? Standing, I yawn and stretch my arms over my head. "I'm going to bed."

Colten nods, gaze on my empty chair. "I'll be up in a few minutes." He forces his gaze to mine. "Will you be okay?"

I nod, not hesitating for a single second. I hate that he feels like I can't be left alone. I feel like a temperamental plant that is always on the verge of dying if it's watered too little or too much, if you change its location in the house or forget to talk to it. I am the exact opposite of independent.

"Good." He reaches for my hand and squeezes it. There's a lot of hand squeezing lately. Colten looks exhausted.

Loving me isn't easy. I can't help but wonder if he ever regrets moving to Chicago. I wouldn't blame him.

CHAPTER
Twenty-Seven

NEW OBSERVATION: The less worthy one feels, the less they *feel* anything.

My parents leave Christmas Eve day after lunch to visit Benji. We'll see them again at the wedding in a few weeks. Becca returns to Texas to be with Chad and his partner for Christmas. It's just Colten, Reagan, and me until Katy picks her up to be with her and Sean on Christmas morning.

"Josie!" Colten grabs the hot pad and takes the pan from me as I hold its searing hot handle. Only, it's not searing to me. "Baby, oh shit ..." He runs my hand under cool water.

I don't feel that either.

"Daddy said a bad word," Reagan observes from her post as present watcher by the tree.

I stare at my hand, red and white. Like Christmas.

"Josie?" Colten presses his chest to my back while keeping my hand under the stream of water. "Say something. How bad is it?"

"I'm … I'm sorry."

"No." He kisses my head over and over. "Don't apologize. But, baby … you didn't drop the pan or scream or so much as flinch."

"I'm sorry."

"Stop. No." He wets a towel and wraps it around my hand, turning me to face him. "I think we should get it looked at."

I ease my head side to side, lifting my unfocused gaze to meet his concerned face. "It's … fine," I whisper.

"Daddy, it's time to open gifts."

"After dinner, Button," he says while continuing to scrutinize me.

"Let's eat." I hug my hand to my chest and turn toward the plates of food.

"Just sit down. I'll finish dishing up the food and bring it to the table."

Reagan hops into her chair. Instead of taking a seat, I stand behind her, stroking her hair with my good hand. "You'd look adorable in short hair."

"Like yours?" she asks, twisting her body to see me.

I smile and nod.

"Reagan, your mom would not approve of cutting your hair," Colten says, setting two of the plates on the table and eyeing me—eyeing my hand stroking her hair. A tiny line forms along the bridge of his nose.

"Baby, have a seat." He nods to the chair across from Reagan.

Every time I touch her hair, he gets that look.

Can he love me and not trust me?

After dinner, Reagan bolts to the tree. "Presents!"

"Give me five minutes. I'm going to get bandages for Josie's hand."

"Hurry up!" She shakes one of the boxes.

"It's fine," I say.

He removes the towel. It's not fine. It's pretty bad. Still, I somehow don't feel it. I felt the look he gave me over Reagan's hair, but not this burn.

"It's not fine. Come with me."

I follow him to his bedroom, taking a seat on the edge of the bed as he grabs first-aid supplies out of the bathroom.

While applying burn cream and gauze bandages, he glances up at me. "You're a little off tonight."

I look at him and nod several times.

"What's up? You're not getting cold feet, are you?"

"About what?"

He grins. "Um ... the wedding. You should have received an invite. I'd love it if you could make it."

"Do you not trust me with Reagan?"

"What are you talking about?" He knows that answer. That's why he's not looking at me.

"Does it make you nervous when I touch her hair?"

He shakes his head, still not looking at me. "No. It makes me nervous when you talk about cutting her hair. I don't want to deal with Katy on that."

"Tonight ... *tonight* I said she'd look cute in short hair. But I've touched her hair other times, and you always give me the same look."

Colten tapes the end of the gauze bandage. "What look is that?"

"Self-doubt."

He grunts a laugh. "Self-doubt about what?"

Before I can answer, he returns the supplies to the bathroom.

"I think it gives you pause. Even if only for a few seconds, you wonder if Winston Jeffries is really dead."

"Nope," he says from the bathroom. "I know he's dead. But..." shutting off the light to the bathroom, he peeks around the corner "...I wonder if you're thinking of my daughter's beautiful hair when you stroke it or if you're thinking of him."

"And if I'm thinking of him?"

Colten frowns, hunching in front of me again. "Do you *want* me to have self-doubt?"

"No. But if you do, I don't want you to lie about it."

He falls to his knees and rests his head on my lap. "No doubts. No cold feet. I love you without a single hesitation. And I trust you with my life."

"And Reagan's?"

"Daddy!" Speaking of ...

Colten jumps to his feet. "Time to open gifts." He holds out his hand to take my good hand.

He's not answering me. That's ... my answer.

We open presents, and Reagan loves all the book

stuff I got her. This brings a smile to my face. And that brings one to Colten's.

"I want to use my sled."

"Button, it's nighttime. Tomorrow, you can use it."

"Tonight. Just once. *Please ...*"

Colten sighs. "Fine. Let's get your stuff on after I run upstairs and get my snow pants."

"I can help her," I say, following Reagan and her sled to the entry.

She pulls on her bib and jacket. I zip it and help her with her hat and gloves.

"Scarf too?"

She nods.

I wrap the scarf around her neck and tie it once, holding one tail with my teeth because I can't grip with my injured hand.

"*I ... can't ... b-breath ...*"

I pull tight. And tighter. And ...

"Too tight, Josie."

I pull a little tighter.

"*Pl-please st-stop!*"

"Let me get that since your hand is hurt." Colten takes the ends of the scarf from me and quickly loosens it. "I don't think you need a scarf. We won't be out there long."

Reagan touches her gloved hand to her neck.

"Are you going to watch us out the window?" he asks.

The girls couldn't breathe. I couldn't breathe. I did to them what was done to me.

"Josie?"

I shake my head, staring at Reagan. Then my attention shifts to Colten, and I nod.

"Go stand by the patio door and watch us sled."

Another slow nod. He's treating me like a child. I would object to this treatment, but I don't have my wits about me enough to build a case for myself. So I turn and shuffle my feet to the patio door.

I wasn't going to strangle her. I was just … fuck. I don't know.

The power of the mind is incredible. Even the best scientists in the world have only touched the surface of its capabilities. If you tell someone something enough, they start to believe it, regardless of its truth. It becomes their new truth.

Winston Jeffries is in my head, a voice whispering to me over and over again. How long before it becomes my truth?

I watch them sled a few times down the tiny hill in the backyard. For a man who thought he didn't want kids because he was afraid of being his father, Colten is the absolute opposite. He's engaged and patient. His love for Reagan shines brightly every second of every day. Occasionally, he glances at me. No smile.

It's sadness.

He loves me, but I'm unwell. He loves Reagan, but she is vulnerable around me because I can't be trusted. If Katy knew any of this, she would take her daughter and never let Colten see her again. That's what a good mom would do. And Katy is a good mom. She's everything I will never be, including the mother of Colten Mosley's child.

I turn away from the window and slide my socked feet along the hardwood floor toward the stairs.

Bang. Bang. Bang.

Reagan's mitten-covered fists drum against the glass. "Watch me on my tummy!" She's not ready to come inside, and he's not ready to let me be out of his sight.

He knows it wouldn't take me long to end my life. And he knows it wouldn't take me long to end hers. Not that I would. I wouldn't. Winston can scream in my head. He can rob me of every ounce of sleep from now until my last breath, but he won't convince me to hurt Reagan. I'm not him.

I'm not him. I'm not him. I'm not him ...

Reagan goes down the hill on her tummy and giggles when her face lands in a pile of snow. "Did you see me, Josie?"

I nod. Fabricate a smile. And wave both hands. That's what someone who isn't out of their fucking mind does, right?

Right? Who the hell am I asking? Is this it? Is this the prelude to the end? Nothing but a series of conversations with myself? Battle of the internal monologue?

I'm not going to die tonight, but I'm tired, so I go upstairs before anyone can knock on the window again and demand my attention. Managing a quick swipe of the toothbrush along my teeth first, I collapse onto the bed in my panties and one of Colten's hoodies. Sleep takes me within seconds while I hug my burned hand to my chest.

I don't know how long it takes, but when it happens, it's sheer panic and nausea. "NOOOOO!" I gasp, but I can't breathe. The pressure on my neck is unbearable. Panic ensues under the noose of my airway being crushed. This is it. This is how I die. It's like I'm drowning all over again, but I'm not. Someone is strangling me. When I peel open my eyes, my heart explodes. It's him.

Colten's strangling me. This is how he's protecting his daughter. I know it's for the best. I deserve this. It's what I've been preparing myself for since the day I should have died in the water. I don't hate him.

No ... I love him. I love him for loving me so completely. I love him for doing the right thing even when I didn't understand it. But this time ... I under- stand it. I'm trying so hard not to fight him, but my hands flail, hitting him.

Just let it happen ...

Fighting the instinct to survive is hard, and it feels so out of my control. I grab his arms, trying to pry them off my neck. I can't. He's stronger.

Stay strong. Finish the job. Focus on my eyes. I'm ready.

I cough. He's not gripping me hard enough. I shouldn't be able to get any air.

Again, I cough.

The hoodie slides over my head.

"Josie. Josie. Josie ... I've got you, baby. I've got you ... Breathe. Just breathe. You're safe. I've got you."

The pressure on my neck disappears, and air fills my lungs. The pounding of my heart overtakes all other sensations while he pulls me against his bare chest and kisses me over and over on my head, my cheeks, my lips.

"I'm sorry," he whispers. "I'm so very sorry."

My good hand touches my neck. "Why did you stop? I was ready."

He pulls back, confusion lining his forehead. "Stop what?"

"Strangling me."

"What? No ... no, Josie. I wasn't strangling you. You were having a nightmare. You woke up gasping and flailing, clawing at your neck like you couldn't breathe."

I sit up, tearing myself from his arms while swinging my legs over the side of the bed. Head bowed. Sweat along my brow. Confused.

"What is happening to me?" I whisper.

Colten crawls out of bed and disappears downstairs. A minute or so later, he returns with a glass of water. "I would never hurt you."

My gaze lifts to his while I take the glass of water. "What are we doing?" I ask, barely above a whisper.

"We're living." He sits next to me on the bed, taking my injured hand onto his lap and tracing the lines of the bandage. "And it's really fucking hard for you right now. If I could take this burden from you, I would. I feel like you're still drowning, and every day I'm trying to save you. Josie, I *have* to save you."

"Colten, I ..." Emotion clogs my throat. "I made Reagan's scarf too tight. I ..."

"It was an accident. She's fine."

"But what if—"

"She's fine," he repeats.

I feel so dead inside, so I hand him the half-empty glass and collapse onto my side, easing my legs onto the bed. "I'm tired."

"Then sleep, my love." He kisses my cheek. "Dream of me. Dream of being legally bound to me forever."

I attempt a smile because he's trying so hard to lighten the mood. I'm walking death, and that sucks for everyone around me.

CHAPTER
Twenty-Eight

IT's a miracle, and because of this miracle, I am a true believer today.

Today I'm marrying Josephine Watts. My heart feels full, overflowing really. Everything I didn't dare to imagine is here in this church.

A daughter.

The woman I've loved since I was ten.

Family.

Friends.

A future.

It's all right here.

"I'm proud of you, son," Josie's dad says to me as I straighten my tie in the mirror. "You've made something of yourself. You are a good man. And I can't imagine anyone better for my daughter." He blows out a long breath. "If your dad was here, he'd be proud of you too. He'd see that you are absolutely everything he never was. And I'm sad for you that he's not here because I think you would have been the dominant influence in his life that he needed. I think he would have been a better man because of the man you've become."

I don't want to think about my dad today. However, hearing Chief Watts say those words to me means a lot. He's reminding me why I always looked up to him over my own father. He *is* the better man.

"How are you feeling about the road ahead?" he asks. "Do you believe her? Do you believe she was that Winston Jeffries guy?"

"Yes." I turn. "I ..." I rub my forehead. "I don't know how it's possible to believe her, but I was there when she found those bodies. There is no other explanation. And here's the thing ... I will follow her down any rabbit hole, no matter how deep or how dark. If I didn't love her and trust her, I wouldn't be marrying her."

Chief Watts nods several times before grinning. "She's never been in better hands."

I don't know about that. If I was totally honest with him, I'd tell him I'm frightened out of my fucking mind that something is going to happen to her again on my watch. She's in this position because something happened to her on my watch.

"Daddy?" Reagan peeks her head into the room.

"Hey, Button, let me see you."

She closes the door behind her and runs to me.

I hunch down and hug her before holding her at arm's length. "I have never seen a more beautiful girl."

She twirls in a circle. God, I love this girl.

"Mommy went to get me a snack."

"A snack, huh?" I stand straight.

"Uh-huh. I'm going to see Josie now."

"Whoa, whoa, I don't want you running around here by yourself. It's not safe."

"Because of bad people?" she asks.

Isaac gives me a look. It's the don't-lie-to-her look.

"Yes. Unfortunately, sometimes there are bad people. Probably not here, today, but you should still be safe."

"But I want to see her."

"Do you know where she is?"

She nods.

"You can go see her, but I want you to stay with her until your mom comes back with your snack. Okay?"

Reagan nods, her curls and ribbons bouncing with each dramatic tip of her chin.

"Love you, Button. You look beautiful."

"Bye, Daddy!" She blows me a kiss with fishy lips.

This is the very best day of my life. Everything has come full circle.

"Do you think you and Josie will have kids together?"

I turn toward Isaac, hiding the confusion I feel from his question. Did she not tell her family that she can't have kids? Did she never tell her parents that she didn't want to have kids?

"I'm not sure it's what she wants. And I have Reagan. My life is complete. Anything else would just be extra. So ... one day at a time." I find a believable smile. I'd have a dozen babies with Josie because it would mean a dozen more pieces of Josie walking the earth, gracing my life with giggles and fishy kisses.

There's a knock at the door.

"Everyone dressed?" Savannah asks before opening the door a crack.

"You're not allowed to see the father of the bride before the wedding," Isaac says.

Savannah opens the door the rest of the way. "Is that so?"

Isaac saunters toward her, wrapping his arms around her waist, hands resting on her ass. If I said I'm not having a blow job flashback, I'd be lying.

"What's that look for?" Savannah asks me when he releases her.

I realize I'm cringing and quickly correct my expression. "Nothing. Just ..."

"Cold feet? Nerves? Your bride-to-be is stunning. Just ..." Savannah gets tears in her eyes. "And Reagan couldn't look more adorable. They're having a private moment right now."

I nod.

"She told Josie you said she needed to stay with her because there are bad people around. I certainly hope there aren't any here today."

"She what? She said that to Josie?"

Savannah nods.

"W-where are they?" My stomach twists into knots. I have a feeling. A terrible feeling.

"You can't see Josie before the wedding, silly."

I take long strides to the door. "Where are they?"

"Colten ..."

As soon as I open the door, my world explodes. That *feeling* comes to fruition in the form of my daughter standing before me with confusion on her face, a short bob, and her long hair banded and hanging from her fist.

I can't fucking breathe.

Reagan holds out her shaky hand with the hair. "J-Josie said I'm safe." She's on the verge of tears. "And s-she said she's j-ust a star."

I take the hair and pull her into my arms.

"She said t-to step backwards ... and I ... think she said there's a galaxy."

"I'm sorry, Button. Your hair will grow back." I hold her at arm's length again like I did when she showed me her dress. "Where is Josie?"

"What's going on?" Isaac asks.

Reagan shrugs. "Her room? I don't know. I unzipped her dress and came to give you my hair."

"Stay right here. Don't move." I kiss her forehead and take off running.

"Colten?" Savannah calls behind me.

When I throw open the door to the lounge just off the ladies' room, an unwelcome emptiness settles into my chest. She's not here. She's not in the building. I feel it. Fishing my phone from my pocket, I call her.

She doesn't answer.

"Colten, where are you going?" Katy asks as I pass her on my way out the door to the parking lot.

I don't answer her. I can't.

Josie is nowhere in sight. She rode here with her parents, and their vehicle is here.

"Josie!" I scream, running my fingers through my hair. She's gone.

Fuck ... I can't breathe or feel anything but my heart losing all control while I turn in a slow circle, my world spinning out of control.

She's gone.

"She's not answering her phone." Isaac says.

I grip my hair tighter and continue turning in a circle.

"Nerves. It's just nerves. She probably decided to walk around the block. She'll be back," he says.

Does he really believe that?

I don't.

She's gone. And I'm so fucking scared she's gone for good.

"Where are my keys?" I search my pockets.

"Probably inside with the rest of your stuff," Isaac says.

I run inside, grab my keys, and run back to my car, ignoring everyone saying my name along the way. They're concerned the bride has cold feet. I'm worried her entire body could be cold if I don't find her soon.

"Just hold on, baby ... please." I speed out of the

parking lot, scouring the area. I can't file a missing person's report, but I can call Rains.

"Hey, I'm trimming my beard just for your wedding. Why are you calling me?"

"I need a favor."

"What's wrong? Your voice is shaking. Colten?"

I clear my throat, the thick pain of reality shrinking my airway. "Josie's missing. And I need to find her."

"It's probably cold feet. Give her a bit. She'll show back up."

"No. You don't understand. She's not having second thoughts about marrying me. She's …" I pinch the bridge of my nose, waiting at a stoplight. "She's suicidal. If I don't find her soon, we won't find her alive."

He doesn't answer for several seconds.

"Are you—"

"I'll get her picture out to everyone. Colten, what hap—"

"Thanks." I disconnect the call.

Over the next three hours, I look everywhere. Rains gives me updates.

Nothing.

Her parents give me updates.

My mom waits at my house.

My brother waits at the church, even after the guests go home.

Her brother waits at her house.

"Colten," Mom whispers my name when I open the back door and shrug out of my jacket, yanking at my tie to loosen it.

"We'll find her."

I shake my head.

"Yes. We'll—"

"NO!" I pound my fists on the kitchen counter.

She jumps.

Then I swipe my arms along the granite, knocking everything to the ground. "FUCK!" My fist lands into the glass cabinet door, then the next, and the next. Blood runs down my arm. "SHE'S DEAD. SHE'S DEAD!" I grab a chair and hurl it through the patio door. "FUCK YOU, WINSTON JEFFRIES!"

"C-Colten ..." Mom sobs, trying to approach me before I break something else.

When my gaze meets hers, I see it. The perfect reflection of my pain. Even if I stopped loving my father, she did not. He selfishly took his life, leaving her with nothing but a million unanswered questions.

"Colten." She takes a cautious step toward me while I pant with the intensity of a rabid animal. When she wraps a towel around my fist, my torso curls inward.

"Noooo ..." I sob.

She hugs me when I fall to my knees. No more promising everything will be alright. Nothing will ever feel right again.

He won. And I lost.

CHAPTER
Twenty-Nine

"ARE YOU AFRAID OF DYING?" Josie asked while we sat in the grass fishing in the pond by the playing fields.

We were thirteen. I didn't think about my mortality as often as Josie did.

"I mean ... I don't want to die."

"Duh. But are you afraid of it? Like a car accident or a tornado? Cancer? Kids get cancer too. Murder ... oh murder would be the worst, especially if it were slow. Like someone tortured you."

"If you're asking if I'm afraid of being tortured, then the answer is yes."

We sat in silence for a few minutes, neither one of us getting a single bite.

"Can you imagine wanting to die? Remember last year when they found that kid hanging from the swing set at North Elementary? The janitor found him in the morning?"

I nodded.

"He wanted to die. That's why he hung himself. A fifteen-year-old who wanted to die. My dad said it's a tragedy, but lots of kids commit suicide."

Another nod.

Just another day in the life of being Josephine Watts' best friend. Death. Death. And more death. Maybe I would have been more scared of it had we not talked about it so much.

"I can't imagine wanting to die." She blows out a long breath. "I suppose that's good, right?"

"Sure."

"But what if you lost everything. Like what if a tornado hit our neighborhood and my parents and Benji died. And you and your family died. And I lived. Maybe I would want to hang myself from the swing set too."

I finished reeling in my line and cast it again.

"Or what if you had cancer and you felt bad all the time. And you knew you were going to die eventually. Would you just get it over with? It might save family a lot of sadness. They wouldn't have to watch you slowly die."

I shrugged. "I don't know."

"You never think about that? You've never thought about how you would kill yourself if you needed to do it?"

"Nope." I had no idea that my dad would one day

drive my mind there. He would anger me and embarrass me to the point of thinking about how I would kill myself.

"At first, I thought I would use a gun because it would be quick. Then I thought about it a little more and realized someone would find me and have to clean up the mess. Now, I'd probably do it in a way that nobody ever found me. They'd never have to see me dead. And they could remember me when I was happy and wanted to live. Doesn't that sound like the best way to go?"

"Or ..." I chuckled. "You could *not* kill yourself. I like that idea best. Don't kill yourself."

"Because you would miss me?" She nudged my arm.

I grinned. "Maybe."

Undoubtedly.

My young brain had quite the imagination, but it couldn't imagine a world without Josephine Watts, my best friend.

"I'd tie bricks around my feet and jump off a bridge into the river. I wouldn't leave a note. Maybe my family would wonder if somewhere I was still alive. They'd have hope. Hope is good. It's better than knowing for sure that you will never see someone again."

I didn't know. Josie's mind worked different than mine and everyone else I knew. Not different bad, just ... different.

"Would you cry if I died?"

I lifted a shoulder. "I don't know. I don't like to cry. Would you want me to cry?"

"Nah. Just sit in my tree and eat a whole candy bar by yourself. Maybe talk to me. I think it's cool when people talk to the dead like they can hear them. Do you believe in ghosts?"

And just like that ... we jumped to another interesting conversation.

"Oh my gosh!" She shot up as I tugged on my fishing pole. "You caught one, Colten! You did it! Don't let it go! It's a big one." She helped me hold my fishing pole as I reeled it in. "If you lose it, you'll never catch one like it again."

I kinda thought the same thing about Josephine Watts.

CHAPTER
Thirty

"Once the snowstorm lets up, we'll go out again," Isaac says a week later.

A week after our wedding day.

A week after Josie lost her battle.

A week after I knew she was gone forever.

"You won't find her." I stare at my untouched plate of food.

Savannah and Mom think I need my strength. I lost it a week ago. I'm the only one facing reality.

The Chicago PD are still looking. Signs have been posted. Her picture's been all over the news and internet.

"Son, we'll find her," Isaac says.

Her body. He means they'll find her body. I think he knows she's gone. They need a body for closure. Should I tell him and Savannah that they won't find her body, which means they can carry this "hope" with them forever? Should I tell them that Josie has been planning her death (even if unknowingly) for decades?

Savannah wipes a tear from her cheek and smiles at her hopeful husband. She, too, knows. My mom keeps to herself. This has resurrected all the memories of my dad hanging himself. At least he left his body in plain sight, which made closure a little easier.

I don't know which is worse: their hope or my certainty.

My phone chimes with a FaceTime from Reagan. I take a deep breath and search for a little smile. "Hey, Button."

"Hi, Daddy. Did you find Josie?" She has a smile for me. And a cute, short hairdo. Josie was right. She's adorable in short hair. "Mommy said she's been sharing her picture and looking for her. I look for her too when I'm at school."

My little girl knows how to hit me in the feels; her words make my eyes burn with unshed tears.

"That's ..." I swallow hard. "That's nice of you and Mommy. Thank you."

"I'm not mad that she cut my hair. Mommy said Josie wasn't well. She said she was sad about something that happened a long time ago."

I nod slowly. "Yeah. That's right."

"Well, she'll get better. And when I see her again, I'm going to show her my hair and tell her that I'm not mad. And I'm going to tell her that Mommy has read me three of the books Josie gave me for Christmas.

And yesterday I took the bag she gave me to the library, and it held eight books!"

"Oh yeah?" I hold my phone away for a second while I stand and head to the stairs, wiping the corners of my eyes with the heel of my hand. "That's great."

There's a tiny but mighty thread I'm holding on to, and her name is Reagan Annabel Mosley.

"Mommy said I need to say goodbye. Can I spend the night with you this weekend? I want to go sledding."

"Reagan, I told you Sean and I will take you," Katy says in the background.

"But I want Daddy to do it."

"Of course, Button. We can go sledding this weekend."

"Maybe we'll find Josie. Maybe she's sledding. I feel better when I'm sledding."

"Reagan ..." Katy takes the iPad away from her and frowns at the camera. "I'm sorry, Colten. She just doesn't understand."

"Bye, Daddy!"

"Bye." I ease my head side to side and rub the back of my neck. "It's fine. I'm glad she doesn't understand."

"How are her parents doing? How is your mom doing? God, I'm sure she's thinking about your dad a lot."

I nod. "Yeah, I'm sure she is. Josie's parents are playing the part. They're going through the motions. Not giving up hope."

"I don't think any of us should give up hope, Colten."

"I think everyone needs to do what's right for them. If that's hope, then I won't take that away. But I knew Josie better than anyone, and that's left me with a lot … a lot of love, a lot of memories, and a lot of emotions. Hope isn't one of them."

Katy frowns. "I'm keeping hope. I think Reagan needs it."

I try to smile. "Agreed." Reagan needs hope. She needs fairy tales. She needs Santa Claus and the Easter Bunny. I need something different.

"I booked my flight." Mom peeks her head into my bedroom. "Home just in time for Valentine's Day by myself."

I smile, glancing up from my notebook, back against the headboard, legs stretched long. "You could stay. I could be your valentine."

She grins, taking a seat on the end of my bed. "Actually, Chad promised to take me to dinner anywhere I want to go since Philip will be out of town."

"Go big."

She chuckles. "I plan on it."

It's been nearly five weeks since the wedding. I work. I spend time with my mom and Reagan, and I send updates to Josie's parents. It's always the same update: nothing.

Rains thinks we might find her in the spring when the snow thaws or when Lake Michigan starts to thaw. It's been frigidly cold. And what he means is we'll find her body.

We won't.

Maybe we were only kids when Josie said she'd die in a way that nobody would find her, but I have no doubt that adult Josie with her vast knowledge would keep that promise. Everything's in limbo. She's a missing person.

No funeral.

Her house sits empty.

Her parents can't collect life insurance until a body has been discovered and one of her colleagues signs a death certificate. Most likely, they'll see the money in seven years. That's how long it takes to collect life insurance on a missing person.

Nobody needs the money.

Nobody needs her house.

We never got the chance to say our vows, so dealing with her possessions is up to her parents.

"Writing me a love letter?" Mom asks, nodding to my notebook and extra fine tipped Sharpie in my hand.

"Do you want me to write you one?"

She shrugs. "It would be nice. I've never been given a love letter."

That's sad. It's sad she married an asshole. I suppose had she not, I wouldn't be here which means Reagan wouldn't exist. So I back up the mental train and let myself be a little grateful that my mom did marry that asshole.

I find a blank sheet and scribble a few things before tearing it from the spiral bound book and handing it to her.

She reads it, tears instantly filling her eyes.

Dear Mom,

Thank you for loving me more than any other human has ever loved me.

Your favorite son,

Colten

While she wipes a few tears she laughs. "I won't show Chad."

I shrug. "He's a big boy. He can take the truth."

She shakes her head. "I do. I love you so far beyond words, it's ... unimaginable." Her hand rests on my foot. "I feel your grief. I feel the hollowness of your heart. I feel your fractured soul. I feel *you*. God, I wish I could take it all away. I wish I could bring her back and make her better. A mother wants many things for her children, but I wanted you to experience love. The kind I never had. And I knew it was Josie. I knew it from the time you were young kids, and I've known it every day since."

Pulling in a long breath, she releases it slowly. "You will be okay. You will go on to do great things like you did when you let her go the first time."

Let her go.

Is that what I'm doing?

I'm not sure I ever really let her go the first time.

For seventeen years, I held on to hope. And she came back into my life. It was a goddamn miracle.

Mom folds the note I gave her in half. "I know you weren't writing me a love letter. What are you writing? If I can ask?"

I toss her the notebook. "I'm writing down all of my memories of her." I shrug as Mom glances through the pages. "I think some people are afraid of moving on because they don't want to forget. I'll admit, I don't *want* to move on without her, but I have a job, a daughter, a mother, and a brother. I have a life even if it's a life with a Josephine Watts-sized hole in it. And whether I want it to or not, life is moving forward. Some days I feel tied to a treadmill. I don't want to move on, but I don't have a choice." I take the notebook back when she hands it to me. "In forty ... fifty years, I might need some of these memories. I don't want them to fade to the point that I don't recall them."

Mom moves to the side of the bed and bends down to hug me. "You're everything your father wasn't. You are a good man and just ... a good human."

CHAPTER
Thirty-One

March.

April.

May.

"You came." Savannah smiles and hugs me.

"Of course." I peer at the crowd seated in the botanical garden for Josie's celebration of life while Savannah whispers, "We're not giving up on a miracle." She releases me and squeezes my hand. "Friends and family need this. We'll have a different kind of celebration when she's home again."

I hide my reaction behind a neutral expression. It's been two months since I've seen Savannah and Isaac. The last time, they visited to go through some things at Josie's house. I was under the impression that they had accepted what I've said all along … Josie's dead.

"Okay." That's it. That's my best response. "Um … I

didn't expect to see so many people here." I narrow my eyes and survey the crowd. There are people from school that I haven't seen since senior year. People who were not friends of Josie's. It's ... weird.

"They're here for you too. A lot of people wanted to pay their respects to you after your father died. Now they can do it for both your father and Josie."

Yep. So weird.

"Would you like to speak? I put your name on the program, but if you can't do it, we'll just skip over you."

Maybe this wasn't a good idea after all. I clear my throat. "Sure." I'm not doing it for Josie. This would drive her crazy. She hated being the center of attention, except with me. She wanted to be my center of attention. And she was ... just my everything. I'm doing this for her parents, to help give them closure I'm not sure they're really looking for yet.

I take a seat in the front row. A collage of photos resides on wood stands lining both sides of the podium. Josie's parents were married in this very spot. Two years later, Savannah was raped on their anniversary. There's too much to wrap my head around in this surreal moment.

Josie's dad speaks first. I tune him out. Then her mom speaks, causing everyone to reach for tissues. Except me. I'm too busy thinking about my life with Josie. Thinking about what I'm going to say.

"Next, we're going to hear from Colten Mosley, Josie's fiancé," Savannah says through sniffles.

Am I her fiancé if she's dead?

I give Savannah a hug while she steps away from the podium.

I'm not the best at winging it, but they didn't leave me with much choice.

Clearing my throat, my gaze slides over the faces of the crowd. "The day we moved into the house across the street from the Watts, my dad told me he met Chief Watts. And then he told me there was a boy named Joe who was my age. I was ecstatic because I hated being the new kid starting school with no friends. I had the whole summer to become Joe's best bud. Then I discovered Joe was Josephine. And ..." I smile, shaking my head. "I was really conflicted. She was a girl. That was disappointing. It was also the day my life changed in ways I never could have imagined.

"Josie poured me a glass of milk and offered me the best chocolate chip cookie I had ever tasted. Then she spent the next eight years threading herself through my heart one stitch at a time. She held me together when my world fell apart around me. Our love was unlike any love I have ever experienced. Unlike any love I have ever seen or any love written with words ... or even in the stars. It's not a father's love. It's not a son's love. It's not even a husband's love. It's that feeling you get when everything is dark, and you can't even see yourself. Then ..." My voice cracks, and I pull in a shaky breath. "She slides her hand into mine and squeezes it." I shake my head, glancing at the smattering of puffy clouds in the blue sky. "And just like that ... I felt *seen*." Closing my eyes, I picture her. That slow growing smile of hers. That knowing smile.

I see you.

When I open my eyes, I release a long breath. "I believe wherever my beautiful Josephine is right now, she's at peace. And making whatever world she's in a better place. That's what she does. She makes everything ... better."

I weave my way between the rows of chairs instead of taking a seat in the front row again. Then I get into my car and drive to the Watts' house.

Through the backyard.

Into the woods.

Up the tree.

Swinging my legs from "our" branch, I laugh. Then I laugh a little more, a little harder. "Tessa Hart was at your celebration of life. Remember her? The placeholder? Actually, there was a surprising number of people from our class, which means nobody moves away from Des Moines unless they are awesome like us. It also means you had more friends than you ever imagined because *you* were awesome. And everything." The smile slides off my face. "Josie ... I'm sorry. I'm so fucking sorry I couldn't fix it. Fix *you*. I'm sorry I only saw you and not him. Had I let myself focus on him, I would have seen you dying long before you took your own life."

Fuck the tears. I set them free.

Everything hurts from my burning eyes to my aching heart. The cold void of nothingness in my soul has never been as chilling as it is right now. It's taken me months to make it here. *Home.* And now that I'm here where she used to be *everywhere*, her absence feels like it's crushing my fucking heart.

I sniffle, tipping my chin to let more tears find their way to the earth below. "Is this how you felt? Alone? Like the best part of you was gone? Stolen?" Nodding slowly, I swallow past the lump in my throat. "Maybe you ..." I grit my teeth when more tears blur my vision. "Maybe you were him ... but he wasn't you. Josie ... He. Wasn't. You." And with that, I pull out a candy bar and eat it all by myself.

"I DON'T WANT to wear that." Reagan scrunches her little nose at me while I hold up her T-ball shirt.

"It's your team's tee. You have to wear it. Everyone else will be wearing theirs."

"Mom said I don't have to be like other kids."

I sit on the end of her bed, chuckling. "That's correct. You are unique. No one is like you. This shirt will not change that. It will make it, so the rest of your team recognizes you as one of the team members. When you're on the field, you need to know if the person standing by a base is the one running on your team or a player from the other team trying to get you out."

With her arms crossed, she huffs. "Fine." She holds up her arms and lets me pull her shirt over her head. "I'm sad mommy won't be at the game."

"She is too. But she'll be at your next game. Now, grab your shoes and I'll get your bag. We don't want to be late." My hands cup her face a second before I give her a big smooch on the cheek. "I love you, Button. Let's go have some fun."

As soon as we get to the ball fields, Reagan bolts toward her team.

"Your glove!"

She turns and stomps her way back to me as if it's my fault she forgot her glove.

"What do you say?"

She mumbles a thank you before breaking into a full sprint again.

"I don't want to play!"

I glance over at the girl throwing a fit in the minivan next to my car.

"I don't like T-ball. It's stupid."

"Find a better word than stupid if you expect me to listen to your little rant," her mom says, grabbing her glove before tossing the girl over her shoulder.

I don't expect that, so I snort a laugh and cover my mouth when she glances in my direction. The daughter pulls her mom's blond ponytail.

The mom ignores her, closing the sliding door and locking the minivan like she's a pro at getting things done with a young girl held hostage over her shoulder.

"I don't know a better word than stupid," the girl says, yanking the ponytail a little harder.

"Then tough luck, little duck."

Tough luck, Mr. Duck.

Following the echo of her words, I make my way to the field where the kids are warming up. A few seconds after I take a seat on the bottom bleacher, that mom takes a seat on the same bleacher a good four feet from me.

She gives me a smile. "Which one is yours?"

I nod toward Reagan. "The one chasing butterflies."

She laughs. "At least she wants to be here."

"Sort of. She didn't want to wear the shirt because her mom told her she doesn't have to be like everyone else."

"Ha. Well, I agree with your wife. But I also feel your pain of trying to get a strong-willed child dressed and to the game on time."

"Well, her mom and I never married, so that might be why I was caught off guard. We should communicate better."

"Oh, sorry. That was a poor assumption on my part."

"Nope." I shake my head. "Totally logical assumption."

She stretches out her hand. "I'm Layla."

I shake her hand. "Colten. And the butterfly chaser is Reagan."

Layla laughs again. "The sack of potatoes I had over my shoulder is Nora."

Several other parents climb the bleachers behind us.

I smile and nod at them.

"Nora's dad was a high school girls' softball coach, so she's determined to never touch any ball that's hit with a bat."

I chuckle. "As the son of a high school boys' basketball coach, I can honestly say I feel Nora's defiance."

"Oh, no ... don't tell me that."

I shrug. "Sorry. Nora's dad might want to lower his expectations in this sport."

Layla keeps her gaze on the girls. "Unfortunately, that will be pretty easy. He passed away last summer."

"Well ..." I, too, keep my gaze on the girls. "Crap. I just ... yeah. Sorry. I stuck my foot in my mouth."

"No. Really. It's fine. I didn't know Reagan's mom isn't your wife. Some assumptions are natural and fair. Joe had cancer. Battled it for nearly ten years."

Joe. Of course, his name was Joe.

"My family and his thinks I need to date. Move on. Blah, blah, blah." Layla laughs. "But some people you don't move on from. I fear my brain knows he's never coming back, but my heart doesn't reason the same way." She tips her chin and blows out a long breath. "Wow ... that was a lot to share with a stranger. Cleary, I needed to get that off my chest, and family isn't the best sounding board. I'm uh..." she makes a popping sound with her lips "...just going to shut up now."

I don't respond because Reagan is first up to bat.

"You've got this, Button!"

Reagan whips her head in my direction.

I cringe. "Oops. I guess I need to call her by her name in public."

Layla laughs, but it's subdued. I should respond to her. But what do I say?

Reagan gets to second base but out at third. She scuffs her feet along the dirt toward the bench, pouting like a champ.

"Nice job. Chin up. Just have fun." Reagan doesn't respond to my pep talk.

A good ten minutes pass while we cheer on the teams. Then one of the girls trips and skins up her knee, so the game is paused.

"I lost my fiancée last January," I say. Through the corner of my eye, I see Layla turn toward me, but I keep my gaze on the dirt by my black sneakers. "I met her when we were nine. And you're right, the brain and the heart don't speak the same language. I don't trust my brain, so I've been writing down things about her, about us, in a notebook because I don't want to forget the good stuff."

"The good stuff ..." Layla echoes. "Yes. I like that. I think I need a notebook too."

"Do you have other kids?" I ask.

Layla's fingers curl along the edge of the metal bleacher while the rest of her body stiffens.

"Don't answer that. In fact, I'm just going to go sit up there before I do any more damage today." I point behind us and start to stand.

Layla reaches for my arm, snagging my wrist. She smiles. It's filled with pain, a desperate kind of pain. I recognize it too well.

"Don't go anywhere. You're stuck with me now, at

least until the end of this game."

I ease back onto the bleacher, and she releases my wrist.

"Six months before Joe died, we used some of his pre-chemo frozen sperm because he wanted to see Nora become a big sister before he died." As tears fill her eyes, she turns away from me. "Go, Nora!"

Nora hits a single, and we clap for her.

Layla clears her throat, managing to keep her tears at bay. "I lost the baby a week before he died, but I didn't tell him. I wore baggy clothes and kept it to myself. Nora didn't know either. I couldn't imagine letting him leave this world with that kind of grief. It gave him peace of mind knowing that after he died, we would have something to look forward to."

I give her words a little space before whispering, "I'm sorry."

We manage to make it through the rest of the game without oversharing anything else.

Reagan runs toward me. "Can we go for ice cream?"

I nod behind her. "Depends. Are you going to get your bag and your glove?"

She gives me her annoyed eye roll and pivots to get her belongings.

"Can we go for ice cream?" Nora runs toward Layla.

Layla laughs. "Is that what your coach told you to say?"

"No."

"Now can we go for ice cream?" Reagan returns with her bag and glove.

"We're going for ice cream too," Nora says.

Reagan frowns. "Is ice cream only for the team that won?"

I shrug. "I don't know. What do you think? Do you deserve ice cream too?"

Her little lips do their fishy pucker. "I think so."

"Good game, Reagan," Layla says. "Tell your dad you definitely deserve ice cream. Oh, and did you and Nora get to meet?"

Reagan shakes her head.

"Well, this is Nora."

The girls share a quick hi.

"There's an ice cream truck a block north of here. We can walk together," Layla suggests.

"Okay," Reagan answers for us.

I grin and shake my head. "Sounds like a good idea. Thanks."

Reagan and Nora walk in front of us, chatting like they've been friends forever. It reminds me of the instant friendship I made with Josie.

Layla and I don't say anything right away. Then she sighs. "Are you as afraid as I am to say anything? I mean, the weather is probably a safe topic."

On a chuckle, I nod. "It's hot. Too hot. Too soon."

"Agreed," Layla says. "We're on the schedule to get a pool next month. It was a promise Joe made to Nora. She's a little dolphin."

"You're getting a pool?" Reagan nearly squeals.

I find myself shaking my head at her again. "How is it you pay no attention to me when I'm talking to you, but the second I'm *not* talking to you, you hear everything?"

Layla giggles.

"My dad died, but he promised me a pool before he died," Nora says.

Six-year-olds talking about death makes me think of a young Josie. So matter-of-fact.

"My dad's Josie maybe died too. The police are still looking for her, but she might be dead. She was sick."

"My dad was sick too," Nora says.

Layla and I share uncomfortable smiles. What can we say? Kids process things differently.

"Look, Mom!" Nora says, pointing to a fire engine.

Layla nods, offering her daughter a tiny smile. "Her dad was a fire fighter."

"My dad's a detective," Reagan says.

"What's a detective?" Nora asks as we approach the food truck.

"He finds bad people and puts them in jail," Reagan says.

Nora nods, seemingly good with that explanation or just too distracted by the ice cream.

"Detective, huh?" Layla says.

"Yeah. Homicide."

"Oh, you put the really bad people behind bars."

"I try."

We order ice cream and eat it on the short walk back to the ball fields.

"Can Reagan come swim in my pool?" Nora asks when Layla opens the minivan door.

"We don't have a pool yet."

"When we do."

Layla glances up at me.

"She gets plenty of trips to the pool. She has a pool pass."

"Well…" Layla shrugs "…we could exchange numbers. Nora doesn't have that many friends in the neighborhood. She'd love to have someone to play with in her pool."

"Yeah, Dad!" Reagan's not giving me a choice.

"Sure." I bring up my contact info and share it with Layla. "Reagan's at her mom's house more than mine. So if you message me when she's at her mom's, I'll give Katy your info if that's okay."

"Perfect." Layla sets her phone on the seat and pulls a wipe out of a plastic tube. "Wipe your sticky hands before you get in the minivan." She glances over her shoulder at me. "Help yourself to a wipe if you don't want sticky hands in your car."

Reagan holds up her sticky fingers and wiggles them.

I frown at her before smiling at Layla. "Thanks."

When both girls are in the vehicles, I head to the driver's side of my car.

"Colten, thanks for being the sounding board I didn't know I needed today."

I smile. "My pleasure."

"Maybe we'll see you when the pool goes in."

I nod. "Maybe. Enjoy the rest of your weekend. It was nice meeting you."

CHAPTER
Thirty-Three

"If your wife dies, will you find another wife?"

"I'm sixteen. I have a girlfriend, not a wife," I said to Josie while we washed my truck in the driveway.

"Jennifer is your girlfriend?" She stopped her motions and stood ramrod straight while the sponge dripped water and suds down her leg.

I shrugged.

"You're an asshole. Do you hear me?"

I was thankful that her parents had gone to dinner, my parents were seeing a counselor, and Chad was glued to the screen playing games because I had a feeling it was about to get bad.

"You had your hand up my shirt and your tongue down my throat last Friday night. And now Jennifer is your girlfriend?"

I glanced around to see if any of the neighbors were outside and within earshot.

"You can't be my girlfriend."

Josie hurled the sponge at my head then grabbed the hose nozzle and turned it onto the hardest stream, spraying every inch of my body. I just stood there with my eyes closed, letting her do her thing. I liked her thing. All of her wild emotions and her willingness to let me stay in her dad's good graces by not telling him about us. Had he really known what we did when no one was looking, she would have had a 4:00 p.m. curfew, and I wouldn't have been allowed on their property past the driveway.

When I didn't give her the satisfaction of reacting, she charged at me, shoving my chest, pitching a fit. I loved it.

"Tell me she's not your girlfriend or so help me, I'm going to end you, Mosley." She continued to shove my chest until we were in the garage.

I grabbed her face and kissed her.

Again, she shoved me. After several seconds of her huffing and puffing her anger, hands balled into tight fists, she threw herself at me.

We kissed for a long time. She had a point to make, or so she thought. I knew the score. I knew what we were even if nobody else did. And maybe I should have said as much, but I enjoyed her attacking me like that. I liked the chase. And then I liked letting her catch me, letting her win.

When she released my mouth and rubbed her lips

together, I couldn't hide my grin. It was a silent victory lap.

"Now I'm wet," she said.

I waggled my eyebrows. "Is that so?"

Her cheeks flamed in shades of red. "Pervert."

"Jennifer doesn't think I'm a pervert."

"If you mention her name again, I'm going to tell my dad that you felt me up last week."

I took a step closer, peering down at her with the usual look I gave her to call her bluff.

"Fine." She sighed. "I'm not going to tell him that, but you will never see these," she pointed to her tits, "again."

I grinned. "Well, why didn't you say that to begin with? Jennifer? Jennifer who?"

Josie's addictive smile swelled until I felt it punch me in the chest. She rolled her eyes and sauntered toward my truck, plucking the sponge from the ground and dunking it into the five-gallon bucket of soapy water. "Now, answer my question. If something happens to your wife, will you find another? Or will your heart only belong to your first love?"

"Well, I told you I'm not getting married."

"No. You said you weren't having kids. Not the same thing."

I used the brush to scrub the tires. I didn't like talking about my future like Josie wasn't going to be part of it. I knew she didn't want marriage and a family, but I guess I kinda wished she'd at least want me.

"I don't know, Josie. I'm pretty sure I'm supposed to

be focusing on college and baseball, not first and second wives. If you got married and lost your husband, would you remarry?"

"I'm not getting married, but hypothetically, sure. I'd remarry. Nobody wants to be lonely, right?"

I chuckled. "Apparently you're okay with it since you don't plan on getting married."

"Doesn't mean I won't date or maybe cohabitate with a man."

"Cohabitate?"

"It means—"

"Yes, Josie. I know what it means. It just seemed like a new dorky low, even for you."

"Says the dumb jock who plays piano all the time."

"I'm not dumb."

"Well, I'm not a dork."

"Why are you asking me about my imaginary second marriage?"

"Because Mrs. Leach is getting married again. Her husband died less than a year ago. So I have to wonder if she really loved him, since she not only found another man, but she's marrying him. Or ... is marriage like a comfort food?"

"Mrs. Leach, the advanced chemistry teacher?"

Josie nodded before tossing the sponge aside and grabbing the hose again to rinse the back of my truck.

"Uh. I didn't know her husband died."

"Where have you been?"

"Playing baseball, hating my dad, and dealing with you."

"Me? Pfft ... whatever. Anyway, I think she's getting remarried because she has two kids and could use some help around the house."

"Or maybe she loves the new guy."

"Well, duh. I'm sure she does. I bet we can love more than one person. Don't you?"

Nope. I loved Josephine Watts. My heart was constructed cell by cell in the womb to one day seek her out and love her forever. "I don't know, Josie," I said instead of my knee-jerk response. "My parents haven't exactly been role models for marriage or love for that matter."

"Well, Mrs. Leach is pretty cool. I think she's my favorite teacher. And if she can move on so quickly and remarry after losing her husband, I think you can too."

I bit my tongue. Really, what was the point of that conversation and my *second* wife?

CHAPTER
Thirty-Four

Dear Josie,

Thought I'd steal a page out of this journal to write you a letter. Today I met a woman. It's not what you think, so just cool your afterlife jets, okay? She lost her husband to cancer last summer, and she has a daughter who is Reagan's age. We chatted during the T-ball game. She said so many things that resonated with me. It made me feel like I was supposed to meet her.

I'm not the only person in the world who feels like love is a one-and-done. At the same time, I recalled the time when we were sixteen and you wanted to discuss my imaginary second wife. Some days are confusing, like today. Am I living the life you would want me to live? Would you hate that those words are even going through my head? I don't know what to think right now. I'm too busy missing you. I'm really good at it, but I don't let anyone else see it.

Anyway, the woman today, her name is Layla (in case you want to secretly hate her in the afterlife), and she made me think. She said her family is pushing her to move on and date. I hope my mom never pushes me to move on, but I fear she will even though she never did after my dad died. I guess I'm struggling with figuring out my new normal.

If it weren't for Reagan, I would have gone with you. I would have left this life. But you knew that, didn't you?

What am I even doing? Writing to you as if your spirit is looking over my shoulder reading this. I need something. I need direction. I keep looking over my shoulder for you, but you're not there. You'll never be there again.

I need my friend. I need "a" friend.

CHAPTER
Thirty-Five

A WEEK LATER, I meet Sean and Katy at Reagan's T-ball game. While grabbing a drink at the concession stand, someone taps me on the back.

I glance over my shoulder. "Oh, hey, Layla. Nora have a game today too?"

"No, I just like the popcorn at the concession stand." She slides her fingers into the back pockets of her shorts.

I grin. "Sorry. Stupid question."

She gestures with a head tilt to the right. "On that field. They're just warming up. You?"

"Same. No game. I just come for the overpriced sports drinks. The blue one is my favorite."

Layla snorts. "The blue is the best."

"Hi. What can I get you?" the volunteer parent behind the counter asks.

"Two blue sports drinks and a popcorn," Layla jumps in and says.

Before I can protest, she throws down a twenty and winks at me. "Let me buy you a drink. It's the least I can do after vomiting my life's tragedies on you last weekend."

I take the blue sports drink and twist off the cap. "It's unnecessary but thank you."

"My pleasure." She takes her change, popcorn, and the blue drink. "Besides, now I can tell my family that I bought a guy a drink, and it will get them off my back for a bit."

I laugh a little because it's a joke. Right? She's not flirting with me. She said she doesn't think she'll move on from her husband. And I'm not moving on from Josie ... probably ever.

"Listen, the pools not in yet, but Nora has been asking to have Reagan over to play. I guess they really bonded over ice cream. Would Reagan like to go with us to the children's museum? I get free tickets."

"Free tickets, huh?" I sip my drink.

"Yes. I work there. I'm their information technology manager."

I nod. "Okay. I'm going to pretend that I know what that means."

She laughs. "Think computer geek and just leave it at that."

"Got it. Well, I'm sure she'd love to go, but I'll need to check with her mom."

"Great. You've got my number. Just shoot me a text after the game."

"Okay. Well..." I nod toward Reagan's field "...I'd better get back before I miss her home run."

"Oh definitely. Bye, Colten." She winks at me again.

Winks.

That's flirting. Right? Or am I reading into it? She's still grieving the loss of her husband. And she knows it's only been five months since Josie died. Yeah, I'm reading into it.

"Reagan made a friend last week. I saw her mom at the concession stand. She invited Reagan to the children's museum after the game. I said I'd check with you and text her," I say to Katy, taking a seat on the bench.

"I'm sure she'd love that," Katy says. "What do you know about her parents? Are we comfortable with them taking our daughter to the museum?"

"It's just the mom. Her husband died last summer. She works at the museum."

"Oh, she's a widow. Is she nice?"

I watch Reagan staring at the sky in the outfield instead of paying attention the game. "What does 'oh, she's a widow' mean?"

"Nothing. Does she know you're single?"

"Yes. She invited Reagan to play with Nora. She didn't ask me on a date."

"I know, but everything has a beginning."

"I'm not beginning anything. And neither is she."

"Katy, it's a playdate," Sean says.

I like Sean. Always have. He's a no-nonsense kind of guy. Works long hours in construction. Adores my daughter. But doesn't act pussy whipped by his wife.

"I'm just saying, you're quickly going to find that Reagan is ... for lack of a better term ... a chick magnet. She'll make lots of friends who have single moms. And single moms love single dads, especially widowers who work in law enforcement."

"Jesus Christ ..." Sean mumbles. "Let the guy properly grieve and figure out his own shit in his own time."

I nod. "Yes, what he said."

Katy nudges Sean's shin with her foot. "Stop. I'm just helping him out, so he doesn't get into a sticky situation."

"He's a homicide detective. I think he's good in sticky situations."

Really, I think I'm on the verge of a bromance with Sean. He just ... gets me.

After the game, Reagan gives an enthusiastic yes to going to the museum with Nora, so I shoot Layla a text.

"I think you should go with her." Katy says. "In all seriousness, it might be too early to send our daughter off with someone you met a week ago for all of two seconds."

I give her a tight grin and a slight nod.

THE GIRLS JUMP from one exhibit to the next with Layla and I close behind them. This feels normal, like something I should be doing. It also feels wrong. I should be here with Josie.

"Say it," Layla says.

I glance over at her. "Say what?"

"All the things going through your head."

"What makes you think anything is going through my head?"

"Because I keep thinking, what if someone I know sees me with you? Will they think I have a boyfriend? Will they think I've moved on? Will they tell anyone? And then I think, what would Joe think? Then, of course, my mind wanders into really depressing territory. Joe died. He will never think anything again. So the real question is, what am I thinking? And when I can't answer that question because I really don't know what to think or what to feel, I wonder what you're thinking. You lost your fiancée more recently than I lost my husband."

My cheeks puff with a big breath before I slowly release it. "You are further along than I am. I'm still stuck in the 'I wish she were here' phase. I guess that makes me terrible company. Who wants to hang out with someone who is wishing they were with someone else?"

"You're right. It's early for you. I still have times when I'd give anything for Joe to be here to see something or experience something with me. But he's been gone long enough that I no longer have moments when I think it's nothing but a bad dream. I'm fully aware that he's gone. I'm consciously moving forward, not merely drifting along. Does that make sense?"

"I think so," I nod slowly.

"So now my brain has started to wander into other directions, somewhat prompted by my family urging me to date. And while this is not a date or anything at all like that, you are a man, and what we're doing feels weird even though we're not doing anything."

I don't respond right away, so an awkward silence fills the air around us while we stare at the girls doing a water race.

"That was the dumbest thing a human has ever said." Layla snorts, covering her face with her hands. "Kill me now."

I chuckle and shake my hand. "You forget I hear a lot of terrible alibis, so you have a ways to go before you're saying the dumbest thing ever. I should have responded right away, but I was letting your words settle, maybe resonate."

"Well..." her hands drop from her face "...that's very kind of you to spin it like that."

"Not kind. Just honest. And if I'm being completely honest with you, I have an unfair advantage at this ... whatever this is."

"An unfair advantage?" She lifts an eyebrow at me.

"When Josie and I were younger, we had a very unusual relationship. We had an on-and-off-again relationship like no other. Then her dad, who I admired and liked more than my own dad, asked me to never be more than friends with her. So when we *were* being more than friends, we had to keep it a secret. And sometimes I dated other people and so did she. It's hard to explain. It sounds crazy when I hear myself say it. But I got used to being around other girls even while I knew my heart belonged to Josie and she knew it too. I guess I can be here, not feeling guilty because I know where my heart is."

Layla hums and nods several times. "I like that. I felt that too. I think I still do, but I feel like there comes a point when you start to feel guilty or maybe a little broken because your heart is what gives you life, and giving so much of it to someone who is no longer in this life feels like ..."

"A waste?"

Her nose wrinkles. "It sounds so terrible, but I read it in a book about grieving, and it stuck with me."

I watch Reagan and think of Josie. She's not her daughter, but I swear she reminds me of her. The curiosity. The smile. The way she embraces her uniqueness. Not trying to fit in, just trying to make her own space in the world.

"I think losing the love of your life is the biggest self-reflection ever," I say.

"It's the me without you."

I nod. "Yes. And I think it's possible to reach a silent acquiescence and truly move on. While I don't want to ever forget, I agree it would be nice if my heart would someday let go ... be fully invested again in this life."

Layla gives me a smile I can't decipher, but it feels like a good one. "We should be friends. Do you have room in your life for another friend? Because you say all the right things at the right time."

I chuckle. I asked if she had other kids, bringing up the memories of a lost child. I'd hardly call that right timing. Still, I feel the same. I feel a little understood. "Friends sounds good."

She winks.

What's with the winks? Maybe it's payback for all the times I winked at Josie while hugging another girl.

CHAPTER
Thirty-Six

"WE FOUND A BODY," Rains says as soon as I step into my office.

I turn slowly. "Hers?" I whisper.

"Don't know yet."

I brush past him.

"You can breathe down their necks all you want, but it won't expedite anything. Mosley, let them do their job. She was one of theirs. They'll want to know just as quickly as you."

"They let her go. She wasn't one of theirs," I mumble, but I doubt he hears me before I step into the elevator.

At the county medical examiner's office, I flash my badge and make my way to the morgue. As soon as I see Dr. Cornwell in the hallway, he shakes his head.

"I don't know yet. We're waiting on dental records."

It's not her. I don't know why I rushed down here. I knew it then, and I know it now. She left this life in a way that her body will never be found. Still, my foolish heart likes to torture me.

"Why do you need dental records?"

He frowns. "Are you really asking me that?"

"She had tattoos."

"I'm aware. But the decedent doesn't have skin or organs if you get the gist."

I swallow a little bile.

It's not her. It's not her.

"How long will it take?"

He pushes through the door to the locker room, and I follow him. "As long as it takes."

"You owe her this."

He laughs while donning PPE. "She'd hate you pestering me, and you know it."

"I hope you take a little responsibility for what happened. You took her life from her."

"Here we go ... I'm impressed it's taken you this long to confront me, Detective. Had Dr. Watts been of sound mind, dealing with a subordinate who was experiencing what she was experiencing, she would have done the same thing I did. Josephine wasn't just gifted; she took her job seriously. She was a professional and understood the need for rules and protocol. What happened to her was tragic, but it wasn't anyone's fault."

"Is that how you sleep at night?"

He glances up at me. "It's been nearly six months. I

grieved her when I had to let her go and again when she went missing. I grieved her for the same reason you're grieving her. We cared about her, and we couldn't fix her."

Fix her ...

He rests his hand on my shoulder before opening the door. "She left her mark on the world, and it was a good one. Honor her by moving on and living a good life, Detective. It's what she would have wanted."

I swallow hard. She's still so close to me. It's a suffocating grief.

"Oh, the body is not hers," Cornwell says.

I turn. "How do you know?"

"There's a gold crown."

"Then why didn't you tell that to Rains?"

He shrugs. "I wanted to check in on you. Josephine would have wanted me to check in on you. Good news. You're going to be fine." He closes the door.

<hr>

THE FOLLOWING WEEKEND, Reagan and I meet Layla and Nora for a Cubs game.

Dinner.

A pool party for the grand opening of their pool.

Coffee just with Layla early on a Wednesday morning before either of us has to be to work.

T-ball.

Movies.

More swimming.

Layla is the sister I never had. She's not Josie, but she's a good friend. And she makes good chocolate chip cookies. I'm not saying better than Savannah, but still ... really good.

Everything feels easy when I'm with Layla. If I'm having a good day, she's eager to hear all about it. But if I have a bad day, she's ready with funny memes and long lists of how my life could be worse. I find myself comparing her to Josie, and that sometimes bothers me. Layla is just my friend. Josie was my everything. There is no comparison, so I don't know why my brain insists on trying to make one.

"Can I be honest with you?" Layla swings the bat in the batting cage and misses.

"Elbow up," I say. "Have you been lying to me?"

She chuckles. "Not exactly." She tosses the bat aside and exits the cage.

"You're not done." I narrow my eyes.

"I am." She sighs. "I hate baseball. And softball. Volleyball. Football. Basically anything that involves a ball. I danced in high school. But mostly, I sat in front of a huge computer and programmed weird stuff. I'm a geek. I like books. Art museums. And the ballet. I *love* the ballet." She gives me a little cringe. "Can we still be friends?"

I blink several times. "Did Joe know you hated baseball?"

"Yes, but he married me anyway. That's why I'm hoping you can still be my friend."

After another long pause, I nod. "I play the piano. Do you play an instrument?"

"No."

I frown. "I've never been to a ballet. But I'd go with you because that's what friends do."

Her smile doubles in a matter of a second. "I'll get us tickets. Do you want to take the girls, or is it just a friend's night out?"

"Depends if I have Reagan."

"Okay. I'm going to just get two tickets and a sitter for Nora."

I have a moment. It's the first real moment I've had in the weeks that I've been friends with Layla. We've been a foursome except for morning coffee, which was rushed because we had to get to work. The ballet feels like a date. But I'm not dating. And neither is she. So why am I hesitant?

"Is that okay?" She eyes me suspiciously.

"Um ... yeah. Sounds great. Fair warning, my job is a fun spoiler, so I might cancel at the last minute or have to leave in the middle of the ballet if some asshole decides to kill someone."

"Got it." Again, she winks.

CHAPTER
Thirty-Seven

"You look mighty handsome," Mom says on our FaceTime call while I tie a red tie that I never wear to work. Still ... black suit. "Thought you said it's not a date."

"It's not. But I think I should wear a suit to the ballet."

"The ballet? That's where you're going? Colten, I think that's a date. Bowling is something friends do. The ballet is romantic."

I narrow my eyes at the screen. "It is? Why?"

"For starters, you're in a suit. That in and of itself says romance."

"I wear suits for work."

"But has this woman seen you in a suit?"

"Yes. We had coffee before work one morning, and I was wearing a suit."

"Fine. Then let's move on to the music. It's romantic."

"Not all music is romantic. Trust me, I know a thing or two about music."

"Are you in denial that this woman might like you more than a friend?"

I check my hair one more time. "No. The reason we're friends is because we both lost people we loved, and we don't have a desire to find a replacement."

"Need I remind you that you thought Josie was a boy, and you said you were only going to be her friend until school started. Look how that turned out."

"Yeah, look how that turned out."

"Colten ..."

"It's not a date. Now, I have to get going so I'm not late to the ballet with my *friend*, Layla."

"Layla? You didn't tell me her name. That's a beautiful name. Is she as pretty as her name?"

"Mom ..." I frown at the phone screen.

"Just tell me you know it's okay to feel something more than friendship for another woman. Josie would have wanted it for you."

I sigh. "It's funny how everyone seems to know what Josie would have wanted more than me ... her best friend. Nobody knew Josie better than I knew her."

"Fine. So you tell me. Would she have wanted you to find love again?"

"No."

"What?" Mom sounds shocked by my answer. "Liar."

"I'm not lying. I'm not saying she wouldn't have said that's what she wanted. But the one thing that seemed to have flown under everyone's radar was how much she loved me. How much she wanted me. How much she hated every girl I ever dated. She'd want me to die a lonely man." I lie. I lie because I don't like the truth.

"Well, Mrs. Leach is pretty cool. I think she's my favorite teacher. And if she can move on so quickly and remarry after losing her husband, I think you can too."

I wanted her to believe we would never find another love like ours. We weren't the Leaches.

"I don't know if I believe that, Colten. She wasn't selfish like that."

"Well, it's a moot point anyway. I'm not ready to date. Don't know if I'll ever be ready to date, but tonight I'm going to the ballet with a friend who knows what I'm going through."

Mom nods. "I'm happy for you. Have a nice evening. I love you."

"Love you too. Night, Mom."

On my way to pick up Layla, it hits me ... picking her up seems like a date.

It's not a date.

There's no turning back now. I've spent so much of my life with the wrong women all the while thinking about Josie. Loving her was as much a curse as it was a gift. Still, I'd do it all over again.

When I pull into Layla's driveway, I'm a little relieved that she's waiting for me outside. I don't even get my car in *Park* before she heads straight toward the passenger door in her red dress that matches my tie. Total coincidence. Red lipstick. And her hair is in loose blond waves. She is pretty.

But she's not Josie.

"Hey, handsome. Nice tie." She closes the door and fastens her seat belt.

"Thanks. You look nice too."

If it were a date, I'd up the nice to pretty.

No ... no, I wouldn't.

You look pretty.

I'd use another word like beautiful or lovely.

"What are the chances that you could run by CVS so I can grab some lozenges? My allergies are acting up, and I know I'm going to get that crazy tickle in my throat during the performance and make a scene with my coughing if I don't have a lozenge."

"Sure. We can do that."

When we get to CVS, I park and follow her inside.

"You could have waited in the car. It will only take me a minute."

"It's fine. I might grab some gum or something myself." I follow her to the aisle with the lozenges.

"They don't have cherry. I'm going to have to go with lemon eucalyptus. Not great, but it will do." She grabs the package.

I turn to head toward the front of the store with her right behind me.

"Oops, sorry." I nearly run into a lady with a walker.

She glances up.

She. Glances. Up.

And I ... I ... can't breathe. I'm so fucking afraid to even blink. This ... this isn't possible.

"Hi," she says in a weak voice I barely recognize.

If it weren't for her eyes and the tattoos on her arms, I wouldn't recognize her. She's so ... *so* incredibly frail. In one breath, she's resurrected, only to look like she's withering away. Loose skin. Hollow-eyed. Haggard.

It takes my brain a moment to decide if this is real.

"Colten?" I barely register Layla's voice.

I don't have one. Single. Word.

My heart has been ejected from my chest and shoved into my throat.

Josie's gaze slides to my right. To Layla.

"We don't want to be late," Layla says.

I didn't think it was possible for Josie to look any sadder, but with the downcast of her eyes, she says, "Nice seeing you." She barely has a voice. Did she lose it?

"Josie, did you find—" A guy stops behind her, midsentence, eyes on me.

I can't tell if he recognizes me. I don't know him. But the way he gently rests his hand on Josie's bony shoulder tells me he knows who I am. Is it just me? So fucking lost in the dark? I don't know if this is a dream or a nightmare.

Again, Josie's gaze drifts to Layla. "You l-look ... pretty."

Emotion punches me so hard, my eyes can barely see past the burning tears in them. "Fuck you ... Josie." My words break into pieces as I barely get them out in a whisper.

As I take a step forward.

As I take her into my arms.

As I support her when her knees wobble beneath her.

As my lips press to her thinning hair.

I don't even have to blink for the tears to release.

She doesn't wrap her arms around me. Maybe she can't.

It wasn't a mistake. It wasn't by chance. I met Layla so that our path would bring us to this exact CVS pharmacy at six o'clock on this very Saturday night. So I would find my Artemis.

Josie was wrong. She isn't a star. She *is* the galaxy.

CHAPTER
Thirty-Eight

THE WEDDING

REAGAN UNZIPS MY DRESS. I turn and press my palms to her face. She's fighting tears. So am I. We are strong for each other.

"I love you. Okay?"

Her lower lip quivers. She's so brave. She will get Colten through this life. Of that, I have no doubt.

When she gives me a tiny nod, I press my lips to her forehead. It's warm, as it should be. She has so much life in her. "Bye, beautiful girl."

A quick change, an Uber, a stop at home, and a long drive across town later, I arrive at Felix Trevino's house. It's a traditional, stone front two-story with a white mailbox that matches the snow and a neatly shoveled drive. Before I ring the doorbell, I kick some snow off my boots.

More than one dog barks before the door opens a crack. "Josie?"

I rub my hands together to keep warm. "Are you going to invite me in or leave me out here to freeze to death?"

Felix shoos the dogs away and opens the door. "I've never seen you with short hair."

I step inside and remove my boots while the dogs sniff me. "I've never seen you with no hair."

He frowns. "There wasn't much left, so I shaved it."

"Happy New Year, by the way. It's been a while."

"Uh ... yeah. To what do I owe the honor?"

I shuffle my socked feet over his hardwood floor, snooping around his main level. "Is your wife home?"

"She's out of town for a week."

"Well, isn't that perfect," I murmur.

"Josie, I'm not trying to be rude, but are you going to tell me what you're doing here? Are you looking for something?"

I turn, just inside his kitchen. "No. Sorry. Just checking the place out. You've done quite well for yourself. I read that you're chief of cardiology, and you married the hospital administrator's daughter. Well done. Glad I could help." I offer him an exaggerated smile despite my heart bleeding out in my chest.

This is my wedding day. I'm supposed to be marrying the only man I've ever loved. Instead, I'm here, cashing in on a favor owed to me.

Felix turns a little paler than he already was.

"It's payback time."

Felix's mom died while he was a first-year resident under me, the chief resident. He spiraled downhill with alcohol and drugs. I got him help instead of getting him kicked out of the program. I covered his ass on multiple occasions. He knows he owes his career to my grace.

"What do you need? A job? I heard you were out of a job. Is it true that you knew the whereabouts of those girls' bodies?"

"It's true."

"And you think you were one of them in another life?" He gives me an unblinking expression like there's a right answer to his question.

I'm about to fail the test. "No." I smile.

Felix relaxes a fraction. Relief washes over his face.

"I was the killer. I was Winston Jeffries."

He's well over six feet, but Felix's back straightening with my answer puts him another inch or so taller. "What's the favor?" He clears his throat. His words are rushed like I stopped by for a quick cup of sugar that he can quickly give me before sending me on my merry way. Debt fulfilled.

"I need you to kill me."

Felix's lips part a fraction while he blinks slowly. Then he chuckles. "What?"

"If it makes you feel better, I also want you to bring me back to life."

His brow furrows, head inching side to side. "Have you lost your mind?"

"Yes. But I'd like it back. And I'm hoping if that happens, it will be mine and only mine."

"Josie ..." He scratches the back of his smooth head and chuckles again. "I don't understand. But I think you've got the wrong guy for whatever job you need help with. Have you looked into counseling?"

"I didn't save any counselor's career. Just yours."

"So payback for me is life in prison? For what? Why the hell would you want to die again? You realize the stats on resuscitation aren't exactly in your favor, right?"

"Yes, I know. But here's the thing, I see dead little girls. I see him—me—poisoning them. Sadly, with the passing of time, these visions or recollections have only gotten worse. To the point that I don't fully trust myself. Some days I have trouble separating the two lives. If I can't erase these memories, then I can't do this."

"Do what?"

"Live."

He laces his hands behind his neck and bows his head. "Jesus, Josie."

"I talked to a parapsychologist in California. She's had a slew of lives. She said my only hope is that I die again, and someone brings me back to life so whatever new near-death experience I have will erase the last one. I have to try."

Glancing at me, he lets his hands fall from his

neck, flopping at his side. "Surely you know there are grave risks."

"Death. Yes. I'm well aware."

"*If* you're resuscitated, you could be in a coma."

"I know. I'm going to go over all of this with you."

A manic laugh bubbles from his chest while he turns and paces the kitchen. "You'll go over all of this with me. Great. That's a relief. I feel much better now."

"Do you want to know where I was a little over an hour ago?"

"Not really. I don't want to know where you are right now, but I do because you're standing in my kitchen after having not seen you in years."

"I was in a wedding dress. Today is my wedding day. *Was* my wedding day. I cut off the flower girl's hair in a ponytail, told her to give it to her dad, the groom, and then I left. I left knowing there is an extremely high probability I won't ever see him or any of my family and friends again."

Felix stops his pacing and stares at me, maybe to gauge the sincerity of my words. Maybe he's stopped pacing because my words are shaky, and my eyes are filled with tears.

"This is my only chance," I whisper, blotting the corners of my eyes. "If I can't get rid of these memories, I can't go on living."

Felix deflates on a deep sigh. "What are you expecting from me?"

Drawing in a shaky breath, I hug my arms to my

chest and pad my way to the wall of windows facing his backyard. "I need you to suffocate me."

"Jesus Christ …"

Ignoring his reaction, I continue. "You will tie me up, so I can't fight you."

"No … no. No. No. Do you know what the chances are of saving your life after asphyxiation?"

"Slim, but I drowned, and they brought me back."

His eyebrows shoot up his forehead. "Great. Let me rephrase it then. Do you know what the chances are of me resuscitating you after being asphyxiated for a second time in your fragile little life?"

"Felix, I'm most likely going to die. Look at it this way. If you knew that your wife's heart was going to stop beating, would you rather it happen when she's alone or when you're right next to her with a defibrillator, oxygen, and medication to restart it regardless of the statistical chances of bringing her back?"

He frowns. "What happens if you don't make it? Or what happens if I restart your heart, but you're in a coma? What happens if—"

"Again, I'll go over all of this with you."

"This is too much." He shakes his head.

"You owe me."

"Not this."

"Look around, Felix. The house. Your family. Your job. Hell, probably even those two dogs. You have this life because of *me*. And for the record, I was never planning on asking you for a single thing. But I'm in a dire situation, the way you were in a dire situation. I need you to step the fuck up and help me. I need you to take a little risk the way I took a risk covering your ass."

He rests a hand on his hip, head bowed. "You are not a good person."

"But I want to be," I whisper. Again, I tear up. "I want to sleep and dream like a normal person. I want to smile because I'm happy not because I'm hiding the pain. I want a job. I want love. I want what you have. I want what I gave you."

I hate this.

I am not this person.

Desperation squeezes every last ounce of humanity from my soul. Maybe I shouldn't have come here. Maybe I should have just ... ended everything for good.

"I have a storage unit with electricity."

My gaze lifts to Felix's. I was right. He was worth saving.

CHAPTER
Thirty-Nine

"I DON'T UNDERSTAND," Colten whispers against my head. "Help me understand."

"This might not be the best place for a reunion," Felix says.

"Colten ... I'll uh ... grab a cab home," the pretty woman in a red dress says.

He doesn't respond. He doesn't move.

Pressed to his chest, I make eye contact with her. She offers a sad smile, touches his arm, giving it a tiny squeeze, and clicks her heels toward the exit.

Colten doesn't stop her. Not a single word of acknowledgment.

He moved on. In his mind, I died, and he moved on. And now a pretty lady in a red dress is broken-hearted because she thinks I'm back from the dead? I can't walk unassisted. I'm skin and bones.

Colten should let me go and follow the red dress woman. She's beautiful and vibrant. She has life in her eyes. I am the echo of death. Alive, but just barely. And it feels like years since I've seen him. I'm still making sense of what I know and what I've been told.

"I don't know who you are, but you can leave," Colten says to Felix.

Oh, Colten ...

With what little strength I can muster, I push against Colten's chest, forcing him to lighten his grip. Taking a cautious step backward, I rest my hands on my walker. He's so handsome in his suit. Tan from the summer's sun, not pale like me. My heart hasn't stopped galloping since my eyes landed on him. I can't imagine a day when my heart can control itself around Colten Mosley. And I can't imagine a day when seeing him with a beautiful woman doesn't sting. Is it just not in the cards for us?

Colten uses one hand to wipe his face.

"I'm glad you're good." I push my way past him. I need conditioner and toothpaste. Felix said he'd get it for me, but I wanted out of the house. I wanted to do something on my own.

"Are you joking?" Colten asks, following me less than a step back. "I thought you were dead!"

"I was," I murmur, choosing the sensitive toothpaste. My teeth have been terribly sensitive lately.

Damn ... the woman in the red dress was so pretty. Such soft skin. So blond. So opposite of me.

My brain won't shut off. Did he kiss her? Have they

had sex? Does she know about me? How did he meet her? Is she like Tessa or nicer than Tessa? And why is my brain comparing red dress lady to high school slut?

"Josephine Eleanor Watts, you left me on our wedding day. I haven't seen you in nearly six months. I spoke at your memorial service or 'celebration of life.' I've grieved you. Your family and friends have grieved you. Yet you're shopping for toothpaste at a fucking CVS like it's no big deal?" He turns toward Felix. "Who the hell are you, and why are you still here?"

"I'm uh ... her ride. Felix. Dr. Trevino. She's living with me. And uh ... my wife. We're helping her rehabilitate."

"Rehabilitate from what? She looks emaciated. Whatever you're doing, it's not working."

"Oh, no. She looks so much better than she did a few months ago."

While they sort through things, I make my way to the shampoo aisle. My hair is disgusting. I need a good conditioner. It's grown out too much. I'm not sure why I ever cut my hair, but I wouldn't mind it shorter again like in the video.

"Josie, let's go. We're going home," Colten says.

"Where do I live?"

"With me."

"I do?"

Colten eyes me like he's sad, like he's trying to figure me out. A puzzle he can't quite solve. I know how he feels. I've been trying to figure myself out for nearly three months.

"Yes," he whispers. "Don't you remember?"

I hand my items to Felix so I can push my walker. Colten snags them from him before I baby step my way to the checkout. "The woman in red is pretty. You always liked the pretty g-girls," I trip over my words. It's so much better than it was even just weeks ago. But it's not perfect. I don't know if anything about me will ever be perfect. Colten scans my items at the self-checkout and taps his credit card to the machine.

"She can't walk that fast," Felix says as I try to catch up to Colten because he has my toothpaste and conditioner.

Colten turns and shoves the bag into Felix's chest. "Take this, and take the walker." He scoops me up in his arms.

"She won't learn to do it on her own if you do it for her," Felix says.

"Shut up, Dr. Whoever The Fuck You Are."

He has no idea what Felix has done for me, but I don't try to explain it now. I'm too busy staring at the side of his face. I want to touch it. I want to kiss it. And that makes me want to cry because I think he's let part of his heart go to another woman. And I'm ... still so broken.

"She needs to come home with me." Felix doesn't back away from Colten. He's invested in my recovery, and for that, I will always be grateful.

"Nope." Colten nods for Felix to open the passenger door of the car.

Felix eyes me.

I give him a slight nod. "I'll get a ride home later."

"No. No you won't," Colten says while setting me on my feet to get into the car.

I sit sideways first, with my legs outside of the door. "Felix is helping me."

Colten gives me a look. The emotion in his eyes tears my heart into tiny pieces. It's painful. He takes the bag and the walker from Felix and puts it into the back.

"You okay?" Felix asks.

I give him a slight nod. He hands me my purse. "My number is in the phone I got you."

I nod again.

"See you in a while, Josie."

Colten closes the trunk and scuffs his black dress shoes to me. On an infinitely deep sigh, he hunches in front of me, resting his hands on my legs. And he just ... stares at me. His gaze slowly brushes along my face. I don't know what to say. My memories are so out of order; therefore, the emotions tied to them are scattered as well. I don't know how to explain this to him. I don't know where to begin.

I just know that my heart is crashing against my ribcage. And I swear I can hear his doing the same.

When he doesn't speak, I expect him to help my legs in the car. I expect him to ask me questions. He doesn't.

He drops his head in my lap. I lift my hands, staring at his head and holding my fingers above it for a few seconds, afraid to touch him because I don't know what's appropriate, how he's feeling, or anything about the lady in red. I draw in a shaky breath as tears flood my eyes. Even if my memories are fuzzy, my feelings are not. I've loved this man my whole life. My fingers find his hair, gently stroking it. His body shakes with silent sobs.

I blink.

All the tears race down my face onto him.

What did I do to us?

What did I do to him?

As quickly as he fell apart in my lap, he lifts my legs into the car, fastens my seat belt, and closes the door. When he doesn't appear on the driver's side right away, I glance behind me. His back is to the car, head bowed, fingers slowly running through his hair as he lifts his chin, gaze to the night sky for several seconds before he moves toward the driver's side.

We make the trip to his house in silence. He retrieves my walker and the bag while I open the car door.

"Need help?" he asks, appearing a little less agitated without Felix's presence.

I shake my head, swinging my legs out of the car and standing with the ease of a sloth. He moves with me, an inch at a time, into the house.

"Is it hard or strenuous to talk?"

"No. Just ... sometimes I can't find the right word. Or I say it wrong."

"Can you walk up the stairs?"

I shake my head.

"Hungry?"

Another headshake.

Again, he scoops me up and takes me to his bedroom, leaving me on the end of the bed while he gets my bag and walker.

I rest my hands on the edge and glance around the room. It's familiar. My mind goes straight to red dress woman. Has she been in this room? In this bed? Is it my business anymore?

Colten sets my walker next to the bed. Then he shrugs off his jacket and loosens his tie. I can't force my gaze to his. I feel too weak.

Too vulnerable.

Too inadequate.

I think my plan backfired. I should have stayed dead.

"Hey ..." He demands I look at him.

So I do, hoping I don't start crying again.

"That woman?" He unbuttons his white dress shirt. "She's a friend. That's it."

Pressing my lips together, I return a tiny nod, again letting my gaze slip to my lap.

When he emerges from his closet in a pair of jogging shorts, he turns on the TV, lifts my legs onto the bed, and fluffs the pillows before hooking his arm around my waist, spooning me to him.

I swallow hard. "I know you have questions."

He kisses my head. "You already answered the only one that matters for tonight."

I stretch my neck around to look at his face.

"You're alive," he says. "That's all I need to know until tomorrow."

My hand makes a slow ascent to his face, cupping his cheek. His eyes redden with more emotion while the pad of my thumb brushes his bottom lip.

He closes his eyes and leans into my touch. How did we get here?

I know, yet ... I don't think I will ever truly understand.

CHAPTER
Forty

"WHAT AM I MISSING?" Felix asks.

I glance around the setup in the storage shed. The "borrowed" medical equipment. Crash cart. Bed. Medications. I hope if he's found out, being the son-in-law of the hospital administrator will help his case.

"Looks good."

He shakes his head. "It's not good. We need a vent."

"I told you, no ventilator. If I can't breathe on my own, you let me die. You know where to dispose of the body. Return everything, and pretend this didn't happen."

"Sure. Because I kill people on a daily basis. No big deal."

"You're a doctor. And you're human. It's probably not daily. I'd hope not. But you kill people," I mumble. The visions. The voices. The burden of accountability has been multiplying with each passing day. I haven't slept more than a few hours in the four days I've been at Felix's.

Nightmares.

Waking up with a racing heart.

Cold sweats.

And then I see Colten. I imagine him looking at his daughter with her short hair. I see all his fears come to fruition. And … I start to hate myself even more.

"Josie?"

I shake my head, coming back to the present. "What?"

"I asked when we're doing this. I'd like to go to prison before my wife gets home, so that she thinks I just left her."

"You're not going to prison. And I need you to record me."

"I'm not recording this. No way."

I shake my head. "Not you suffocating me. I need to tell myself a few things in case this works."

"I'm not following."

I pat my pockets. "I don't have a phone. I destroyed it. We'll use your phone."

"We'll use an old video recorder that used to belong to my parents."

I frown. "Fine."

An hour later, Felix has the video recorder dug out of his attic, and I'm perched on the borrowed hospital bed recording a message for my post-suffocated self.

"Hi, Josephine. If you're watching this, then you're alive. Give Felix a huge hug."

Felix rolls his eyes while recording me.

"I hope you're okay. I'm recording this because I don't know what you'll remember. If my plan works, you won't remember why you had to die and be brought back to life. You had a near-death experience months ago. You remembered a previous life. And you might see news articles about you and claims about that previous life. Here's all you need to know. You were having terrible visions and nightmares. You lost your job. You couldn't sleep. Your life was miserable to the point that you didn't want to be in this life most days. You were going to marry Colten, but you didn't trust yourself. He has a daughter, and you never wanted to put him in a position to choose between being with you or being with her. I hope what I'm saying sounds unreal to you. I hope you can hear me but not feel it. I hope you're detached from that life. That was the purpose."

I think about what else I want to tell future me. I've got nothing. The chances of a future me is really slim. I nod to Felix to stop the video.

"If I'm in a coma, end it."

"You could be in a coma for a few days, maybe a week or two."

I nod. "Two weeks, not a day longer. You have a life. Your debt will more than be paid."

Deep worry lines cut across his forehead. I think they're nearly permanent by now. I know I'm asking something so much bigger than what I did for him. But I'm desperate.

"When?" he asks.

"After dinner."

His Adam's apple bobs before he nods.

"Let's eat."

Another nod.

We order food from my favorite restaurant. Dessert too. As he pours himself a glass of wine, I give him a look.

"I need your mind clear to save me," I say.

He laughs, pouring the wine to the very top of the glass. "I need to relax so I can go through with this. If I can't suffocate you, I can't resuscitate you."

I chew a bite of food before wiping my mouth. "I bet that's a phrase you've never said before now."

Felix frowns just before taking a long swig of his wine.

"You'll be good at this. Winston Jeffries used to drink heavily before poisoning the girls. I remembered that a few weeks ago. Never told anyone. But now I know why I've had no desire to drink. He was so messed-up. Everything's come in pieces to me. A puzzle. A heinous puzzle. Eventually, I stopped sharing the pieces with Colten because I saw it in his eyes. The doubt. I know it pained him to have those moments, but I didn't miss the subtle flinches, the extended looks when I interacted with his daughter. We got so good at pretending everything would be fine if we just kept ..."

"Pretending?"

I nod.

"Winston was abused by his mom. Always being compared to his sister. And I think his mom got so mad at him one time, she tried to drown him in the tub. She shaved his head because he didn't comb his hair. I never see her in the vision, but I *feel* his fear. One day I feel his anger, his wrath toward the girls, and the next day I feel his despair. Every inadequacy. Every inclination to end his own life."

I poke at the food on my plate, but I've lost my appetite. "That would have been the better choice. It would have saved so many lives." I glance up at Felix. "I've started to think that about myself. I often wonder if there's a switch that could flip, and I'd be more him than me. What if I go from imagining self-harm to harming someone else? An animal that needs to be put down."

"When does a killer become a killer?"

I nod. "I don't know, but it's always fascinated me. The conception of a killer. I used to fixate on mass shootings. I'd do so much research on the killers, trying to get inside of their heads to understand. My parents used to say understanding a killer would be impossible. Yet I felt like I could. Not like I wanted to kill anyone, just ... I understood. You know?"

Felix takes several more gulps of his wine. "I'm about to find out."

I reach for the bottle of wine.

Felix raises an eyebrow. "Shall I get you a glass?"

Bringing it to my nose, I take a slow whiff. Then ... I take a sip.

And another sip.

And eventually, I consume the rest of the bottle. A nice buzz. Felix can't kill me if his mind is clear, and I'm not sure I can die with one.

It's bizarre how methodical we are while we finish dinner and dessert. We clear the dining room table and wash the wine glasses. I put the silverware in the dishwasher while Felix takes out the trash. Then I take a shower, shaving everything but my head.

Floss.

Brush my teeth.

Dry my hair.

I trim my fingernails and toenails.

Deodorant.

Lotion on my legs.

Why? I have no idea. It feels necessary.

We drive in silence to the storage unit. I completely undress, and Felix doesn't question it for a second. He knows it's easier to use the defibrillator, perform any necessary procedures, or administer medications if I am naked.

I never prepared to die the first time. I know people do it. Suicidal people. Terminally ill people. Inmates on death row.

"I need to say this," Felix says, holding the bag in his hands while I sit on the edge of the hospital bed. "*If you survive death, you will likely have severe, permanent neurological damage. Language, behavior, mood,* and cognition disturbances. I don't know what kind of life you imagine, but the chances of you miraculously coming out of this without those issues is so close to zero, I can't put enough zeros after the decimal. I need ... really *need* to know you understand this. I need to know this is what you want. I need to know you are making this decision with a sound mind."

I think his buzz has worn off. Mine is still swirling in my head, but it doesn't numb my conscience to the words he's saying.

"If you weren't doing this for me, I would take my own life. And I'd do it in a way that no one would be around to save me. So please always, *always* remember that you didn't kill me. I'm already dead. And while I can't be *him* in this life any longer, I've loved my life. I love my family. I loved my job. And I love Colten to the very deepest parts of my soul. So for this life I love, this life I don't want to leave, I owe it one last chance. I owe it the greatest risk, no matter how tiny the chance might be. I am making this decision with a sound mind, even if slightly buzzed." I manage a small grin, but Felix struggles to find one of his own.

"No keeping a vegetable. Understood? Throw out the vegetable."

After a few seconds, Felix nods.

First, he inserts an IV and makes sure the crash cart and epinephrine are ready.

Then he walks behind me and ties my wrists together so I can't fight him. My heart jumps, gallops, takes off like a fighter plane. When he walks around to the front of me again, I blink, and several tears work their way out.

Felix isn't immune to the harsh reality either. His Adam's apple bounces over and over while he glances toward the ceiling to keep from blinking.

"Thank you," I whisper when I can't find a strong voice behind the emotion.

The adrenaline.

The fear.

I'm scared. I don't want to die. But I can't be him. I say this to myself over and over again. I wish it made it easier to let go, but it doesn't.

Felix stares at the bag in his hands. A gun would be easier and faster. Carbon monoxide would be more peaceful. A drug overdose would increase my chances of coming back. But this ... this is how *he* has to die. This is how he has to leave me. Of that, I am certain. Winston left that life by hanging. I'm not asking Felix to do that to me, but this will be close. Close enough.

When Felix lifts his gaze to mine, I nod once.

He puts the bag over my head and seals it with a tight grip and several firm twists. Felix's jaw clenches while he holds the bag in place and closes his eyes. I don't want to fight, but I do. I don't want to panic, but I do. I don't want to feel pain, but I do. My oxygen hungry retinas cause my vision to blur while my mind tries to change its mind. It's too late. There is no going back now. There is only ... darkness.

CHAPTER
Forty-One

Felix

"GOD, I MISSED YOU." Isabella jumps up from the sofa when I get home from work.

"I would have picked you up from the airport," I say when she hurls herself into my arms.

"I know, but I took an earlier flight, and I knew you were working." With her arms draped around my neck, she grins and gives me a slow kiss.

I need her kiss.

When she reaches for my tie, loosening it, I decide I need that too. I need her in every way. I need her body to distract my mind. I need her soft moans to spur some life back into my black soul.

Our clothes pile up at our feet, and we make it up three stairs before I'm inside of her.

"F-Felix ..." She giggles, wriggling away from me.

She gets up two more stairs before I hook her waist and take her from behind, her knees on one step, her hands two steps higher. This time she doesn't giggle. Her fingers dig into the runner rug, and she grunts with each thrust.

Fucking my wife like an animal on the stairs is a good way to not think about Josephine Watts in my storage unit ... in a coma.

"Oh god ... Felix ..." She wiggles her ass, doing the work for me as the sound of skin slapping fills the room.

I grip her hips and enjoy the view. Her long auburn hair splays along her face as she looks over her shoulder at me, mouth slightly agape with each tiny grunt.

Uh. Uh. Uh ...

They're little staccatos drowning the memory of Josephine trying to scream inside the plastic bag.

She gives me a tiny smirk and pulls away from me, running the rest of the way up the stairs. I chase her down the hallway and into the bedroom, where I pin her beneath me and wedge myself between her spread legs.

My tongue flicks her nipple, and she whispers, "Tie me up." She lifts her hips and grinds against me while stretching her arms above her head toward the bed posts in surrender.

My erection dies, her words a marksman with a direct hit. In all the years we've been together, I've tied her to the bed maybe ... twice? And tonight ... out of all fucking nights, she asks me to do it.

I crawl off her and drag my limp dick to the bathroom.

"Felix? Where are you going? What's wrong?"

"I haven't had dinner, and I need a shower."

"What? Are you serious? We didn't finish!"

I close the door, knowing she'll be opening it in a matter of seconds. What am I supposed to say? I grab my cock and stroke it over and over, thinking about my Isabella, my sexy wife. Her tits. Her pussy. When that doesn't work, I think about Heather, one of my nurses. She's twenty-four. A double D. And she's always wearing a fucking pink thong under her scrubs that I see every time she bends down to tie her shoes when she's not wearing her lab coat. I don't want to fuck her in real life. I'm a happily married man, but in a pinch, I think of her, and it always does the job.

Not tonight.

The tire is flat, and I don't have a spare.

"Felix." Isabella opens the door and traipses up behind me as I turn on the shower.

I cringe when I jump in before the water has a chance to warm up.

"Brr ..." She squeals, following me into the shower.

There's no escaping her hand reaching for my flat tire.

She frowns when I turn toward her.

"Sorry." I shrug. "Cold water." I squirt shampoo into my hair and work up a lather.

Isabella drops to her knees and pulls me into her mouth.

Nothing.

This is emasculating. She's been gone for over a week. She'll think I don't want her, or worse, that I'm cheating on her.

"Ouch!" She pulls away when I not-so-accidentally squirt body soap into her eye.

"Oh, Izzy … I'm so sorry, honey." I help her to her feet and guide her face under one of the jets.

"Oh my god. It burns!"

"I'm *really* sorry." I hand her a washcloth.

She takes it and exits the shower.

"I'll be out in a minute. I can help rinse out your eye," I say, resting my forehead against the tile.

I suffocated a woman four days ago. By some miracle, I brought her back. But now she's in a coma in my fucking storage unit with stolen equipment from work. Losing my job is the least of my concerns right now. If someone found Josie, would I be arrested for … attempted murder? I have no alibi. And there is not one good reason why she's in my storage unit. If the electricity goes out during the night, she'll freeze to death. If she wakes when I'm not there and is disoriented, she could try to leave on her own. What have I done?

Eleven more days. Josie has eleven more days to come out of her coma before I take her life for a second time and dispose of the body where no one will ever find it. And I have to do all of this while saving lives at work and trying to act like a normal husband who can properly fuck his wife.

Regardless, we are even. More than even. What I did for Josie was so far above and beyond what she did for me. There's no way to adequately measure it in one lifetime.

TOMORROW IS the last day for Josie unless she wakes up before then. I've had a shit day at work because I can't stop thinking about burying a body for the first time in my life and hopefully the last. I can't stop thinking about what prison will be like.

On the way to my car, Izzy calls me. "I can read your mind. You want me to pick up dinner." I open the driver's door.

"Felix, I'm in our storage unit."

Fuck. Fuck. FUCK!

Isabella has been to our storage unit once in the seven years we've had it. ONCE!

"I'm on my way. I'll explain when I get there."

"Felix," she says with a shaky voice. "W-why is there an unconscious woman in our storage unit? In a hospital bed? T-tell me!"

"I'll be there in less than twenty minutes. Don't touch anything."

"Touch anything? What am I going to touch? The

unconscious woman? Felix, this is the woman that's been on the news and online. She's the missing woman! What the hell did you do?"

"Izzy, I *need* you to calm down. Stay put. Don't call anyone else. And just wait for me."

When I get to the unit, Izzy's standing at the end of the bed, arms hugged to herself. "Felix! What is she doing here? What have you done?"

I hold my finger to my lips, wishing she'd keep her voice down a bit. "Do you want a lie or the truth?"

She frowns.

I thought of a lot of things, but I didn't imagine having to tell Izzy without first being arrested. "When I was a first-year resident, Dr. Watts, Josie, was my chief resident. After my mom died, I struggled with addiction, and Josie saved my ass on more than one occasion. She saved my medical career. While you were gone, she showed up at our doorstep, out of the blue. You see, I owed her a favor after what she did for me. And so I had no choice."

"Why is she unconscious in our storage unit?" Izzy asks like she's on the verge of losing it.

"Shh ..." I cringe again. "Can you keep it down?" I say while checking Josie's vitals, her IV, feeding tube, and catheters. Over the next fifteen minutes, I proceed with the whole story, as unbelievable as it is. Then I show her Josie's video because I need her to believe that I'm not a true killer.

"Felix ..." Izzy whispers my name, dazed as she shuffles a few steps away from the bed.

Is she distancing herself from Josie or me?

Her fingertips touch her parted lips, gaze on Josie between slow blinks. "You c-can't kill her t-tomorrow," she stammers.

"That was her wish. It's been two weeks. We are, in fact, in a storage unit. It's winter. I have a full-time job. Her chances of waking up are slim. Her chances of waking up without neurological deficiencies are nearly zilch. I will follow her instructions. Return the equipment. And go on with my life. With our life."

Izzy's gaze flits to me. "We can't let her die. No. It's only been two weeks. She could wake up. You know this. And she might have minimal or no neurological deficiencies. It's not impossible."

Izzy's experience as an ICU nurse isn't helping this situation. I need her to feel helpless and reliant on me, not like a superhero.

"She has family ... a fiancé looking for her. What if we can save her? What if she doesn't remember her past life? Felix, what if we can do this?" She laughs. It's a shaky laugh before she releases a long breath.

I'm glad she's hopeful or relieved, but it's not realistic.

"I'm following her wishes. The way I'd follow a living will. It's the legal and ethical thing to do."

"Legal and ethical? Are you joking? We are in a *storage unit*. You have a former medical examiner in a coma because you tied a bag over her head. Her fiancé is a homicide detective. You stole thousands of dollars' worth of medical equipment, and now I'm either a witness who is going to report you or I'm an accessory."

I unbutton the top of my shirt with my sweaty hands. Her assessment has my heart quickening. Reality fills the room, stealing all the oxygen.

"I'm proud of you," Izzy says, donning a pair of blue gloves and rechecking everything I just checked, except she's also checking for bed sores. She's focusing more on the contents of the catheter bags. She's assessing Josie like a nurse would do if she were caring for someone's loved one ... to return them to their family—alive. "Most people don't seek the truth because it's too messy. Most people don't stretch their minds to make room for things they haven't experienced and can't see. I'm proud of you for listening to her. I'm proud of you for believing her."

"Who said I believed her?"

Izzy glances over at me while holding Josie's wrist, feeling her pulse. She traded in nursing to become an acupuncturist. "She's in our storage unit. You tied a bag over her head. You believed her."

"I owed her."

Izzy chuckles, resting Josie's wrist at her side. "Not this. Nobody owes anyone *this*."

She's right. I believed Josie.

"It could be months," I say just above a whisper. "We *have* to let her die."

Izzy doesn't look at me. She messes with Josie and her bedding, sliding her one way and then the other way. "The bed doesn't adjust."

"It's not plugged in."

She unplugs the crash cart and plugs in the bed to adjust Josie. "How did you get all of this here?"

"The janitor helped me load it into a moving van."

"Without question?" She glances over her shoulder.

I shrug. "I said it was going to one of the clinics."

"And how did you get it in here by yourself?"

"The bed? I paid Jonah to help me. I told him there was some renovation happening at the hospital, and we had to store some things until it was done."

She snorts. "The neighbor kid? And he believed you?"

"He's seventeen."

Crossing her arms, she stares at Josie. "You tied her hands behind her back ... that's why you had *issues* the night I came home, when I asked you to tie me to the bed."

When I don't answer, she glances over her shoulder at me.

I nod once.

"We're going to take care of her, Felix. We're not going to give up on her." Her head dips into a resolute nod.

"That's not what she wanted."

"She didn't want to inconvenience you any longer than possible."

"She asked me to kill her. I think fear of inconveniencing me went out the window at that point."

Izzy turns and wraps her arms around my neck.

"I'm going to work on her tomorrow. Acupuncture. I'm going to get some essential oils, objects with different textures. She needs to be moved, adjusted, bathed, talked to like she's not in a coma. Maybe a little music from time to time. Let's bring her back."

There's no use arguing with her, so I nod.

A MONTH PASSES. I start to lose hope even with Izzy feeling optimistic.

"Her brain is healing," she says.

She's braindead, but I don't say that.

Another month passes. It's official. I've kept the vegetable. I'd say Josie will be pissed off at me, but she won't. Not in this lifetime. I don't blame Josie for wanting to try, to exhaust every last effort. I would do the same thing to stay in this life with Izzy. But time is up.

"No," Izzy says when I come into the storage unit after work. She knows what I'm going to say.

"No one's immortal, Izzy. You've blown me away with your generosity, your kindness to a complete stranger. But—"

"She squeezed my hand today."

"Palmar grasp reflex. You know this."

She takes Josie's hand, running her finger along her lifeline.

"Izzy, I don't want her to wake up."

"Why would you say that?"

"You know why. She wouldn't be able to physically function. She'd be, at the very best, I'm talking truly miraculous best, mentally impaired. It's unlikely that she'd be able to speak."

"That's what therapy is for. Speech. Physical. Occupational. It will take time, but I believe she will recover."

"Time? You mean years? What are we supposed to do? Take her and dump her off at Colten's front doorstep? At her parents' front doorstep? Are we going to rehabilitate her? Izzy, you have to be realistic. The humane thing to do for her and everyone is to let her go."

"Would you let me go?"

"I would if that's what you wanted."

Izzy turns toward me, mouth slightly agape.

I shrug. "I think you forget about your years as a nurse. I think you forget what I see and do every day. And..." I smile "...I love that about you. I imagine us having kids and how lucky they will be to have you as their mother. I want that life, Izzy. I don't want to go to prison. I don't want anything to jeopardize our future. Maybe that's selfish of me, but when it comes to my life with you, I feel protective and selfish."

She holds out her arms while she makes her way to me. I embrace my world. And then ... it's as if the world stops for a breath. More like a blink.

Josie opens her eyes.

CHAPTER
Forty-Two

I WAKE UP ALONE. No Josie. For a few seconds, I rub my eyes. Was it real?

She's alive.

She uses a walker.

She's incredibly thin and frail.

She's. Alive!

I climb out of bed, grab a T-shirt, and go downstairs. She's nowhere in sight and neither is her walker. How did she get down the stairs ... with her walker? Did Felix pick her up? How did I sleep through everything? I run back up the stairs, and just as I head into my bedroom, I hear her.

"I'm in here."

I follow her voice to Reagan's room. She's perched on the end of Reagan's bed, staring at the cat mural.

"Who painted this?" she asks.

"I did." I bend down and kiss her head before sitting next to her.

"Did I know that?"

"Yes. You did."

"Huh ..." She continues to stare at it.

"Josie," I whisper, taking her hand in mine. "It's time. I need to know. Where have you been? What happened?"

"I'm not sure."

"What does that mean?"

"There's what I know and what I've been told. I've been trying to piece everything together, but it's been hard. I know I loved my job. I know you moved to Chicago, and it was the first time I had seen you in seventeen years. I know I was mad at you. I know you did a weird proposal over donuts. I know I said no. But I watched a video I made before I died, and I guess I was going to marry you, so I must have said yes at some point. The video version of me said that I had a near-death experience where I remembered a past life, and it was giving me horrible visions. I was suicidal. I was afraid of making you choose between your daughter and me. I must not have thought we could coincide in your life. Felix has filled in some more information as well. I have memories from before the first death, the shooting, but I think everything from after that until I woke up from the coma is gone."

"Josie ..." I stand, running my hands through my hair before turning toward her. "You were in a coma?"

She nods.

"Wh-how ... for ... Jesus ... for how long? Why am I just now hearing about this? Why didn't your name come up when you were admitted to the hospital? I've been looking for you for months!"

She winces.

I feel instant regret. I'm angry, but not really at her. I'm confused. My chest aches, and I feel so lost and helpless.

"I didn't go to the hospital."

"What?" I shake my head. "That makes no sense."

"I told you what I know. Now this is what I've been told. I left you on our wedding day. I showed up at Felix's house. He was a first-year resident when I was chief resident. He had some issues, and I saved him and his career. I went to his house because I thought he owed me. I asked him to kill me. He restrained me and tied a bag around my head—"

I shake my head over and over before running to the bathroom and hurling. Not much comes out because my stomach is empty. Everything from the pit of it to the top of my throat aches and burns. I've seen truly horrible crime scenes and barely blinked at the carnage. But imagining someone restraining Josie and tying a plastic bag over her head ... it's gutting me.

She left me on our wedding day... to die.

"I'm sorry," she whispers.

I stand and rinse my mouth in the sink. Pressing a towel to my lips, I glance at her in the mirror, standing with her walker in the doorway.

"I should leave."

I turn and clear my throat. "How long were you in a coma?"

"Two months. In a storage unit filled with equipment Felix *borrowed* from the hospital."

Two fucking months in a coma ... in a goddamn storage unit. And I thought she was dead.

"I was confused as to why Felix kept me alive that long. I thought I surely gave him instructions, but I couldn't remember. When I pressed him, he told me it was two weeks. His wife found me, and she refused to let me die. I think ..." Josie's gaze drops to the floor, eyes narrowed.

I turn, resting against the counter.

"I think ... sometimes ... that they should have let me die because I'm nearly four months post coma, and I look awful. And I can't walk without a walker. And my memory is slow some days. And piecing things together is painful. I'm trying to form these connections in my brain, and it's so very hard." She takes in a shaky breath. "It's statistically unlikely that I'll ever be what I was before the coma ... before I died a second time. Most days I wonder why. What is the point? Why did I want to stay in this world so badly?"

I run a hand through my hair. "For me. You wanted to stay for me. Because you know I love you. Because you know I need you."

Her head eases side to side. "You wanted me. But you didn't need me. You didn't *need* me when you broke my heart our senior year, even if you wanted me ... you didn't need me. And you didn't need me when we reconnected seventeen years later. I know this because you made it seventeen years without me, without making any effort to find me. You had other relationships. A career. A daughter. All without me. So I wanted to stay for me. I wanted to stay because you came back into my life, and I liked the version of me with you. I've always liked that version of myself. But now I'm barely a ghost of what I used to be. And I hate it. I hate that I allowed this to happen. I hate that I didn't have the courage to just let go. Let *you* go. Let this life go."

How can she be alive yet I hurt more than I did when I thought she was dead?

Something chimes from the bedroom. She turns and pushes her walker toward the bed, taking her phone off the nightstand and answering it. "Hello? No. I haven't done my exercises yet. No. I haven't—yeah, I know. I will. I know." She closes her eyes for a few seconds and blows out a long breath. "Fine. I'll meet you out front." Ending the call, she glances up at me. "I have to go. That was Izzy."

"Who's Izzy?"

"Felix's wife. I go to therapy four times a week, but I have exercises to do at home every day. Izzy feels very responsible for my recovery since she's the reason Felix didn't let me die."

"Sounds like I owe her a debt of gratitude."

"No." She frowns. "You don't. I'm not her. I'm not the woman you asked to marry you in a donut shop. I'm the car that needs to be sent to the junkyard because my parts are worth more than the whole of me. I'm nothing but a liability."

"Don't say that. Don't ever fucking say that again."

Pushing her walker toward the door, she mumbles, "Izzy's coming to get me. Give my apologies to your date from last night. Felix was right; I should have let him run my errands."

I follow her to the stairs. "It wasn't a date."

"Can you get my walker?" Josie holds the banister and lowers herself to the top step.

"I'll carry you."

"I can do it." She takes it one step at a time on her butt.

I watch her. I used to watch her cut into dead bodies and help solve cases. I used to watch students study her, envy her, want to be her. Now, she's scooting down my stairs on her butt. She wishes she would have stayed dead. Maybe she's right. Maybe that woman is gone. Still, I just ... fucking love her so much. Reason 683 why everything hurts right now.

"Are you going to tell your parents, or am I?"

She glances over her shoulder when she reaches the bottom stair and stands with the assistance of the banister.

"For that matter," I say, carrying her walker down the stairs, "when were you going to tell me? Never?"

"I'll call my parents." She frowns. "And the plan was to come back to you when I was functional again."

"And if you're never functional?"

She takes her walker and heads toward the front

door. "Then that will suck for me, but it doesn't have to suck for you." She opens the door. "Call the woman with the red dress. Apologize. And move on with your life like you were doing before you saw me at CVS."

"Stop. Just ... stop!" I ball my hands, ready to send one of them through the wall. I'm ready to crawl out of my skin. How can Josie be alive and it feel like a nightmare? Where is *my* Josie? "I told you she's a friend. That's it. I don't want to talk about her again. I want to know why after *six months* I found out you're alive by pure luck. Happenstance. I was supposed to be your husband. Your. Husband."

She stares at the floor. It's hard to read her. Is she numb to what I'm feeling?

"A serial killer. That's weird, right? I mean, I've had such a fascination with death. I was really good at my job. Dr. Cornwell used to say 'eerily' good. He said I thought like a killer when I worked on cases." She chuckles. "I suppose every soul has to find a new life. At least this life has been mostly worthwhile. Good deeds this time."

I deflate. She's unfocused, almost indifferent to the words I say to her. I want to hold her. I want her to hold me back. I want to feel her love. I need to feel missed. I need to feel *us*.

What happened to *us*?

"Izzy's here. Thanks for taking care of me. Please let me tell my parents first."

Taking care of her? Does she have any idea how much it's killing me to let her leave?

"I need the address," I say. "I have to go in to finish up a few reports, but I can pick you up by three."

"I'm staying with them for now. So if you pick me up, they'll just have to come get me again tomorrow."

My heart has been stuck in my throat since I saw her yesterday at the CVS. I hate that she's three feet from me. She's *alive*. Yet she doesn't get that she belongs with me.

"I'll pick you up at three. And I'll return you to their house tomorrow," I say.

And I'll drop you off the next day. Pick you up. Drop you off. Repeat. Repeat. Repeat.

"If you have plans later, don't let me disrupt them."

I LOVE YOU! Stop pushing me away!

Controlling every crushing emotion racking around inside of my chest, I give her a simple nod. "I'll see you at three."

"Okay. Have a good day." She steps outside and closes the door behind her.

"A good day," I whisper to myself, taking a seat on the stairs, resting my hands on my knees while shoving my fingers into my hair. "You're alive, baby. It's a fucking *amazing* day."

CHAPTER
Forty-Three

"How are you?" Izzy asks, backing out of Colten's driveway.

"Good. Why?"

She puts the car in *Drive* and gives me a quick sideways glance. "Well, yesterday your fiancé—who thought you were dead—saw you at a CVS. He had to be in shock. I can only imagine. Completely stunned. It's been six months. And Felix said he was there with another woman. You must have some feelings about all of this. What did Colten say when you got back to his house? Is he serious with the other woman? What are your feelings at the moment?"

"Colten was ... in shock. I think. As for my feelings? I feel bad. And I feel guilty. And I still feel confused. Insecure. Frustrated. Brokenhearted. You name the emotion and I'm feeling it. Angry ... I'm definitely angry."

"At Colten?"

"No. I'm angry at myself for not ending my life, for not thinking this through. It's good that I don't have memories of Winston Jeffries. It's bad that I'm crippled. It's bad that Colten knows I'm alive, and he feels responsible for me ... just when he was moving on. And now I have to tell my parents before he tells them. I'm mad at myself for thinking that my existence in this world was necessary."

"Josie, I don't know if anyone's existence in the world is necessary. It's life. The good, the bad, and the ugly."

I can't stop thinking about the woman in red. "She's beautiful," I say. "The woman. They were clearly going someplace nice. They were way too dressed up for 'just friends.' In his head, I died. And I *did* die. Do I think six months is a little early to be dating someone new?" I shrug. "I don't know. My memory is so messed-up. I'm having trouble sensing time. Six weeks. Six months. Six years. It's all about the same to me."

"How did it make you feel when you saw the other woman? Were you angry then?"

"I was surprised to see *him*. She was an afterthought. And I think ..." I sigh. "I think it brought back memories of all the times he was with some other girl when we were younger. I got so used to being silently jealous and irra- tionally angry. I never felt good enough for him, and it had nothing to do with him. Colten never made me feel anything short of the most special person in the room. But *I* felt different than the other girls. He was so talented, and everyone adored him. It was easy to want him yet feel inadequate, like he deserved someone better than me."

"That's sad, Josie."

I nod. "It was sad. Inadequacy is a soul-robbing emotion. It was then, and it is now. When we were younger, it took me a while to feel like he wasn't being my friend or my boyfriend because I was the default girl next door or the chief's daughter. And no sooner did I let that feeling of inadequacy fall away, he let me go. Seventeen years passed, and we were back in each other's lives. I didn't need anyone to tell me that I hated him. I remember all too well. I also didn't need anyone to tell me that I still love him. I remember that all too well. So this second chance at being with him gets trampled by, yet again, something else that spirals me back into that soul-robbing feeling of inadequacy. Fuck my life. Really ... just fuck my life."

"Are you saying he's no longer interested? No longer in love with you?"

"He loves me," I whisper. "He's hardwired to love me. I know this. But sometimes we're hardwired to do things that aren't in our best interest. Some would say addiction like alcoholism is something hardwired within people. So sure ... Colten loves me. He'd leave the pretty girl from last night to be with me. But who am I? I'll tell you. I'm a mutated version of my original self. I'm a salvaged vehicle. I don't know if I'll ever be mentally the same. Or physically the same. He's ..."

I laugh despite the pain. "Colten is so sexy. In his prime. Virile. And deserving of a woman who ..." I shrug. "A woman who looks like a gift from God in a red dress with magnificent heels and long flowing hair. He doesn't need, nor does he deserve, someone who can't climb the stairs. She has sexy shoes. I have a walker. Which one do you think gives a guy an erection?"

"I highly doubt he saw you last night and thought, 'There's the love of my life. Finally, I can get a proper erection.'"

I snort, staring out my window at the congested sidewalks. It feels inappropriate given the events of the last twenty-four hours—or the last year for that matter. But I can't help it. It feels good.

"He was hours, minutes, from promising to love you through sickness and health. You are getting better, Josie. You will continue to improve. Do you know how many times Felix has said you're a miracle?"

I scoff. "It's a miracle that I survived death twice. I am not miraculously using a walker. Not miraculously piecing together memories or thoughts. Not miraculously trying to find myself again. All of that is nothing short of a tragedy that could have been avoided had I just left my wedding and left this world for good. He just ..." My voice fades into a whisper. "He deserves the red dress and heels."

THAT STRONG, wide-shouldered, handsome, virile man comes to the door at three. I watch out the front window like I'm fourteen and my dad is letting me go on my first date.

"I'm proud of you for remembering our address," Izzy says, sneaking up behind me.

"I didn't. Colten is a detective. Felix introduced himself."

"For someone who doesn't feel adequate, you didn't hesitate to pack an overnight bag." Izzy picks up said overnight bag.

Pushing my walker toward the door, I frown. "I told you; he's hardwired to love me. He thinks I belong with him. It's going to take a while for him to see that I no longer fit. That I can't give him what he deserves ... what he wants even if he can't see it clearly now."

Izzy reaches for the door handle. "What if he can see it now?" She opens the door and smiles. "You must be Detective Mosley. You met my husband, Felix, last night. I'm Isabelle." She holds out her hand.

Colten, in all of his sexiness, offers his hand. "Nice to meet you. Thank you for all you've done and are doing for Josie. I owe you a huge debt of gratitude."

Oh, Colten ...

She hands Colten my bag. "It's been our pleasure. She's a miraculous human, this one here." Izzy winks at me while I maneuver my walker out the door.

"Bye, Izzy," I clip before she can sing my praises for another second.

"See you in the morning."

"I'll drop her off," Colten says. "We should talk about her therapy."

"Absolutely," Izzy says. "Have a good night."

The boy who used to race me on our bikes or to my favorite tree is now waiting for me to slide into his car so he can take my *walker* and put it in the back of his vehicle. I'm not eighty. I'm thirty-six.

When he gets into the driver's seat, he eyes me with a smile so big it's almost clownish. "It's good to see you."

I can't quite match his smile. This isn't the happily ever after I dreamed of having with Colten Mosley. It's not happy. It's not even forever. It's simply after. After I did something I should not have done.

"That's my line," I say for lack of a better response.

Colten slides his hand to the back of my head and leans over the console, not letting his smile waver for a second before pressing a soft kiss to my cheek. He hasn't kissed me on the lips yet. Maybe he's conflicted —as he should be if he found someone else. That's not true. He shouldn't be conflicted. He should simply choose her.

I died. I should have stayed dead.

"Stop," he says, fastening his seat belt and backing out of the driveway.

"Stop what?"

"Thinking whatever you're thinking that's feeding your self-doubt."

"I'm not doubting myself." I stare at my hands folded in my lap. "I have no doubt that I made a mistake. I have no doubt that I shouldn't be here. I have no doubt that I may never be mentally or physically normal again."

"Josie ..." He rests his hand on mine.

I can't look at him. He symbolizes everything I will never be. It's a more debilitating pain than reteaching my body to function properly again.

When we get to his house, I shake my head over and over. "No. Stop. Why did you tell them? I'm not ready." Panic overtakes my whole body, shocking my heart into an irregular rhythm.

My parents' car is in his driveway.

"I didn't tell them. I asked them to come today. It was a big ask with no explanation. They did it for me."

My head continues to shake. "You had no right. I said I'd tell them on my own time."

He kills the engine, gets out of the car, and comes around to my side. As soon as he opens the door, he rests his arms on the roof and sighs slowly while closing his eyes for a brief moment. "If it were Reagan, I'd want to know. If you were my daughter, I'd want to know without hesitation. I'd have a hard time forgiving anyone and everyone who kept it from me. Josie, we all lived through your tragedy. We've been grieving you for months. It's cruel to let them grieve for another day ... for another second."

When I unbuckle my seat belt, Colten retrieves my walker. He lets me step out of the car on my own, in my own time. Then he leads me to his front door.

I take a deep breath as he opens it.

"Oh thank goodness. We've been dying to find out the surprise—" My mom's words die like they stepped off a cliff when she comes around the corner and sees me. Her hand slowly covers her mouth, eyes unblinking while they fill with tears.

"What's the surprise—" My dad turns the corner right behind her.

I force a smile while wiping a few tears from my own face. "Hi."

My mom's gaze inches along my body, stopping at my hands gripping the walker. "Josie," she exhales while her hand falls from her mouth and tears cover her cheeks.

Before I can take another step forward, my parents rush toward me, sandwiching me between them, casting my walker aside.

"Oh my god ..." My mom cries. "You're a-alive ..."

My dad doesn't speak. I don't think he can speak without breaking down. When their hold on me finally loosens, I grip my dad's arm, reaching for my walker with my other hand.

He catches me, scooping me up into his arms like he did when I was a little girl.

I wrap my arms around his neck and smile. "I can walk ... with a little help."

He drops his forehead on my shoulder and just ...

breathes. It's reminiscent of Colten having a moment when he put me in his car at the CVS.

Disbelief.

Shock.

Utter speechlessness.

I give him the moment, as does my mom and Colten. Nobody says a word for a few seconds.

Canting my head toward his, I rest my cheek on it and whisper, "I missed you too."

His head makes a slight nod without lifting it from my shoulder. When he sets me back on my feet, sniffling to keep his emotions in check, Colten has my walker waiting for me.

"Well..." I glance up at the three of them "...I'm sure you have questions." I smile.

Over the next hour, I tell them what I know, what I've been told, how Colten discovered me, and what Felix and Izzy have been doing for me.

"You'll come home," Mom says with a sharp nod.

"Yes," Dad seconds.

Colten stiffens on the sofa beside me.

"I have therapy."

"We have therapists in Des Moines," Mom says. "There's no need for you to be a burden on Felix and Izzy anymore."

I open my mouth to argue, but I can't. She's right. I don't want to be a burden on anyone.

Colten clears his throat and sits up straight before leaning forward to rest his hands on his knees. "She should stay with me. I'll hire help for when I'm at work."

Who's going to take care of me? I hate this conversation. I hate how helpless I feel. I hate that I'm now this decision that has to be made.

"Or I can live in my own house. Everything is on one floor. I can pay for rides to therapy. I can have groceries delivered, or I can set up a meal service while I'm recovering."

There's a collective no. My parents and Colten eye each other as though I'm not in the same room.

My mom moves from the chair to the sofa, taking ahold of my hand. "Come home, just temporarily. Stay a few weeks. A month? Stay until you're feeling more confident."

Colten readjusts in his spot again. "Why is everyone acting like I can't do this?"

"You have work," Mom says to him.

"I said I'd hire someone."

"And you have a daughter," Dad adds.

Colten gives my dad a look. I think he's used to him being his ally.

"I'll come home," I say, giving my parents a sad smile and slight nod. I'm thirty-six and moving back home so my parents can take care of me. It's a new low.

Colten stands and walks out of the room.

"Colten?" my mom calls after him.

He goes upstairs without a word.

Mom squeezes my hand. "He'll be fine. This is just a lot right now. Give him time, and he'll see this is for the best. When you get better, you'll be able to move back to Chicago. Go back to work. Get married. We just want to help you get your life back." She hugs me. "Josephine ... you're alive," she whispers in my ear, her voice cracking beneath the weight of the day.

"I'm alive," I whisper back, not feeling the same level of gratitude or relief.

"WE COULD GO FISHING next weekend. That would help with strength and coordination of your arms, Jo," Dad says while we eat dinner.

Colten hasn't said more than a few words to anyone since the food arrived, and he came back downstairs with us. Even now, his head is bowed toward his plate while he picks at his food.

Just as I start to speak, Colten's phone vibrates.

"Hey." He listens for a few seconds. "Yeah, sorry. I was going to call you. What time is her game? Okay. Yeah, I'll be there. Thanks, see you tomorrow." He ends his call.

"T-ball game?" my dad asks.

Colten nods, taking another bite of food.

"I'd love to see her. Can I go?" I ask.

Colten glances over at me. He doesn't say anything at first, so I shrug.

"It's fine. I don't have to go. I should probably go to my house and sort through things before I go back with my parents."

"You can go. She'd love to see you. I haven't told her that you're ..."

"Alive?" I assume that's what he's trying to say.

"She thinks you're missing. That's all."

I nod.

After dinner, my parents decide to head to my house. "You should stay with us since you can't take the stairs," Mom says.

"I carried her last night," Colten says.

"Yes, but that's silly when she can sleep in her own bed."

I know my mom doesn't mean to disregard all of Colten's suggestions. She misses me. I guess they all miss me. Why don't I feel more missed and less of a burden?

"I thought my bed was her bed," he mumbles. I'm not sure she even hears him as he grabs my overnight bag from the bottom of the stairs where he set it when we arrived.

My dad takes the bag while my mom holds open the door.

I smile at them. "I'll meet you outside in a minute."

They nod and shut the door behind them.

"You brought them here. And I'm grateful, truly. But you can't expect them to say hi and leave like it's no big deal. Would you do that to Reagan?"

Colten slides his hands in his front pockets and inches his head side to side. He's incredibly quiet. I don't know how to make this better. Make this, whatever *this* is, go away. There's no roadmap for this.

"Do you want to pick me up tomorrow, or should I meet you at the park?"

"I'll pick you up at ten." He stares at the floor between us.

"Sounds good."

There's an awkward silence.

"Good night," I say, opening the door barely an inch before he steps behind me.

His hands rest on my shoulders, and his lips press to the top of my head, staying there for several long seconds. I draw in a shaky breath and blink back my tears. I just want to be in his arms. I want to be me before all of *this*. I want to have him chase me up the stairs and jump on the bed as I try to get away from him, giggling and taunting him before he captures me.

Before we lose our clothes.

Before he loses himself inside of me, and I lose myself so completely to him.

"Good night," he whispers before taking a step away.

The loss of his touch feels like an unwelcome chill.

CHAPTER
Forty-Four

I'VE STOPPED TRYING to hold it together. Josie's going back to Des Moines. My heart is nothing more than pea gravel on a playground, getting trampled without a second thought.

Before my fist makes contact with Josie's door, Isaac opens it. Josie smiles at me for a brief second, then she frowns. "Don't say anything about my hat. Izzy let me sit at her vanity to do my hair. I don't have a seat. So … it's a mess."

"You look pretty," I say.

Her gaze shoots to mine. I offer a tiny smile that feels forced because I don't know if references to our past matter anymore.

"Thanks," she says softly.

"See you after a bit," Isaac says.

She doesn't wait for me. Not my help. Not even for

me to offer her help. It's hard to see her fight for independence when I know she's feeling so helpless. I don't know where I fit with her right now. She's leaving Chicago, so that feels like a strong sign that I don't fit anywhere in her life at the moment.

"How's her team doing?" Josie asks on the way to Reagan's game. She asks a lot of questions that have nothing to do with us. Anything to fill the void, I suppose. That painful silence.

"We can go over the gravel or take the long way on the sidewalk. I can carry you," I say when she steps out of the car.

"I'll take the sidewalk. You can take the gravel. I don't want you to miss any of her game."

"We have time." I lock the car, and we take the long way to her field.

"Hey."

I glance up. "Hey," I reply to Layla.

"I was going to check in on you, but I didn't want to pry." Her gaze ping-pongs between Josie and me.

I'm a dick. I should have called her or messaged her. My brain has been spinning for the last two days. How do I explain Josie coming back from the dead? "I should have messaged you. Sorry." I nod toward Josie. "Layla, this is Josie. Josie this is Layla. Her daughter Nora and Reagan are friends."

Layla's eyes narrow just a fraction, maybe to see the ghost I'm introducing to her.

"Nice to meet you, Layla." Josie stabilizes herself

and shakes Layla's hand. "My apologies for inter-rupting your date the other night. I feel bad."

Date.

It wasn't a date. I told her that.

Layla slowly shakes her head. "It's ... uh ... don't apologize. I got a ride home. It's ... fine."

She doesn't correct Josie and say that it wasn't a date. Was I stupid? Naive? Was it a date?

"Well, you two can chat more without me, but I'd better keep moving since it will take me a bit to get to the right field." Josie smiles at Layla but doesn't give me so much as a quick glance.

"Nice ... meeting you." Confusion masks Layla's face while Josie hobbles down the sidewalk.

"I'm really sorry," I say again. "She just ..."

Layla tucks her hands into the back pockets of her jean shorts, head cocked to the side.

"She went missing. We thought she was dead. So the other night ..."

Layla's eyebrows crawl up her forehead. "Oh my god ..."

I nod while she shakes her head. "That ... I mean ... you must have thought you were seeing a ghost."

"Something like that."

"I'm happy for you. I hope she's going to be okay." Layla glances in Josie's direction, as do I.

"Me too," I whisper. "Tell Nora I said hi. Okay?"

Layla nods. "Of course. She still wants to have Reagan over to swim."

"Sure. Just ... call me." I say before jogging to catch up to Josie.

"Hey, sorry about that. Do you want me to grab you anything from the concession stand?"

Josie continues to push her walker down the sidewalk and shakes her head. "Nope. I stopped being a fan of concession stands when I saw you making out with Tessa behind one."

"Well, I'm pretty sure I can get you some popcorn or candy without making out with anyone."

"You sure?"

Layla.

I step in front of Josie a few feet from the bleachers, forcing her to stop. "Look at me."

After huffing a breath, she lifts her gaze.

"Layla invited me to the ballet. That's where we were going that night. We were *friends*. She lost her husband a year ago, so we had something in common, or so I thought."

Josie frowns, but I ignore it.

"We met at a game. The girls bonded. It's that simple. I didn't make out with her behind a concession stand. I didn't ask her to homecoming. I haven't had sex with her. We haven't kissed. We haven't held hands. We've been *friends*."

"I don't care." She pushes past me.

I drop my shoulders and glance at the sky, looking for help, looking for answers.

"Josie!" Reagan comes barreling toward her, dropping her glove onto the ground while her team continues to warm up. I'm so glad I called Katy this morning, explaining things so she could give Reagan a heads-up.

"Easy," I say to Reagan as she hugs Josie.

"Cute hair. When did you decide to cut it?" Josie asks.

Reagan releases her and steps back. "You cut it, silly. Don't you remember?"

"Reagan—" I try to interrupt, but Reagan ignores me.

"On your wedding day. You put it in a ponytail and cut it off. Then you told me to give it to my dad. Then ..." Reagan's smile vanishes. "You disappeared."

Josie remembers none of that. I can tell from the loss of all color in her face.

"Reagan, you need to get back to your team. The game's about to begin." I shoo her toward the field.

"Hey, Josie. So good to see you," Katy steps down from the bleachers, followed by Sean, and hugs Josie.

"I'm ..." Josie shakes her head. "I'm *so* very sorry."

"Sorry for what?" Katy squints at Josie and then at me.

"I ... I shouldn't be here." Josie tries to push her walker over the gravel toward the parking lot.

"What did I say?" Katy presses her hand to her chest.

"Nothing. Just ... nothing." I take long strides toward Josie and grab her just as her walker catches, and she starts to tumble over it.

Pulling her into my chest, I rest my hand on the back of her head while she cries.

"I'm sorry ... I'm so s-sorry ..."

"Shh ..." I kiss her head. "There's nothing to be sorry for."

"I c-cut her h-hair. Who does th-that?" She shakes in my arms.

"We'll tell Reagan something came up, and you'll call her later. Okay?" Sean says from behind me as he bends down to pick up Josie's walker.

I give him my best thank-you smile and a slight nod. Resisting the urge to pick her up, I keep Josie hugged to me and help her to the car while Sean follows us with the walker.

Josie slumps against the door while I drive toward home. "Take me to my house," she says, her words void of life.

When we get to her house, she opens the door before I have her walker out. She stands on shaky legs, holding tightly to the door to keep upright. "Layla is beautiful and normal. She's not a monster. She would never cut Reagan's hair. She would never leave you at the altar. I'm giving you a pass, Colten. Just ... take it."

"Shut up, Josie. Just shut the fuck up." I grab her face and kiss her.

Taste her.

Inhale her.

With her lips pressed to mine, I come to life for the first time since our wedding day. The gaping hole she left in my heart fills with her touch, expanding my chest, healing it one slow breath, one slow beat at a time. When I release her mouth, I whisper over her lips, "You died for *this* life. You died to give up that life, to forget it. So please ... *please* let it go. Be who you are, not who you think you were. Be mine. Not his."

"I'm broken," she whispers in a shaky voice.

"Baby, we're all a little broken. I'll take *you* chipped, cracked, or shattered into a million little pieces."

Josie wouldn't go with me to homecoming our senior year. Over the summer, I got a fake ID, started drinking on the weekends, and dove headfirst into self-destruction. She also didn't tell anyone. Not my parents. Not hers.

I never knew why she kept my secrets yet refused to do something as simple as go to homecoming with me. Either she liked me, or she didn't.

Nothing was that simplistic with Josie. I should have known that, but I was too self-absorbed in my own miserable life to see her—really see her.

"Jason is a dick. Why would you go with him to homecoming?" I leaned my back against the lockers while Josie swapped out her books before her calculus class.

"Because he asked me."

"So you'll go out with any guy who asks you out as long he isn't me?"

She slammed her locker door shut and glared at me. "I want to graduate. I want to have a clean record to get into college. I want a future that doesn't involve addiction. And before you decided to let your dad win, I thought I wanted you." She took off down the hallway.

"What's that supposed to mean? Let my dad win?"

"Colten, I have to get to class."

"What's that supposed to mean?" I grabbed her arm to stop her.

She sighed. "Let go of me. I don't have time for this."

"Time for this? You mean time for me. No time to talk to me. No time to go to homecoming with me because you no longer want me? Really? We've come this far and you're done? We're done?"

"I'm going to class. I don't know what you're doing." She took several steps and turned her head, resting her chin on her shoulder while her dark eyes lifted to mine. "Do you, Colten? Do you know what you're doing?"

I let her go. I had a way of letting her go when I knew she was right, and I was too stubborn to admit it.

So Josie went to homecoming with Jason, and I spent the evening drinking under the bleachers. Alcohol on school property. Not my finest hour.

When I felt adequately buzzed, I sauntered toward the school entrance and waited for Josie and Jason to leave the dance. They were kind enough to not keep me waiting too long. An hour before the dance ended, Josie pushed through the doorway, giggling like Jason was somehow entertaining her. She looked pretty in her white dress and hair pulled back with ringlets around her face. Her nails were painted light pink like the color of her lip gloss.

I didn't go to homecoming with Josie because my dad wanted me to go to the dance since it was my senior year. Fuck him. I wasn't going to the dance *because* he thought I should go.

"Josie ..." Her name slurred from my lips as I stumbled toward her. "Did you have fun with Jason?" I asked as if Jason wasn't standing right next to her.

"Have you been drinking?" she asked, but she knew the answer.

I held up my fingers and tried to measure an inch. "A wee bit."

"How are you getting home?"

I patted my pocket, then my other pocket, then my back pocket before I felt my keys. "My truck."

"You can't drive."

"Well, you wouldn't go with me, so I had to drive myself." I laughed and shrugged, finding it nearly impossible to hold still because everything around me seemed to be moving.

"Dude, you're going to get suspended. Just call your parents."

"*Dude* ... I didn't ask for your fucking opinion. I didn't ask for you to take *my* girl to homecoming, and

I'm sure as shit not going to call my parents because you said I should."

"Colten ..." Josie reached for my arm.

"Uh uh uh ... don't touch me. We're not allowed to touch because you didn't say yes to me. And I told your dad I wouldn't date you or kiss you. Maybe even screw you. I can't remember for sure." I scratched my chin.

"God ... you're a mess. Give me your keys."

"Can't. Gotta go. Don't fuck him, Josie. I heard he has crabs."

"Fuck you, man. I don't have crabs." Jason took a step toward me, but I was bigger and stronger, and he knew it. Even slightly inebriated, I could have knocked him flat on his ass.

"Just ... let me handle this." Josie stepped between us.

"Handle?" I smirked "Are you going to *handle* me?" I grabbed her hand and pressed it to my cock. I wasn't even hard.

"Back the fuck off!" Jason shoved me.

I laughed, stumbling backward. "Josie's my girl. Did you know that? She's mine. She's been mine since we were nine." I laughed some more. "That rhymes. Mine since we were nine. Ha! I'm a poet, and I don't even know it." I turned, still chuckling at myself.

"Colten!" Josie chased me, but I pulled away every time she tried to grab my arm. "You are not driving!"

"Are you handling me again?" I clucked my tongue. "Don't tell Jason."

"Colten."

"Josie," I parroted.

Then she was gone.

I turned.

"Josie?"

She wasn't in sight, and neither was Jason. It took me several attempts to not only fish my keys out of my back pocket, but to get them into the door of my truck to unlock it. More time was wasted trying to poke the key into the ignition. The truck sputtered to life, and I shoved it in *Drive* before speeding out of the parking lot. I barely made it to the stop sign before bright cherry lights flashed. Someone snitched.

"ARE you trying to blow your whole goddamn future? If so, congratulations, Son, you're hitting it out of the park," my dad lectured on the way home from the police station. "If it weren't for Chief Watts stepping in, this would be on your record. You'd be in jail overnight. And god only knows what kind of fine we'd have to pay. When are you going to start thinking about someone besides yourself? You could have killed someone. You could have killed Josie. Did you think about that? What if she would have been out on the road and you crashed into her car? Do you think the chief would have saved you? No. He would have let your pathetic, careless, irresponsible ass rot in prison."

Even though the alcohol was the reason for my situation, I was oddly happy that I had it in my system.

I wasn't nearly as buzzed as earlier, but it kept me from losing it with my father and his self-righteous lecture. God ... could he taste the utter hypocrisy in his words?

When we reached the house, I marched past my mom to my room, ignoring her tear-stained cheeks and forlorn expression. Yes, I was a disappointment. Yes, all the men in her life were fuckups and disappointments. She was partially responsible. She allowed it to happen. She was too damn forgiving ... of all of us.

When I heard my parents arguing about me, I opened my window, hopped onto the lower roof, and shimmied my way off the edge of it, body dangling for a second before letting go and dropping to the ground. It should have surprised me that Josie was standing two feet away from me, still in her white dress, arms crossed, but it didn't. "Did you turn me in?" I grumbled, walking down the street.

"Yes."

I whipped around because I didn't really mean it. I didn't really believe she turned me in. "Are you fucking kidding me?"

"No." She shoved my chest. "No, I'm not *fucking* kidding you, you stupid asshole." Josie cut through the neighbor's yard and wormed her way to the woods, but not to her favorite tree. I wasn't sure where she was going. I don't think she knew either. "You could have killed someone!"

"You could have killed Josie."

I stopped next to a tree, slumping beside it and sinking to my ass, knees bent, head bowed. "I hate my life," I murmured. "I hate it so much there are days I don't want to be here."

Josie clung to denial when it came to me. She never really believed I wanted to end my life, maybe because she didn't know what to do with that potential reality. For the most part, she protected me.

She protected me from her dad.

My parents.

Officials at school.

Other kids.

Everyone ... but myself.

I was my own worst enemy, my biggest threat.

"Don't say that," she whispered.

"It's the truth."

"It's not. You just ... you just need to get through this year. Go to college. Get away from your dad. Things won't seem as bad. High school is like a prison. Just hold it together for one year, Colten. Not even ... more like eight months."

I stared at her shiny black shoes, and I thought she might wear them and that dress if she died, if some asshole like me killed her in a drunk driving accident. Then I wondered if they put shoes on dead people when they dressed them up for visitations and funerals. It was very Josephine Watts of me to wonder morbid shit like that. She'd clearly rubbed off on me.

My gaze worked its way up her legs. She had the best legs. Her dress. Her kissable lips. Her pretty hair. Under the wedge of moonlight finding its way between the trees, she looked ethereal.

Unexpected emotion caught in my throat, making my chest ache and my stomach roil with regret—or maybe it was too much beer. "I feel so b-broken." My words cracked under the weight of guilt, under the weight of her perfect existence in my fucked-up world. It was an awful feeling to know that you were not good enough for someone, yet you selfishly wanted them against all sound judgment.

Josie stepped closer, forcing my legs out straight while she straddled my lap. Her hands slid around my neck, and she kissed my forehead, my nose, my cheeks. I didn't deserve her. How did she not see that?

Her next words ripped a sob from my chest, and I hated her and loved her in equal parts for saying them. "We're all a little broken. I'll take you chipped, cracked, or shattered into a million little pieces. You're my Colten. And I'm your Artemis."

CHAPTER
Forty-Six

"Hɪ," Colten says as soon as I answer. He says it before I answer with my own greeting.

"Hi." I can't help my smile while sitting in a chair, doing my physical therapy exercises before bed.

"How have you been?"

I chuckle. "I left Chicago yesterday."

"And I already miss you."

I don't know how to respond. Of course, I want to scream the words, "I miss you too!" But I don't because I feel like we've reversed roles. I'm the one feeling like I need to let him go for his own good. Only, I can't find the actual words to say it to him.

"I called my mom and told her you're alive. She's dying to come see you. Don't be surprised if she calls you. I gave her your new number."

"I'd love to talk to her."

He doesn't say anything for several seconds. Have we already exhausted the small talk?

"Listen, Josie ... what Reagan said to you—"

And here it is.

"Is it true?" I ask. "Did I cut off her ponytail before leaving you at the altar?"

"You didn't leave me at the altar. We didn't make it to the altar."

"Colten ..."

He sighs. "Yes. It's true. She wasn't mad. Nobody was mad. We were concerned. That's all."

"I ..." My eyes close while I lift a bent knee. I'm slowly getting stronger ... physically. Mentally, I'm struggling with who I was and what I did to get rid of the images of another lifetime. "I'm sorry."

"I told you, Reagan's not—"

"That's not what I mean. I'm sorry for thinking this insane plan I concocted would work."

"But it did."

I laugh. "I can't walk unassisted. I had a speech issue for several months. I don't have a job. Everyone I loved thought I was dead. And now that I'm alive, those same people, who spent months grieving and moving on, have to figure out how to take care of me like a child. I've caused so much pain only to now be a burden."

"You're not a burden."

"My dad is sixty-six, and he's going to have to carry me to my bedroom if he's uncomfortable with me sleeping on the sofa."

"That's why you should have stayed with me."

Switching legs, I grimace because I'm pushing myself through another set of leg lifts. I don't want to be dependent on anyone. "We can be friends. You know that, right? We were friends before we were more than friends. In fact, we spent our childhood being friends and then more than friends and back to friends again. If you move on, I won't be mad. I'll be happy for you. And that would be something new. I was never really happy for you when you had other girlfriends. This time would be different. I swear."

"Can you just say that you love me too? Can you do that?"

I press my hand to my face and rub my eyes. "It's late. I should go."

"I don't want to be friends, Josie."

"Have a good week."

"Josie—"

I end the call.

"You can't avoid him forever," Mom says a week later after I've religiously ignored Colten's calls and texts.

"I'm afraid of giving him false hope," I say on our way home from therapy. Today, I practiced using a cane instead of a walker. Now I feel eighty instead of ninety.

"False hope? Why would you give him false hope? He's your fiancé."

"Yeah ..." I whisper while my blank gaze affixes to nothing in particular out the window.

"Josie, what's going on with you? You're alive. I feel like I'm the one who's been given a second chance at life. It's something so much greater than a miracle. Why are you so sad? Did Colten do something?"

With a tiny headshake, I release a slow breath. "It's ... hard to explain. When I was with Felix and Izzy, before anyone else knew I was alive, I felt the tiny improvements in my health. We celebrated every milestone. The world looked different. With Colten, I don't see that version of myself. I don't see everything I am or everything I've become. I see everything I'm not and maybe never will be. When I'm with him, I miss the old Josie, and I know there's no way he doesn't miss her too."

"I didn't ..." Wiping a tear, I try to swallow past the thick pain in my throat. "I didn't think this through."

"Josephine Eleanor Watts, that boy loves you. I'm not sure I've ever seen so much as a glimpse of anything but love and adoration gleaming across his face with your presence or just the mention of your name."

I think about her words. And I'm not denying that he loves me, but that doesn't mean that he wouldn't be better off without me. "He met someone."

"What?" Mom pulls into the garage and shuts off the engine.

"When we told you what happened? How we saw each other at the CVS? What we didn't tell you was that he was there with another woman. A beautiful woman in a red dress. I saw her again at Reagan's T-ball game. They met there, at a game for Reagan and her daughter. She lost her husband a year ago. And they became friends."

"Well, yeah ... *friends.* So what?"

Glancing over at her, I offer a smile that doesn't feel right on my face. "They were dressed up for the ballet. Just the two of them. I'm not stupid. I know where things were headed whether Colten would ever admit it or not. And I'm not mad. I died. He deserved to move on. And if it's her or someone else, my point is ... Colten *did* move on. He took those first steps which means he can live without me. And I think he should live without me. I want this for him. Eighteen years ago, he thought he knew what was best for us, for me. And maybe it was or maybe it wasn't, but we survived. I went to school and landed my dream job. He served his country and fathered a beautiful little girl. We can have a future without it being *ours.*" Those words hurt. They hurt so much my heart feels like a ball of sandpaper working its way up my throat.

"Were they ..." Mom clears her throat.

"He said nothing had happened between them."

"Do you believe him?"

I nod. "But I don't believe nothing would have happened had we not run into each other at the CVS."

"Did you ask Becca when she called?"

"Mom ..." I shake my head. "She was too busy crying. I didn't think it was a good time to ask her about Colten's dating life. And I saw what I saw. Maybe he never told her about Layla."

"Who's Layla?"

"The other woman."

"Josie, don't say it like that. That makes it sound scandalous."

I open my door, sliding out my new cane to stand. "It's not scandalous. It's life. His life. I just want him to have everything." It takes me a second to shift my balance to using the cane instead of the walker. "I am his past. The past is something, but the future is everything."

CHAPTER
Forty-Seven

"Earth to Detective Mosley," Rains says.

I jerk my head in his direction.

"They found a gun in the dumpster." He nods behind him as we canvass the entire block after the three bodies have been removed from the alley.

"Okay."

"Gang related?"

"What?"

He chuckles. "Sorry, am I disturbing you with work. Where are you?"

I shake my head. "Nowhere. Here. I'm ... I'm fine. Sorry. Let's check the cameras at the convenience store."

Rains follows my lead. "She'll come around, man. You just have to give her some time."

"She wants me to move on. That's not coming around. That's the kiss of death."

"Give her time."

"Time?" I shoot him a look, squinting one eye. "It's been over six months. That's half a year she's been alive when I thought she was dead. She didn't come knock on my front door. I saw her at a CVS. And the look on her face…" I shake my head "…it was guilt. Not surprise. Not excitement. It was guilt. An 'oops, didn't think I'd run into you' look. She said she was trying to get better before coming to see me or her family, but that's bullshit. If you love someone, you don't let them exist, thinking you're dead, for even a second if you have a choice. And she had a choice."

"Okay, you're mad. That's probably a good thing. Josie, in her physically impaired state, will naturally get the most attention and sympathy, but you've been through hell too, and repressing those feelings is not good."

"Are you giving me therapy?" I open the door to the convenience store.

Rains offers me a wink. "I'm a man of many talents. That'll be a hundred and twenty dollars."

<hr>

OVER THE NEXT TWO WEEKS, I start to spiral out of control. When I'm not working, I'm drinking. Katy and Sean took Reagan on vacation, so I don't have her to distract me from thoughts of Josie. I need a distraction that doesn't involve beer.

No such luck.

It's just me and my thoughts of Josie.

Me and my anger.

Me and my resentment.

It's her refusing to reply to my texts, refusing to answer my calls. It's me and my irrational behavior like now as I call Savannah at 10:00 p.m.

"Colten?"

I take another swig of beer from my sofa with the TV on mute: Cubs vs Dodgers. "Is Josie there?"

"She's in bed. I know she's not taking your calls or responding to your messages. We're trying to convince her that she needs to just talk to you. But ... she's struggling."

She's struggling?

"How are you, honey?"

"Me?" I chuckle. "I'm uh ... great. Yeah. Never been better. How are you and Isaac? I bet it's nice having Josie back. It was nice when I had her back, but now I don't. I don't have her anymore."

"Colten ..."

"But it's good. I've been hanging out with my friends." I glance at the bottle in my hand. "My buds. Budweiser. Bud Light. His cousin Michelob."

"You sound a little ... over-served."

"Do I?" I finish the last ounce or two of the bottle. "Huh. I didn't realize that. Is she asleep or just in bed? Did Isaac carry her to bed? I carried her to bed when she was staying with me. But ... she's not with me. She doesn't want to be with me."

"Colten, she needs time. Give her time. She'll come back to you. She always comes back to you."

"She didn't come back to me. She died. Came back to life, but not back to me. Doesn't it piss you off, even a little, that I found her by accident? We all thought she was dead. Nope. She wasn't dead. She was living with essentially two strangers. She was eating pizza and watching Netflix while all of us thought she was dead. You don't feel even a little hurt by that?"

She doesn't respond. I glance at my phone. She's still on the line.

"She wants me to move on with my life. Did she tell you that? Maybe you and Isaac should move on too. You know? Let Dr. Felix and his wife be her new parents, her new family. I mean ... they probably love her more than you guys do."

"Colten ..."

"I won't keep you. I just wanted to talk to her, but maybe I'll never talk to her again. I deserve it, right? I broke up with her before graduation. I was a dick. I didn't tell you and Isaac how much I loved her. I didn't tell my dad to fuck off. I let her go. This is payback. A nice little 'fuck you, Colten.'"

"Listen ..." She sniffles.

Shit. I've made her cry.

"I'm trying to hold on. It's that simple. I have a million feelings about the events of the past six months. I've had my moments of elation, relief, confusion, frustration, even anger. But at the end of the day, I'm just *so* grateful that she's alive. Every day I see her fighting depression. Every day I watch her work her butt off to walk on her own. To get stronger. Watching my independent girl hobble around with a cane breaks my heart. I spend every waking second putting on a brave face for her. So instead of drinking away your feelings, come visit her. Show her that you are committed to her no matter how much of a martyr she's trying to be right now."

"She doesn't want to see me."

"So what? Don't come for her; come for you."

I try to think over her words, but I can't think right now. "Night, Savannah."

CHAPTER
Forty-Eight

"I don't need a life jacket."

Dad chuckles, casting his line from his fishing boat while I reel in my line. "You keep saying that."

"And you keep ignoring me."

"I'm not ignoring you. I said you don't have to wear one when you can walk up the stairs by yourself."

"I did!" I angrily recast my line.

"Five. You walked up five steps. We have twelve."

I set my pole aside and whip off my life jacket, tossing it into the water.

"Christ ... what are you? Five?" he grumbles, quickly reeling in his line while glancing over his shoulder to the shore. "Oh good. Maybe he can talk some sense into you."

I follow his gaze to Colten strutting his way toward the dock.

What is he doing here?

A dozen emotions collide and tangle somewhere between my head and my heart. Then ... I rock forward and summersault out of the boat. The whoosh of water fills my ears. I feel weightless for the first time in a long time.

Peaceful.

Serene.

My nerves relax, letting go of every ounce of stress. I'm alive and unburdened. I'm unafraid.

In the next second, I'm yanked from my cocoon. An arm hooks under mine, dragging me to the surface. "JOSIE!" Colten's voice booms as he pulls me like a tugboat. His free arm and legs frantically working to take me to the dock.

"Stop," I say.

"Josie!" Dad's voice sounds from the opposite direction. He's in the water as well, right behind us.

"Stop," I repeat, but no one listens.

Dad bypasses us and climbs up the dock. I kick and wiggle.

"Josie, it's okay. We've got you," Dad says while Colten passes me off to him and he plucks me from the water. A hooked fish. His biggest catch of the day.

"What are you two doing?" I bat away Dad's hands and sit up on the edge of the dock with my feet dangling over the edge.

"Are you trying to kill yourself? What the hell was that?" Dad asks just as Colten lifts himself onto the dock, clothes drenched.

I slowly shake my head. "I ... no. No ..." I continue shaking my head. "I wanted in the water. Not ..." They thought I was trying to drown myself? "I just wanted to be in the water."

Both men wear panicked expressions. Pure torture.

"Jesus, Jo ..." Dad runs a hand through his hair before trying to wring out his clothes. "Watch her," he says to Colten. "I have to go get my boat and take it to the loading dock. Bring her home, please."

Colten nods while trudging to the end of the dock next to me.

"What are you doing here?"

He scrubs his hands over his face, letting them flop to his sides, tugging his shoulders down a couple inches. "Why did you do that?" He ignores my question. There's a world of anguish in his words.

Why did I try to kill myself?

"I told you. I wanted in the water."

"You can't swim."

"I can swim."

"You use a walker. I doubt you can swim."

"I'll have you know I don't use a walker anymore. And I most certainly can swim."

"I'm tired of pulling your lifeless body out of the water."

I wince, and instantaneous regret covers his face. Resting my hands on the side of the dock, I hang my head. "You shouldn't have saved me the first time," I whisper. "And I wasn't drowning this time, but even if I were ..."

"I should have let you drown? Let you die?"

I nod.

"That's ..." He turns his back to me, stabbing his fingers into his hair. "That's fantastic, Josie. So fucking fantastic! I save you, but you don't want that. I try to marry you, but that wasn't right either. I find you, but now I'm not supposed to want you." He turns back to me, letting his hands slide to the back of his neck. "Whatever I did to you eighteen years ago? It's over. Debt paid. Time served. I let you go, but I didn't fucking let you believe I died. I didn't let you mourn me for months. And I sure as hell didn't hide from you. Just say it. You were never coming back to me."

I shake my head, tears in my eyes. "I was," I whisper.

"NO!"

I jump.

Colten's shaking. Hands fisted. Jaw clenched. "I don't believe you. I don't trust you. And I don't feel your love anymore."

I visibly jerk my head, his words kicking my chest, cracking ribs, and bruising my heart. "Colten ..." I blink, letting go of my tears.

"You keep pushing and pushing and pushing ... just ... *pushing* me away. And I'm exhausted. I feel like a fool for coming back." He laughs a little, shaking his head. "I did this when we were young. I was the boomerang that always came back to you when you held out your hand. I willingly, anxiously came back every single time because I knew you always wanted me. I knew the game. The hoops. The secret. It was simply *us*.

"But I don't see us anymore. I don't feel your open arms. I no longer know the game. All I feel is unrequited love. The darkest fucking hole. And I'm so very sorry that you've had these terrible things happen to you. But if you can't let it be me who helps you through this, then I'm done. I'm done waiting. I'm done hoping. I'm just ... done."

Curling my lower lip between my teeth to keep it from quivering, I swallow as many of these suffocating emotions as I can. Colten blurs on the other side of my tears.

He scoops me up, his motions almost robotic. And he carries me to his vehicle. No words are exchanged. He doesn't even look me in the eye. Nothing between us has ever felt this final. When we get to my parents' house, he disappears inside the house, leaving me without anything to assist me to walk into the house. My dad's truck is still gone. He must have returned the boat to the marina. And Mom is grocery shopping.

I guess Colten could have left me on the dock. Still, this feels like a silent, although gigantic, fuck you.

When nobody comes to get me or bring me my cane, I open the door and find my wobbly legs. Taking a deep breath, I move one foot forward. My hands fly out to the side, but there's nothing to grip. Still, I'm still on my feet.

Another step.

And another step.

My legs tremble. Unsteady. Unsure.

I use the rail to climb the four steps to the front door. Three more jelly-legged steps to the door. Grabbing the handle, I press my other hand flat to the door and catch my breath. Sweat beads along my brow. When I open the door, I don't hear anything. I follow the wall, using it to steady myself to the stairs.

It's a mountain. My Everest.

One.

Two.

Three.

By the seventh stair, I ease to my knees, resting my forearms two steps above the one at my knees—head bowed, breathing labored. After a few seconds, I lift my head and climb to my feet again.

Eight. Nine.

Ten.

Eleven.

Oh dear god ... I'm dying.

Twelve!

I cling to the banister, resting my forehead on it. When the floor creaks, I glance up. Colten's a few feet away, a duffle bag slung over his shoulder, wet clothes exchanged for dry ones. He must have been here before he came to the lake. He was going to stay, but not now. He's leaving.

Leaving me.

Forever.

His eyes are red. I see the boy I fell in love with. I see the teenager who hated life as much as I do right now. I see every *us* we've ever been. With each blink, it gets harder to breathe.

The only thing more unimaginable than dying is living without Colten Mosley.

Today I don't want to die.

And I know ... I *know* that tomorrow and every tomorrow after I will not want to live without him.

His throat bobs once while he walks down the short hallway toward me, chin tipped to avoid looking at me any longer. "Tell your parents goodbye for me."

When he reaches me, lifting his foot to descend the stairs, my hand closes around his wrist. Colten's gaze slides to that hand.

"I can't do it," I whisper, waiting for him to look at me. When he does, I feel every drop of emotion trickle down my face. "I can't live without you." I sniffle and choke on my next words. Pulling in a shaky breath, I let my hand slide from his wrist to his hand, lacing our fingers. "I don't need anyone ... except you."

Colten's gaze sweeps across my face a beat before he kisses me. It feels new. He feels new. It took twenty-seven years for me to fully open up my heart to him. It took twenty-seven years for me to feel worthy of his love. I think it's taken twenty-seven years and two deaths to love myself.

Who we are is not what we've become. It's a beautiful reflection of everything we've always been. I've always been his, and he's always been mine.

Colten wraps his arms around my waist and walks me backward into my bedroom, kicking the door shut behind us. Our kiss breaks long enough for him to peel off our clothes. In a naked embrace, he lays me on the bed, settling between my bent knees, pushing into me while my eyes drift shut. This feeling ... it's perfection.

"Open your eyes, beautiful."

On a deep inhale, I gaze at him.

He grins, slowly moving inside of me, one hand planted next to my head while his other hand slides between us, making my breath hitch from its touch. "We're enough. You and I. We are—"

I lift my head and kiss him, dragging his lower lip between my teeth before whispering. "We are everything."

He pauses for a moment. Something serious steals his expression. Whatever it is tugs at my heart. And I hate that for even a single second, he had a reason to doubt my love.

"I love you," I say.

He nods slowly.

My fingers feather up his back and frame his face. "I *love* you," I repeat.

"Say it again," he murmurs, kissing down my neck.

"I love you ..."

"Again." He flicks my nipple with his tongue.

"I love you ..." My words mingle with a soft moan.

"Again." He slides out of me and lowers his body, his tongue dipping into my navel.

"I ... love you." I squirm, anticipating his next move.

"Again." He descends a few more inches, one hand

cupping my inner thigh while his other hand squeezes my breast.

"Oh god ..." My head rolls to the side, and my fingers thread through his hair.

He swipes his tongue between my spread legs and mumbles. "That works too."

———

"Let's go, baby, before your parents get home." Colten forces me to sit up. He pulls my wet tee down over my head and threads my legs into my shorts, minus my panties.

"What are you doing?" I'm drunk.

Drunk on sex.

Drunk on him.

Drunk on life.

"You'll see." He hurriedly carries me down the stairs and to his car.

"Colten ..." I fasten my seat belt while he backs out of the driveway.

He doesn't answer me.

I don't protest. I'm too busy watching him. Studying his features. Resurrecting dreams of our future and piecing them together with superglue. Occasionally, he gives me a quick sideways glance and grins. It's so mischievous and handsome.

"We're fishing again?" I say when he pulls up to the dock in the secluded cove where we were a little over an hour earlier.

Colten says nothing. Instead, he plucks me from the car and carries me to the water's edge.

Off with my shirt and my shorts.

"Colten ..." I glance around, buck naked.

"Can you stand?"

I nod.

He releases me and removes his clothes. Then he scoops me up again and carries me into the water. I stiffen as the cool water covers my body.

"What are we doing?" I giggle.

"You wanted in the water. So I'm giving you the water." His lips find mine, sharing a slow kiss before he releases me. "I'll give you everything, as long as you promise to stay."

Live. As long as I promise to live.

I straighten my body. Arms relaxed. Legs supple. Ears in the water bestowing peace again. I gaze up at the fluffy clouds outlined in blue and then close my eyes and float.

Exist.

Draw breath from this life.

Draw strength from the only person who has always set me free. And I always ... *always* find my way back to him.

I find my way home.

Epilogue

A year later ...

"I'm not going to lie. I'm a little intimidated," Dr. Gellhaus says on my first day as Deputy Medical Examiner for Johnson County in Iowa City.

I laugh, taking a seat at the conference table to go over the one case for the day.

One case.

She already determined the other three don't require autopsies.

Things are a little slower here than in Chicago.

"Intimidated?" I question my superior.

"Yes." She sits across from me. "Dr. Cornwell was my mentor as well. But he never called me the best. He never said he learned anything from me. He never called me special."

I feel an invisible fist clenching my heart. It's been a long year of recovery. I wasn't sure I'd get here. And I never imagined here would be anywhere but Chicago.

When Katy and Sean decided to move to Iowa City, Colten didn't think twice. He insisted we follow Reagan, even though it's only a four-hour drive. I was on the cusp of begging Dr. Cornwell for my old job. The timing was undeniably perfect.

"I'm flattered." I smile, a little unsure of myself. Will I bring the same level of expertise now that so much has changed in my life?

"Have you taught before?"

I shake my head. This new job includes a clinical professor position at the University of Iowa.

"You have a gift, Dr. Watts. Go share it," Dr. Cornwell said when I visited with him just before the move.

"I'm sure you saw a lot in Chicago. Lots of stories to share."

A tiny smile curls my lips. She has no idea.

SIX HOURS LATER, I'm home. Home before five on a Monday. I might like this new job.

"Mommy's home. How's my baby?" I deposit my bag inside the back door and hunch down to nuzzle my nose into Artemis's neck, taking a deep inhale. She's the reason I don't mind short workdays. I get to be with her before Colten's off work. We get our special girl time. "Let's take a walk before Daddy gets home. What do you think?"

Her fluffy golden retriever tail whips side to side while she licks my face.

After an hour walk, I shower, make dinner, and wait for Colten. His new detective position is nearly as sleepy as my new job, but that means he has time to coach Reagan's rec softball team. It means we eat dinner together nearly every night. It means we get sunset bike rides and lots of time to fish on the weekends.

I rarely think about Winston Jeffries. Colten was right. I was him, but he isn't me. I'm the quirky girl who fell for the popular boy. I'm still fascinated by death. I love climbing trees and finding a shady spot to read. And ... I love being kissed by Colten Mosley. The best things never change.

"Tell me you're going to be under my naked body without telling me you're going to be under my naked body," Colten says from the deck door behind me while I sip sweet tea and read my book, occasionally gazing into the trees of our wooded lot.

I grin, setting my drink and book aside before standing.

His gaze roves along my body covered in a thin, flowing cotton sundress. Nothing underneath but my naked body.

"What makes you think you're going to be on top, Coach Mosley?"

Colten smirks.

I love that he leaves the house in a suit and tie and returns in jogging shorts and a tee.

"Did you walk her?" He leans down to scratch Artemis's head.

"I did."

"Dinner smells amazing."

I grin. "It does."

His teeth scrape along his bottom lip while his gaze takes another trip along my body. "Will it keep warm for a bit?"

I saunter toward him. "It will. But I'm hungry now."

Colten's hands snake around my waist then to my butt while he pulls me flush against him. "I am too, but not for food." His fingers gather the thin cotton of my dress, hiking it up my legs.

"Tough luck, Mr. Duck. Food first."

He buries his face in my neck, his hands finding bare skin along my backside. I'd be lying if I said my heart isn't racing, my knees aren't weak, my need isn't just as impatient and real as his.

"You're not even going to ask me about my first day?"

Colten pauses his motions, kisses my neck, and begrudgingly releases me. "How was your first day?" He adjusts his erection and blows out a long breath that ends in the best smile.

I match his grin and brush past him to the kitchen. "There was one case. It took me less than an hour." I pull dinner out of the oven. "I had a meeting at the university to discuss this fall's schedule. I made three new friends. And I think my associate professor has a crush on me. He's pretty cute, so we might have to break up for a bit while I let him be my boyfriend for a few months. Don't worry; we'll probably get back together."

Colten fills water glasses from the fridge dispenser. "That's cool. I ran into Tessa Hart. Remember her? She's recently divorced and hasn't let herself go one bit. Tits for days. She asked if I was married. And since you won't marry me, I told her the truth. I have her number. I'm thinking of meeting her for a drink this Friday."

After setting the Cornish hens onto the stovetop, I slowly turn and tug the oven mitts from my hands. "She's a placeholder, and you know it."

Colten smirks. "My, my ... all these years later and you still go a little feral at just the mention of her name."

"Tits for days? Really?" I narrow my eyes.

He sets the waters on the table and turns, offering me a one-shouldered shrug. "How *cute* is your assistant professor?"

I slide my arms around his waist and tip my head back to look at him. "They can't compete with *us*."

His palms cup my face, fingers teasing my short hair while he grins. Has it always been this simple? Did we get caught up in materialistic dreams, the mind games of success, and the expectations of everyone else, when the grandest thing we can possibly experience in life is love?

"Indeed. There is no competing with *us*. We are more than pieces of a life ... more than memories of a life ... we are ..."

I grin. "Everything."

The End

ALSO BY
Jewel E. Ann

Standalone Novels

Idle Bloom

Undeniably You

Naked Love

Only Trick

Perfectly Adequate

Look The Part

When Life Happened

A Place Without You

Jersey Six

Scarlet Stone

Not What I Expected

For Lucy

What Lovers Do

The Fisherman Series

The Naked Fisherman

The Lost Fisherman

Jack & Jill Series

End of Day

Middle of Knight

Dawn of Forever

One (*standalone*)

Out of Love (*standalone*)

Holding You Series

Holding You

Releasing Me

Transcend Series

Transcend

Epoch

Fortuity (*standalone*)

The Life Series

The Life That Mattered

The Life You Stole

Pieces of a Life

Memories of a Life

Acknowledgments

Jenn, I shall start with you because I feel like we start and end every day together. You were a true sounding board for this story on more than one occasion. If readers don't like it, I think we should share the blame. ;) Either way, you are the amazing talent behind my teasers, book design, formatting, newsletters, and a million other things. I love our friendship. You are The World's Best Assistant!

To my publicist, Nina, her daughter "That," and the rest of the magical team at Valentine PR, it's always a pleasure to work with you. Thanks for the forks!

To my editor and agent, Max, thank you for always believing in me. That sounds so generic, but after thirty books together, it's fitting.

An enormous thank-you to the rest of my editing team: Monique, Amy, Leslie, Kambra, Bethany, Shabby, Sian, and Shauna. I feel like every book gets messier just like my thoughts, and you swoop in to save the day.

Thank you to my ARC teams, Instagram team, bloggers, social media influencers, and EVERY

SINGLE READER who took a chance on this story. It's an honor to write for you—a dream.

Finally, thank you to my family and close friends for a lifetime of love and support. I'm blessed beyond words.

ABOUT THE
Author

Jewel is a free-spirited romance junkie with a quirky sense of humor.

With 10 years of flossing lectures under her belt, she took early retirement from her dental hygiene career to stay home with her three awesome boys and manage the family business.

After her best friend of nearly 30 years suggested a few books from the Contemporary Romance genre, Jewel was hooked. Devouring two and three books a week but still craving more, she decided to practice sustainable reading, AKA writing.

When she's not donning her cape and saving the planet one tree at a time, she enjoys yoga with friends, good food with family, rock climbing with her kids, watching How I Met Your Mother reruns, and of course...heart-wrenching, tear-jerking, panty-scorching novels.

www.jeweleann.com